MARYSUE
RUCCI
BOOKS

THE STORM WE MADE

A novel

VANESSA CHAN

**MARYSUE
RUCCI
BOOKS**

NEW YORK   LONDON   TORONTO   SYDNEY   NEW DELHI

MARYSUE RUCCI BOOKS

Marysue Rucci Books
An Imprint of Simon & Schuster, Inc.
1230 Avenue of the Americas
New York, NY 10020

This book is a work of fiction. Any references to historical events, real people, or real places are used fictitiously. Other names, characters, places, and events are products of the author's imagination, and any resemblance to actual events or places or persons, living or dead, is entirely coincidental.

Copyright © 2024 by Vanessa Chan

All rights reserved, including the right to reproduce this book or portions thereof in any form whatsoever. For information, address Simon Element Subsidiary Rights Department, 1230 Avenue of the Americas, New York, NY 10020.

First Marysue Rucci Books hardcover edition January 2024

MARYSUE RUCCI BOOKS and colophon are trademarks of Simon & Schuster, Inc.

Simon & Schuster: Celebrating 100 Years of Publishing in 2024

For information about special discounts for bulk purchases, please contact Simon & Schuster Special Sales at 1-866-506-1949 or business@simonandschuster.com.

The Simon & Schuster Speakers Bureau can bring authors to your live event. For more information or to book an event, contact the Simon & Schuster Speakers Bureau at 1-866-248-3049 or visit our website at www.simonspeakers.com.

Interior design by Hope Herr-Cardillo
Jacket designed by Vi-An Nguyen, art by Fadilah Karim, with thanks to TAKSU Galleries

Manufactured in the United States of America

1 3 5 7 9 10 8 6 4 2

Library of Congress Cataloging-in-Publication Data has been applied for.

ISBN 978-1-6680-1514-8
ISBN 978-1-6680-1516-2 (ebook)

For my mother and my grandmother, who always chose life

Dear kind reader,

In Malaysia, our grandparents love us by not speaking. More specifically, they do not speak about their lives from 1941–1945, the period when the Japanese Imperial Army invaded Malaya (what Malaysia was called before independence), tossed the British colonizers out, and turned a quiet nation into one that was at war with itself.

The thing is, our grandparents are chatty about everything else. They tell us about their childhood—the neighbors and friends they used to play with, the teachers they loved and hated, the ghosts they were afraid of. They tell us about their adulthood—the blush of first love, the terror of parenthood, the first time they touched our faces, their grandchildren. But of those four years of World War II they rarely speak, only to tell us that the times were bad, and they survived. Then they tell us to buzz off and not be nosy.

Before writing *The Storm We Made*, I could count on one hand what facts I knew about the Japanese Occupation. I knew that the Japanese ingeniously invaded from the north via Thailand riding bicycles, while the British cannons were pointing south at the sea. That the Japanese were brutal and killed without mercy. That they dropped red propaganda flyers about an "Asia for Asians" as they invaded, both a warning and a call to arms.

As the first grandchild on my father's side, I spent an inordinate amount of time with my paternal grandparents, asking them many questions, to which they dotingly replied. From these childhood interrogations I gleaned just a few more facts from my grandmother: How to avoid getting hit by an air strike ("Stay flat on the ground, and don't get up till the plane is completely gone because they drop their bombs when they are diagonally ahead, not when overhead").

How to become your mother's favorite ("Be a handsome boy like my brother, get kidnapped by the Japanese during the war, come back and say nothing happened"). How to make your husband jealous ("Receive a calendar in the mail every year for twenty-five years from a rare, kind Japanese man who used to work with me at the railways during the war").

As I grew older, excavating truths from my grandmother about her teens in occupied Kuala Lumpur was like playing an oral scavenger hunt. When I would ask her what life was like during the Occupation, she would always reply, "Normal! Same as anyone."

But eventually, over the years, in an even voice that delivered only facts, I learned more—that people struggled to feed their families, schools were shut, and members of the violent Japanese secret police, the Kenpeitai, imprisoned British administrators in Singapore and quashed the Chinese rebellions in the jungles.

I put these facts away for years. I had other things to do and other places to be, I thought. I had jobs to keep, money to make, my own stories to tell. Until, in 2019, in a homecoming of sorts, I started writing the stories of Malaysia.

During a writing workshop in late 2019, I wrote what I thought was a throwaway homework assignment—about a teenage girl struggling to get home before curfew, before Japanese soldiers storm the streets. I remember the handwritten comments from the instructor: "Keep this precious thing close," she wrote, "and keep writing it."

So I did. I wrote through a global pandemic in my small apartment, through the premature death of my mother, through the deep loneliness of being unable to go home to Malaysia. I wrote about inherited pain, womanhood, mothers, daughters, and sisters, and how the choices we make reverberate through the generations of our families and communities in ways we often can't predict. I wrote about carrying the legacy of colonization in your body, about being drawn to a toxic man, about complicated friendships, about living a life in fragments, about the ambiguity of right and wrong when survival is at stake. That throwaway homework assignment is now the fourth chapter of my novel.

I hope you enjoy *The Storm We Made* and how Cecily, Jujube, Abel, and Jasmin make their way in their world. I hope that you will feel love, wonder, sorrow, and joy as you read. And mostly, I hope you will remember their stories.

Thank you for reading.

Yours,
Vanessa

HISTORICAL TIMELINE

1820s • The British begin a more than one-hundred-year rule of Malaya, succeeding two prior Western colonizing powers, the Portuguese and the Dutch.

1936 (November) • Nazi Germany, Fascist Italy, and Imperial Japan enter a treaty of friendship.

1937 (August) • The Battle of Shanghai begins. Japan invades China at the start of the Second Sino-Japanese War, precipitating the Nanjing Massacre, also known as the Rape of Nanjing.

1941 (December) • The Malayan campaign begins. The Imperial Japanese Army, under the command of Lieutenant General Tomoyuki Yamashita, invades Malaya from the north, via Thailand. As the country falls, the Occupation of Malaya begins, alongside the Second World War in Asia.

1945 (August) • The US detonates two atomic bombs over the Japanese cities of Hiroshima and Nagasaki, killing hundreds of thousands and leaving detrimental long-term impacts.

1945 (September) • The Imperial Japanese Army surrenders and the British return to Malaya. The Second World War ends.

1957 (August) • Malaya receives independence from Britain.

1963 (September) • The modern federation of Malaysia is formed.

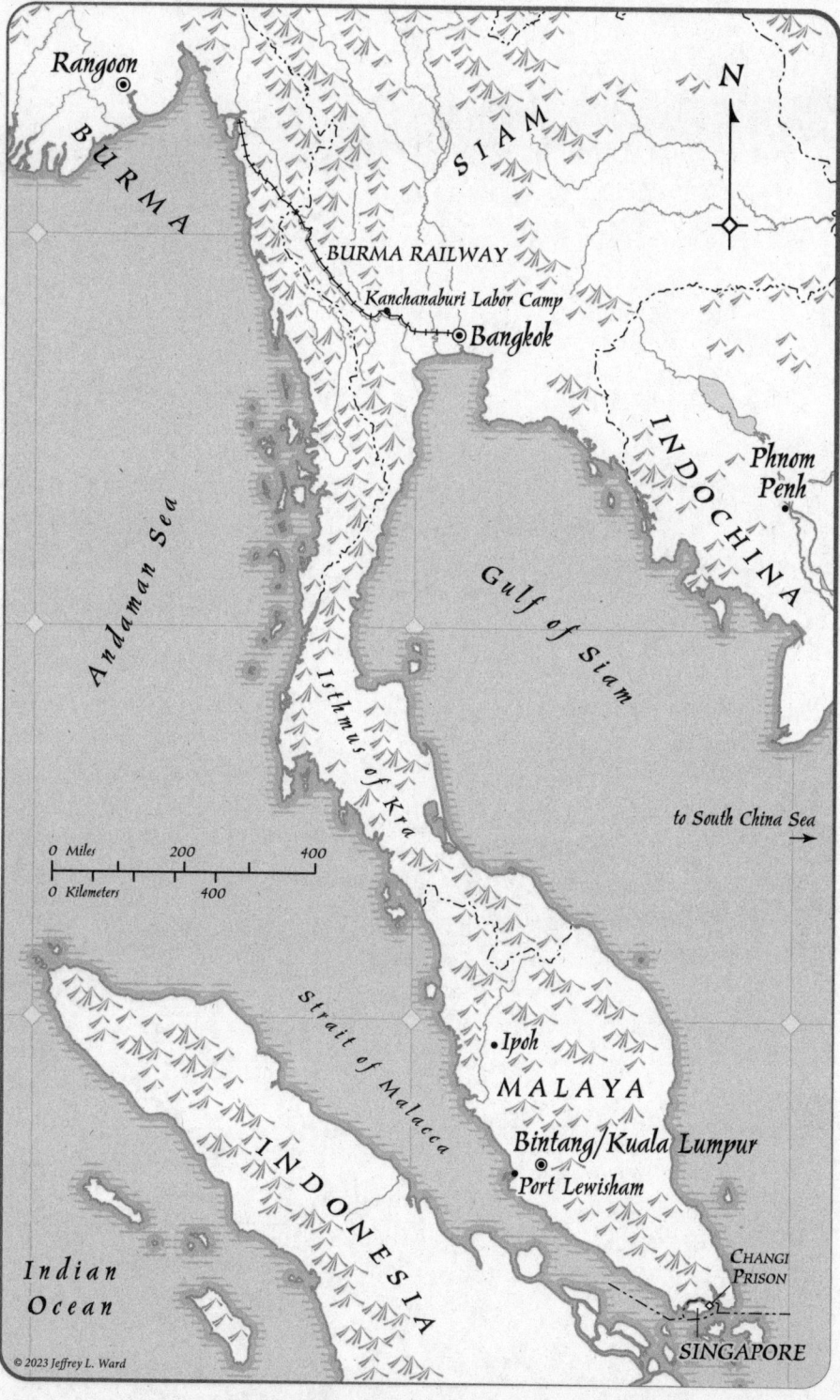

CHAPTER ONE
—

CECILY

Bintang, Kuala Lumpur
February 1945
Japanese-occupied Malaya

Teenage boys had begun to disappear.

The first boy Cecily heard of was one of the Chin brothers, the middle of five hulking boys with narrow foreheads and broad shoulders—they were Boon Hock, Boon Lam, Boon Khong, Boon Hee, and Boon Wai, but their mother called them all Ah Boon, and it was up to the boys to know which one she was calling for. Throughout British rule, the Chin boys were known for being rich and cruel. It was common to see them crowding in a circle behind the Chins' gaudy brown-and-gold house. They'd be standing over a servant, one of the boys with a switch in his hand and all the boys with glints of excitement in their eyes as the switch made contact with the servant's skin. When the Japanese arrived before Christmas 1941, the boys were defiant: they glared at the patrolling Kenpeitai soldiers, spat at the ones who chose to approach. It was the middle boy, Boon Khong, who disappeared, just vanished one day as though he had never existed. Just like that, the five Chin brothers were four.

Cecily's neighbors wondered what had happened to the boy. Mrs. Tan speculated that he had just run away. Puan Azreen, always a cloud of gloom, worried that the boy had gotten into a fight and was lying in a drain somewhere, which made the neighbors peek fearfully into drains as they went about their errands, unsure what they would find. Other mothers shook their head; that's what happens to bullies, they said, maybe someone had simply had enough. Cecily watched the Chin boys' mother, curious to see if Mrs. Chin was stationed by the door waiting for news, or if she performed the hysterics of the terrified mother, but Mrs. Chin and the rest of the Chin family kept to themselves. On the rare occasion they left their house, the four boys surrounded their gray-faced parents in an enormous wall of sinew and muscle, keeping them out of sight.

Only once did Cecily encounter Mrs. Chin, very early in the morning at the sundry shop. Mrs. Chin was staring at a bag of squid snacks, face glistening with tears. Cecily marveled at the quietness of it all, no sobs, no shaking, just bright, damp cheeks and wet eyes.

"She's been like that for five minutes now," said Aunty Mui, the shop owner's wife, delighting in being able to share her discovery with someone else.

After a few weeks, because there were no further public displays of anguish, no other gossip to be gleaned, people stopped wondering about the Chin boys. Soon the neighbors even forgot which Chin brother was missing.

The next few disappearances came in quick succession. The thin boy who worked as a sweeper at the graveyard, who Cecily was convinced stole the flowers that families left on gravestones and sold them at the market. The plump boy behind the sundry shop who smudged his face with dirt and pretended to be lame by tying up the bottom of his pants leg, to beg passersby for coins. The ghoul-eyed boy who had been caught trying to peep into the toilets at the girls' school. Bad boys, Cecily and her neighbors murmured. Maybe they got what they deserved.

But by the middle of the year, sons of people whom Cecily knew also began to disappear. The nephew of the couple who lived in the house next to Cecily, a boy with an enviable baritone who won all the oratory contests at school. The son of the town's doctor, a quiet boy who carried a small chessboard with him everywhere and would set it up to play with anyone who asked. The laundry lady's boy, a diligent teenager who laundered all the Japanese soldiers' uniforms, and whose mother was now forced to take over because the Japanese did not have the time for bereavements.

With only one major road bisecting the town, one chemist, one sundry shop, one school for boys and one for girls, Bintang was a town small enough for worry to mutate. The whispers began again, pointed glances at the families of the missing boys, lowered voices wondering about their fate. In fact, the boys' disappearances were discreet, as though they had sneaked away, afraid to offend. This bothered Cecily because teenage boys made the most noise when they moved—they bumped into things, they stomped when they walked, they shifted uncomfortably even when standing still, unable to control the new power in their physique, the new length in their limbs.

"Is it not enough that they starve us and beat us and take away our schools and our lives? Must they come for our children too?" hissed old Uncle Chong, who owned Chong Sin Kee's sundry shop, the local store in the middle of Bintang where everyone bought supplies, from spices and herbs to rice to raw soap. His wife, Aunty Mui, slapped his mouth. Those were treasonous words, and the Chongs had a son too.

It had not always been this way. When the Japanese first arrived three-ish years before, Cecily, her husband, and their three children had been one of the families to line up outside their house and wave at the military convoy, a welcome party. Cecily remembered the blossoming in her chest as she pointed out the bald, squat Japanese general, Shigeru Fujiwara, at the front of the parade. "That's the Tiger of Malaya!" she told her children.

General Fujiwara had brought the British forces to their knees in under seven weeks, orchestrating a brilliant and unexpected land invasion, cycling in on bicycles from the north where Malaya bordered Thailand, across rough, hot jungle terrain, while the British Navy, anticipating a sea attack, pointed their guns and cannons south and east toward Singapore and the South China Sea. To Cecily, it had felt like a dawn of a new age. But her hope for a better colonizer was short-lived. Within months of the Japanese arrival, schools began to shut down and soldiers made their presence felt on the streets. The Japanese occupiers killed more people in three years than the British colonizers had in fifty. The brutality shocked the quiet population of Malaya, accustomed by then to the stiff upper lip and bored disinterest of the British, who mostly stayed away from the locals as long as the tin-mining and rubber-tapping quotas were reached.

Fearful of what was to come, Cecily started doing a roll call every evening to make sure each of her three children had made it home. "Jujube," she would call over the din of dinner preparations. "Jasmin! Abel!"

And every evening they answered—Jujube irritably, face twisted in the seriousness of an eldest child, Jasmin cheerily, small feet skittering across the ground like a puppy's. And her middle boy, Abel, who worried her the most, who would shout, "Ma, of course I'm here!" careening toward her with a big, loping hug.

For a while the system seemed to work. Evening after evening as the sun set and the mosquitoes began their nightly chorus, she called for her children, and they replied. The family would gather at the scratched dining table and tell each other about their day, and for a few minutes, listening to Jasmin snort-laughing at one of Abel's theatrical jokes, watching as Jujube pulled at her short curls that looked so like Cecily's own, Cecily could forget the severity of their circumstances, the terror of the war, the barrenness of their lives.

But then, on his fifteenth birthday, on the fifteenth of February, Abel—who had light brown hair so unlike the rest of the siblings, Abel who was ravenous all the time because of the food rationing, Abel who had grown six inches the previous year and was now taller than everyone in the family—had not answered her call, had not made it home from the store. And as the waxy birthday candle melted into Abel's dry birthday cake, Cecily knew. Bad things happened to bad people; and she was exactly that—a bad person.

The truth was, for the last couple of years, Cecily found she could not hide the distinct fear that controlled her existence; the knowledge that all the things she had done would come for her, that retribution was always a day away. This fear manifested in her anxious, twisting fingers, in the way her eyes darted over her children, in the distrust with which she greeted anyone unfamiliar. Now that the catastrophe had come to pass, she felt every piece of taut energy in her body simply give way. Jujube told her later that she had released one long howl, low and anguished, then sunk into the rattan chair without further sound, her expression calm, her body motionless.

Around her, the family was a hive of activity. Her husband, Gordon, paced, shouting to himself or perhaps to her, at the top of his lungs: "Maybe he went to the shop; maybe he got stuck at a police checkpoint; maybe, maybe, maybe." Jasmin held on to her older sister's thumb, her face too stoic for seven years old. Jujube, ever practical, had sprung into action. She extricated herself from Jasmin and ran to the back of the house, called over the fence to the neighbors on both sides: "Have you seen my brother? Can you help me find my brother?" But it was past the eight o'clock curfew, and none of the neighbors dared respond, even if their heart broke at the sound of Jujube's cries.

Cecily said nothing. For a few minutes before the guilt took hold of her, it was a relief to see her terror realized. It had finally come to pass, and this was all her fault.

She had caused this, all of it.

The morning after Abel's disappearance, Cecily's neighbors swung into action. The Alcantaras were a respectable family, and respectable families did not deserve tragedies this monumental. The men organized daytime search parties, carrying signs and roaming around hollering Abel's name. They looked in storerooms behind houses, they looked in the corners of Abel's favorite shops, they looked in playgrounds and in abandoned factories. They looked but didn't enter the old school that had been turned into a Japanese interrogation center. The men stayed in small groups, bent their heads low when the Kenpeitai soldiers in muddy-green uniforms looked their way, but felt a secret smugness because there was safety in numbers, and this search for the boy felt like their own tiny revolution, a small uprising against the Japanese. The women treated the incident like a birth or a death, bringing over an endless supply of food and consolations to the Alcantara house. They assured Cecily that all would be well—that Abel was just a careless boy and had probably fallen asleep somewhere and would find his way home soon, that Abel had lost track of time and was staying with one of his friends, that boys like Abel—so handsome, so charming, and with so much promise—didn't just disappear.

Cecily, the other women thought, was surprisingly ungrateful. She did not say thank you when they delivered the food, she did not make them tea when they waited at the door to be invited in, she did not cry or confide or collapse in the way that would be understandable. All she did was look so terribly alert, eyes darting everywhere, as though ready to pounce. On what? They didn't know. Of course, they felt for her, they whispered to one another, but Cecily really took things too far sometimes. Remember the terrible stories she used to tell her children?

"The one about the man who was forced to drink soapy water till his stomach hung out from his body, then the Japanese soldiers balanced a wooden beam on him and jumped on either side of the beam like a seesaw till he burst? That one?" said Mrs. Chua.

"Aiya, do you really need to repeat that awful story? Yes, that one!" said Mrs. Tan. "It gave my children nightmares for weeks!"

Sometimes, they thought, Cecily really didn't know how to act right. They were all mothers; they knew how mothers should act. And when a mother loses a son, she should cry, she should collapse, she should seek comfort in other mothers. She should not just hold her pain as a shield, act so prickly that everyone was afraid to come near.

Still, they reminded themselves, they needed to be good neighbors. Mrs. Tan continued to send steaming bowls of soupy noodles to the Alcantara house and tried not to be offended when she saw the bowls standing in the exact place outside the gate when she passed by the next day. Mrs. Chua offered to watch Jujube and Jasmin so Cecily could get a break. Puan Azreen, who loved the dramatic, told stories about everyone she'd ever heard, who'd gone missing, but she couldn't resist adding a sheen of horror to her tales—people coming home absent limbs or with disfigured faces.

To the neighbors, at least Gordon, Cecily's husband, seemed grateful enough. He tramped through town with the other men, called for his son, slapped the backs of other husbands, thanked everyone for their time. He has become so much nicer now, the neighbors told one another. Of course you don't want such a thing to happen to anyone, of course not, they tsk-tsked, but they preferred this iteration of Gordon Alcantara, taken down a peg, without the pompousness they had disliked about him in the before times, when the British were in charge and Gordon was an administrator who fancied himself better than all of them.

The days of Abel's absence stretched into weeks. Daily searches by the men became sporadic, and the house visits from the women began to dwindle. As more and more boys began to disappear, the neighbors stayed home, hid their own sons away from the barbed glares of the Kenpeitai soldiers. The brief joy of revolt died down, and the neighbors remembered once again that during a war, the only priority was one's own family. They could not waste their time on the missing children of others.

A week before he disappeared, Abel had come home with an armful of ugly, weedy-looking flowers that he'd clearly plucked off the side of the road. But he had been so proud, that Cecily had put them in a vase and pretended they were the most beautiful flowers she had ever seen. In the weeks after he disappeared, the weeds became dry and brittle, but still, Cecily couldn't bring herself to throw them out. Then, one afternoon, she forgot to close her bedroom window during a thunderstorm, one of the noisy, wall-rattling tropical storms that Malaya was known for. The room became misty with rain, and the wind knocked everything over, shattering the vase of Abel's dried weeds. That evening after the storm subsided, Gordon found Cecily bleeding from her fingers as she tried to glue the pieces of the vase back together, tried to arrange the broken weeds to stand as tall as a boy. But, as with the pieces she had set in motion ten years before, there was no fixing to be done. There was no coming back from this.

CHAPTER TWO

CECILY

Bintang, Kuala Lumpur
1935
Ten years earlier, British-occupied Malaya

Cecily's family was Eurasian, descended from Portuguese men, the first in a series of white colonizers who had come to Malaya's shores in the 1500s, armed with guns and ships and an ambition to control the region's spice-trading routes and immense natural resources. Cecily's mother relished the speckle of white in their names and their blood, would sweep her eyes, dark with judgment, over others around them. Her mother's refrain: "We did not come here as laborers like the Chinese and Indians to work the land and the mines, and we were not conquered like the Malays. We were made by white men, we are Christian, we worship their same gods, and they gave us their names, Rozario, and Oliveiro, and Sequiera."

As a child, Cecily was confused because their Eurasian friends and family came in all colors, brown, black, yellow, but she couldn't think of a single person with the same white and pink blotchy skin she saw in the British.

"Ah, but we are nearly white, like them," Cecily's mother would insist, gazing adoringly over at the nearest British person, usually sweating in the unfamiliar heat: a teacher, an administrator, a priest.

Cecily had never felt entitled to the beautiful and superior. Growing up, she was a nice girl but an unnoticeable one, not pretty enough to attract much attention. It showed in the way her mother appraised Cecily's muddy-brown hair, eyes, and skin with indifference and, on some days, disappointment. Her sister, Catherine, four years older, was the aspiration. Catherine, with her olive skin and green-gray eyes, ended up marrying a British officer called Abbott who took her back to England to claim his lordship. Just like that, Catherine became Lady Abbott. But plain girls like Cecily, even if she was Eurasian, born into small houses with thatched roofs in stiflingly hot British colonies in the early 1900s, were meant to lead quiet lives that fulfilled all the roles set for them—first as a girl, learning all the skills that would attract a good husband, then as a wife, keeping the household organized, getting along with the neighbors, then as a mother, bearing and raising the appropriate number of children to prove her worth.

And Cecily did all those things with quiet tenacity and, by age thirty, found herself with two children, Jujube and Abel, and a husband—Gordon, once a plump Eurasian boy who lived two roads away and who provided her with decent comforts. They lived in a small house with an orange roof, not at all beautiful but very functional. And yet she was unbearably discontent. Every morning she would stand in the hot kitchen making half-boiled eggs for her husband and children. She would pour black coffee into little tin mugs, a smile on her face, sometimes a song on her lips. But while cooking, singing, and doing all the chores that simulated a quiet, small world of domestic bliss, she would fantasize about cracking the boiling eggs on her husband's head and throwing hot coffee in the children's faces. It made her sick with shame. She did not know when, why, or how the shift occurred inside her; she did not know how to fix herself. Even outside the home sometimes, when she was at the market trying to haggle with stallholders over the price of fish or brinjal, she would feel a sudden urge to scream and tip the tables filled with scaly fish and bleeding pork onto the proprietors.

On the last Tuesday of November in 1935, Cecily watched the sky suspiciously. It was about to rain, gray clouds gathering like a congregation. She was knee-deep in stinking refuse, pressing so hard into her slippers for stability that her toe joints shone white. The air was humid, as late afternoons in tropical Malaya tended to be, even more because the rain clouds lurked, threatening release. She was worried she wouldn't finish her assignment before the rain arrived. She dug through the trash heap, through cabbage leaves, fish bones, and something that looked suspiciously like an animal's testicle. The heat blasted the smell of all the rot straight up her nostrils. She suppressed a gag, cursed the assignment, and prepared to give up before she saw the document she was looking for, a sheet of notebook paper sitting calmly atop a bag of garbage that she had just torn through. It was stained but smooth, lying there as though waiting to be claimed. She thumbed the paper and flapped it a little, then regretted her action because whatever trash juice was on the paper flicked droplets onto her face. At least the squiggles, diagrams, smudges, and lines on the paper, written in her husband's handwriting, were intact.

"Good work, Cecily."

The brittle voice startled her, caused her feet to slip in her squat. She widened her stance to steady herself from toppling headfirst into the trash heap, which would have been a revolting outcome. She stood and whirled around, holding her hands in front of her so her fingers wouldn't drip on her clothes. "What are you doing here?"

Fujiwara stood three strides behind her. His hands were fair and clean, a stark contrast to Cecily's own, which were brown and damp with garbage juice. His linen suit was creased enough to show signs that he had walked through town. He stepped toward Cecily, one arm outstretched, gesturing for the notebook paper. She frowned at him. This was not their agreed-upon process, and he knew she didn't like it when he acted unpredictably. It destabilized the carefully constructed nature of their relationship, and that, in turn, destabilized her.

Fujiwara pinched an unstained corner of the notebook paper from her hand and flapped it in the air to dry it. This did not work. The humidity dampened the flapping sheet even more.

"Put it away or you'll get us caught," Cecily said. She tried to stanch the jumpiness in her stomach with as much frost as she could muster in her voice. Her words came out high-pitched and reedy. A swell of frustration rose through her throat.

That day, as on all other days, Cecily was supposed to drop off the sheet of paper at the Chongs' sundry shop, where she would slide her fingers between the splintery wall and rickety shelf that housed sanitary napkins, feeling for a tiny nook, and press whatever intel she had picked up that week into the little space. It was an ingenious drop-off point—hidden in plain sight at one of the most trafficked businesses in town—simply because men avoided the aisle and that shelf, afraid to have anything to do with female reproductive parts, and women scurried in and out, not wanting to be noticed there. Fujiwara's trusted cook would pick up whatever intel was in the nook as part of her shopping and deliver it to him. They'd been doing this for months; there was no reason for Fujiwara to switch up the procedure on her.

"I don't like this," Cecily hissed. "I could get caught talking to you." Her eyes flicked to the main road perpendicular to the alley they were standing in, usually a busy thoroughfare. A motorcar passed, then a rickshaw, then a bicycle, but no one seemed to be paying attention to them.

"Cecily," he murmured. Of the many things that frustrated Cecily about Fujiwara, one of the biggest was that his voice never really rose above a whisper. She wondered if he was aware of his power, that the quiet tenor of his voice was its own aggression, forcing people to stop what they were doing in order to lean in and listen.

She turned away from him and from the chisel of high nose that always made her stomach leap. Fujiwara was not a beautiful man, but there was a cleanness and symmetry to his face that lent him the air of the aristocratic. She focused on reaching for the nearby hose to wash the smell of fish scales off her hands. As cool water gushed over her left palm, a stinging pain shot through her arm, and bubbles of blood flowed pink along the stream of hose water.

"Cecily, you're bleeding."

As he stepped forward to look, the mint scent of his hair cream coated the warm air around them, reminding her that she was always in his capture.

"It's nothing, just a scratch," said Cecily. *Because* you made me dig in the garbage, she thought but did not say. Instead, she arranged her face into a calm smile, almost a smirk, an expression she hoped would belie her desire to grasp his wrist, to communicate the yearning she felt for him. It had been like this for months, her stomach toppling insensibly the few times that they met, making her feel both hungry and drunk.

"I'm sorry, I know you don't like when we make changes," he said.

Cecily ran her hand under the water and flinched as the sting of the cut roiled through her.

"It's just that I have to tell you something. I couldn't wait," he said.

There it was again, that delicious curdle in her stomach. He had never given her a clue that he felt the same way. In fact, he had never given her a clue as to how he felt about anything.

Fujiwara raised his right hand and pressed his fingers against the stained sheet of notebook paper, smoothing it against his thigh. Cecily removed her own finger from the stream of water and wiped it, the cut already beginning to clot, on her floral skirt. The splotch of blood darkened the petals of a flower on the fabric, but the stain could barely be seen, a monster hidden in plain sight.

"What do you have to tell me?" she asked, hating that she sounded like she was begging.

"These numbers will be useful to us," he said, staring at the notebook paper, ignoring her question, furrowing his dark eyebrows.

Cecily studied Fujiwara as he studied the notebook paper. A tiny bead of sweat clung to the top of his eyebrow, unusual, as he always looked fresh, as if he had just bathed. Cecily wanted to stick out her tongue and lick it away, taste the hot saltiness.

"I will have to take this back to be analyzed," he said. Because he had stepped back away from her, she could barely hear him. "But it looks like part of a log your husband made of tides and hourly water depths at the port. He must have written his findings into a larger report and thrown away these notes."

Cecily nodded, half-listening, trying desperately to draw her eye away from the bead of sweat. Her bloody finger stung with shame.

"Well. If you're not going to tell me what's going on, I'm leaving now," she said. "It's dangerous, hanging about like this, and I have to get back to the children." She turned away, her breath catching. She was a woman who could walk away, she told herself.

"Wait, wait." Fujiwara's breath whistled through his teeth. Close by, a mynah bird cackled as though mocking their impasse. "I have heard about a German man, who is both a good man and a bad man, and he will win us the war from the British." Fujiwara's voice vibrated with excitement, making him even harder to hear.

Cecily stepped back and turned to face him. This was unusual. The nature of their relationship was transactional; Fujiwara was her spymaster. She, the informant, gathered intelligence, mostly stolen bits of information from her husband, Gordon, whether from the discarded bits of paper in his trash or from conversations she overheard. Gordon was an unsuspecting middle manager for the British administration in the public works department, focused on geology and land use. It was a job he did not love, but the title, "land superintendent," offered Gordon sufficient respect among his friends, so he tolerated it. Fujiwara took Cecily's intel back to his superiors, little pieces in a convoluted puzzle that the Japanese were trying to put together to overthrow the British, who had been in Malaya for over a hundred years. Fujiwara rarely fed back information to *her;* anything she knew, she surmised from crackling wireless dispatches, about German and Japanese invasions in places so far away as to seem not real. Sometimes, on nights she felt lost, she wondered if Malaya would ever be liberated, as she hoped.

"Isn't every man a good man and a bad man?" Cecily asked. "That seems like an unnecessary riddle."

"Cecily." The corners of Fujiwara's thin mouth curved upward. "This is what I like best about you. I am a dreamer; you are always practical."

Cecily felt a burning sweep through her and color the tops of her ears. That was perhaps the most direct compliment he'd ever paid her. *Like,* he had said, *like best.* She pressed the frizz of her hair against her ear and hoped he would mistake her blush for a reaction to the sweltering afternoon heat.

"You should know. I want you to know. There is an alliance . . . between Germany and Italy and Japan that will be so powerful. It will shape the future." His voice shook, sparkling with energy. Cecily felt it too. From the beginning, Cecily and Fujiwara had talked about a world in which Asians could determine their own future, a world in which one's status in society did not mean calculating how many points of separation there were between them and a white person. An alliance like this, between the Germans and Italians, who had been making immense progress overthrowing their British counterparts, and Japan, whose leaders had vowed to free Asia from the scourge of the British, would make all these become an actual possibility. She released the breath she hadn't realized she was holding. His words were so few, yet she felt propelled, like change was just one wave away, and she could see the crest coming at them as they stood on the shore. And maybe, for now, that was enough.

Fujiwara had entered Cecily's life during the monsoon season of 1934, had blown in like the gusting winds from tropical storms that whipped at trees and threw everything out of place. It was the week before Christmas. The air was filled with the promise of a new year ahead, the nights full of parties to celebrate the end of the old one. That particular night felt cool because it had stormed all afternoon, for which Cecily was relieved; it would ensure that she didn't sweat through her party dress. For the first time ever, they were guests at the resident's house, to celebrate the appointment of an assistant British resident in Bintang. Gordon had already made her change three times, settling finally on a cream dress with a light pink stripe down the sides, neither too fitted nor too loose, one he felt was both appropriate and approachable.

The longtime resident, a dour man called Frank Lewisham, was the local administrator responsible mostly for keeping peace and for making sure Bintang made its tin-ore and rubber-tapping quotas. Cecily studied the new assistant resident, a thin, silly-looking man called William Ommaney who, perhaps because he licked his lips when he was nervous, had the most chapped lips she had ever seen. Gordon was pleased with this appointment. Gordon was a British loyalist and believer; he conjectured that Ommaney's appointment signaled Kuala Lumpur, the city that contained their town of Bintang, was on its way to becoming, like the neighboring islands of Singapore and Penang, a key administrative station for British Malaya.

"The Crown finally sees our full potential!" he had bellowed to Cecily when he learned of the news.

At the party, people milled about, and the air filled with a rising orchestra of conversation, punctured by the occasional high-pitched squeals of British women echoing off the clean white walls. The resident's house was an imposing structure that stood in the center of a smooth, clipped lawn dotted with lush angsana trees whose leaves fluttered in the post-storm breeze. The gramophone sent strains of Billie Holiday streaming into the manicured lawn, and the night felt languid, softened by the mists of the after-rains. Cecily surprised herself by stepping gently side to side, the closest thing to dancing that she had ever done. This was uncharacteristic; she'd always felt dancing was a pastime for prettier girls. Plain women like her didn't get to feel the joy that having physical beauty bestowed.

In the swirl of introductions, the flicking of gratuitous hand touches, Cecily encountered Fujiwara for the first time. But that was not the name he went by at the time. His accent was British, one she later learned was not native to him.

"Bingley Chan," he said, enunciating the "-ley" so hard his throat clicked. He extended an arm for a handshake, and someone introduced him as a merchant from Hong Kong specializing in the trading of goods from the Orient.

Cecily studied him, this Asian man who seemed to command a curious respect from the British. He did not have the rounded features she had learned to recognize in the Southern Chinese men brought to Malaya by the British to work in the mines. But she hadn't met many Asians outside of Malayan people.

"So, Mr. Chan, do you do any business with the Germans, or do you keep your business strictly for Crown and country?" Gordon asked, puffing out his chest and inserting a clip in his accent, the one he thought made him sound posh in front of the Brits. Cecily suppressed a wince.

"The Germans surely have no use for a merchant who sells spices and rugs," Bingley Chan replied, his tone arch, one eyebrow raised.

"Blasted Germans!" someone shouted, and all the men in their circle roared in the way that men do, more in masculine solidarity than in any kind of mutual understanding of a joke. The man then known as Bingley Chan twisted his lips upward in an approximation of a smile. But Cecily noticed that he, like her, did not laugh.

After the resident's party, Bingley began calling at the Alcantara house during the after-dinner hours when the children were in bed. Gordon, enthralled with the idea that a connected British man, even one of Asian descent, would aspire to become a part of the couple's circle, was delighted to have him visit, reveling in what he perceived to be their increased status. The two men would lean back in the cushioned rattan chairs in the front room of the house. They would swirl and sip brown whiskey that Bingley had brought, Gordon marveling at the quality, Bingley demurring when asked if he got it on the black market. An hour would pass, then two, then three, the men laughing uproariously at nothing, and Cecily sitting opposite them, smiling indulgently, nursing her first and only glass of the night.

Soon came nights when Gordon nodded off sitting up, fingers still clasped around the dripping glass, thighs open wide against the sides of the rattan chair, face slack with whiskey sleep. At first Cecily was embarrassed, making excuses for Gordon: "Oh, he had a long day at work," she would say, apologizing for what she worried Bingley would perceive as a slight, and ushering him out the door. But after three nights of struggling to haul her husband to their bed, Cecily accepted Bingley's offer of assistance. And thus it began, night after night—the two of them dragging Gordon, sometimes gently by the shoulders and sometimes roughly by the arms, into the bedroom, plonking him on the bed fully dressed, giggling like children at Gordon's snoring. Just friendly, Cecily told herself. A nice gentleman, helping her get her husband to bed after a friendly night.

But as all things evolve, so too did this. Bingley began to linger after Gordon had been put to bed. At first just a few minutes of standing by the door chatting about things happening in the neighborhood, eye-rolling at the latest antics of Mrs. Carvalho, the nosy next-door neighbor, or commiserating together about the humidity in the air that didn't seem to dissipate at night. Very quickly, the conversational mundanities turned to confidences that required Bingley to sit down and listen.

There was Cecily's increasing disillusionment with the British, a view that was at odds with her mother's and her husband's reverence. The older she got, the more she noticed the underachievement of the white men around her—third and fourth disinherited sons, failed soldiers, alcoholics, expelled by their families or their regiments and sent to far-flung places like the Malayan peninsula in order to regain a modicum of dignity for their lineage. And while here, in their weather-inappropriate wool suits, they marched around, stinking, she thought, with an air of unearned superiority, unless they spotted a particularly well-shaped set of local breasts, in which case their watery eyes would brighten.

There was the pinch of shame she felt twisting in her chest when she found herself being sidestepped by a British wife at the shops, or every time her husband came home thrilled by a crumb of validation he had received from a white colleague who could barely remember his name.

And there were moments that clouded her hopes for her children's future. The day when six-year-old Jujube had come home all flushed cheeks and big eyes, pulled her baby brother, Abel, into her lap, and started screeching "UN-CI-VI-LA-IZED" into his ear till Abel too began screeching, then crying, his gray eyes shiny like the surface of a swamp.

"Jujube!" Cecily yelled, appalled. "Where did you learn that?" Hearing such an ugly word come out of such a young mouth had sent a wave of shock through Cecily.

"The teachers at school said that's what we are! That's why they came all this way on a ship to help us! And that's why we have to go to church, so that God can see we are—reformed!" Jujube singsong-screeched, and pronounced "reformed" as "ray-formed," scrunching up her face in concentration to regurgitate everything she had learned. Cecily flinched, but beyond shushing Jujube and consoling the confused Abel, she didn't know how to explain to her daughter that even if they told themselves they were white-adjacent, even if they held on to the flecks of European in their veins, it meant nothing.

Gordon and Cecily's mother had hoped that the whiteness in their blood would supersede the brownness of the skin, that if they waited and served their British masters patiently enough, their European lineage, faint as it was, would be recognized by the white men, that they would be elevated above Malayans of other races. But no matter how hard they scrubbed at their skin to get to the lighter layers, no matter how well they formed their vowels around the English language, no matter how loudly they said their surname, no matter how hard they tried to be the right kind of civilized, they remained, in the eyes of their white imperialists—less than.

Bingley confided in her too. He told her in his soft, uncomplaining voice about the consistent put-downs he faced from the British—the names they called him, the mockery they made of his eyes. He told her about his son who'd died weeks after being born, how a relationship, his relationship, could not survive that kind of pain. She heard a crack in his usually even voice as he swallowed. Long after everything had come to pass, she would realize this was the moment when any resistance she'd possessed had been worn down. His vulnerability felt like something stolen, that everything she would do henceforth would be owed because of this one moment of brokenness he had let her see.

Years later, Cecily tried to remember the details of the night when he revealed his identity to her. Were the mosquitoes buzzing? Was the moon full or crescent-shaped? Was the air warm or cool? She could not recall. All she knew was that he must've understood he'd peeled her back enough, exposed the tender layers, primed her to be ready. With her husband asleep in their marital bed, Bingley revealed himself as Fujiwara. His accent transforming, he spoke in brittle Japanese-accented English, and she learned his true affiliation with the Japanese Imperial Army, his dream of an Asia for Asians, a world in which white men didn't always win.

All she remembered was that after his revelation, she listened raptly, breath held, to Fujiwara and his ideals, which managed to be both logical and romantic. He talked about a world in which people who looked like them were no longer imperial subjects, an Asia that looked out for its own, led by its own, a society that dismantled the structures of white men she had been told for so long were the only things that mattered but that she had never felt comfortable with. And as their clandestine nights continued, Cecily found that she too could envision a world taken back from the British, a future in which she, and her children, and their children, could be more than just unnoticed, bland, ornamentation.

CHAPTER THREE
—

ABEL

Kanchanaburi Labor Camp on the Burma/Thailand border
August 16, 1945
Japanese-occupied Malaya

When Abel came to, he was in a chicken coop, his head buzzing with the chittering of scratching webbed feet walking around him. One chicken, a brown hen with a spray of white feathers on her underside, stopped above his nose to peer at him. He held himself still—he did not want to get pecked. When the hen had enough of her inspection, she shuffled away and Abel sat up to feel his face, which was crusted with dried blood. He looked around. The wire mesh of the coop created an enclosure that was not much larger than eight feet across and five feet high. There were four chickens in the coop: the brown hen from earlier, two white hens pecking at each other, and a rooster that lay on its side. Dying, Abel guessed from its fetid smell.

Even though he'd been at the labor camp for six months now, this was his first time in the chicken coop. He realized he would not be able to stand. He pulled himself into a squat. As his bent knees touched his chest, he felt a searing pain in his abdomen. Lying back down on the dirt, he lifted his torn brown shirt to investigate and saw a web of purple and blue bruises, crisscrossing lighter pink, yellow, and green ones. His tongue felt dry and huge, like it was threaded with splinters. He tried to clear his throat to find his voice, and he heard himself croak a little. The brown hen turned around to glare at him again.

Abel had first heard of the railroad the day before his fifteenth birthday. He was turning fifteen on February 15, which seemed particularly momentous to him, even if the war meant he wouldn't be celebrating that much. He'd been on his way back from the sundry shop—his buddy Yao Chun who worked there had given him a cigarette and one of the old Lucky Strike posters of a pretty girl smoking. With a wink, Yao Chun had rolled up the poster and said, "Make good use of this, my friend," and Abel had winced in embarrassment. But he had grabbed the poster anyway; pictures of pretty girls were hard to come by. As he walked home inhaling the smoky tar from the cigarette, he thought about what it meant to be fifteen. It meant that in a year, he'd be able to enlist and push the Japanese back to where they belonged.

It bothered Abel to watch his father, who used to be portly, get thinner and paler each day, with scabbed-over cuts on his hands multiplying from the job he was forced to do at the sheet-metal workshop. It bothered Abel even more to see the frown line between his mother's eyebrows get deeper and deeper as she looked at the scarce rations his father brought home after work. Just the week before, his father had stood in line for four hours only to be given a bag of bloody bits that turned out to be bull testicles. Abel had found it hilarious and collapsed into a fit of guffawing laughter, yelling, "Bullballs bullballs," when his father had shamefully revealed the contents of the bag to their mother. Even serious Jujube had allowed herself to crack a smile. But instead of joining in the family mirth, their mother had screamed, "I GIVE UP!" Abel remembered watching her lower lip tremble as she marched away to the small room she shared with their father, refusing to come out for the rest of the evening. That night the family ate boiled bull testicles covered in soy sauce for dinner, while pretending not to hear their mother's muffled sobs coming from the room down the hall. Abel could still taste the gaminess of the meat.

"You!" a booming voice had bellowed, interrupting his birthday walk. He was surprised to see Brother Luke. Before the Japanese had arrived, Brother Luke was his history teacher. With the exception of the priests, who went by "Father So-and-so," the British missionaries who lived among them gave themselves the honorific of "Brother," which implied both solidarity with fellow white British men and a designation superior to the brown people. Brother Luke had been shipped over to Malaya as a teacher and had helped found St. Joseph's Boys' School, which Abel attended. A member of the Jesuit order, Brother Luke was a strict schoolmaster. This did not suit Abel, a terrible student.

"Name me three inventions from the Industrial Revolution, boy!" Brother Luke would bellow at Abel, sweat bubbling along his sideburns. He called all the students "boy" so that he did not have to figure out how to pronounce their names.

"Steam engine. Cotton gin," Abel sputtered before drawing a blank. He squeezed his eyes shut, willing his memory to deliver the third invention, but it would not come. Knowing what came next, he held out his hand, bracing for the stinging pain and turning his face away as Brother Luke's wooden ruler made contact with the softest part of his palm.

But the Brother Luke who had stood in front of Abel on the eve of his fifteenth birthday looked like a shadow of the robust, red-faced teacher with large round shoulders whom he remembered. This iteration of Brother Luke was gaunt, the base of his cheeks hollowed, one eye smaller than the other, swollen.

"Boy, do you mind?" Some things hadn't changed, Abel supposed. Brother Luke still didn't know his name.

"Yeah, Brother Luke?" Abel held the lit cigarette at his side, trying to hide it from view.

"Yes, boy, may I?" He gestured at the tendril of smoke that Abel had failed to conceal. Abel, resigned, handed over his birthday cigarette.

Brother Luke took a long drag, his cheeks sinking even farther into his face as he inhaled. "You do me good, boy." He sat down on the curb and held on to Abel's cigarette. "Have a seat next to me."

"It's good to see you again . . . sir," Abel said nervously. It was shocking to see Brother Luke; Abel had assumed that, like most of the other British administrators and missionaries, Brother Luke would have been taken away when the Japanese arrived, jailed at Changi Prison down south.

"Sir, did the Japanese let you out?" Abel asked.

Ignoring Abel's question, Brother Luke shielded his good eye from the afternoon sun, which poured its heat directly on them. "Listen, have you heard of the Burma Railway?"

Abel shook his head. "Have you been freed, sir?" he pressed.

"Boy, you were always so terrible at learning. It's a railroad the Japanese are building. To transport supplies."

Abel frowned at Brother Luke, unsure what a railroad had to do with him, irritated that he wasn't getting the answers he was looking for.

"Look, boy, do you want to help your family? They're looking for workers, coolies. It's easy work, good pay, and they will even give you a place to stay."

Yao Chun and Abel's other friends had heard about people coming around recruiting boys to work for the Japanese, with promises of easy jobs. A couple of their friends had even taken the offers, packing their meager belongings in hard trunks and hopping on the back of lorries, bound, they thought, for good jobs. They had never returned.

Still, this was the first time Abel had heard of a British recruiter; the others were more often local men who needed rations to feed their families. Abel inched away from Brother Luke and tried to stand up.

"Where are you going?" Brother Luke reached out the hand not holding the cigarette and gripped Abel's right forearm with surprising strength.

"Sir, I should go. My mother will worry."

"Look, boy, come with me, do it for me." Abel noticed that the outer corner of Brother Luke's good eye had begun twitching uncontrollably. "I need you to come."

"Sir, no, I must go." Abel pulled his arm away from Brother Luke's grip and stood so quickly he nearly tripped.

"They will put me back in the prison, boy. Please." Brother Luke's good eye was leaking tears; a desperation clouded them, so dark that Abel had to look away.

He ran home, leaving Brother Luke, a crumpled mess on the curb.

―

They came for him the next day, on the fifteenth, on his actual birthday. His mother had run her fingers through his hair that morning and promised him a surprise. He knew it wouldn't be much, they didn't have much these days, but maybe she'd whip up something sweet; his mother was creative with their limited rations.

He'd also been thinking about telur mata kerbau, a fried egg with a perfectly yellow center like the deepest part of a buffalo's eye. That morning, at the store again, Yao Chun's father, who owned the place, had given him five perfect brown eggs for free.

"But, uncle, we can't afford—" Abel said.

"Take it, birthday boy. It's from our chickens," Yao Chun's father had said.

Abel was daydreaming about the taste of the crunchy brown edges of a fried egg when a voice bellowed, "There he is!"

Turning toward the sound, Abel saw Brother Luke again, though the man looked even worse than he had the prior day. He pointed at Abel with his good arm. The other arm, his left, hung useless by his side, twisted at an odd angle. His good eye now had dried blood crusted on the lower lid; the other eye was swollen nearly shut. Brother Luke had clearly taken a fresh beating.

"Brother Luke!" Abel called out.

"Boy."

Before Abel could react, two Japanese soldiers in green army fatigues circled him. One was an inch or two shorter than Abel and stocky; the other was unusually tall, with a limp. They looked like caricatures of evil henchmen from the comic books Abel used to read.

"Come with us!" the taller one said. The shorter one pulled at Abel's shoulder roughly. Abel gripped the bag with the five eggs tightly, refusing to give them up.

The tall one made an impatient noise at the back of his throat that sounded like a rattling engine. He brought his heavy boot to the back of Abel's knees. Abel heard a sickening crack. He wasn't sure if it was the eggs or his knees hitting the hard, hot gravel.

As the two men dragged him away by the shoulders, Abel looked back at Brother Luke, bent over, tongue on the ground, lapping up raw egg yolk before it was absorbed into the ground.

From his crouching position in the coop, Abel heard the footfall of heavy boots. A familiar, pungent aroma of body odor and stale cigarette smoke swirled in his nostrils. He shrank to the back of the chicken coop, as far away from the latched door as possible. Earlier in the day, while he was working, he had found his knees shaking and his fingers losing their hold on the hard-to-grip edges of the wooden box he was carrying. He had stopped to put the box down and squatted on the ground, his head to his knees, trying to quell the dizziness that filled his head, having not eaten anything for two days. The line of boys behind him had come to an abrupt halt.

"Come on, man, you gotta get up." Rama nudged Abel's toe. "He's coming."

"White boy," the Japanese supervisor, Master Akiro, had shouted in Malay. "Move!"

Abel had felt his throat tighten.

"WHITE FUCK!" The supervisor advanced toward him, the sweat pool under his armpit darkening, his lips curving into a snarl.

Abel stood up as tall as his thin frame could muster. He glared down at Master Akiro. "Japanese fuck," he'd muttered.

That was how he had ended up here in the coop, bleeding alongside a dying rooster.

Abel had always been taller than everyone and fair, his eyes a hue of gray so light that his mother told him she could see the stars reflecting back at her when she looked at him. He was the only one. Both his parents had skin the color of murky coffee, as did his siblings, Jujube even darker than that, a fact she sometimes lamented.

He had always loved being fair. When he was a toddler tugging at his mother's arm, older ladies on the street would stop, pet him, and surreptitiously hand him his favorite sour-plum candy. When he grew taller, girls from the neighborhood tittered and pushed each other when he walked by, even the older girls. Abel's fair skin, his looks, and his disarming smile meant that he was always able to get what he wanted. He understood the concept of charm long before he knew the word for it.

But here at the camp, his fair skin was a curse. The supervisor assigned to his quadrant, Master Akiro, took a particular loathing to Abel, perhaps because Abel was the closest to his visualization of the white enemy. Master Akiro was thinner and slighter than Abel, so it made Abel furious to be so afraid of him. Every time the supervisor's small, sharp eyes turned in Abel's direction, Abel would feel his stomach lurch, and whatever tiny bit of food he had consumed for the day would rise and pool at the back of his throat, threatening escape.

For the first couple days after Abel arrived, Master Akiro engaged in simple cruelty. He would walk by the line of boys digging or carrying heavy loads, and when he reached Abel, he would drag his rifle on the ground so it knocked Abel around the ankles, causing him to trip and slide into the dust. Eventually, days became weeks and weeks turned into months, and the cruelties Master Akiro inflicted became more complex. Like the time when Master Akiro had made him and Rama stand side by side: Abel, his fair skin flushed by sunburn and mottled with dirt, and Rama, broad-shouldered and dark-skinned, the tips of his fingers dotted with white spots where cuts and calluses accumulated.

"Do you think their blood is the same color, huh? Blackie and Whitey?" Master Akiro said to himself. Then he raised his voice so all the boys and men in the quadrant would look up. "Let's see!"

Abel wished he had passed out like Rama had when the blunt knife blade scratched back and forth over his arm, frustrating Master Akiro because it was taking too long to draw blood. But Abel would not scream, biting his tongue so blood flowed in his mouth too.

"The same! Their blood is the same!" Master Akiro yelled, holding both Abel's and Rama's arms in the air like victorious fighters, dark, thick streams of blood running down their elbows.

In the chicken coop, Abel watched Master Akiro's boot tips, muddy and discolored, kick the door open. It was almost sunset. The other boys would be going to the mess hall now for dinner. Abel noticed his battered body cast a crooked shadow on the ground; the air had become still, windless, the buzzing of mosquitoes around him a rageful harmony. The dirty boots came to a stop in front of Abel.

"Up," said Master Akiro's thick voice.

Abel raised his eyes and stared up into the supervisor's nose. A drop of sweat from Master Akiro's face improbably dripped onto Abel's lip, forcing him to taste the salt and dirt from his tormentor's body.

"Get. Up." Master Akiro shoved his boot under Abel's body and forced him onto all fours. The mosquitoes seemed to buzz louder, drowning out the horrifying realization that ran through Abel's body as the sound of Master Akiro's belt buckle hitting his holster rang through the quiet evening. Abel felt the tiniest of breezes as Master Akiro's pants fell on the dusty ground. He tried to crawl toward the door, toward the dying rooster, anything to get away from what he knew was coming, but the supervisor pulled him back by the shirt. The two white hens squawked and the brown one stared at Abel, her eyes blank, knowing. As Master Akiro's penis scraped Abel's insides, Abel heard him mutter, "Same as white lady, same as white lady." Through a gap in the coop door, Abel stared into the orange ball of sunset in the distance, willing his knees not to buckle.

CHAPTER FOUR

JUJUBE

Bintang, Kuala Lumpur
August 16, 1945
Japanese-occupied Malaya

Jujube was having a rough day at the teahouse. It wasn't her first rough day; she'd been working at the teahouse for almost a year, and she was used to a certain level of rudeness from the soldiers who patronized the shop, leering glances, rough hands, spitting words. But the last couple of weeks had felt different, a tension threatening to break like a dam.

Three soldiers gathered at a table in the center of the teahouse, shoulders slumped, eyes glazed.

"They will leave us in this godforsaken place to die," said one of the soldiers, a stout man with patchy hair. The soldiers assumed she did not understand Japanese.

"They may bomb us, but Americans are no match for our men," another one, younger, said hopefully.

"Either way, we drink," the third one muttered, pulling out a bottle of murky liquid and passing it around.

Jujube looked helplessly at her teahouse manager, Doraisamy. It was only eleven o'clock, and they did not permit alcohol at the teahouse. She assumed the soldiers had gotten the sharp-smelling liquor on the black market since it was so difficult to come by otherwise. Doraisamy shook his head. *Let them,* he mouthed. Jujube nodded. Doraisamy was right; nothing good would come of reprimanding the soldiers.

—

The previous week, on the evening of August 9, just as her family had sat down to dinner, her father had screamed in excitement when the static crackled through the illegal radio he kept hidden in a flowerpot. As the static cleared, a voice broke through, announcing that the Americans had dropped nuclear bombs on Nagasaki. Their neighbor Andrew Carvalho, a little man who worked alongside their father at the sheet-metal workshop, burst into their house waving a telegram.

"I'm told it looked like a mushroom cloud. The towns will not survive!" Mr. Carvalho pulled their father to his feet.

"THE AMERICANS!" her father had said, rising shakily from the floor. "If they win this war, I will go to America to shake President Truman's hand."

The two men crowded around the radio, food forgotten. Jasmin, with a wink at her sister, tipped the last of their father's food onto her own plate.

"Ma, what do you think? Should I clean up the dinner?" Jujube said.

But her mother had disappeared, footsteps echoing down the hall, the sound of the bedroom door slamming shut. Jujube sighed as she began stacking the plates, clearing the table. She would take care of everything, as always.

———

As Jujube walked back to the teahouse kitchen, averting her eyes from the table of soldiers, she heard a soft voice murmur, "Sorry for they are embarrass." It was her favorite regular customer, Mr. Takahashi, stumbling over his tenses.

Mr. Takahashi had first come in on a rainy day the previous December, after she'd been working at the teahouse for about three months. Unlike the soldiers who grabbed her by the strings of her apron or spat at her feet, he had stared shyly at the table and said, in Japanese-inflected English, "My name is Takahashi." He pointed down the street. "I teach. At the school over there."

Over the next few days, Jujube had watched him from the glass window that separated the kitchen from the dining area. She noticed that he avoided the low, rickety wooden tables that the soldiers gathered around, favoring instead the small green one in the left corner, a little bit away from the rowdy soldiers. He wore the same brown blazer every day, the sleeves scuffed, the fabric beneath his pits stained dark from sweat. Always alone, he would flip through the local newspaper absently, rubbing the newsprint off his fingers and onto his gray pants, leaving little smudges that Jujube wondered if he knew how to clean. He was only an inch or two taller than she, and whispers of gray dotted his sparse mustache. His ears pointed a little too far forward, and those, in combination with his thick but too high eyebrows, gave him the air of an owl, she told Jasmin later. He always said "please" and "thank you" in English when she poured his tea.

One day as she passed his table, he'd looked at her above the rim of his teacup and said shyly in Malay, *"Apa koh-bar?"*

"KHA-bar," Jujube corrected in spite of herself.

Every morning after that, he would come in and greet her, *"Apa khabar,"* in his soft lilt, and Jujube found herself nodding. One day after his greeting, she surprised herself by responding, *"Khabar baik."*

His eyes lit up like a child's. "I'm doing well also!"

About two weeks after he first arrived, he waved Jujube over.

"More tea, sir?" she'd asked, pointing at the ornate blue kettle she was holding, steam rising from the spout.

"Can I give you something?" he asked. As her eyes met his, he looked down, inviting her gaze to the white saucer under the teacup, and on it, she saw the tattered edge of a red food ration coupon.

"For you." He smiled. "For a Christmas present."

Jujube's family, like every family for the last two years, was allocated one food coupon that entitled them to a quarter bag of rice every week. It was a struggle; sometimes her siblings' stomachs growled so loudly they could be heard in the next room. Jujube's mother had taken to mixing waxy tapioca root with their rice, creating a congealed sticky texture that Jujube hated. It filled their stomachs, so it didn't feel like sour acid gnawing a hole in there, but it made everything taste like glue.

Before his disappearance, Abel had grumbled endlessly about the tapioca, coming up with a new reason every day for their mother to stop mixing it into their rice. "Ma," he would whine, "do you know that raw tapioca root is dangerous?"

"Boy, do you think I was born yesterday?" Their mother would roll her eyes and pull Abel into her arms.

"Ma," he would squeal, wriggling away, "it has cyanide! It will kill us, you know." He stuck his tongue out the side of his mouth and crossed his eyes like a cartoon character. "Dead!"

"Only if I don't soak the root well enough, silly. Now help your mother rinse it."

Mr. Takahashi's red food coupon would double their ration, and Jujube's mouth watered at the thought of fluffy rice, rice that could soak up curry and spices, rice that didn't congeal, thick at the back of her throat. She grabbed it off the saucer, crushed it in her palm, and started to walk back into the kitchen. Then she paused. "Thank you." She could feel Mr. Takahashi smile into her back.

From then on, every couple of days, Mr. Takahashi brought her a new gift. Sometimes he brought books, children's books full of pictures that Jasmin loved, or novels, Penguin Classics like *The Swiss Family Robinson* and *Jane Eyre*, that Jujube devoured. Sometimes he brought meters and meters of cotton, which her mother used to make them all new shirts; sometimes he came with a beautiful but useless ornament like a carved wood turtle or a porcelain ashtray. But Wednesdays were the best day. Each Wednesday morning, Mr. Takahashi came into the teahouse with a single tattered red food ration coupon, and each Wednesday evening, their family ate like kings. Jasmin laughed, her lips crinkling on her sallow skin, and if they were lucky, Jujube's mother smiled all the way up to her eyes.

At first Jujube had thought he wanted sex, like the rest of them. She'd asked her mother what to do if one day he were to take her into the back of the teahouse, throw her onto the pile of wet garbage, and hold a knife to her neck. Her mother's advice had been simple: "Stay still." For the first few weeks, Jujube waited, hands shaking, for Mr. Takahashi to claim his prize. But all Mr. Takahashi did was talk. He would sip his tea, the steam blowing up his nose, and chat about this and that. Sometimes they discussed the relationship between Jane Eyre and Mr. Rochester (Jujube thought it romantic, Mr. Takahashi felt it inappropriate); sometimes he told her stories about his family in Nagasaki (everyone worked in the Mitsubishi factories, making ships and munitions—they were all metalworkers who were good with their hands, except Mr. Takahashi, who used to get made fun of for reading all the time). And then at exactly 10:20 a.m., he would stand up abruptly, say, "Recess is over!" gulp down his tea, and go back to his school.

The soldiers roared, their drunken bickering echoing through the teahouse.

"Do not be worry," Mr. Takahashi said as he got up.

"Are you going back to the school, sir?" she asked.

"Yes, and I will see you tomorrow," he said.

The truth was she didn't like growing fond of Mr. Takahashi. She had heard about the kind ones, of course. The sergeant who, when told to ransack a home and clear everyone in it, had left the youngest baby alive, hidden behind a dustpan. Or the doctor who had injected his young comfort-women patients with harmless viruses that gave them a rash, so they would become undesirable enough not to have to go back to servicing the soldiers. And now Mr. Takahashi. But kindness did not excuse mass violence, kindness did not bring Abel back, kindness wouldn't keep her safe. She consoled herself by telling herself she was getting something out of it, the red coupon that helped keep her family alive.

Also, Mr. Takahashi could be pedantic sometimes, his teachery ways coming through unexpectedly. Six months into their curious friendship, he'd asked her what she hoped to do after the war ended. Jujube had been startled; she hadn't spent much time thinking about this for herself. She knew that she wanted Jasmin to go back to school, she knew that their mother hoped Abel, before he disappeared, would go on to join the civil service—it meant a stable, safe office job that guaranteed the grant of a tiny but serviceable tract of land where he could build a house for his eventual family. But for herself? Jujube shrugged at Mr. Takahashi's question. She might be too old to go back to school; she could not see herself married. It didn't matter, she didn't matter, and no one knew when the war would be over anyway.

At her shrug, Mr. Takahashi's eyes had flashed. "You need to see more for yourself," he said, which had surprised her. "You can be scientist, journalist, you just need to get the . . . the . . ." He wavered over the word, then said it in Japanese: ". . . credentials."

Then he was standing up, chair pushed back, voice raised. "You cannot survive this and live a dead life." Beads of sweat dotted his forehead.

She felt her hand holding the kettle become clammy. It felt like it was slipping. She willed herself not to drop it. "Sir, Mr. Takahashi, sir, I didn't mean to upset you. I'm sorry," she murmured.

The air in the already stuffy teahouse thickened. Other customers, soldiers mostly, had put down their teacups and turned to look at them. A tall soldier with an uneven mustache reached for his weapon.

"Sir, I'm sorry, I didn't . . . What can I do to make this better?" Jujube pleaded. She felt the soldier move closer.

Doraisamy waved frantically from the kitchen window. Do not make trouble, Doraisamy's eyes said.

Mr. Takahashi sat down heavily and shook his head at the advancing soldier. "No need." Then he turned to Jujube, eyes dark with remorse. "I am sorry," he said. "My daughter is in Nagasaki. We are just two. Her mother is no more. My daughter, you and she are— What is English word? Alike."

As the months wore on, her conversations with Mr. Takahashi continued with quiet regularity. Sometimes he would invite her to sit and read the plays of Shakespeare together, doing voices, Mr. Takahashi stumbling over words like "forsooth." Sometimes he would write letters to his daughter in Nagasaki, in English ("I want her to learn!" he said). He was worried because lately his daughter's replies had waned. Perhaps the letters were not arriving? Perhaps the mail carriers were being shot down? But faithfully, he wrote, calling over the sound of the whirring fans in the teahouse to ask Jujube for words: "What is word for when a child grows up into an adult?" ("Matures," Jujube would reply.) Sometimes he would have her read over his letters.

"Make it more loving, like a father to a daughter," he would say. "Affection is not something I learn for teaching."

She would reply, "Add this: 'I miss you all the time.'"

Things were not going well at home either. About two months after Abel disappeared, a pair of soldiers had shown up at their front door, rapping angrily. Her father, face ashen, had answered.

"*Ada guniang kah?*" one of the Japanese soldiers said in Malay, tapping his rifle on the ground.

Jasmin, in the kitchen, stopped chopping the onions she'd been tasked with and turned toward Jujube. "Sis, what's a *guniang*?"

"Basement. Now," Jujube whispered, grabbing Jasmin's arm and rushing them down the rickety wooden steps into the tiny cellar space her father had dug to hide valuables and food in the event that their house was ransacked. Jujube heard her mother click the wooden door above their head and, a minute later, the footfall of heavy military boots.

"You have girls?"

Jasmin opened her mouth as if to cry, and Jujube clamped her hand over it.

"No, sir, only boys here. Maybe you try next door?" Her father's voice echoed above them. Jujube admired how still and unwavering he sounded. The strength of his voice reminded her of what he was like before the war, convincing and fearless. Now most days her father shuffled through the house coughing, his face creased with worry. He told their family that they were the lucky ones; most of his British colleagues had been taken away to Changi Prison, some killed en route, but even if his words said so, he did not sound grateful, only brittle with sadness.

Jujube knew about comfort women. After the Rape of Nanking, the Japanese tried to prevent rape crimes in occupied regions. Instead of allowing the soldiers to go out to cities and villages, the women would be brought to them, to "comfort stations" where the soldiers would be allowed to relieve their urges. At first Jujube had started wearing two bras to flatten herself as much as possible. But she soon learned that the recruiters preferred younger girls, pre-pubescent, as they lay more still and did not get pregnant. These recruiters, rough-skinned soldiers, would walk through the neighborhood, knocking on doors. *"Guniang,"* they would say. "Bring out the young girls."

Minutes felt like hours, but soon Jujube heard the front door slam. As they crawled out of the basement, Jujube's mother had grabbed Jasmin roughly by the shoulder and pushed her down into a squat on a bucket.

"Cecily," her father had pleaded. "Stop."

"I will not lose another child," her mother had cried, grabbing a pair of scissors and chopping off all of Jasmin's fine black hair. Jasmin, brave and old beyond her years, had blinked back tears in silence and held Jujube's hand. From that day, Jasmin wore Abel's old clothes—grimy pants and large white shirts—and was not allowed to leave the house.

That night, on the mattress they both shared, Jujube had held Jasmin, running her fingers through her sister's short, uneven hair. Jasmin wept so quietly that no one would have known anything was amiss unless they felt the wetness on Jasmin's cheeks. Jujube laced the fingers of Jasmin's left hand into her own and pointed them up at the sky outside their window, gleaming with stars.

"There are people out there, fighting for us," she said, running her free hand through her sister's shorn scalp.

"Where?" Jasmin whispered. "Where are they fighting?"

"Normandy," Jujube said uncertainly. "Dunkirk. Antwerp."

"Ant—" Jasmin whispered. "How do you say it? Ant—"

"An-TWERP, silly. Do you know what 'twerp' means?"

Jasmin shook her head.

"A twerp is a silly person. Like you!" Jujube pressed two fingers into Jasmin's ticklish side and her sister giggled through her tears.

Maybe they have forgotten us, Jujube thought, these Western fronts, places with names that rolled strangely on her tongue, places she could find on atlases but couldn't visualize. Maybe people like her, Jasmin, and Abel did not matter—here in a tiny tropical corner in the East, being brutalized by people who looked almost exactly like them.

As evening bled into dusk, the soldiers at the teahouse grew more and more raucous, culminating in several vomiting all over the floor. The smell of their bile filled the warm air. Doraisamy helped the swaying soldiers out of the teahouse, then handed Jujube a gray mop.

"You know what to do," he said, nodding at the streaky mess on the floor. "Remember to lock the door when you leave."

Jujube's throat seized with panic as she looked first at the clock, then at the setting sun, an orange ball filling the window. Her eyes pricked, but she didn't have time for sentimentality; she just had to finish up and get home. It was a straight shot to the house, a twenty-minute walk at most, but as night fell, Japanese soldiers roamed the streets trying to catch anyone in violation of the eight o'clock curfew.

Jujube filled a bucket and dipped the old gray mop into the water. As she cleaned, arms aching from working as fast as she could, a quiet, familiar voice pierced the air. "I come after school. I thought maybe you need help so you will not be late. For the curfew," she heard Mr. Takahashi say.

"Sir, how did you get in?"

He gestured at the unlatched back door. "Next time close door, Jujube. For the safety."

"Sir, I cannot—" Jujube protested. Doraisamy would fire her if he knew that a customer, and even worse, a regular customer, had picked up a mop.

"I will not tell anyone. A secret," Mr. Takahashi said, holding a finger to his lips.

It was completely dark by the time they finished mopping. Jujube glanced at the face of her red leather watch—ten minutes to eight. The watch was a gift from her parents for getting straight A's in the general examination a few years earlier, but of course there was no more school now. Her school, like many others the British had set up in the city, had been converted by Japanese forces into an interrogation center. The once-bright windows now stood shadowed, and as she walked by, she could smell the sourness of blood and sweat squeezing through the seams. General Fujiwara had now dispatched his soldiers to roam the streets. Anyone deemed suspicious—a bow not low enough, a look perceived to be insolent—was thrown into one of the many dank rooms in the interrogation center and beaten until a confession, any confession, was extracted.

When the Japanese first arrived, her father, a devoted empire loyalist, had told them that the British would come back and sweep out the Japanese like the trash he said they were. But that hope seemed to be extinguished when, six months into the Occupation, her father was ordered to work at a converted sheet-metal workshop, carrying piles of sharp, newly cut pieces of metal across the workshop floor. Now her father's hands were cut with scars, his throat expelling a constant rasping cough, and his defiance a distant memory. He had taken to carrying a photo of Emperor Hirohito in his wallet, as proof of his fealty to the Japanese, hinging forward to bow so low that his head nearly touched the ground every time he saw a soldier. To Jujube, this seemed like the true treason.

She had declined to go to the few Japanese language schools that had been opened. She hated learning the language, and every time she greeted anyone in Japanese, it felt like bile rising in the back of her throat. Some people were subtly defiant, of course. Instead of saying *"Ohayo gozaimasu"* in greeting to the Japanese soldiers, Abel used to bow and whisper, *"Ohayo gosok* my arse" (*gosok* being the word for "scrub"). The joke always made Jasmin giggle, but Abel's insolence just made Jujube want to twist his skinny arm—was a silly pun worth dying for? Thinking about Abel made her heart ache so painfully, she had to close her eyes for a second.

"Jujube?" Mr. Takahashi said. "Work finish?"

Pulling off her apron, Jujube replied, "I must lock up."

"Come," he said. "I will walk along you. It will be safer."

"No, sir," she protested. He was old. He would slow her down.

"We will go," he said.

She gave in. It was too late to argue.

―

Five days earlier, Mr. Takahashi had arrived at the teahouse with the same gray face that Jujube had seen on her mother the night Abel had not come home. Mr. Takahashi had sat down at his usual table, but instead of waving her over, he stared at the smudge on the splintery wooden surface with blinking eyes, his left shoulder twitching.

"Do you need any tea, sir?" Jujube asked.

He lifted his arm as if to wave her away, then dropped it as though he'd lost the will to move. "They . . . they got her, Jujube. My daughter. The bomb . . . they say no one . . ."

Mr. Takahashi's anguish was interesting to Jujube. Whereas the light had gone out in her mother's eyes, Mr. Takahashi's eyes were wild, darting around in their sockets. He stood up and started pacing.

She noticed that instead of wearing shoes, he wore blue slippers and only one sock.

"How could the Americans do this? The people there are innocent, INNOCENT!" His voice cracked, and in spite of herself, Jujube felt a splinter of pity in her heart. "I will write to the general. There is a chance, a small chance. Perhaps she was somewhere else. Perhaps..."

And then Jujube realized what the difference was. Her mother's eyes held no hope. But Mr. Takahashi was not yet broken in the way her mother was; he could believe that his daughter was alive.

"It will be all right, sir," she said, pouring him some tea. "Have faith."

After all, his people could still afford to have faith.

Mr. Takahashi continued to come to the teahouse each day. He wrote letters to everyone he knew: ambassadors, generals, friends, family. He wrote letters in English and Japanese, Jujube reading over the English ones.

"I write to you of a matter of very urgency," he would write.

"Utmost urgency," Jujube would correct, glancing over while refilling his tea.

"Utmost," he would scribble before looking up at her with gratitude in his eyes. "You are my hope."

―

The two walked in silence, Jujube as briskly as she could not to offend, eyes trained for soldiers. Suddenly, she felt the ground begin to rumble beneath her. With instinct born of necessity, she flattened herself against the dirt.

"Down," she cried. "Sir! You must get down!"

She watched as he mirrored her, flattening himself against the dusty road, both bracing for an air strike. If she were home, everyone in the family would have been running outside to avoid being killed by falling debris, the noise of the planes above them looming. Warplanes, her mother had taught her, are not most dangerous when they are flying directly above you, casting a dark shadow over your head. In fact, they are most dangerous when they have flown diagonally ahead of you, because the bombs they shed from their tail fall to the ground at an angle, destroying everything in their path.

The earth continued to shake beneath Jujube's chin but then stopped. The night sky remained dark.

"Just a plane flying low," she said, standing up and dusting herself off. She pulled Mr. Takahashi to his feet, the old man's shoulders trembling. "Sir, don't worry. It was not an air strike."

"Thank you," he said, dusting himself off. "How do you know what to do?"

She did not know how to answer Mr. Takahashi. To explain that after past explosions, Jujube and her family would stand up and peer past each other to see which one of their neighbors' houses had survived and which ones had been blown up. They would kick through the rubble for bits of friends and family to find something, anything, to bury with dignity.

"Do you think——? Was it like this—in Nagasaki?" Mr. Takahashi said, his voice shaking.

Jujube felt empty, consoling words rushing to the tip of her tongue, but she knew they would be useless. It was probably much worse in Nagasaki.

"Let's keep going," she said.

Up ahead, lights flashed. A checkpoint. It was swarming with soldiers, checking the long lines of people for munitions, knives, black-market medication, and food. As they approached the barrier, a soldier yanked her arm so roughly she felt a twist in her shoulder. It would hurt tomorrow.

"You are late! You know what happens to girls who are out after curfew?" The soldier shone a flashlight at her chest as his eyes rolled up and down her body.

Jujube bit down hard on her lower lip. She would not shake before this soldier, this pale, angry man scouring her loose clothes for traces of a curve, for something on her body to lay his disgusting hand on.

"Hey, sir, no need for that," she heard Mr. Takahashi say in Japanese. "She is with me."

"Don't you know how to respect your elders? Bow," the soldier said to Jujube. To Mr. Takahashi, "Old man, what is this scum doing with you?"

Jujube felt hot with rage. She knew what she had to do, but her body would not obey; instead of bending into a bow, she straightened in defiance, her back stiffening.

"Bow," Mr. Takahashi hissed in Japanese, pressing long, bony fingers into her back, the first time he had ever touched her. His voice softened into a plea. "Please. Please bow."

He was right. Her family needed her. They had already lost too much. Gritting her teeth, Jujube bent her head so low it grazed the dust. But as the flashlight above her head pointed elsewhere, Jujube narrowed her eyes and spat a quiet trail next to the soldier's boot.

The soldier pulled her up to standing by her hair. "Get lost." He pushed her through the barricade.

When she looked back, she saw Mr. Takahashi waving before he turned and walked slowly away.

CHAPTER FIVE
—

JASMIN

Bintang, Kuala Lumpur
August 16, 1945
Japanese-occupied Malaya

"Mini! Eenie-meenie!" Jasmin heard the familiar shrill whistle of the Japanese girl's voice flitting through the open window that she and Jujube lay entangled under.

"Come ousside," said the whisper.

In a series of practiced motions, Jasmin pulled first her left ankle, then her right, out of the tangled nest of legs that she and her sister often found themselves in when they slept. That night, the moon, obscured by the clouds, provided only a sliver of light, but Jasmin was used to spending time in the dark. With the stealth of a cat, she crept to the front gate, gathered her nightdress at her waist, and clambered over.

"Yuki! Shhhh! You're too loud, we'll get caught!" Jasmin scolded.

"I couldn't sleep. Aunty Woon won't put on the fan, and it's so hot." Yuki fanned herself dramatically, her yellow nightie, too big for her, bunching under her arms.

Jasmin rolled her eyes at Yuki, but she could never stay angry at her friend.

Jasmin had met Yuki in January, just weeks before her brother disappeared, when Abel had taken her to the chemist to get something to help with their father's coughing. That afternoon had been a scorcher, Jasmin remembered, the sky wide and cloudless in a way that was rare. As they walked, Jasmin had pushed her nose upward, the steamy air flowing through her nostrils, sweet from her namesake jasmine flowers, and sour from the stale river water slopping around the muddy estuary where the Talim and Merbok rivers met. Her brother had looked over at her sniffing and chuckled.

"My silly sister." Abel pinched the tip of her nose.

"Abe! Stop!" She pulled her nose away from his fingers.

"Well, stop sniffing the air like a dog, Langsat," he said, mumbling his nickname for her—a reference to the fruit they used to share. It was Abel who had taught her how to nibble an opening in the outside skin and squeeze out the translucent flesh inside. They'd munch on the pile of fruit till their fingers were sticky. But of course, that was in the before times.

When they reached the chemist, Abel had lingered much longer than he needed at the counter. Jasmin noticed he always took too long when Peik Lum, the buxom assistant, was on shift. Their father, prone to the pun, called the girl Peik Plump.

"You tied up your hair today," she heard Abel say to Peik Lum, a nervous wobble in his voice.

Jasmin suppressed a laugh. Even if it was a little idiotic, she liked seeing her brother smile. Everyone smiled so little these days. Jujube walked around with her lips squeezed so tightly together that Jasmin wondered if she even remembered how to smile. Jasmin missed her sister, her sister from before—she missed how Jujube would fold her body in half and barrel her head and fingertips into Jasmin's stomach until Jasmin fell onto the cushions a giggling, ticklish mess. Now all her sister did was hold on to Jasmin's hand so tightly she left fingernail imprints on Jasmin's palm.

"*Bodoh,* isn't he?"

Jasmin whirled around to find out who dared call her brother stupid. That was a privilege reserved for her and Jujube only. Yes, he was a little silly, but his jokes, and his impressions of Leher, the giraffe in Jasmin's favorite comic, were the only things that could make their mother chuckle these days.

When she turned, Jasmin came face-to-face with the strangest-looking girl she'd ever seen. The right side of the girl's face was fair, that clean paper-white coloring she had learned to recognize in the rare Japanese woman she saw on the street, with a thin line of fine hair marking a faint eyebrow above her single-lidded eye. But the left side of the girl's face looked as though it had been mashed in with a spatula—the skin was darker, rough, and ridged down the cheek, and her eye seemed stretched to the side of her face. There was no eyebrow, thin or otherwise, on the left side. Jasmin felt herself beginning to recoil, but she pushed that thought away, held herself still, afraid to upset the other girl.

"Jasmin, you ready to go home?" Abel called, and Jasmin ran to meet him.

The strange, insolent girl followed them home. Jasmin noticed the girl flitting behind her and Abel, starting and stopping, as they did, on corners. Abel, distracted by his conversation with Peik Lum, hadn't noticed, and Jasmin didn't say anything. When they got back to the house, Jasmin turned around to confront the girl, but she had vanished.

Then, in May, three months after Abel disappeared, the girl had shown up at the house. Jasmin, curled up against her sister under the window, heard a whisper: "Wake up!"

Pulling herself out of Jujube's tight embrace, she looked over the window ledge and saw the strange girl standing below, her head barely grazing the bottom of the wooden windowsill.

"Come out," the girl said. "Let's play."

Jasmin eyed her suspiciously. The night air felt cool and delicious in the window, and the moon was lopsided, three quarters and bright. She wanted nothing more than to run around barefoot and feel the damp grass creep between her toes. But she didn't know this strange spatula-faced girl.

"What's wrong with your face?" Jasmin had asked.

"What's wrong with your hair?" the Japanese girl replied, and stuck out her tongue.

Jasmin tugged at the uneven patches on her head. After the recruiters had gone away, Jujube had assured her that she had nothing to be afraid of if she stayed at home and wore Abel's old clothes. But then the recruiters returned, once the next week and three times the following week. At first her family used to have her father answer the door as Jujube rushed her into the basement to hide. But they began to worry that they wouldn't get to the basement in time, or that the recruiters would push past her father, who seemed tireder and sicklier by the day, and the men would see Jujube smuggling her into the basement. So now, every morning after she and Jujube woke up before sunrise, Jasmin would kiss her sister goodbye and head to the basement, where she would stay all day until curfew, when it got dark and the men stopped their house-to-house interrogations.

Her family tried to make the small space comfortable. Jasmin's father moved a little table in there, and a chair with a cushion on it. Sometimes when she was bored, Jasmin traced the batik patterns on the cushion cover from memory, little yellow circles on an affronting red-pink fabric, but because it was so dark in the basement, the red looked brown like rust, like blood. Because they didn't want any light to seep through the floorboards, Jasmin often sat in the dark, watching the shadows move on top of her as her family walked around the house. Sometimes she imagined a different family living above her—one with superpowers, a brother with the strength to lift a tree or throw a million soldiers over his shoulder, a sister who could run as fast as light, and herself, with the power of invisibility so she could observe people.

Jujube brought Jasmin as many books as she could get her hands on, some from her new Japanese teacher friend at the teahouse, but it was often too dim to read, and it made Jasmin's eyes hurt to squint. Sometimes her father would poke his nose through the floorboards and make loud sniffing noises like a dog, which made her laugh, then made her sad when he would inevitably cough. Jasmin knew they were trying—she loved her family so much it hurt her chest sometimes. Her mother brought food down at intervals, and they would eat together quietly. Since Abel had disappeared, her mother, who used to chatter and grumble incessantly about everything—the weather, the laziness of her children, the difficulty of raising a family during a war, the neighbor who annoyed her by allowing his mangy dog to roam around, and so on—had ceased to talk. When Jasmin looked at her mother, she felt a sadness so deep it radiated from her, little pinpricks that shot through anyone her mother encountered. And once a week, Jasmin's mother would lock her jaw and take a pair of scissors to Jasmin's hair. Jasmin still cried every time.

But the worst thing was that Jasmin worried she was forgetting Abel. When she first started wearing his clothes, she would feel like she was cloaked in his scent, like she could never get away from him. But the clothes had started to smell more like her, and when she tried to conjure up memories of Abel, she felt like his face was fading. She would squeeze her eyes shut to remember something, a joke he made over breakfast or how he used to take off only one sock when he came home from school, running around with one smelly sock and one smelly bare foot, but even if she could remember his veiny foot, the edges of his face, the contours that made his cheeks rise when he spoke, the little hole on his chin—a "dimple," her mother called it—the memories all seemed blurrier, harder to recall.

And no matter how much her family cleaned the basement, it was always dusty, the air heavy with a dampness she couldn't escape—like it was crawling with something, creeping into her throat every time she inhaled. She had taken to breathing as shallowly as she could, her body trying its best to refuse the air. It was difficult trying to stifle her cough; she knew that a single sound at the wrong time could mean she would be sent away.

She had asked Jujube once, what the recruiters wanted.

"You heard them, Jas, they want young girls."

"But, sis, what for?" she'd pressed.

Jujube's face went dark, her brown eyes clouded black. "Bad things. They'll hurt you"—Jujube pointed to Jasmin's private area—"there."

The following afternoon when she was alone in the basement,

Jasmin slipped her cotton panties off and felt around the lips of her vagina in the dark. "What could they want?" she wondered, bringing her fingers to her nose. "It just smells like piss."

"Come on! Come play!" the Japanese girl had whined that first night.

"No." Jasmin shook her head. "My sister will hear me."

The girl held her hand up to the window. "I have marbles." She held three small shiny balls in her palm. They shone against the moonlight, colorful slivers of light, pink, blue, white, green, yellow, bouncing and mixing in the glass spheres, the palette mesmerizing Jasmin. It was Abel who had taught her how to play marbles, how to hold the cool glass on the tip of her hand between her thumb and index finger, and how to flip the marble off with a tiny thumb raise, just enough pressure to scatter the other marbles but not so much as to send her own marble bouncing. He'd lost his temper with her only once, when she'd been practicing with his favorite marble, a black one with yellow stripes, his *guli harimau*, he called it. She'd flipped the marble too hard onto the grass, and it had rolled into the drain outside their house; they'd heard a tiny splash as the marble sank into the shallow water, settling into the silty, brown-stained drain.

"Abe, I'm sorry," she began. He'd pushed her aside and stormed off.

Over the next few days, she saw him climb into the drain and balance precariously on the ledge, flinching as he plunged his hand into the stinking water, feeling around for the marble. She'd offered to help, but he would wave her away wordlessly with his free hand, nose screwed up against the wafting smell of dog shit, sodden refuse, and rotting vegetables that coated the drain's edges.

The day before Abel's birthday, it had rained torrentially in the evening, the kind of storm their mother always said portended an angry god. "God is crying, my babies, because someone upset him," she would murmur as they flinched from the loud thunder. Abel had watched mournfully as the drain water roared ferociously in the storm, the current pushing its way along the ledge, dragging everything with it, trash, animal feces, rot, and probably the marble, to the river.

"I'm so sorry," Jasmin had cried, hugging her brother at the waist, her small arms barely reaching around even though Abel was thin.

"It was just a stupid marble anyway," he said quietly to her, the first words he'd spoken to her in days. They stood by the window watching the raindrops splash.

When he didn't come home the next day, Jasmin had hoped he was out looking for his marble. Perhaps he'd just followed the drain current out to the river and was rooting around the riverbank, nose scrunched up against the smell.

Now it had been months. Jujube's eyes had turned hard, her father barely spoke, and her mother had stopped talking altogether.

Jasmin and Yuki developed a routine. They would curl up opposite each other on the grass patch on the side of the family house, just out of sight of both Jujube's window and the road where soldiers occasionally patrolled. Jasmin would pull out the congkak board she had hidden behind the bougainvillea bush and set it down between them, a carved wooden boat-shaped board with seven holes on each side, and two larger empty divots that operated as "home caves" at the ends of the board.

Congkak was a game of mathematics in which two players moved marbles across the holes in the oblong board and accumulated as many of these brightly colored spectrums of light and beauty into one's home cave as possible. But instead of viewing it as winning or losing, Jasmin liked to think about congkak as a game of saving, like she was guiding each marble back to its home.

One night Jasmin played a game of pretend with herself, wondering, if she had seven seats on a boat to herself, whom she should allot them to. There were five people in her family, so that left just two spare seats in the imaginary boat. Whom would they go to? Perhaps Peik Lum, the plump girl at the chemist? That would make Abel so happy, and Jasmin figured they could always get medicine. Or what about the old Japanese owl-man whom Jujube talked about, the one she seemed fond of from the teahouse? For a while they would get food coupons from him, and he sent presents, including this very congkak board. It would be nice to have a kind man with presents around. And how about Yuki? Yuki with her bright eyes and bumpy face who looked the same age Jasmin was but somehow felt much older, Yuki who tried to hide the cuts between her fingers and who limped sometimes as though she had been punched between the legs, Yuki who always started little stories about her day, her life, the people who lived with her, but never finished them. Then Jasmin remembered that she actually had three extra seats, not two, because Abel had disappeared, and their family was now four. Abel did not need a seat on the boat. Remembering that made her stomach hurt.

She and Yuki set up their game as always, the board between them, the grass scratching the backs of their knees. Jasmin adjusted her nightie so it shielded her from the blades of grass that sometimes left itchy welts on her thighs. Yuki seemed distracted, pulling at the grass and scattering it on her dress.

"Yuki, you're bleeding." Jasmin pointed down the inside of Yuki's leg.

Yuki tugged at her dress. "It's not painful anymore."

"Yuki, what's wrong with you? Don't you want to play?" Jasmin was used to seeing Yuki with cuts here and there, but the blood down her leg seemed fresher and the shine in Yuki's eyes a bit dimmer.

"There was an uncle today. He was rough."

"What do you mean, an uncle?"

Yuki shook her head and picked up a handful of marbles. "I'll start the game," she said.

A few days earlier, when Jasmin had asked Yuki where she lived, she'd stared at the congkak board and said, "In a different place, smelly."

"My basement's smelly too sometimes," Jasmin had said. "Jujube says it's rat poop."

She'd thought the grossness would make Yuki giggle, since most everything else did. But Yuki had just looked away. It was always like this. Jasmin knew that Yuki lived in a house with a bunch of other girls and an older woman called Aunty Woon. Sometimes she would complain about the other girls—how they stole her things or were mean to her. One time she told Jasmin she had thrown one of the girls' hair combs into the dustbin, then thrown hot oil on it just to make sure the other girl could never use it. Jasmin was appalled; her family would never be this nasty to one another. Jasmin thought Yuki should be more appreciative. Jasmin loved curling up with her sister in their little corner at night. In the moonlight she felt like she could see the Jujube she used to know—the one who read stories, who wanted to be someone big, like a doctor or the principal of a school. To Jasmin, it seemed that having many more sisters like Jujube would be wonderful.

After clacking her marbles into the divots on the board, Yuki said, "Do you know the feeling when something goes in there?" She pointed at Jasmin's vagina.

Jasmin thought of when she'd pressed her fingers into the folds and it had smelled like piss. She didn't want to tell Yuki that. "No. Why? Is it itchy?" Sometimes if she didn't wipe properly, or if the family ran out of toilet-paper rations, Jasmin got hot red marks down there. Jujube would help her rub ice on it to make it feel better.

"It feels like vomiting the wrong way," Yuki said. "Like someone punching you all the way inside till it comes out your mouth."

Jasmin felt the bile rise in her own throat and tears prick the back of her eyes. She had never heard Yuki's voice shake this way. Jasmin thought of her sister, serious, strong, always knowing what to do. Even if their mother was yelling, all Jasmin needed to do was feel Jujube's fingers on her palm to know she would be safe.

"Yuki, do you want to talk to my sister? She won't tell."

"She'll be angry you sneaked out," Yuki said. "Anyway, I don't want to play anymore." Yuki tipped the congkak board and watched all the marbles roll onto the grass. Jasmin was shocked. She opened her mouth to protest, but Yuki spoke first. "This game is boring. Come, I'll show you something." Yuki jumped to her feet, rubbed the blood from her leg. It left a brown streak on her yellow nightie that Jasmin couldn't look away from.

"Come on! Let's go!" Yuki pulled Jasmin to her feet and slipped her rough, fair hand in Jasmin's brown one.

As she ran alongside Yuki, the moon spilled at their feet. Their nightdresses swished together, yellow and white, almost one, a tiny bouncing apparition. Jasmin felt like her head was spinning, like there were many things that had happened in their talk and she was missing pieces, even though she knew she'd understood the few words they'd said to each other.

"Where are we going?" Jasmin panted, struggling to keep up with Yuki. Being confined in the basement had made her breathing shorter, and it was hard to run as quickly as she used to. Her legs felt like rubber, not moving as steadily.

"I want to show you my favorite place in the whole world." The moon had ducked behind a cloud, and Yuki was darkened by shadow except for the glitter in her eyes. "It's a secret place. They can't find me there."

The grass was wet and soaked through Jasmin's thin slippers. Yuki always did this, speaking in riddles. *Where* was this place? So that *who* can't find her?

"Yuki, I'm tired. Are we there yet?" Jasmin panted through her teeth, sweat pooling down a thin line on her back. They had run up a hillock, past the river, and the smell of mud swirled in her nose with the scent of her and Yuki's sweat, making her dizzy and irritable. She was starting to get worried. What if Jujube woke up and could not find her?

"Almost. You run so slow; you're lucky you don't live with Aunty Woon, or you wouldn't be able to run away from her cane!" Yuki said.

Jasmin felt her throat catch. "Stop making fun of me!" The exertion of yelling and panting making her choke.

Yuki's face fell, and her lip trembled on the side of her face that was patchy and rough. Lit by the moonlight creeping through parted clouds, the crevices on Yuki's face looked especially deep. Jasmin felt immediately sorry. She had learned to be attuned to moods. If a voice was raised, if someone's eyes filled with tears, if a room felt thick and hot with tension, she always knew that if she smiled, made her eyes bigger, and crawled into someone's lap, the feeling would change.

Jasmin opened her mouth wide and crossed her eyes. A little saliva dribbled out of her mouth down her chin, and she made an exaggerated show of flopping onto the ground. "I'm deaddddd," she moaned theatrically.

Yuki burst into a fit of giggles, the peals of her laughter echoing through the quiet night like wind chimes. Jasmin felt her body relax. They resumed their trek.

After a few minutes, Yuki stopped. "We're here! Be quiet!"

A sign on the corner said: WELCOME. A few feet in front of them stood a row of identical wooden shacks with thatched roofs covered in nipah leaves, each shack with one window and a narrow wooden doorway. Some of the doors were open, but most were closed. Jasmin raised her right index finger and counted fourteen doors. The ground on the road leading to the shacks was muddy and marked with many deep boot imprints, their ridged lines crisscrossing, lit by the moon. There was a smell in the air like sweaty bodies, blood, and a staleness Jasmin wasn't familiar with. Yuki put a finger to her lips and beckoned to Jasmin. As they ran along a path next to the shacks, Jasmin tried to peek into the ones with open doors. It was dark, but in one shack, she saw a girl, perhaps twelve years old, lying on her side. A man in military fatigues was standing over her, his back to the doorway. As Jasmin and Yuki scurried past, the man pulled the door shut, but not before Jasmin locked eyes with the girl on the floor, the girl's eyes empty, black.

"Yuki, I'm scared." Jasmin huddled closer to her friend, smelling the sweat in her armpits, sour.

"Why are you such a scaredy-cat!" Yuki pulled Jasmin over to a curve in the path. "Come with me; I'll show you my hiding spot."

Jasmin whimpered. "I want to go back. Jujube might wake up."

"But we're here, Mini! Just climb in there!" Yuki gestured at a stationary wheelbarrow, bright blue, standing upright, tucked in the corner of a tiny patch of grass. They were barely ten steps away from the shacks, but because of the curved path, it was on its own, completely out of sight of the main pathway. The wheelbarrow itself was surprisingly clean, even new.

"The wheel is loose," Yuki said, pointing at the front of the wheelbarrow. "No one uses it."

"What do you do with it?" Jasmin asked.

Yuki pulled her yellow nightie up and hoisted herself into the wheelbarrow. She held out a hand to Jasmin. "Come on! This is where we play. This is my castle. It's far away from everything, and no one can find us here."

"This is a wheelbarrow, Yuki. My pa has one."

"It's where we can be safe," Yuki said. "Grown-ups can't see it because it's magic."

Yuki was smiling that bright, toothy smile that reminded Jasmin of looking at the sun. Jasmin hoisted herself into the wheelbarrow and sat across from Yuki, cross-legged, their knees touching. Yuki then pulled what looked like a bedsheet from under her knee and flapped it open so it covered them both inside the wheelbarrow, leaving only slivers of moonlight seeping in through the thinner parts of the sheet. Jasmin couldn't see much of Yuki except her eyes, and when she caught Yuki's glance, they both burst into a fit of giggles.

"Shhhh!" said Yuki, trying to swallow her laughter. "I don't want anybody to hear us!"

Jasmin didn't know why they were giggling, or why she was overcome with a burst of joy, but here in Yuki's castle, this small blue wheelbarrow, crouched together under the warm sheet, she felt like they had built a world for just the two of them, and no one could get to them; no one could take it away.

CHAPTER SIX

CECILY

Bintang, Kuala Lumpur
1935
Ten years earlier, British-occupied Malaya

Espionage suited Cecily. She had a knack for invisibility, combined with what Fujiwara called an "instinct for the important." This in concert with Gordon's rise to third in command at the public works department meant Cecily had graduated from combing the garbage for notes and letters to delivering intel overheard at important meetings, and to stealing information, not just from Gordon but from his superiors.

Cecily often wondered whether Fujiwara had weaponized her feelings and her. It humiliated her, the idea that he could feel her want, and that sometimes it felt like when he said her name, the pores in her body began to leak—with sweat, desire, hunger, everything base, the whole of her simply ooze. Yet it seemed as though her yearning made her a stronger spy, the need to press past the roiling panic inside her causing all neurons to fire on all cylinders, finely tuning the brain to work exactly as it should.

But her idolatry was not blind. The truth of it, she thought, was that men lose interest when the veil falls off and they learn the normalcy of a woman—that she urinates and bleeds and cries and snores like everyone else. But women grow fonder when a man feels within reach. Women do not worship gods; they yearn for broken toys they can mold and imprint on. It was so stupid, and she hated herself for it. Yet perhaps this was what a woman's idealism is: not the reach for a utopia—everyone had lived long enough to know perfection was beyond reach—but the need to transform one thing into something better.

He came by the house just over a year into their collaboration. From the kitchen window, Cecily watched his swift yet ambling walk; he was a man who strode quickly without seeming to, rapid but somehow languid and relaxed. It was quiet on the street because it was the awkward in-between time in the late morning, when the men had gone to work and the women thought it too hot to do their errands. Cecily pressed a hand against a particularly stubborn curl that had escaped its nest behind her ear. It had been a few weeks since their conversation by the garbage dump, and over a year since his last visit to the house, their communications reduced to stilted missives attached to bits of intel she stashed behind the sanitary napkins at the sundry shop. Still, she wasn't surprised to see him. The next evening was her biggest assignment to date.

Fujiwara knocked on the grille of the gate behind the house. It clattered noisily, and the cacophony of children from the front of the house halted. Jujube called out, "Ma, who's that?"

"Just a friend here to see me. You children get back to playing."

The cacophony resumed, all the neighborhood children engaged in what sounded like a loud and incredibly competitive tournament involving top spinning. Even without looking, Cecily could see them: Abel, big gray eyes focused on spinning the colorful saucer-shaped top, and Jujube, ever responsible, keeping an eye on him while she devoured whatever book she had gotten her hands on from the British library.

"What are you doing here?" Cecily pulled the rusty gate open but stood in Fujiwara's way.

"We need to discuss the assignment tomorrow. At the resident's house."

"It's risky to meet like this—" she began, but then gave up. She always did. She ushered him in and washed her hands in the kitchen sink. She positioned him behind the spice cupboard, angled so that he could make a quick escape via the back gate if one of the children walked in.

A shout echoed from the playing children.

"They are joy," Fujiwara said.

Cecily nodded. In the last year, she had become a better mother to them, and for that she was grateful to Fujiwara. The urges she used to have, wishing that they would disappear, that she would disappear, seemed to have faded. She was also a better wife to Gordon—she listened, she cared, she ran the house, she did not ignore the neighbors, even the nosiest, Mrs. Carvalho. She was polite to Aunty Mui at the sundry store, even when the woman always seemed out of stock of the things she needed. She taught her children how to read and write. Jujube took after her, consuming books so quickly that Cecily had trouble keeping up with Jujube's pile. And Cecily was surprised to hear herself laugh so much those days. She laughed at her children's incongruent stories, she laughed when a rat and a cockroach chased each other around the house, she chortled when Abel and his father jumped on the tables in terror as Jujube chased the rodent and bug out. She laughed when Gordon tickled her at night, and she was even able to bring herself to his body—her happiness enough of a shield. Gordon loved it, of course. "You are content now," he would say, pleasure rounding his shoulders.

"Tell me again about the dinner tomorrow," Fujiwara said right as Cecily asked, "Would you like some tea?"

They looked awkwardly at each other, and Cecily suppressed a frustrated sigh from escaping her nose. What had happened to the two people who'd talked and laughed effortlessly, all night, about family and ideology and the future? Now they were wooden, like strangers.

Gordon was now a senior superintendent in the public works department, just "three, maybe four steps below the boss," he had told Cecily proudly when he was promoted. He had a particular expertise in sand, tides, and most important, understanding the ability of ships—both naval and supply—to anchor at port. Gordon had spent many hours poring over soil samples at Port Lewisham, named rather unoriginally for the British resident, built on the once-swampy, mangrove-laden Talim River. Gordon came home some nights, arms covered in angry red bites, a meal to mosquitoes as he squatted on the mouth of the port, taking notes. Cecily worried he would get malaria.

She handed Fujiwara a steaming cup of tea. "Be careful, it's hot," she said, then regretted mothering him.

He flattened his fingers against the cup as though he hadn't heard her.

She barreled through her intel brief. "The dinner will be at the resident's house. Gordon says that the resident general will be there. A fellow named Sir Woodford."

Fujiwara's face was taut and at attention. She had known this intel was important, but watching him now, she felt like nothing else mattered. She reveled in the moment, felt his eyes sear through her, unblinking. "Lewisham wants Gordon to present his findings on the port to see if it'll be a suitable location to bring in Allied aircraft that needs servicing. For the RAF."

When he had told Cecily about this dinner, Gordon had practically vibrated with excitement from the thrill of the resident general's name on his tongue. "Sir Algernon Woodford. Algernon. Woodford. Woodford." He rolled the name off his tongue.

"This matters. This matters a lot," Fujiwara said, blowing the top of his tea.

Cecily nodded but cast her eyes around nervously. This information was more important than any piece of notebook paper she had ever lifted out of Gordon's trash. That the British air force was planning to bring Allied planes to the port meant it would become a point of their vulnerability. The dinner, and the men's meeting that would follow, would be rife with information, diagrams, maps, coordinates, a veritable treasure chest of intelligence. But still, the audacity of Fujiwara to stride into her house in the middle of the morning? She felt a burr of fear twist in her stomach, but she held her lips still.

"This could be a turning point for Japan," he said.

A roar echoed from the front of the house. One of the two top-spinning teams must have claimed victory. Cecily noticed a smile pricking at the edge of Fujiwara's face.

"I'm sorry, they're just excited."

"No, Cecily. I'm sorry to have come here. It just seemed . . . I wanted to . . . It was important to discuss in person." A line crested between his eyes, a dwarf of frowns. Absently, he picked up a clove of garlic from the wicker basket on the counter and tossed it between his hands like a ball.

Cecily's body surprised her by laughing. "Stop that. You'll never be able to get the smell out of your fingers."

He tossed the garlic back into the basket and missed. A wave of fondness swept through her.

"Do I smell bad?" He held up his hand to her nose.

"Rank," she said. They both laughed.

Cecily stood still, aware of every limb. She crossed her arms, uncrossed them, then became self-conscious. But she didn't say anything. If there was one thing she'd learned, even in their few conversations, it was that with Fujiwara, she had to exist in the quiet spaces. Often information was only one beat of silence away. So she waited, the air pungent with garlic and morning sun. The children outside became quiet too, as if everyone held their breath.

"I am very grateful for all you do," he said.

Cecily swallowed, nervous.

"I'll see you at the dinner," he continued.

"I'm worried. Maybe I should just go alone, eavesdrop on what I can. We shouldn't be seen together," Cecily said.

"There's too much at stake. With two of us, we can get so much more. Besides, I don't want you to have to do this alone. You're—it's—too important."

You're. Her heart flooded with blood. That was enough for now. It had to be.

By the time they arrived at the resident's house for dinner, things were in full swing. It was crowded and stuffy, even with all the windows open. More than once, Cecily found herself swatting away a stray mosquito that buzzed too close to her ear. Gordon's excitement manifested in an uncontrollable need to empty his bladder, so Cecily was left on her own many times while he scurried away after holding it in too long, taking tiny steps to prevent leakage. The other wives in attendance were mirrors of her: floral dresses, tittering laughs, the invisibility cloak of femininity.

Within the cohort of women was a divide—the white women stood some distance away, backs to Cecily, a circlet of pale arms. Cecily stood among the other Asian women whose husbands worked as colonial subordinates to the white men, including Mrs. Lingam, whose husband worked at Guthrie, a British trading company handling the rubber and oil palm export; and Mrs. Low, whose husband had risen from tin miner to commercial head of Jardines, which traded cotton, tea, silk, and opium. The loudest of their circle was Mrs. Yap, whose husband, Yap Loy San, was the kapitan cina of the town, a gangster who owned a third of the land in Bintang and controlled much of the tin-mining business by organizing Chinese labor for the mines. An uneasy truce existed between Yap Loy San and the British resident—Yap had to pay levies to the British in order to maintain his businesses, but in return, the British acknowledged Yap's leadership and claim as kapitan of the Chinese clans, legitimizing him and enabling him to squash uprisings from other clan leaders. Kapitan Yap's leadership maintained a shaky peace among the clans, which in turn fed the British coffers.

Cecily found Mrs. Yap insufferable. To Cecily's ear, Mrs. Yap's voice existed one octave and multiple decibels above where it should be, and everything she said reverberated off the walls and against eardrums, making them ring in protest. She couldn't have been more than a handful of years older than Cecily, but she always seemed like an annoying aunty, constantly grasping for gossip.

Mrs. Yap was in her element that night, hair pulled back in a puffy bun, smelling of sweat and expensive black-market perfume—strong, overbearing. In the cluster of women, Mrs. Yap turned away from the whispering she was doing with Mrs. Lingam and leaned over. "Eh, Cecily, you know who is that man there?" She shoved her finger so hard into Cecily's side that Cecily felt it in her throat.

"Who?" Cecily said, feigning innocence.

"There lah, that man." Mrs. Yap gestured at Fujiwara. "Why I never see him before ah," she hissed in Cecily's ear, attempting to whisper while pointing, without any subtlety, at Fujiwara across the floor.

The cloistered air in the room was so still; Cecily felt a line of sweat tickle the small of her back. Around her, people touched elbows and greeted each other amid a swish of skirts and British officer uniforms. Cecily raised her eyes to look directly at Fujiwara, who wiped something off his linen pants, then looked straight back at Cecily, as though intuiting her fear.

"Aiyo, he's coming here now!" Mrs. Yap whispered so loudly that even the Englishwomen turned to look, all female eyes on the merchant known as Bingley Chan. His linen suit rustled slightly as he walked.

"Ladies," he said. "I hear there is some interest in understanding what the fashions of Europe are looking like right now. I have just returned from a brief visit to Paris and London."

It turned Cecily's stomach sour to hear him revert to a clipped British accent.

Within a few minutes Fujiwara as Bingley Chan had all the women, English and local alike, milling around him, lapping up his every lie about the length of gloves and the height of hats worn by European women on the continent he hated. Cecily held back the urge to roll her eyes. Where was the impervious, indifferent man with a lilting Japanese accent whom she knew? As debonair merchant Bingley Chan, he smiled crookedly, he told stories, he filled silences with witty quips in clipped English, he flirted with the women by touching their elbows and looking in their eyes. She needn't have worried about him.

Dinner passed in a haze of irritation for Cecily. Lady Lewisham, enamored of her new couture adviser, made a big deal of switching the place cards so that Fujiwara sat next to her, near the head of the table. Cecily and Gordon were seated at a separate table entirely, with the other local engineers and wives. Normally she wouldn't have minded. It wasn't new, the way the British treated the locals like scabs they needed to live with until they could pluck them off and discard them. But that evening, a quiet envy bubbled along the top of Cecily's skin, making her scratch at the sleeve of her dress. Gordon was so nervous about the after-dinner presentation that he could barely eat. Usually she would feign concern, fuss, throw food on his plate, make little spoonfuls of rice and shove them in his mouth like she did with her children. But that night she couldn't bring herself to. It took all her effort to hide her aggrieved seething every time she saw the hands of a woman caress Fujiwara. His comfort with these white people disconcerted her. It was a sharp contradiction from the angry frustrations he had shared during those moonlit nights at her house.

Logically she knew that she and he were both doing a job—he, playacting the charming foreign guest, she the dutiful housewife—but the systemic dismantling of what little equality they had built up between them, their tenuous partnership, made her feel like her whole body was curdling into something bitter, rotten.

To her left, Mrs. Yap swiveled her head to watch what was happening at the British table behind her. "Bingley is such a funny name, don't you think, Cecily? I didn't know Hong Kongers even read Jane Austen," and she chuckled to herself, which surprised Cecily, who hadn't thought that the kapitan's wife read anything beyond the European fashion catalogs that always showed up in Bintang six months late.

"Yes, funny name," Cecily repeated back to Mrs. Yap. This was one of the many things that Fujiwara had taught her—to maintain a low-effort conversation without offending someone, you just needed to repeat back what they said to you. At the time Cecily had found this groundbreaking, but she realized now that it made sense; people were vain and boring.

"These dinners get tiring sometimes," Mrs. Yap said, a small sigh pressing through her lipsticked mouth. Her breath tickled Cecily's ear. It smelled like shallots and milk, not unpleasant.

"Yes, quite tiring," Cecily said. Fujiwara's low laugh echoed across the room.

After digestifs, amid a clattering of pushed-back chairs and maids removing plates from the table, the two tables split themselves into three groups: Group One, the men who were meeting to discuss Gordon's findings and the suitability of the port for RAF aircraft repair; Group Two, the non-administrative men who were peeling off to smoke cigars and discuss whatever it was that men discussed in armchairs in smoking rooms; and Group Three, the women, both white and local, who would be forced to socialize together in the parlor, making small talk about the length of hairpins and the importance of spices in food.

Gordon puffed out his chest and marched purposefully off to Group One, stopping quickly at the toilet to relieve his nervous bladder again, before moving to a large blue-wallpapered meeting room down the hall. All the men of Group One swept off with some urgency, leaving a continued mingling of Groups Two and Three. Fujiwara stood off to the side with the other men moving to Group Two; the heady smell of cigar smoke and sweating leather chairs had already begun to seep into the dining room.

Cecily felt Fujiwara trying to catch her eye. She watched his polished shoe tap lightly against the floorboards, a tic he had when he was impatient but trying not to show it. The next part of the mission depended on her, but Cecily had not been able to shrug off her irritation. She looked away, studying the pristine white of the wall, trying to focus her spinning mind on the table fans, match her breathing to their rhythmic whirs. The women of Group Three began their leisurely stroll, arms entwined, skirts swishing—seemingly united but naturally divided by skin—into the parlor. Cecily could feel Fujiwara's eyes burning into her back. The crowd dispersion would soon be complete.

She swallowed and curled the pinkie of her left hand under the ring finger, pressing the two fingers into each other until they hurt. This was her own tic—the physical pain drowning out the other, less tangible one. She raised her face to meet Fujiwara's eye, gave him the tiniest nod. His nostrils flared. It was a controlled exhale, but it thrilled her, the relief flooding his face quickly, his jaw loosening.

Was this power, to hold a man's fate in this way? She didn't have time to wonder. It was her turn to be the spectacle. She sucked in her breath, reached for the end of the tablecloth, groaned as loudly as she could, and fell to the ground in a faint.

The next few minutes were a buzz of confusion. With her eyes closed and body still, Cecily had only her ears and nose to make sense of her surroundings. She heard the shouts of the women, Mrs. Yap the loudest of all, "Aiya, she FAINT! Get her water and salts!"

The men of Group Two had spilled back into the dining room as she and Fujiwara had hoped, everyone focused on Cecily. When they had first discussed this strategy, Cecily had been unconvinced. Her primary advantage, she told Fujiwara, was her invisibility. No one would care if she fainted. He had smiled one of his rare smiles and said, "You're not invisible. Being underestimated and being invisible are two different things."

Eyes pressed shut, she envisioned him now, creeping quietly down the hall while everyone's attention was focused on her. Her mission was simple: to hold still. But she had not accounted for everyone's clumsy attempts at helpfulness—people were trying to lift her by the legs, then by the arms. She worried they would bruise her or, worse, tickle her. Others were spraying her face with water and with sharp, floral-smelling salts. Everyone was yelling at such a loud volume that it became difficult to isolate the voices and identify them. She resisted the urge to wipe the spit that sprayed at her face.

She imagined Fujiwara, crouched somewhere outside the blue-walled room, trying to eavesdrop on Gordon's meeting. She imagined him pulling himself to his feet, with some effort because he wasn't a man who was used to crouching. This inadequacy made her tender toward him. She knew he was about to burst into the meeting room, wave his arms in a comical, frantic way, tell Gordon that his wife had fainted and pulled the entire dining table down with her. Gordon would turn red, then purple, his moment of glory rudely interrupted by his wife. Sir Woodford, Sir Lewisham, Mr. Ommaney, and the others would file out of the room decorously, feign polite concern at a fainting brown woman. Fujiwara would stay behind, use the mini German imaging device whose name she could not remember, and create duplicate images of the maps, diagrams, notes, and intel left behind in the men's haste.

One of the women threw what felt like a bunch of herbaceous-smelling leaves at Cecily's face. Mrs. Yap's milk-and-shallot breath hovered above her; Cecily's nose itched, and her heart thrummed unpleasantly against her chest. She bit her tongue to calm herself down, again invoking physical pain to quiet the noise inside her. She became alarmed at the feeling of callused hands grabbing her ankles, an attempt to drag her to a sofa, a chair. A splinter from the floor ate into the exposed soft flesh of her cheek. Even though she couldn't see, she could feel the disapproval on the faces of the white women, Lady Lewisham's mouth pursed tight, whispering about the *hysterical* nature of the local women, frustrated at the indignity of the whole thing happening at her party. Cecily imagined the men trying to see up her skirt. She tried to remember at what angle she had dropped her legs.

"Cecily!" Gordon's voice, Gordon's mouth breathing, then Gordon's sour scent hovering above her as the voices lowered to a murmur. Her mind's eye saw a crowd parting for him to make his way through. This was her cue.

"She's waking up!"

"Goodness, that was a long faint!"

"Gordon," she breathed. "I don't know what happened. I was so dizzy. I'm sorry to have ruined the night."

Her eyes struggled to focus, and she blinked rapidly. Around her, shoes, skirts, and pants hems shuffled as everyone stepped back to make space for the couple. When she looked up, she saw several people looking away politely, but most stared curiously.

She expected Gordon to be furious; after all, she had taken away his moment in the sun, his moment to shine just for a few minutes with the white men he so admired. But Gordon, as he did sometimes, surprised her.

"I was so worried, my love. Don't frighten me like that." And after a pause, he whispered, "Perhaps you are pregnant."

She saw Fujiwara kneel, close to where Gordon was cradling her head but still a respectful distance away. The mint of his hair cream made Cecily so dizzy that she thought she truly would faint. The two men helped her to her feet, her back cricking angrily. She cast her eyes at everyone. A few lowered their eyes in shame; the rest just stared, insolent in their nosiness. Fujiwara clasped his hands in front of his chest. He nodded at her. He had the intel.

They had actually pulled it off.

CHAPTER SEVEN

ABEL

Kanchanaburi Labor Camp on the Burma/Thailand border
August 17, 1945
Japanese-occupied Malaya

Most of Abel's memories of arriving at the camp were blurry. He remembered lying in the back of a lorry. He remembered many days on a bumpy road, the smells of rot, body odor, and blood in the air. He remembered being handed a shovel and told to dig, keep digging, till the sun went down each day. He remembered that same sun burning painful red imprints into his back, he remembered the rain at first feeling like cool relief but then quickly growing dangerous as the mud became slippery and rolled down the sides of the mountain in landslides, taking screaming boys with it. He remembered staggering back to their quarters at night, his back a knot of pain, weeping sores on his arms and legs. He remembered falling on the cement floor in the crowded room with all the other boys and realizing that no matter how small he curled into himself, he could not quite fit his six-foot-tall frame into the two-foot-wide space he was allocated to sleep in. He remembered forgetting what day it was, long nights staring into the dark atap ceilings as the rain pelted the roof, the stench of pus and piss around him, feeling so tired, so demolished, that he could neither sleep nor cry.

"Psst."

Abel started, his eyes flying open, feeling the mud caking around his ankles. Sunrise. He'd been in the chicken coop for almost a day. He looked around for the source of the whisper and, once more, caught the eye of the brown hen from earlier. She was staring at him again; he must've passed out a second time. Master Akiro was gone, and Abel noticed that his own thin gray pants were pulled up, thankfully covering him.

"Abe. Abel." Abel squeezed his eyes open and met the unmistakable blue ones of Freddie, who was crouching outside the wired coop, his knobby knees pushing up against his chin.

"Here's water," said Freddie, pushing a metal cup through the wire, spilling some liquid on the dying rooster, who didn't react. "Man, this little guy is gone."

Abel crawled over, feeling the mud scrape his knees. "Thanks," he croaked, sipping, sloshing the water around on his tongue, the liquid filling the dry divots in his mouth.

"They really beat you up," Freddie said, his eyes wide, scanning Abel, top to bottom.

"It's no big deal," Abel said. The bruises across his stomach throbbed.

"It turns out Vellu can play the accordion," said Freddie of one of their campmates.

"Did I miss another singalong last night?"

Freddie shook his head, his eyes cloudy with concern. "You miss a lot these days. It's all that stuff you drink."

At the mention, Abel felt the craving come back—the sour swirl in his stomach, the first sweet burn as the liquid coated the back of his throat, the lull of his limbs, the way his wounds and his heart always felt a little less painful.

"Did you bring any, Freddie?" Abel pleaded. "I gave you that bottle to keep. I could use some." He gestured vaguely at his wounds.

"You really shouldn't, Abe. This stuff is junk. You fall down. You say stupid things."

How little Freddie knew, Abel thought, feeling the pool of blood on the back of his pants. Instead, he said, "Well, Akiro's not the boss of me."

"Here." Making a face, Freddie handed him a bottle covered in a dirty rag. Abel looked around to make sure no one was approaching, then pulled off the rag to reveal the murky liquid swirling in the bottle. As the sickly-sweet smell hit Abel's nose, he felt a familiar rush and took a large gulp, then another. The toddy coated the back of his parched throat and burned down his empty stomach. He felt the familiar smooth calm wash over him.

The toddy had been a lucky addition to the camp in the recent months. The rumor was that one of the guards had a black-market connection, so whenever the supply trucks arrived each month with rice and other food items, crates of toddy were included. Once in a while, the boys unloading the trucks were able to steal a few bottles without being noticed; accounting of supplies was not the soldiers' strong suit.

Before the camp, Abel had known toddy by many names. The British newspapers had called it the "workingman's opium," an irony, since it was often used by the British rubber estate owners to control the Indian migrant workers. His father disdainfully called it the "laborer's drink" because it was always the cheapest of all the liquors. In the before times, his older friends sometimes sneaked a bottle for the boys to share when it was someone's birthday. But that was back then—back when he still sipped the sweet drink, content with a quick, warm buzz that faded fast. The toddy at the camps was more potent, palm wine fermented longer, mixed with other unknown liquors that deepened its color from a cloudy white into a murky beige. Also, Abel now drank in gulps, in large swigs.

At the camp, many of the boys drank, but unlike him, they drank a little bit at a time, scrunched up their faces at the taste, and swallowed with fingers pressed against their nostrils to cut the burn. For them, drinking was something to do to pass the time, something to help injuries hurt a little less. And at first that had been how it was for Abel too. A sip here, a splash there, a way to wash the days away. But then the cravings began—wishing he had something to drink at night before bed, to unsee the horrors of the day and fall asleep. The need went from a dull ache to a sharp pain, from sipping leftovers when he woke up sweating and craving, to wandering the camp looking for abandoned bottles that he would hoard and hide from the others or, when he couldn't hide them, guzzle them as fast as he could. It helped him feel less, of course, but most of all it helped him dull that incessant desire he had to stand up and shout, to defy, to make himself heard. It didn't always work, which was why he'd ended up in the coop, but most days the toddy helped him care less and comply, which helped him survive, and perhaps, Abel told himself, that was the most important reason of all.

"You need to go now, Freddie. Akiro could come by." Freddie didn't need to know that Akiro had already been by.

Freddie grabbed the metal water cup and looked pointedly at the toddy bottle Abel was cradling. Reluctantly, Abel handed it over, through the fence, nearly emptied. Shaking his head, Freddie pulled himself up on his skinny legs. "Stay away from the dead rooster, brother."

"It's not dead yet, is it?" Abel looked over at the rooster. It was dead.

Freddie had arrived at the labor camp two months after Abel. Like Abel, he had been thrown off the back of a lorry with a bunch of other boys, grubby and bloodied, eyes wild. Abel had noticed Freddie because of those eyes, bright blue, unusual even among Eurasians. At camp, however, Freddie's stormy blue eyes and pink-and-white skin, even fairer than Abel's, were the source of all his troubles.

"White Boy Two!" the supervisors would call before smacking Freddie across the face with the butt of their rifle, leaving large bruises on his fair face. "This is what we do to your kind."

At first Abel was relieved. It was good to have someone else be the subject of the supervisors' ire. It meant that he could stop to take the occasional breath when he was tired, without getting beaten. It meant that he could take a swig of toddy and focus on the sharp, hot tang in his throat. It meant that he could occasionally catch the eye of Rama or Vellu or Azlan or Ah Lam making dumb gestures like pretending to punch someone in the balls, or miming a penis being jerked off, and actually stifle a laugh or roll his eyes without being knocked to the ground and kicked within an inch of his life.

But even as his days improved marginally, the nights were a struggle. Assailed by sweat smells and the sound of snores at night, Abel found himself haunted into wakefulness. Often his mind took him back to the days before his fifteenth birthday. He wondered what he would have done if he had known that would be the last time he would see his family, the last time he would know any kind of happiness. Would he have told someone about Brother Luke, taken a different route home, been a little warier? Would he have rolled his eyes at Jujube for being so uptight? Would he still have yelled at Jasmin when she dropped his striped tiger marble in the monsoon drain? Would he have tuned out his father's nostalgic, self-important stories about the "good old times" in the British administration? Would he have complained less to his mother when she mixed disgusting tapioca with rice? His mouth watered at the thought of rice. Now he was always hungry. A gnawing animal seemed to live in his stomach, but the bowls of gruel that were slapped down in front of them at camp, grains in gray water, were sometimes dotted with sharp things—splinters, dust, and one time, the end of a nail that had cut up his mouth before he could spit it out, leaving the taste of iron and dirt at the back of his throat as he swallowed the blood that pooled on his tongue.

One night about a week after Freddie's arrival, as Abel lay staring at the ceiling, he heard a shuffling sound that was different from the snores, the kicking legs, and the occasional whimpering he'd come to expect from the other boys. In the corner of the room, on the other side of Rama, where a slice of moonlight crept through the gaps in the roof, someone was sitting up, his head bent in concentration. Abel sat up and pulled his long, skinny legs under him so he wouldn't kick his neighbor. Straining, he could see it was Freddie, just out of reach because of the large lump that was Rama between them. Nose lit by the moonlight, Freddie held a small stick in his left hand and appeared to be staring at something on the floor, occasionally bringing his stick to the surface. He did not notice Abel, or if he did, he gave Abel no heed. The shadows cast by the moon and Freddie's body obscured what he was doing on the floor.

Abel lay back down. He felt foolish watching.

Every few nights after that, Abel would hear a shuffling, and when he looked over, he would see Freddie sitting up and staring at the floor. Sometimes Freddie looked like he was squinting; it was hard to tell. One particularly bright night, Abel caught a glimpse of an enormous bruise on Freddie's cheek, blue, black, yellow, a kaleidoscope of pain on flesh.

Freddie was small for his age and often struggled in the field. Abel remembered being surprised to learn that Freddie was fourteen, only a year younger; he had thought Freddie was at most eleven, twelve. Abel noticed Freddie was often assigned tasks that required less brute strength and finer motor skills, things like welding and fitting pieces of metal together, but he struggled even with those.

After three nights of watching, Abel's curiosity got the better of him.

"Hey, Rama, wanna swap places?" Abel said. "There's a hole in the roof above me. It's cooler. More air."

Abel steeled himself for Rama's questions. He wasn't sure how he would answer them. But Rama just shrugged, disinterested. He rolled over to the spot that Abel used to sleep in, closed his eyes, and immediately started snoring.

Once in Rama's spot, Abel assumed his normal position, his back on the floor, eyes to the ceiling, studying the outline of the nipah leaves lashed together on the roof. Freddie lay next to him, facing away. Out of the corner of his eye, Abel saw that Freddie's shirt was torn, the hole exposing shadowy lines of spine coiling through his thin flesh. Abel squeezed his eyes shut, trying to find sleep, trying to escape his own foolish curiosities.

Soon after he lay down, he heard the familiar shuffling. He opened one eye. Freddie was sitting up. Now that he was right next to him, Abel could see that Freddie was holding a sliver of toilet paper, a little rectangle no larger than the size of his palm. At camp they were given a few inches of this rough yellow-brown paper every day to wipe the shit from their asshole. It was a new effort, apparently, after boys started dying of cholera. In his other hand, Freddie gripped what looked like a badly made paintbrush. The shadows and moonlight made it hard to see, but Abel noticed that the toilet-paper rectangle appeared to have figures on it.

"You switched places." Freddie looked down at Abel with steely, unfazed blue eyes.

Abel was surprised. There was a lack of fear in the boy's face that he had not expected, and Freddie delivered his pronouncement in a calm, almost disinterested whisper. Because Freddie was sitting up, they were so close that Abel's face was within inches of Freddie's knee.

Abel pushed himself into an upright position, so he was eye level with Freddie. "What are you doing?"

"I'm drawing."

"Why?"

"So that I don't forget things here." Freddie reached for his paintbrush.

Abel didn't understand. All he wanted to do was forget the camp. What was this boy trying to remember?

"Where did you get that?" Abel pointed at the brush. "Can I see?"

"I made it." The boy's eyes seemed to blaze with something—anger? Abel wasn't sure. "Don't break it." The boy handed the brush to Abel.

The stick end of the brush was a rough twig. But the brush side had light brown fibers lashed to the end with a piece of string. Abel ran his fingertip across the brush. "Is this—hair?"

The boy pointed to the top of his head, which Abel now saw was patchy, certain areas pink and scabby, the hair plucked clean.

"What . . . ?"

"I make do."

The floor in front of Freddie was dotted with rectangles of toilet paper. Seeing the question in Abel's eyes, Freddie smirked. "I use leaves when I have to go."

"And what do you paint with?"

It was then that Abel noticed the cuts on the boy's arms. Some were fresh, some scabbed over, jagged brown lines on his fair skin. Blood; he was painting with blood. Abel shuddered. It was one thing to be injured out in the fields as they worked; just today one of the boys had his foot sheared clean off by a huge piece of falling metal. But somehow this boy's self-injury, the cuts Abel assumed that he made on his arms to create a palette, seemed more horrifying. It reminded Abel of the day after the "bull's balls" incident when their father had come home jubilant, a baby goat trotting on the end of a string.

"I got it at the black market. Tonight we'll eat well!" Abel could still see the shining pride on his father's face as he gazed at their mother, trying to make up for the previous night's debacle with the bull's testicles. "Abel! Jujube!" their father had yelled. "We'll have to drain it."

Abel remembered watching in horror as their father slit the goat's neck, then cut neat, long lines into the goat's chest. He remembered dipping his hand into the warmth, how it was smooth, sticky, as it flowed out of the goat into their muddy yard, filling the air with the smell of rot and iron.

Abel looked away from Freddie's arms. "Does it hurt?"

"Not really." Noticing Abel's discomfort, he said, "Look, it's just for the color. I use mostly tree sap and mix them together." Freddie gestured at his bloody arms. "They're not even deep."

"But why?" To cut oneself just to engage in a hobby seemed masochistic.

"It's for when we get out of here. So we can show people. To explain." Freddie stuck out his jaw obstinately, his colorful cheek bruise rising out of the shadow.

Abel studied the squares of toilet paper on the floor in front of Freddie, all dotted with faces sketched in rusty brown. Despite the rudimentary nature of the tools Freddie used, in the dim moonlight, Abel recognized the faces. The drawings were surprisingly detailed, arched eyebrows, single-lidded eyes, noses shaped and shaded. Master Akiro with his sharp, thin eyes. General Fujiwara with his round chin. Other supervisors and Japanese officers whom Abel had seen roaming around the camp, eyes, noses, ears, lips expertly formed on the thin pieces of toilet paper. One of the pieces of toilet paper fluttered away as a tiny night breeze swept into the room. Abel reached out to hold the piece in place. Lifting his palm, he saw a face that made a hot rage rise in his chest.

"You know him too? He brought you here?" Abel whispered, voice shaking, the ruddy face of Brother Luke staring back at him.

"If I see him again, I'll kill him," said Freddie, his voice quiet, unwavering.

—

Abel was surprised by their friendship. It felt almost illicit. By day, the most they would do was nod at each other, acknowledging the other's existence as they worked, carrying heavy boxes of supplies or laying metal to make tracks on the railroad. Even in the mess halls, Abel would sit with the other boys slopping the goopy gruel into their mouth, while Freddie would sit on his own, quiet but seemingly unconcerned by his aloneness. His eyes were always clouded with something, Abel didn't know if it was rage or disinterest. But then every night for hours, they would whisper in the corner of the barracks. Abel learned that Freddie, an only child, had an English father and a Eurasian mother; that after the Japanese arrived, Freddie's father had called Freddie into his room one day, told him to take care of his mother, and disappeared that night. Freddie had no idea if his father had run away or had been captured by Japanese soldiers. Very soon after that, Brother Luke had brought the soldiers right to the door; one dragged Freddie away as another soldier pinned down his mother, tearing at her clothes. Abel found himself biting his cheek to stop himself from shaking as he listened, but Freddie talked without blinking, his voice even and still.

Freddie tried to teach Abel how to draw, but that was a doomed enterprise, as Abel lacked the talent. Instead, Abel watched his new friend paint, the rusty smell of blood filling his nostrils. He whispered his memories to Freddie, who drew them—his memories of camp, of the other boys, of Master Akiro's cruelty, of Brother Luke's betrayal. From faces, Freddie graduated to scenes, snippets of camp brought to life on the bloody toilet-paper canvases. It felt important, what they were doing, making a record. Freddie had even begun drawing Abel's family. Abel described the curve of Jasmin's eyes and the flare of her nostrils. Freddie painted a crimson sketch of her. The nose wasn't quite right, and there was no way to describe the light in her eyes, the innocence that made everyone else around her smile with their whole face. And yet it was Jasmin, recognizable, his littlest sister. Abel felt the tears well at the back of his eyes. He was grateful for the night shadows so Freddie couldn't see.

Nightfall arrived, and the mosquito chorus in the coop had reached a fever pitch. The chickens, daytime creatures, seemed to have fallen into an uneasy rest, no longer chittering and squawking. But when the moon peeked out from behind the clouds, he could see that the brown hen was still looking at him. Abel's exposed arms were covered in itchy red bites, and no matter how he swatted, the mosquitoes found places on his skin to land and feed. Perhaps it would be best if he just lay still and allowed the mosquitoes to have at it—could one die from too many mosquito bites? Perhaps that would be ideal.

"No, no, stop, let me go! I'll make it worth your while. I'll bring more boys, like before!" Outside the coop, a man's clipped English accent broke through the buzzing of the mosquitoes, which seemed to stop as if to listen to the commotion. The voice was muffled, but Abel felt a swell of recognition in his chest. He knew that voice. The odor of sweaty soldiers wafted into the coop first, followed by the echo of their boots. The yelling voice had become a very loud series of whimpers. The heavy latch of the coop door swung open, and a flashlight shone in Abel's eyes, blinding him at first.

"Get inside!"

A loud thunk followed.

"We can leave the two whites here till morning," said the voice of Master Akiro.

Abel shrank away, avoiding the harsh glare of the flashlight. Before he could do anything else, the door to the coop closed. As his eyes adjusted once more to the darkness, a crest of moonlight crept through the clouds and shone like a spotlight in the coop. A familiar body crouched in a heap by the dead rooster; bulging eyes in a ruddy face looked back at Abel fearfully. The Japanese had thrown Brother Luke into the coop with him.

The mosquitoes began buzzing again.

CHAPTER EIGHT

JASMIN

Bintang, Kuala Lumpur
August 17, 1945
Japanese-occupied Malaya

As Jasmin clambered stealthily back into the bedroom after her night with Yuki, the little clock on the table told her it was already the next morning, both hands pointing at two. She was smelly and would need to change before she crawled back into bed with Jujube. Padding about as quietly as she could, Jasmin found a new nightie, cream-colored, the closest she could find to her current one, and changed. She threw the other nightie, covered with specks of dust, mud, and a conspicuous splotch of blood that must have rubbed off Yuki or some other surface at the shacks, into the top drawer of a chest she shared with Jujube. She was so tired that her eyelids felt like they were being pressed down. She crawled onto the mattress, careful not to jostle Jujube, who sighed but didn't wake up. Jasmin would figure out what to do with the dirty nightie when she woke up.

"Jasmin!"

Jasmin opened her eyes blearily and saw Jujube's face hovering above and breathing hot morning breath onto her. Outside the window, the sun was a faint orange ball, barely peeking over the horizon. It wasn't even sunrise yet. Her whole body screamed out for her eyes to close; she felt like she had barely had any sleep.

"Get up, sis! I need to show you what to do."

"Wha . . . ?" None of Jasmin's limbs wanted to move. She turned over and covered her eyes with her hand. The air was still cool; she wanted to enjoy a few more hours of it before she had to wake up and go back down to the moldy basement.

"Sis, seriously, wake up. I have to talk to you before Mama sees."

"Go away," Jasmin mumbled.

"I found this." Jujube was holding Jasmin's soiled nightie from last night in front of her. It unfurled in front of Jasmin like a smelly curtain, a patch of blood visible on the back.

Jasmin felt her throat drop. Why hadn't she washed the nightie? Why had she thrown it in the drawer? And now her sister, always responsible about everything, had found it.

Jujube's voice softened, and she sat down beside Jasmin on their lumpy mattress. She pulled Jasmin into her lap and tossed the nightie on the floor.

"Your body is changing, baby sister," Jujube began. "I found your nightie. The blood must've scared you."

Jasmin stared at Jujube, rubbing her eyes, not comprehending.

"Did you—?" Jujube twisted her fingers together uncomfortably. "Did you start bleeding last night? You're so young . . . I thought we'd have more time before I needed to explain." Her sister's words rushed out of her in a gust of breath.

"No, that isn't my blood," Jasmin said. "It's from . . ."

Jasmin's sleepy mind spun. She stared at the crack in the cement floor, curving around her foot like an earthworm. She didn't know how to lie, but she wasn't sure how to tell the truth. Jujube would be furious. Lately, everything was so much harder. Every time someone talked, there was always another meaning to the words that she struggled to understand. Now Jujube was talking about blood and bodies, but this was not her blood, nor was it from her body.

"You don't need to be afraid, Jas." Jujube squeezed Jasmin's shoulder. "It happens to all girls. I'll show you how to wear a pad. In fact, you must have stained your panties too." Jujube pulled Jasmin to her feet. "I don't want you to stain the mattress. It'll upset Ma."

Jasmin had seen the bloody napkins and rags around the house that told her either her mother or her sister was bleeding. Jasmin felt humiliated, ashamed that her sister was being kind when she was lying. "It's not my period," she said.

Jujube looked shocked, as though Jasmin had said a bad word. "How do you know it's called that?"

"I'm not a baby, you know. I know things."

"Well, then, why is your nightie dirty?" Jujube's gentle tone had shifted, a furrow coming between her eyes, the one that Jasmin knew meant she was confused or upset.

"I . . . I . . ."

"Did you—Did you—go outside?" Jujube's voice was even, soft, but it sounded dangerous. Jasmin would almost rather Jujube yell.

"I went to see my friend," Jasmin said in a small voice.

If Jasmin didn't know her sister better, she would not have

known that Jujube was upset. Her sister sat completely still on the edge of the mattress; her feet pressed flat on the ground. Jasmin noticed the tops of Jujube's feet were dry and peeling, little flecks of white disturbing the normally smooth brown surface. The only part of Jujube that moved was her throat, which appeared to be swallowing rapidly, undulating ripples down her neck. Jasmin wanted to smooth down those ripples, cut the tension.

Then, without a word, Jujube grabbed a tuft of Jasmin's hair and pulled her to her feet. Jasmin screamed, more from fear than from pain—Jujube had never, ever been rough with her. Jujube grabbed her by the arm, so hard that Jasmin could hear the seams of the thin nightie strain as Jujube pulled her out of the bedroom.

"Stop, Jujube, I'm sorry! I won't do it again!"

Jasmin could hear Jujube breathing heavily through her nose.

"Ju, what are you doing, what's going on?" Her father came running out of his room, his pajama pants sagging on one side. "Why is your sister yelling?"

"Don't." Jujube fixed him with an icy glare, but even scarier to Jasmin was her voice, again completely even, not raised, without expression. It filled Jasmin's whole body with shakes. She felt her arm begin to sweat through the nightie where Jujube gripped it.

"Let me go, Ju! I won't do it again!" Jasmin wailed.

Jujube kicked open the wooden door to the basement. "Go inside," she said, looking at Jasmin for the first time since pulling her off the bed.

"I want to bathe. I'm smelly. Are you gonna let me out for dinner?" Jasmin's voice lowered to a piteous whine.

"You forfeited your chance when you sneaked out. You're going to stay here till you learn your lesson." Jujube raised her voice so the rest of the family, now gathered around, mouths agape, could hear. Their father, hair sticking up on the back of his head, stepped toward the sisters, but Jujube held out a hand to block him. Then Jujube darted into the basement and stood on a chair. She reached for the tiny lightbulb in the low ceiling and unscrewed it.

"Jujube, what are you doing? That's cruel. This is your sister." Her father's eyes widened.

"She has been sneaking out. She might've been seen last night. They might have followed her home. We have to make sure there's no chance they can see her!" Jujube's even, cold voice shook just a little. "There is no other choice."

Her mother held out her arms, as if to reach for her daughter, but then dropped them. Jasmin felt her eyes burn as she stepped into the basement and squatted on the floor, her head in her hands. The wooden door clanged above her, and she heard the latch click, and a new sound she hadn't heard before: a padlock, clicking twice, locking her into the darkness.

Jasmin's whole body exploded out of her eyes, the tears, giant rivulets rushing down her cheeks, the aching of uncontrollable sobs rising through her body. She let out a sound, somewhere between a gasp and a howl, that vibrated at the back of her throat. She wiped the snot away from her nose with her hand, but more flowed. How could they do this? Lock her in here forever? In complete darkness? Would she even get to eat? Were they going to kill her? The thoughts that rushed through her head shocked her. Even in their saddest, angriest moments, Jasmin had never been treated this way. Jujube *knew* she was afraid of the dark—that was why she had moved their mattress close to the window, so Jasmin could feel the moonlight seeping through her closed eyes; it was the only way she didn't feel as though someone or something was going to grab her in the night. And now she was in this horrible basement forever. At night it would be pitch-black. Jasmin choked back her fear. As her eyes adjusted, she could see the vague outlines of the chair and the table, but she felt frozen, her body rooted in the squat—she could not move, she could not do anything but heave the sobs.

Above, she heard muffled yelling, her father shouting, her mother walking around in circles. Then she heard Jujube's voice, clear as a bell, authoritative, frightening.

"She needs to learn. She is the only one who doesn't know how to survive. I'm done trying to protect her from everything if she won't listen."

At first Jasmin wanted to yell, "I'll listen, I'll listen, let me out!" But a wave of defiance she didn't recognize, fiery, furious, washed over her. She held her head up and bit the side of her cheek to stop herself from heaving and gasping. If she was going to cry, she would not let them hear her, her family who had thrown her into the basement like a rotten vegetable. As the arguing voices above her quieted, so did Jasmin's crying. She would not let them win.

―

"Baby girl?"

Jasmin opened her eyes; she must've fallen asleep. She stretched her mouth to clear her throat, the dust bits sticking. She heard the sound of the latch being dragged, then her mother was standing in a puddle of light on the steps of the basement, holding the door open.

Her throat scratched. "How long have I been in here?" she said, struggling to adjust to the light.

"Silly child, it's only been a few minutes. Your sister just left for the teahouse. It was a nonsense fight! Come out, I'll make you a Horlicks." Her mother held the door open.

Horlicks, a malty, sweet drink, was extremely expensive and hard to get on the black market—they each got half of a cup on their birthday, and that was it. Jasmin coughed. The dampness in the basement made it feel like someone was sitting on her chest. It had felt a lot longer than a few minutes since her sister, the one she loved and who had sworn to always keep her safe, had locked her away in the dark. As she passed her mother on the steps, her mother pulled her close, so Jasmin could smell the sweat under her arms and feel the dampness of her cheeks: from sweat or tears, she didn't know.

"We'll talk to your sister, okay, baby girl? You are sisters; you'll figure it out. It's the war that does this. It does bad things to us."

Jasmin pulled out of her mother's grasp. Normally she liked hugs, sweaty or not, but today was not a normal day. The shock of Jujube's betrayal had made her body feel different—like there was a heavy rock in her chest, like a sheet had been lifted off her eyes and she could see clearly for the first time. This family, the one she had loved all her life, the one she tried to smile for and stay happy for, had tossed her away. Jasmin's mother went to the kitchen, and Jasmin heard the familiar bubble of boiling water and the tinkle of a spoon stirring the malty Horlicks mixture into a ceramic mug with condensed milk. "A nice hot drink; it'll make it all feel better," her mother said, turning to face the window.

It was quick, but Jasmin knew what she had to do. She pulled her nightie away from her ankles and ran soundlessly across the small house and through the front door. She could hear her mother murmuring little comforts as she stirred the Horlicks. But her murmurs became a loud yell when she realized that Jasmin had disappeared.

Jasmin ran as fast as she could across the grass outside the house. Her breath streamed out of her, wet and steamy, and she realized she had put on mismatched slippers—one orange and one blue. She kept running, as fast and as far as she could, in zigzags into the lane that led to town, flinching whenever she caught the sound of her mother shouting her name.

Eventually she could not hear her mother anymore, and she stopped, wheezing, her breath escaping her throat in quick, painful bursts. She was sweating through the nightie, and it stuck to her back, her underarms. It was a cloudy day, as far as days went, but the air was still, no breeze to break up the humidity. She'd been running more or less into the center of town, but she had tried to zigzag and stay off the main street in case her mother dispatched neighbors on bicycles to come look for her. Once or twice, she'd seen soldiers loitering under trees, smoking, but they didn't seem to notice her. Her left foot ached, and she noticed it was because the base of the orange slipper, already thin, had worn off, and her foot was scraping against the hot ground. Limping, her adrenaline dying down, Jasmin looked around and realized she was close to the chemist. She didn't have any money, but maybe Peik Lum would give her something to cover up the blisters already forming.

The little bells hanging on the door clinked as she entered. Peik Lum walked around the counter toward Jasmin.

"Girl, you're all sweaty. Come sit down." She pulled Jasmin by the arm into a chair, usually occupied by one of many old people waiting for medications. "What's going on?"

Jasmin stared at the floor. She didn't know how to explain her family's betrayal. Instead, she said, "My brother is gone. Away."

"I heard. I'm sorry, little girl." Peik Lum pressed her head into her hands. "My cousin, he went away for a job too, but now we don't hear from him anymore, no letters, nothing."

She pulled Jasmin into a squishy hug till Jasmin squeaked. Peik Lum released her and dabbed her own damp eyes gingerly before noticing the mismatched slippers. "Aiya, what did you do?" She disappeared behind the counter and came back with a paper bag. Squatting, she said, "Give me your foot."

Jasmin extended her hurt left foot, and Peik Lum pulled it toward her, clucking the whole time and not even flinching at the smell. Jasmin screwed up her nose, the sour, musty odor of her own foot making her gag. Peik Lum dabbed her sole with a soft, damp rag, then put an ointment on the blistered arch that stung at first but quickly softened into a cooling sensation. She covered what looked like the beginning of a blister with a plaster. Then she rustled in her bag again. "Nah, here." Peik Lum pushed a stray piece of stick-straight hair that had escaped her ponytail off her face with one hand and tossed Jasmin a pair of new blue-and-white slippers, which she slipped on eagerly.

"Thank you," Jasmin mumbled, not knowing what else to say.

The bell on the door clinked again. Peik Lum rose to her feet and turned toward the door. Jasmin saw the smile she usually put on to greet customers fall from her face.

"General, sir." Peik Lum lowered her eyes and pressed one hand over the other, Jasmin noticed, to stop them from shaking.

At the door stood a short, round man in a soldier's uniform. But unlike most of the soldiers' uniforms Jasmin had seen, this man's wasn't grubby or stained—it was pressed, knife creases in the pants legs and starched stiffness on the collar. For a short man, he held himself straight and tall, a curling frown splitting his face in two as he scanned the room. Jasmin watched his gaze start on his left, past the shelves of herbs, the white bottles of pills, the glass bottles of colorful liquid, the counter where Peik Lum had stood, over the calendar with red Chinese characters on it, which deepened his frown, finally resting on Peik Lum and then her. Jasmin tugged at her nightie uncomfortably—it felt strange to have a man who wasn't her brother or her father looking at her in nightclothes.

"And who are you?" he asked, his Japanese-accented English curt, soft.

"She's just a neighbor girl, General. Just a no one." Jasmin had nearly forgotten about Peik Lum, such was the draw of this small man who seemed to suck the air out of the room, while also forcing her to look at him.

"How old are you?" he asked, ignoring the shaking Peik Lum.

"I'm almost eight," Jasmin said. "My birthday is in January."

The general cocked his head to one side when she said that. "Who are your parents?"

"I—I—" Jasmin stammered. Peik Lum had stiffened her neck so much that Jasmin could see her collarbones. Peik Lum was shaking her head as subtly as she could.

"You. Go back to work." The general waved Peik Lum away, and she shrank back behind the counter.

His voice softened just a bit, and he bent one knee so she could look more closely at his face. "I'm not going to hurt you. My name is General Fujiwara. I just want to know who your parents are." He pronounced "hurt" as "hut."

"My daddy is Gordon," Jasmin began. The general waved that information aside with his hand, as though swatting a fly. "My ma is Cecily . . ."

The general's forehead frown deepened so much Jasmin thought his face would break in two. "What is your surname?" he said, nearly breathless. Behind her, behind the counter, she heard Peik Lum inhale. "Is it Alcantara?" he asked.

Jasmin nodded mutely. Because she was so close to General Fujiwara, she could do the thing she did best, see things. She saw that his frown was melting away from his face. She saw the beginnings of a smile pull apart his sparse mustache, causing a small crumb on the top to fall onto his lip. She saw him brush that crumb away, then use the same hand to wipe his forehead, although he wasn't sweating. And then she heard it before she saw it, a huge, bellowing laugh, rocking through his stomach, past his chest, and out of his mouth, shaking his entire uniformed body to and fro.

"I have been looking for you everywhere! Come!" He stood up from his kneeling position, with ease and without help, Jasmin noticed, unlike her father, who usually needed one of his kids to pull him to his feet.

"Sir, this is a nobody girl. I don't think you're looking for her." Peik Lum's shaky voice rang through the room.

"It's all right. I know her parents," he said. He held out a hand to Jasmin, who shrank away. "Come on, little girl, tell me your name."

He turned her around with surprising gentleness and tugged at the label on her night dress, at the names that Jasmin's mother always stitched into their clothes. He read the blue stitches. "Jasmin, I see. Come, little Jasmin. I promise I won't do anything. Are you hungry? I'll get my houseboy to make you a good lunch."

Jasmin was confused, dizzy. The general, who a few minutes ago had seemed like a scary man, now sounded like a kind uncle or neighbor offering to feed her. She was indeed hungry; she hadn't eaten since Jujube had thrown her in the basement. At the memory, she stuck out her lip bitterly. She wouldn't go home; she didn't want to be with a family who didn't want her. Her stomach growled. She dropped her hand into the general's, surprised at his smooth skin. The door clinked as they left the chemist.

Outside, a blue car stood idling. A driver with a pointy black cap rushed to open the door for the general and cast a questioning eye at him before receiving the nod to keep the door open for Jasmin. Jasmin hesitated. Her mother and sister had warned her many times about getting into any kind of vehicle with a stranger, and her thoughts swirled back to the day when the soldiers had come banging the door asking for *guniang*. But she'd never been in such a nice car. The seats looked comfortable. Plus, the cooling ointment on her left foot had faded, so it was beginning to hurt again.

"Come on." The general smiled at her, making his mustache curl up comically like a worm. Jasmin stifled a giggle and got in. The car was lush, the brown seat holding her like a hug, even more comfortable than her mattress at home. It seemed like he wouldn't stop staring at her. They sat side by side on the car's bench seat, and she could feel him studying the side of her face. Jasmin straightened up to meet his inspection. She wished she weren't wearing this dirty nightie, and she crossed her arms over her chest. Hot wind blew through the open window; it felt good on her head.

"Why does your mother cut your hair like this?" the general asked, pointing at a small bald spot where her mother had been careless with the scissors the previous week.

Jasmin opened her mouth but shut it again. She didn't know how to explain to him about the men coming, and her mother pushing her onto the bucket, and wearing Abel's clothes, and all the grown-ups talking about hurting "down there." Not waiting for an answer, he muttered to himself, "Odd of Cecily to do this."

"Do you know my mother?" Jasmin asked.

"In a way," he said, looking out of the car at an angsana tree they passed. It felt to Jasmin like he didn't want to say anything else, so she too stared out the window. The next five minutes passed by wordlessly, but Jasmin didn't feel uncomfortable. She liked to think she had a sense about grown-ups, that she could tell when they were mean or nice. The lady at the pisang goreng stall who always rolled her eyes—mean. Peik Lum the chemist's assistant—nice. The soldiers who came banging down their door—mean. Her only mistake had been with Jujube, who had always been at the top of her "Nice" list but had quickly become the meanest person she knew. And now General Fujiwara, who, even at his coldest, felt nice to her. Comforted with her assessment, she nestled into the seat.

A hand was shaking her gently. "Wake up, we have arrived."

"I wasn't asleep!" Jasmin yelped. Before she had time to feel embarrassed, the driver opened the door, and the general held out a hand to Jasmin, who took it and exited the car.

They had stopped in front of a large white house, the largest that Jasmin had ever seen in her life, larger even than the house of their richest neighbor, Raja Zain, and his wife, Aunty Faridah, two roads down. Raja Zain was descended from Malay royalty, and his house had a second story and a big growly dog that Jasmin was afraid of. She saw they had driven up a long curving road that led to the house, which sat on a soft green lawn. The house itself was not attached by the walls to the neighbors' houses on the left and right; it stood alone.

"Your old British resident used to live here. I took it over when . . ." General Fujiwara paused. "Never mind, come inside." He waved her in.

Inside the house, her feet encased in soft cloth house slippers the general had handed her, she stood awkwardly at a pillar. The general had disappeared, and in his place, a Japanese houseboy stood, dressed in starched white. The houseboy, who looked about Abel's age, bounced on the balls of his feet. He mimed with his hands, making a little cup and bringing it to his lips.

"Is it water?" Jasmin asked.

He nodded and handed her a tin cup filled with cool water and waved her into a rattan chair with the most comfortable cushions Jasmin had ever sat on. They felt like they were wrapping her in a soft, cool embrace. The houseboy soon reappeared with a large steaming bowl of rice, and on top, Jasmin saw a piece of fish covered in garlic and soy sauce. The fragrant smell filled the room and made her head spin. The houseboy waved the bowl under her nose. "You," he said, handing her a spoon.

The general came back down as she was spooning the last of the rice into her mouth, her tongue pulling a grain that had gotten stuck on her upper lip, not wanting to waste even the smallest bit of this meal, the tastiest she'd had in a long time. The general wore loose light-colored trousers and a singlet, his armpits exposed in the large armholes. To Jasmin, he looked so much smaller this way, and older, even older than her father, who was the oldest person she knew.

"How do you know my mother?" Jasmin asked. It surprised her that her mother would know anyone outside of their family and their neighbors, because for as long as Jasmin could recall, her mother had always seemed afraid to go outside. During heavy storms, when little cracks of lightning broke through the sky before the loud shout of thunder, the fear of what was to come made Jasmin shiver. It seemed to Jasmin that her mother lived in this in-between place—always shaking, about to crack open, always waiting for the thunder.

"Ah, well," said the general, his voice gentle, quiet, lulling Jasmin into a peaceful calm. "Your mother changed me, and the world."

CHAPTER NINE

JUJUBE

Bintang, Kuala Lumpur
August 17, 1945
Japanese-occupied Malaya

The sun streamed through the teahouse's slatted shutters. Usually Jujube opened the shop at sunrise. But she was still reeling from the rage she had felt when she learned that Jasmin had been sneaking out; even now a sharp knob of guilt pressed against her chest. She wanted to run home and let her sister out of the basement and encase her in a hug. She knew Jasmin could endure only a few hours of hiding in the basement each day. She told herself she would let Jasmin out in the evening, and everything would be all right—she just needed to learn a lesson. Jasmin was so naive at times, and Jujube was torn between wanting to preserve her sister's innocence and wanting to shake some sense into her, teach her how to take care of herself. She knew there was always a chance she would not be able to be there for Jasmin, and Jasmin, silly, naive Jasmin, needed to learn how to trust less, or else, or— She shuddered at the thought and pushed it out of her mind.

As Jujube swung the rickety wooden shutters open, Mr. Takahashi came bounding in, stepping into a puddle of sun and casting a long shadow across the cement floor.

"Sir, you are early today!" She noticed he wasn't wearing his usual brown blazer and gray pants. He was in a white singlet, the armholes exposing the unmuscled flesh of his arms. She averted her eyes.

"Jujube, I have news! I wanted to tell you first!"

The light, she saw, flickered in his eyes in a way that had been absent the last week, filled with letter writing, anxious energy, and mismatched shoes.

"Sir?"

"She lives! My daughter, she was away!"

His daughter, supposedly lost to the war they were both living through. His daughter, the reason for her sympathy, their kinship.

"She is visit my sister in Osaka!"

It was a strange feeling, as if a slow, heavy wind had struck Jujube in the stomach. Her brain, fast-moving and always alert, knew to arrange her face into a jubilant smile, to push from her mouth a quick succession of happy congratulations. "Sir, that's such wonderful news! I am so happy for you!"

She could see and feel everything—the orange stain on the ground from when another tea girl had spilled saffron tea on the floor, the ache in her shoulder where the soldier at the checkpoint had grabbed her the night before, the parts of Mr. Takahashi's white singlet that seemed grayer, as though it had been washed in dirty water. She should be happy, be able to smile at this man, her friend, a kind man whose innocent daughter was given another chance at a life, which they both deserved. He brightened her days with his literature and his ambitions for her and his care and his food coupons. When hopeful things happened to good people, you were supposed to hold on to the little joy you felt, to grasp it to you, knowing that it may not happen again soon. The pulsing anger that pressed through her body shouldn't be there.

"Jujube! Jujube!"

The shout shook Jujube from her thoughts. She was shocked to see her mother standing in the teahouse doorway. The stark morning light against her mother's back made her figure a dark shadow. "Ma! What are you doing here?"

"Your . . . your . . ." Her mother was breathing so hard little bits of spit flew out of her mouth into Jujube's face. Her nose was running, a glob of snot loosely holding on to her left nostril. For the second time that morning, Jujube looked away from the desperation of an adult.

"Your sister ran away!" her mother finally managed to squeeze out.

Jujube did not expect her own response. A normal person, she thought, would start peppering her mother with questions—how did she get out, did you let her out, where did she go? A normal person would start yelling or crying or expressing any kind of appropriate fear-filled emotion. A normal person would, simply, react. But Jujube felt rooted to the ground, her head full of waves of something that seemed to rise through her body, through her chest, up into her throat, straight into her head, an anger so strong it almost blinded her, pressing against the bone and flesh of her skull, without which, she felt like, it would've spilled out all over the teahouse floor, burning everything in its path.

She didn't realize that she had closed her eyes. When she opened them, Mr. Takahashi was consoling her mother, who was a bereft pile of hiccupping tears on the teahouse floor.

"You should go, Jujube," Mr. Takahashi said, his voice thick with sadness. "I'll let the manager know that you had to leave."

Doraisamy emerged from the kitchen, and Jujube's heart sank; she expected to be scolded, told to stop causing a scene and get back to work.

"I'm sorry, my sister—my mother just told me—" she stuttered.

"Go," Doraisamy said. He waved her out. "I can handle the place today."

The kindness shocked Jujube. She nodded mutely and grabbed her mother by the arm, more roughly than she had intended. She turned to face Mr. Takahashi and opened her mouth to say something, but she couldn't muster up enough gratitude for a thank-you.

All Jujube could think was, these people—their invaders—when they dared to hope, they were rewarded for it. He would get his daughter back, and the price, it seemed, was something *she* had to pay—with Jasmin. The knot in her chest swelled through her, like an arsonist's fire.

The house was steaming by the time they got home. It was about eleven o'clock, and every wall was warm to the touch. A trail of ants crawled up the kitchen counter and swarmed a small green enamel mug with a round blue face on it—Jasmin's favorite. Some of the ants had drowned themselves, gulping down the abandoned Horlicks drink. Before Jujube could reach for the mug to throw out the remnants, her mother flattened her hand like a knife blade and swept her fingers across the counter, knocking everything over—spatulas, a bottle of cooking oil, a wok, a wooden-framed family photo, the mug of ant-ridden Horlicks. Objects crashed on the floor in a cacophony of different sounds, the wok clanged, the spatula tinged, the cooking oil thudded softly and didn't make much sound but spilled yellow liquid everywhere, the framed family photo made a sickening crack, and the green mug emptied itself, causing little ant dots to scurry for shelter amid human feet and spilled fluids. The mug bounced once, twice, before landing by Jujube's feet like an offering.

"Ma, please stop, you're making a mess," Jujube pleaded, stepping over the sticky malt of the Horlicks and the slippery, rancid cooking oil as they began congealing into each other on the cement floor.

"I did this," Jujube's mother muttered.

"No, Ma." Jujube pressed a fist into her chest. It was not her mother's fault, it was hers. She had driven Jasmin away, frightened her sister into thinking that she had nowhere else to turn. Jujube tried to make her way over to where her mother was now squatting with her feet flat on the ground, head buried in her hands. She breathed heavily, frenzied. Her mother didn't seem to feel the little black ants that were using her feet as a pathway to escape the mess on the ground.

"I'll go get Pa at the factory," Jujube said. Someone, she thought, had to take charge.

In between panicked gasps, her mother said, "He owes me; he will know."

"Who will know? Ma? Who?"

Jujube's mother fell silent, but she twisted the fingers of her left hand so much that Jujube worried they would break. Jujube sank to the floor and crawled through the oil to her mother, knowing somehow that if she didn't manage to get through to her, things would only get worse.

Unlike other Eurasian mothers, Jujube's mother had never been focused on Jujube's looks, or her marriage prospects, or any kind of ability to attract boys. When Jujube had gotten the job at the teahouse, she had thought she would have a tough time convincing her mother that the extra money would be worth it. Instead, her mother had smiled a rare smile and looked almost proud.

Still, for so long, Jujube's mother had exhibited a nervous anxiety that often dampened the mood of any room she walked into. She was always twisting one hand into another, a deep frown line cleaving her face in two. But Jujube knew her mother had not always been this frantic, nervous woman. She was old enough to remember a time when her mother had smiled full smiles and thrown back her head when she laughed but they were faint, these memories, scuffed on the edges, the way shoe scratches against walls leave an imprint but not a mark. Jujube remembered crouching in her favorite hiding place, the little shaded drain under the kitchen window, and from this window, hearing the voice of a man she didn't recognize wafting out, and even more surprising, hearing a deep belly laugh—familiar because it was her mother, unfamiliar because her mother so rarely laughed that way. In her mind, Jujube had called the man Uncle Toothpaste, because he smelled like the bracing cool scent her mouth emitted after she'd brushed her teeth. She'd seen him one time, standing outside the sundry shop. She'd recognized the minty scent from her days sitting under the window, and she'd whirled around to see a short, smooth-faced man watching them both. Jujube's mother must've noticed too; her hand had tightened across Jujube's and became clammy and unpleasant. Her mother had closed her eyes briefly and inhaled in a small, rattling way down the back of her throat. Then she'd opened her eyes and pulled Jujube into the shop, walking by Uncle Toothpaste as though she didn't know him.

As Jujube grew older, Uncle Toothpaste became one of the many made-up stories that Jujube told Jasmin at night when they curled together studying the moon. Uncle Toothpaste will help us if the soldiers come, Uncle Toothpaste will bring Abel home, Uncle Toothpaste will stop Pa from coughing.

"What does Uncle Toothpaste look like?" Jasmin had asked one day, big blinking eyes looking up from her perch in Jujube's lap. But try as she might to recall, Jujube couldn't remember a single defining feature of the man's face. Only that mint scent, tickling the back of her nose.

CHAPTER TEN

CECILY

Bintang, Kuala Lumpur
1936
Nine years earlier, British-occupied Malaya

Cecily was a woman who liked categorization, who found solace in order. Even the dichotomy that her life had become—housewife and spy—felt like tidy boxes she could open and close as the circumstance warranted. Most days she played her role as the unspecific, forgettable wife of a local administrator, tolerated, unquestioned, barely noticed. She was an irreproachable mother to her children; she mingled with other mothers, gossiped about minor neighborhood scandals, fed, clothed, and read to her children. Gordon was known to describe her as everything one would need in a wife and mother, one who anticipated and fulfilled needs, lived unremarkably, almost happily.

And, as an informer for the Japanese Imperial Army, she was appropriately diligent—she knew how to parse the intel from the unnecessary, had a knack for flitting in and out of Gordon's meetings and overhearing just enough for her to put together the pieces with Fujiwara. Informing was like a big puzzle, little pieces here and there: a scrap of a log, a torn map, a murmured tail end of a conversation. And when she and Fujiwara put it together, parceled the morsels of information into a tangible report of intelligence for his bosses, it felt like so much power, like she could do anything in the world.

This proclivity for order meant that Cecily did not enjoy yearning; she did not enjoy its lack of solidity. On some days her yearning for Fujiwara felt hopeful—the days when he smiled, the days when he told her that everything was coming together, the days when they cracked a particularly tough piece of intel. But on other days her yearning felt panicky, like everything depended upon her ability to get his approval and she would not be able to function without it. In one of these throes of panicked yearning, she had kissed the tiny sliver of skin above Fujiwara's upper lip, above the faint mustache he'd tried to grow to look more dignified. As her lips pressed into him, he had held himself completely still, neither leaning nor recoiling. And when she'd pulled away, tasting salt, the smell of mint hair cream all around her, he had looked at her, said, "Thank you," and continued their work deciphering the map of the swamplands they had been reviewing, as though she had simply handed him a dossier or said hello.

She took her yearning out on Gordon, much to his delight. "You exhaust me," he said once after a particularly vigorous night, his sweat coating the sheets and her, the open window blowing a tepid breeze over them. "Could a man be luckier?" Cecily had tightened her jaw and scowled her dissatisfaction into the dark bedroom.

In early 1936, when the monsoon winds began transitioning from northeast to southwest, the arson at the port was the talk of the town. It had been just about two months since their daring intel grab at the resident's dinner. That morning, the newspaper arrived with angry block letters:

FEBRUARY FIRES AT PORT LEWISHAM, FOUL PLAY SUSPECTED

The night before, everyone in the neighborhood had rushed out and watched as the orange flames curled through the night sky as though trying to touch the moon. To Cecily, the ashy air smelled like victory. The newspaper talked about what a crippling blow this was to the British air force, how many RAF planes were laid waste, that only someone with *inside* information could have known that the port was designated for RAF plane repair. A *mole*. She saw photos of blackened remains of the hangar structures looking like skeletons shaking against the backdrop of the muddied river water. Cecily pressed her hands against the newsprint, fingers dusted gray. She licked the newsprint off her fingers when Gordon wasn't looking. It tasted like Communion wafer, like nothing. She steeled her lips in a thin straight line across her face, maintained an expression of concerned seriousness, but inside her was a gush of warmth at their success, the direct impact her intel had on the Japanese effort. Later that day at the sundry shop, she dropped an off-white piece of notebook paper, her newest piece of intel, Gordon's logs of vegetation at a nearby stream. On the back corner of the crumpled paper, she scribbled:

Overjoyed. What next?

For the next two weeks Bintang became a rush of agitation and breathless speculation. All around Cecily, men were being hauled in for interrogation as the British desperately tried to weed out the mole. Rumors swirled in the neighborhood, fences were whispered over, husbands would fail to return home in the evenings, and their desperate wives would go knocking on doors begging neighbors for information. But the doors were slammed; no one wanted to be seen colluding with the wife of a suspected traitor.

Meanwhile Cecily's initial exultation passed quickly. Gordon returned home every day with eyebrows pressed together, lines of worry creeping under his eyes. She peppered him with questions— who was hauled in for questioning, where did they think the leak came from, how would they know when they had the mole, how did they get information out of the people they took in? Gordon was patient. He did not have many answers, but he did his best: Today they took Lingam in; it's hard to pinpoint the origin of the leak because there were no missing documents, just evidence that specific high-value areas of the port were targeted by the fires; they think they'll just know who the mole is when they catch him. But when Cecily pressed him for just *how* they would get this information out of the men, Gordon's face darkened. "There are ways," he said. "You don't want to know."

But Cecily did want to know. And in the absence of news, her sleep was filled with imagined torture, faceless men beating her within an inch of her life, her children screaming as they watched. She became preoccupied with the limitless ways there were to die.

"Gordon," she asked one night after putting the children to bed, "would it be better to be hanged or to be drowned?" She immediately regretted her question when the bottom of Gordon's jaw began to quiver, and his eyes glistened, suspiciously wet. "I'm sorry," she said. "I'm just scared."

Gordon wrapped his arms around her. "We are safe," he murmured into her hair. "I've never given them any reason to doubt my loyalty."

Cecily knew she should have felt guilty that poor, ignorant Gordon was trying so hard to give her comfort from his body, to shield her from the very worst. But instead, she prickled with loathing, skin hot with disgust. Fujiwara never would have given in this way, never would have shown her such weakness.

But where, in fact, was Fujiwara? For fifteen days after the fire, she had waited for a sign from him, some sort of instruction on what to do, even if it was to lie low. This was the longest they had gone without communicating in the two years she had been informing for him. She startled at every noise, sweeping every corner of the town for a glimpse of him. But she could not seek him out. It was always he who found her, who told her what to do, where to meet, and without his anchoring, she was lost. How loathsome to rely on a man this way. His silence threw her into a spiral of confusion—sometimes anger, sometimes shame, sometimes fear. The emotions roiled in her, settling into a hard rock at the base of her stomach that made everything—eating, shitting, sleeping, existing—a huge effort.

It took every wisp of energy she had to maintain normalcy: to feed her children, to greet her husband, to go to the market, to gossip with the other wives, to say hello to people on the street, to make dinner, to playact simplicity, all the while her body screaming for a man who had seemingly left her at a time when she needed him most.

After a series of starts and stops, the British began focusing their attention on the Chinese population, convinced that Zhou Enlai had embedded Communist agents within their ranks. Kapitan Yap, Mrs. Yap's husband, was their most immediate suspect; it didn't take long for rival clan chiefs to give up the hiding place of their embattled kapitan, who had been holed up at his widowed daughter-in-law's house. The British officers who arrived to arrest him chained him by the neck like an animal and threw him into a lorry. That was the last anyone ever saw of Kapitan Yap.

Kapitan Yap's arrest unleashed a spate of violence in Bintang. With their leader out of the way, the Chinese clans began fighting among themselves to take his place, and people began whispering about civil war. Mrs. Lingam, whose husband, Arun Lingam, managed palm oil and rubber estates, was furious at the English. "They only suspect us! What about the gweilos themselves? Why don't they suspect their own?"

In the days following the arrest, the wives gathered at Mrs. Yap's house in a show of support, murmuring consolations and bringing her hot tea. Cecily had always hated this pantomime of care; no one actually cared. They were all just itching for information, little nuggets they could discuss among themselves later, gems they could shine up and bring back home to their husbands, who, despite pretending not to care about neighborhood gossip, also wanted to know everything.

Mrs. Yap was nearly catatonic, rocking back and forth on the floor, face swollen and bulbous, a shameful sight. Though all love was humiliation, in a way, Cecily supposed. All love was someone breaking their soul into smaller pieces and offering the broken pieces of themselves as a puzzle to someone else—*help me put myself back together*. Sitting as a part of the circle of cooing, fussing women, she studied the back of Mrs. Yap's head. Usually Mrs. Yap's hair was parted in a straight line down the middle of her head and pulled back smoothly into a very high bun. But today her part was jagged, bumpy, raised like angry snakes.

"Can I get you anything?" she whispered to Mrs. Yap. She did not expect a response.

"Get me out of here," came the whispered reply. Mrs. Yap's breath no longer smelled like shallots and milk; it was bitter and sharp, the breath of someone who hadn't gargled in days.

Cecily knew she should feel guilt, this family torn apart for her crime. Yet she felt nothing for Mrs. Yap; all she ached for was Fujiwara. That was the most humiliating thing of all: Fujiwara had changed her, and because he had changed a tiny bit of her into something she was proud of, he had left something of himself in her. He had given her a bigger, brighter version of herself, and once she'd had a taste of this new self, she craved more, so much more.

"I'll get you some water," she said to Mrs. Yap. Cecily rose, walked to the kitchen, and without looking back, opened the back door of the house and left.

CHAPTER ELEVEN

ABEL

Kanchanaburi Labor Camp on the Burma/Thailand border
August 18, 1945
Japanese-occupied Malaya

Abel's eyes flew open. It was morning again, his third day in the chicken coop. It felt like he was living in a loop, one where every morning he was greeted by the angry pecking of a brown hen who did not enjoy having him encroaching on her space. The night prior, he and Brother Luke had assumed opposite sides of the chicken coop and glared at each other across the darkness. Abel had thought about crawling over to Brother Luke and beating his face into a pulp—the man had sold him into this horrible life, after all—but he didn't think he would win the fight, broken down as his body was. Brother Luke, for his part, did not seem to recognize him, which infuriated Abel even more; how many families had Brother Luke done this to? How many more boys had he snatched from their families and sold to the Japanese, and in return for what? Brother Luke was trapped in the same coop that he was.

The door to the chicken coop was unlatched again. Both boy and man shrank to their respective corners, preparing for the worst.

"White Boy!" Master Akiro said, bending his head to fit under the coop.

Abel noticed that Brother Luke's shoulders dropped in relief, which made him clench his own fists in anger. It wasn't fair.

"You like this? You want this?" Master Akiro had opened a flask and was swishing the liquid around inside. The unmistakable sweetness of toddy swept toward Abel, over the humidity and smell of chicken feces. Abel wanted to grit his teeth and look away, to hold his own against this man who had beaten him into a bag of broken bones, who had, just hours ago—No, he didn't even want to think about what had happened. But Abel's body betrayed him; he craved the drink so badly that he found himself sniffing the air like a rabid animal, crawling toward the door, toward Akiro, toward the toddy. He needed to feel the burn scorch its way down his esophagus; he wanted the warmth to spread through the nerves that were screaming now from the cuts, bruises, bites, and breaks; he wanted to drink until the shouting in his head became an even buzzing that wrapped around him like a blanket.

"Ah, ah, no." Master Akiro ducked away and capped the flask. "Not free of charge, White Boy." Akiro reached for something on the ground and tossed it toward Abel as if throwing food into an animal pen. It made a loud thud as it hit the ground. All the chickens except the dead rooster squawked, flapped their wings, and moved toward the edges of the coop in indignation. Master Akiro had thrown a slim, long piece of rebar. Abel had touched, carried, and laid down steel rebar many times before as part of the work he and the other boys did to build the railway tracks.

When he looked up, Abel was surprised to see that a small crowd had gathered at the doorway and around the chicken coop fence, both Japanese soldiers and camp boys alike. They crammed against one another, pushing to get a view. He scanned the crowd: Ah Lam was there, and Azlan, and Rama. Then he saw Freddie standing slightly away from the crowd, as usual, blue eyes narrowed and fixed on Brother Luke. Abel opened his mouth to ask what he was supposed to do with the rebar, but his voice came out as only a choke. Master Akiro laughed a little cruel laugh.

"You kill. I give you drink. I let you out," Master Akiro said.

The camp boys and soldiers outside the chicken coop roared, "Fight, fight, fight!"

Brother Luke was screaming by this point. "No, please, boy, no."

The world is cruel, Abel thought. Here before his feet was the instrument to do the thing he had wanted to do—kill the man who had destroyed his life, sold him into slavery, taken him from everything he had ever loved. But now he was to do it for sport, for the entertainment of everyone around him, with his violated body, under the glare of Master Akiro. Abel knew he should feel guilty, he should feel fear, he should feel something, but all he felt was bone-crushing exhaustion. He wondered if he even had the strength to pick up the rebar.

"Do it, White Boy, or you stay in here. Then *he* kill *you*." Master Akiro pointed at Brother Luke, who was squatting on his haunches, inching away from Abel. Abel looked around the coop as the faces huddled close to the wire, boys and men alike, stamping their feet and making so much noise that the coop vibrated. The brown hen was clucking and flapping her wings in terror. With every vibration, the dead rooster's body jumped, and Abel wished they could swap places, that he could be a shell of himself rotting in the corner, not holding the life of a man he hated in his hands.

"Abe, you have to." A voice behind him, just beyond the fence: Freddie, having made his way to the part of the fence nearest to Abel. Freddie looked at him unblinking, a disquieting calm in the chaos.

Absolution, Abel realized, could come in all forms. Brother Luke had taught the boys at school that absolution came only from god. But where was god when Akiro broke him from the inside, where was god when Brother Luke sold little boys to save his own skin, where was god now when his options were to murder or await a fate worse than death? Freddie, fourteen-year-old skinny Freddie, who had lived so many lives before his time, was giving Abel a way forward. He would do it for Freddie. After all, Brother Luke had taken from Freddie too.

Abel stood up, his knees and shoulders bent to prevent his head from hitting the top of the coop. He watched his shadow pick up the rebar, sway, press all its strength into his arms. His shadow held the rebar aloft, then slammed it into Brother Luke's teeth.

"Someone vomited." Abel's vision was hazy, his nose assaulted with the smell of bitter bile.

"Sit up, I can't lift you." Freddie's voice broke through the haze. Abel felt a shoulder against his back, a person forcing him into a seated position. Abel tried to straighten himself and immediately heaved, a wave of vomit threatening to expel itself through his mouth. Right, so the vomit was coming from him.

"Abe! You have to sit up or you'll choke."

"What happened?" Abel's head felt like someone had stuffed it with cotton.

"Lean on the wall," Freddie instructed, shoving Abel's left shoulder into the side of what he realized was the outside of their sleeping quarters. It must've been midafternoon, based on the crooked sun and the way his shadow curled at an angle. "You drank too much of that stuff all at once."

Flashes of the morning came back to Abel. The cracking sound the rebar made against Brother Luke's teeth, one of those teeth flying at him and embedding itself into his arm. The cheer that went up through the camp when Brother Luke, face full of blood, had rolled onto his stomach and tried to drag himself away. Abel instinctively looked at his arm. Brother Luke's tooth was no longer embedded in his flesh, but in its place, a bloody indentation and the beginnings of a ball of pus in the infected wound. The second crunch when Abel slammed the now-bloodied rebar into Brother Luke's retreating back, and how the man had lain there twitching afterward, Abel not knowing if he was dead or alive, the smell of rust everywhere, the chickens screeching, the air pungent with sweat and death. Limping toward Master Akiro and grabbing the flask, then drinking and drinking and drinking, the burning sensation down his throat and into his empty stomach, the spinning in his head, the sun finding him no matter where he tried to shelter his head, and finally release and darkness.

Abel slid back to press his shoulders up against the wall. The stone was painfully warm from the sun, but the toddy continued to have its effect; Abel barely felt the scald on his skin. Something poked him in the back, burning hot, as he tried clumsily to shift his weight. Looking down, he saw it was the piece of rebar; the end of it had become a deep rust color, dried blood. The middle of the bar was bent where it had struck Brother Luke.

"Is he—?"

"They took Brother Luke away to the field." The field. The killing field where the Japanese piled the bodies of dead boys one on top of the other in deep holes, then filled the holes with soil once they were full of carcasses, rotting in the sun.

"Thank you," Freddie said so softly that Abel could barely hear him above the cotton in his head.

"For what?" Abel asked.

Freddie pulled the rebar away so it wasn't poking Abel in the back anymore, yelled as the hot metal touched his fingertips. Freddie threw the rebar toward the trees. Abel heard the swish of leaves and a thud as it fell into some bushes, out of sight.

"Just thank you," said Freddie, looking him in the face for the first time since Abel had woken up, his blue eyes clear as the sky. "Now let's try to get you to stand up."

After one kills a man, one's days and nights start blending together. Each new day was punctuated with long periods of time when Abel's mind would replay the crack the rebar made when it hit Brother Luke's teeth. The indent on his arm where Brother Luke's tooth had struck him had begun to weep in earnest, oozing pus and blood down his arm. And every time it began to heal and scab over, Abel would pick at the wound. There would be no healing for killers, no healing for him.

And yet the days resumed at the camp. During the day, he did the same backbreaking work as always. The railway tracks were almost complete—neat, even lines of wood and metal. But at night, there was a newness in the air, a desperation that the boys couldn't put a finger on. Rama, whose Japanese was more fluent than most of the boys', overheard the soldiers talking about Japanese cities being bombed, about American soldiers, about giving up. Each day they noticed fewer and fewer soldiers monitoring their tasks. They realized that many Japanese soldiers were deserting the camp, leaving night after night, complaining that now there was no more use building a railway to transport supplies between Rangoon and Bangkok when there were no more supplies to transport. The soldiers who remained became both crueler and kinder—more kicks and beatings if they were bored, but also much less interest in monitoring the boys working. Master Akiro was one of those who stayed, but his face grew haggard, and he seemed to lose interest in both Abel and Freddie. He was glued all day to the tiny transistor radio he carried, listening to staticky news in Japanese.

The nights became livelier, and the Japanese didn't appear to care. The boys would gather in the sleeping quarters, mashed against one another with a curious intimacy. Here at the camp, what else did they have but one another? Legs over legs, arms over arms, dirty feet curled under bodies, sticky armpits pressed against shoulders and necks, the proximity, the smell of sweat almost a comfort, a reminder, I am alive, I am still here.

These gatherings were also superseded by something new, something rare—tiny moments of joy. The stuffy nights became filled with music and song as their occupiers stewed and drank in their own quarters. Notes of harmony rising in the air like the heat. It turned out that Rama could sing, bellowing melodies that were both sweet and powerful out of that belly of his, old Malay folk songs, but also Jimmie Davis, Cliff Edwards, Frank Sinatra. Azlan with his long, dexterous fingers had fashioned a makeshift accordion out of discarded wood and pallets from the camp. The two would sing and play, and the other boys would howl along, some with more talent than others. Sometimes when they were feeling particularly bold, they would shout the song "Der Fuehrer's Face," but swap "fuehrer" with "emperor," and feel decidedly defiant.

Freddie's favorite song was "When You Wish Upon a Star," a naive tune about dreamers and hope that, to Abel, sounded a little cloying. Freddie, who never sang out loud, would come to life at this song and mouth the lyrics fiercely, his eyes a bright, earnest blue that made Abel think maybe, just maybe, they could survive.

One night, after a particularly rousing rendition of the song from Rama, Freddie had turned to Abel. "That's us, Abe. We can be the dreamers after all"—he gestured around the camp—"this."

"What dreams, Freddie?" Abel scoffed. "Dreams of something other than this stupid camp? Here where we're gonna starve, where we're gonna die?"

"I don't think it's a bad thing to hope, Abe," Freddie said quietly.

"Why do you even like this song so much?" said Abel crossly. Sometimes the toddy made him irritable.

"I hate talking to you when you're like this." Freddie shifted his shoulders away from Abel.

Distracted by their own problems, the Japanese soldiers were far more careless with their alcohol. Lately, they'd begun leaving partly finished bottles around, the toddy evaporating in the sun. Abel would gulp down these dregs. Sometimes he was able to steal almost full bottles, left beside outhouses when the soldiers went to take a piss. It was a new kind of wonderland, being able to exist in the thin, watery space where nothing hurt, everything swayed, and he didn't have to remember the sickening crack the rebar made against Brother Luke's teeth, or the pool of blood that stuck to his feet after.

"I wish you'd quit the stuff," Freddie continued.

"Come on, what's your problem?" Abel surprised himself by grabbing Freddie's arm so hard that a little jolt of pain shot through his still-festering wound.

"Stop it." Freddie pulled his arm away from Abel, his tone hard.

"I'm sorry," Abel said, his tongue thick, his eyes watery. He looked away. He wished he could quit, wished his body didn't start shaking and sweating when he went more than a few hours without a sip. Also, these days he couldn't control his eyes as much. Maybe it was the toddy, maybe it was just the effort it took not to remember, but when he got upset, his eyes would well up shamefully and he would have to leave so the other boys wouldn't see. He rushed out of the quarters barefoot, the ground soft and muddy but cool against his feet. He swayed a little; the contents of the half bottle he'd sneaked earlier behind the outhouse finally hit, and everything roiling inside him washed clean. The voices in his head became quieter, and the night sounds—the crickets and the laughter of the boys—became smoother. Abel stumbled down the path away from the barracks, past the construction, past the piles of wood and metal, past the near-complete railway tracks.

Even if he could use toddy to stop reliving the crack the rebar made against Brother Luke's body, nothing stopped the strange way he had begun to lose hours. That night, for example. He remembered leaving the raucous singing of his friends, the happy sweat of their bodies. He remembered feeling tired and slowing his stumbling run to a walk. He remembered regretting snapping at Freddie, remembered thinking he should apologize. Then the next thing he remembered was hours later, rocking back and forth, Freddie by his side, again in the chicken coop. How long had he been there? Why was he there?

"Come on, Abel, you came back here again. We have to go."

What did Freddie mean—again?

"When did I last come here?" Abel asked.

"You come back here every night, Abel."

"I don't know why. I just— Since—" The words were jumbled in Abel's throat.

"Since Akiro put you in here. I know."

Abel felt his stomach drop, a wave of shame and despair so overwhelming he felt like he was drowning. Did Freddie know what Master Akiro had done? Abel shuddered, remembering the swish of the belt buckle hitting the dusty ground, the mosquitoes squealing, the brilliant sunset.

"Because of Brother Luke." Freddie's voice, soft and low, seemed to crack. "I know you didn't want to do that to him."

Abel's breath hissed out of his gritted teeth in relief. Freddie didn't know about Akiro, a small mercy but a mercy nonetheless. Abel could only deal with so many humiliations.

"Freddie, do you come get me every night?" he asked.

"Always," said Freddie.

CHAPTER TWELVE
—

CECILY

Bintang, Kuala Lumpur
1936
Nine years earlier, British-occupied Malaya

Right around May 1936, the hottest month of the year, Aunty Mui, who, along with her husband, ran Chong Sin Kee's sundry shop, told anyone who would listen that Cecily Alcantara was losing it. She told Puan Azreen, who worked at the secondary school, that Mrs. Alcantara was looking more disheveled by the day, that her hair smelled oily and unwashed. She told Mrs. Chua, who ran the haberdashery, that Mrs. Alcantara came to the shop twice a day, maybe three times, and always hovered around pretending to buy ice cream, even though goodness knows, if her children were eating all the ice cream she was buying, what would become of their teeth?

And in fact, some days Cecily felt like she *was* losing it. She waited day after day for someone—officers, army men, British intelligence—to come drag her away. She jumped whenever someone slammed a door in the house, flinched when the children pulled at her skirt. They demanded stories at bedtime, but she found she could not stop her voice from quivering as she read, so she stopped. She refused to leave the house except to go to the sundry shop to stick her hand fruitlessly into the splintery nook where she used to correspond with Fujiwara, her heart beating with the same anticipation every time, even though she knew she wouldn't find anything. She practiced what she would say to Gordon as he watched the officers arrest her: "I'm sorry, you deserved better, take care of the children." She played all sorts of scenarios in her mind—someone had found her letter to Fujiwara, someone had seen her talking to Fujiwara and put two and two together, or worst of all, Fujiwara had been caught and sold her out. She lived in this haze of desperate, sharp anxiety, not knowing what day of the week it was, the knots in her stomach growing tighter.

"Disgraceful how unkempt she is!" Puan Azreen said to Aunty Mui, leaning over the counter at the sundry store.

"At least I hear the daughter is very capable, luckily walking to school all by herself," Mrs. Tan said, joining the conversation.

"What must the husband think? Remember that time she fainted at the party?" wealthy Faridah Mansor said, but the other two shook their heads. Their husbands were not important enough to have been invited.

"I hear Eurasian ladies can be unstable, all that mixing blood, you know?" said a particularly bitter Mrs. Lingam, though no one listened to her because everyone knew she'd set her sights on marrying a Eurasian man for the mixed babies, but none had wanted her.

But no one ever came for Cecily. Kapitan Yap was executed, so they heard. People said Mrs. Yap had packed a bag and slipped away quietly one night, leaving no note and no forwarding address. They assumed she'd gone back to her mother's house in Ipoh; no one expected to hear from her again.

"Good riddance," said Mrs. Low, "she was always too loud."

"I won't miss that crass woman," said Lady Lewisham, the resident's wife.

And once it was all over, people quickly forgot the fear and resentment they had felt when the British had torn into their homes looking for the traitor, went back to their day-to-day trivialities—the price of vegetables, the unlikely wedding of the butcher's girl and the schoolmaster's boy, the scandalous abdication of the English king, Edward VIII, for the "American," as Gordon would say, not able to utter Wallis Simpson's name without grimacing.

Gordon did worry about Cecily, in his way. For a few weeks he would cycle to and from the office to check in on his wife—a break in the midmorning, an hour at lunch. He wavered between pleading and rage.

"Cecily, please tell me what's going on?" he asked one day when she cringed away from his touch. "Does hysteria run in your family?" Another day he yelled so loudly that it made Mrs. Carvalho stick her head over the fence: "Snap out of it! You're not being a good wife!" Most days he pleaded, "Come back to us. We need you."

But Cecily needed Fujiwara. That was not a switch she could turn on and off. Gordon loved her, she knew. Still, it was inconceivable to him that there was an external reason for her behavior, that it was guilt and fear eating at her. He simply did not perceive her as someone capable of doing anything extreme enough to create guilt. Her "moods," as he called them, always boiled down to some quirk of temperament, some built-in flaw in her system causing her to act in undesirable ways that belied the parameters of their little domestic world. She knew it was easier for Gordon to see her this way—it meant he would never suspect her of anything—but it made her scorn for him even more virulent. Loving without seeing, she thought, was simply delusion.

Cecily replayed the stolen bits of time she'd had with Fujiwara, that night under the moon when he'd told her who he really was. Throwing garlic at each other in her kitchen the day before their triumphant intel grab at the resident's house. A brush against a shoulder while walking through town pretending not to know each other. A stolen meeting at a seedy hotel room where they'd flinched anytime they heard a moan from one of the rooms next to them. Was he being beaten this very minute for information? And if pushed hard enough, would he name her as an accomplice? She told herself that he would not. But if she was honest with herself, she did not know. She knew only of his fervor to Japan, his willingness to sacrifice anything for the imperial ideals. As for his loyalty to her? Cecily did not know if she mattered to him at all.

Nevertheless, as life returned to its small, meandering normal in Bintang, for the Alcantaras, it also brought surprising fortune, in the form of another rise in rank for Gordon, who had been promoted to the highest possible position a non-British person could hold in the public works department, bringing with it income, recognition, change. They were able to hire a servant for the household who put food on their table and dressed the children for school. Their clothes, once taken in and out with rough threads by Cecily, now saw the smooth stitching of the town tailor they were able to use, alongside the white men and women. They hired a contractor to add two small rooms to the back of their house—one so Jujube and Abel could each have a room and one more "for possibility," said Gordon, his eyes shiny with hope.

Perhaps this is what growing up was, thought Cecily. To give up one's ideals in exchange for comforts, to understand that one of these cannot exist in tandem with the other. And as the months passed, as her family's life improved, as Fujiwara's silence persisted, she stopped going to the sundry shop, stopped feeling around the shelves hopelessly for instructions, stopped waiting to be called. And with time, the Fujiwara-sized knot in her stomach became a dull ache, one that she felt only rarely—on days when the monsoon rains flared, like an old healed-over injury.

The Club, for those in the know, was an abbreviation for The Federal, a whites-only country club. The building was a giant monstrosity, combining Tudor architecture around the windows and the curved bull-horn edges of a traditional Minangkabau roof. This combination of East and West architecture was supposed to symbolize unity, but as far as Cecily could tell, The Club served as respite only for white men, a place where they could retreat from the agonies of having to mix with the masses, a place where they sipped melting gin and tonics and played rounds of cards while discussing whatever inanities men discussed when they were slumped lazily in armchairs trying not to sweat.

There were rare nights, however, when The Club opened its doors to a select few local administrators and their wives. The Monsoon Ball was a twice-yearly event held in March and October to celebrate the change in the monsoon winds. This was hardly a reason to throw a ball, Cecily thought. But the English, she had learned, needed little excuse for a party. At these parties, they would gather with the same people they saw every day, to whisper the same gossip they always exchanged. The only difference was that at these balls, they wore finer clothes.

Gordon's rise in stature admitted him into the upper ranks of British society and its parties. Cecily found that where once they were thrilled to be invited to a single party every few years, now they were inundated with invitations, more than they could partake in or afford to attend. But the Monsoon Balls were unmissable. As they readied for the night, Cecily gave her maid the usual instructions, stopping for a moment to marvel at how different their lives were from just months prior. Then, hand in hand with Gordon, she stepped out into the monsoon-damp night. They had evolved. Cecily's coarse black hair was cut in the latest style, shorter, curled on the ends, and barely skimming her shoulders. She wore a long-sleeved chiffon dress in a shade of green that flattered her skin, its wide shoulders giving her the illusion of a waist. Gordon, in a double-breasted herringbone suit not unlike those worn by his English counterparts, had his suit tailored to conceal his plumpness better. If not beautiful, they were at least a handsome couple. The months had also softened her disdain for Gordon, the distraction of her added comforts leading her toward, if not love, at least a vague fondness for her husband.

"My lady, are you ready to board our trusty steed?" Gordon held out his arm to help Cecily into the car.

"I'm yours, my lord," she said, taking his proffered hand before they both lost their composure and laughed. It was nice to laugh.

The Club was dressed up like its guests, silks artfully draped along its arches and fluttering in the October-evening breeze. A live band played in the corner, and Cecily paused to admire the stillness of the trombone player, waiting his turn at the music. She had a soft spot for the ignored. White women in pale gowns drifted on the floor, tittering among themselves. For a minute she felt a squeeze of self-consciousness. Her gown, while well made, looked plebeian next to the haute couture she saw, satin dresses from Paris and London, many sleeveless and revealing, styles she did not recognize.

When the gloved hand swept against her elbow, interrupting her momentary insecurity, she turned, rearranging her face to hide the mild derision that had crossed her mind—which silly white woman would think that gloves were appropriate attire for the painfully humid tropics? But derision turned to shock, and the delicate-stemmed martini glass she held between her fingers slipped, sloshing gin over the woman's gloves.

"Aiya," the woman said, her eyes sweeping over the wet spot. "Oh well, never mind, I have so many!" she tittered. "Hah, Mrs. Alcantara, you look so pretty tonight!"

A replica of Mrs. Yap stood in front of Cecily. The woman had a similar face: the same soft cheeks, the same too-far-apart eyes, the same height of forehead, but the Mrs. Yap whom Cecily remembered—the gangster's wife—had been pungent with perfume, her clothes clashing and bright, her person brash and loud. This woman was also unignorable, but her skin and her dress were so pale, so close in color, that she looked like she was not wearing anything. The only note of contrast was on her lips, stained red like fruit. She was thin in the way that was fashionable in Europe now, her dress grazing her body like water, slippery and curveless. And her hair. The Mrs. Yap whom Cecily remembered had long hair she pulled into a tidy bun, but the woman in front of Cecily had hair so dangerously short as to be inappropriate. Women and men around her turned to stare. Cecily saw astonished recognition on some of the other women's faces, mirroring her own.

"Mrs. Alcantara, aiya, you really look wonderful," said the copy of Mrs. Yap. Even her voice was transformed, once shrill enough to give Cecily a headache, now a velvet throb.

"Mrs. Yap," said Cecily.

"No, no, call me Lina! I don't like to use . . . that name." A crest of pain slivered across the woman's forehead. Cecily was mortified, readying apologies. Mrs. Yap took Cecily's hand and placed it in her gloved one, damp with spilled drink. The brown of Cecily's palm looked like a mouse nestled in Mrs. Yap's wet white glove.

"Don't worry," the former Mrs. Yap breathed. "Come, come, I'm so glad to see a familiar face." Cecily wondered at the warmth of this chic woman who led her through the party by the one arm, barging through throngs and conversations without the slightest inclination of self-consciousness. Cecily moved as quickly as she could to keep up, anxiously sipping the drink she held in her other hand to prevent it from spilling over the top of the wide-mouthed glass.

"Let me introduce you to my new husband." She craned her long neck, and Cecily felt a jolt of recognition; it was the same movement Mrs. Yap, no, Lina, used to make when scouring parties for people and gossip. Cecily extended the stem of her own neck as she stretched through her body, finding herself curious to know more about the man who had transformed a gangster's wife into a Chinese ingenue.

"Husband, you mischief maker! Where did you disappear to?" Lina scolded, folding her arm into the elbow of a man's linen suit.

A familiar scent blew against Cecily, the sting of mint wafting through her nose into her throat. A pit opened below her stomach, her body recognizing desire before she even sensed his presence.

"Mrs. Alcantara, it has been too long," a voice murmured, a voice so soft it demanded you lean in to hear.

Cecily's chest crumbled into her stomach. The stem of the glass she was still holding made a small cracking sound before it hit the ground, her fingers stinging as a gush of blood bubbled through the cuts from the shards.

It couldn't be Fujiwara. She'd seen only his sleeve when Mrs. Yap, no, Lina, had tugged at it. Not even his face. After all, she'd barely had time to react before the glass she was holding had shattered and she'd been rushed away, bleeding from her fingers. It had been almost a year since she'd been physically near him. But even as she told herself otherwise, she knew. She'd smelled him, she'd heard him, her whole body had sensed him. And now she found herself sitting in The Club's small library with Lina fussing over her.

"Those kinds of glasses are a hazard! You're lucky it's only a few cuts, Mrs. Alcantara!" Cecily noticed that Lina had removed her gloves, which were draped neatly over a chair, the fingertips dotted with blood. Lina's fingers were fair and chubby, a reminder of the weight she used to hold.

"I'm sorry about your gloves," Cecily said.

"No, no, I feel terrible that I shocked you," Lina babbled while pressing a wad of tissues to Cecily's hand. When she pulled the tissues away, a corner stuck and tore itself away from the wad, a bloodied string hanging off Cecily's hand.

"I'm all right, Mrs. Y— Sorry, Lina, I am just so clumsy."

Strains of music from the party leaked into the library; the trombonist from earlier was playing a solo, and although he was blowing hard, he wasn't very good, lots of pitchy flat notes. Lina sat down next to Cecily and pulled Cecily's injured hand into her own to peer at it. Cecily noticed that Lina's hands were callused, the fingertips hardened with work. Cecily wondered—did she run those hard tips over Fujiwara's body? Did those hands press into his smooth palms, fingers interlaced in the quiet intimacy of marriage?

"It must be such a surprise after all this time," Lina said. "Of all the men, I end up with Bingley Chan." She paused, quiet. "I myself can't believe it sometimes."

So Fujiwara was married to Lina under his cover identity. Lina did not know who he was, or did she? Cecily opened her mouth to ask something, what, she didn't know. She closed her mouth, played with the string of tissue stuck to her hand.

"After my husband . . . after my ex-husband was executed, I left Bintang. I stayed with my mother and thought, that's it, that was the end of me. Sometimes I thought I would die, that I should die. But Bingley came to visit me. Every few days he would come and just listen to me. No one else did. It was like everyone thought I would infect them. He persuaded me to come back to Bintang. And I did."

Cecily stared at the floor. So that was where he had gone, all that time she was looking for him, all that time she lived in a state of vibrating panic, trying to will a letter from him to appear at the sundry shop.

"I know your husband probably didn't let you write to me," said Lina, mistaking Cecily's silent rage for guilt.

All that time she had worried about his well-being, she had worried about his capture, about her own—all that time he was comforting and cultivating another woman. The tips of her ears felt hot with humiliation.

"He was just so kind to me, you know?" Lina looked beseechingly at Cecily, eyes damp. It made her look younger, almost childlike, like she was asking permission. Cecily remembered a time when Bingley was kind to her as well. She saw the anguished vulnerability in Lina's face, the tremble of her cheeks when Lina recalled the pain she had endured at the hands of the British, the press of her teeth together as she steeled her jaw to perform strength. Cecily wondered if she had looked the same all those years ago in the old kitchen of her house, breathing tales of her sorrows and mistreatment to Fujiwara. Was that all it took for him to ensnare a woman—kindness? If so, how weak a sex they were, how gullible, she thought, twisting the bloodied tissue string hanging off her finger into a pulpy, disintegrating mess.

"I'm talking too much now. I'm sorry. It's just so hard to come back and with everyone staring at you," Lina said. "Ah, looks like the bleeding has stopped." She pulled out a bandage, one that Cecily didn't even realize she had, and wrapped it around Cecily's hand, covering up the evidence of Cecily's turmoil. As she tucked the corner of the bandage in to secure it, she held Cecily's hand for a beat longer than needed and glanced up at her. In a small voice, not shrill like before, not the velvet tenor that she had adopted but a new shyness, she said, "I hope . . . I'd like for us to be friends."

Before Cecily could fully register Lina's request, the men burst into the room, all bluster and bellows. "Cecily, are you all right?

You disappeared! And look who I found, good ol' Bingley!" Gordon yelled.

Cecily stood up quickly and the room spun, making her ankles soften as though they would give way.

"My dear, are you all right?" said Gordon, sweeping to her side, arm pressed against her back, steadying her.

"Haiya, I think she's dizzy. She lost some blood, she cut her hand, you know?" Lina gestured at Cecily's bandaged arm.

"Let's go, Cecily, I'm taking you home," said Gordon, steering her to the door.

"I'll bid you good evening, then, Mr. Alcantara." Fujiwara extended a hand, grasping Gordon's into his own. "Mrs. Alcantara." Fujiwara's hand hung in the air, awaiting her responding clasp. For the first time the whole night, Cecily raised her eyes to meet his. He was thinner than she remembered, his cheeks more sunken, but with that same chiseled nose, that same still voice. She grasped Fujiwara's hand weakly. She did not react, even when she felt the stiff corner of a piece of folded paper in his palm pressing against her hand, a barrier between them. She bit her lip to stop it from shaking. The physical touch felt like a current.

Later that night, Cecily uncoiled her fingers and smoothed out the triangular note he had written her.

ORIENTAL HORIZONS.

TOMORROW.

3 O'CLOCK.

She pressed the corner of the paper on her nose and flicked her tongue on it. It smelled like mint. Tasted sour.

The next afternoon, Cecily arrived in room 7A before Fujiwara. The room was close to the stairs for a quick exit, should the need arise. The walls reeked of postcoital cigarettes; the flowery bedspread was tucked into the ends of the bed to hide stains. The ceiling was low, as though bowed with the weight of everything it had seen. They'd met only twice before at the Oriental Horizons, a seedy gray hotel on the outskirts of town where no one wanted to be seen, not even the staff. It was where the British went with their prostitutes, where lovers met for liaisons, where politicians stored their Asian girlfriends and children when their white wives arrived by ship.

The sordid impropriety of the hotel as a meeting place had always given Cecily both a rush and a feeling of disgust. When they had met before, they'd always assiduously avoided the bed—he would lean stiffly against the door or window on one end of the room, and she would sit in the ugly green chair in the corner on the other end. Both times their meetings had been quick, a perfunctory five minutes: staccato instructions about their mission at the resident's house, a request for more intel on the tide patterns at one of the smaller northern ports. Both times she had stared at the mold spots on the carpet, felt itchy from whatever germs she was sure lived in the unwashed chair she sat in. And both times, when Cecily had gone home, she had found her underwear soaking with desire, her body aching with need.

That morning she found herself angry that he was not already waiting for her when she arrived. After all, he was the one who owed her— What did he owe her? She didn't know. But something. She was owed.

The night before as she lay in bed, listening to the air rise and fall through Gordon's chest, she'd rehearsed in her head what she wanted to say to Fujiwara.

"Why did you leave me?" Too needy.

"What happened to you?" Too aggressive.

"I expected more." Too much the disappointed mother.

"Where do we go from here?" That could work. But there was no "we," not even the possibility thereof, now that he seemed to have moved on with Lina. Cecily wondered why he had picked Lina, the disgraced wife of a Chinese clan leader. Cecily did not see what Lina could possibly have to offer that would help with the cause. Lina was shunned in the town. The only reason she was even able to show her face at the Monsoon Ball was as the wife of Bingley Chan. Perhaps he needed information from Kapitan Yap's dealings with the British, but that was easy enough to steal or glean, it didn't require marriage, a contract, a relationship. Cecily knew that sometimes the truth was the simple thing not cloaked in conspiracy, the painful thing that she didn't want to conceive of, that she didn't want to know—perhaps he had, quite simply, fallen for Lina. This truth made her feel pain throughout her body like she had never felt—a constant ringing in her ears, a rising fury in her chest, a head that felt too heavy to stay up on its own. She stood up to pace around the dank room. Sitting was making her feel sick.

The door creaked, and as usual, the smell of him hit her before she saw him.

"Thank you for coming," he said, coiling himself into the green armchair she had been sitting in.

Cecily shifted her weight awkwardly from one foot to the other. Fujiwara was ablaze that day, linen suit crisp, hair even mintier than usual. She resisted the urge to press down a cowlick that he had missed with his hair cream. It curved away from his neck like a fishhook. He rocked back and forth in the chair, tapped his fingers against his trousers. His face, usually a mask of stoic indifference, seemed to burn—two patches under his ears were pink, and he breathed shallowly.

"I thought you were dead," Cecily said.

"You know I couldn't—" he said, his voice strained and testy.

If she couldn't make him feel desire, she could at least make him feel something. "You couldn't let me know you were all right? You couldn't tell me they wouldn't come for me? You left me to rot." She pressed her hands against the peeling wallpaper; little bits of yellow stuck to her palms like specks of jaundice. "And then you come back with . . . with her?"

Cecily knew she sounded hysterical, but her body had overtaken her mind, the anger bursting past the shame. "And I'm the one with something to lose here. I've got a family. You don't—you don't have anyone who gives a shit about you. Is that why you married her? So someone would care if you died?"

She saw him suck his cheek in; it looked like he was biting the inside of his mouth to restrain himself. The body knows a wound before the mind does, and she watched herself press into his.

"You have no one," she repeated. "That's why you hang around silly women."

"Stop it." He pressed his hand against his side as though it ached. "Stop saying these things."

"And a dead son doesn't count. Some of us have living children to care about."

She watched him as if in slow motion: Fujiwara rising from the chair, his knees bending and then straightening, the crease of his pants smoothing out, his feet crossing the floor, his arms outstretched, coming for her. She was afraid, but the deep hole below her stomach and above her pelvis opened even more; it was hungry, and it was thrilled to watch him break, to feel this kind of power over his feelings, to see perhaps just for a second how it felt to be the hunter.

He slammed her against the grubby wallpaper, one arm mashing against her shoulder and the other wrapped around her neck. She breathed choppily, watching the muscles in his neck bulge. Because they were the same height, she stared directly into his eyes, watching the black of his irises grow large, dilating, as his breath, sourer than she had anticipated, blew against her cheek.

"Do you do this to all your girls?" she taunted. "Do you do this to Lina?"

She longed to bite the throbbing vein in his temple, have him press all of him into her, break her. She watched his chest expand, felt it press against her own as he took a long, shaky breath. He was hard, she could feel him against her thigh. She had never wanted someone so much.

Then he stepped back and took his hands off her. His left hand was shaking. He curled his fingers into his palms, fisting them before pulling his hands behind his back, face gray with shame.

"I must. I must leave," he said.

As the door to 7A slammed behind him, Cecily opened the window and took a deep breath, the smell of the street's humidity simmering through her, her body tingling, bruised, and wet like ripe fruit.

CHAPTER THIRTEEN

JASMIN

Bintang, Kuala Lumpur
August 22, 1945
Japanese-occupied Malaya

For the fifth day, Jasmin woke up at General Fujiwara's house. She loved the big, airy place, full of nooks and corners to play in; she loved how the houseboy always had a delicious snack or a cold, sweet drink for her whenever she wanted it; but most of all, she loved when the general came home each day. He would sweep in, dusty in his uniform, smile at her. Then she would hear the water splashing, and a few minutes later, he would emerge freshened and cooled down, in a singlet and loose trousers. They would sit on twin rattan chairs outside, sipping cold drinks from glasses wet with condensation—his glass filled with something that smelled bitter, and hers full of a sugary drink like Horlicks. The houseboy would lower the mosquito netting around their chairs like a tent, but it was unlike any net that Jasmin had seen. It was gauzy and light, almost invisible. She would still feel the dusk breeze slipping through the fine holes, and while the mosquitoes buzzed around them, none got through the net; they were safe from bites. The mosquitoes sounded like an orchestra, making nighttime music. As the crickets began to sing too, the sun would slowly sink itself into the horizon.

The general didn't say much for a grown-up. Jasmin was used to people yelling around her all the time—the neighbors, her siblings, her parents, each striving to speak louder than the others, always worried about not being heard. But General Fujiwara did not seem concerned with being seen or heard. He didn't have to try. He just was. She felt safe with him in a way that she had not felt with any grown-ups in a long time. At night, in their mosquito-net cocoon, he filled the space with his warm, minty scent. Around him, she was reminded of when Jujube would hold her close at night and tell her stories about a man she called Uncle Toothpaste. "Uncle Toothpaste will come save us," Jujube used to say, "he will keep us safe, he will make it all better." Jasmin imagined Uncle Toothpaste as a plump, jolly creature, not unlike Santa Claus, who would deliver all the wonderful things to them, presents and feasts and her brother back. Sometimes at night when she said her prayers, Jasmin would swap out Jesus's name: "In Uncle Toothpaste's name we pray, amen." And for a long time after Abel disappeared, she would peer at the gate every time it opened, expecting Uncle Toothpaste, with his comforting kindness and his minty smell, arm in arm with her brother, bringing him home safe.

When General Fujiwara had told Jasmin he knew her mother, she had been worried he would take her home, where she would be in deep trouble. But he'd brought up her family only once. On the second day of her stay, he'd looked at her and said, "Are you afraid of me?"

She'd shaken her head, no.

"Do you want to go back to your house?"

Jasmin had shaken her head even more vigorously. "No!" she screamed. She couldn't go home; they would lock her in the basement forever, until her throat closed up from the dust and she could no longer speak or breathe. "Can I stay here? Please? For a little while?"

"Are you happier here?"

She'd nodded vigorously, yes. She knew they would panic to find her gone, the way they had when Abel disappeared. It made her heart pinch to think she could cause this kind of pain, but she pushed it away. What she knew about a family was that a family was supposed to make her feel safe and loved. But since Abel had disappeared, it felt like all the joy in their family was gone—her mother, father, sister a shadow of their former selves, eyes dark and unseeing with pain. But I'm here, she often wanted to scream. I'm still here!

Now, after what Jujube had done to her, any desire she had to stay with her family was gone completely. The general, even if she didn't know him that well, helped her feel safe, comfortable. He made the painful flutter in her heart slow. Around him, the world felt quiet. She wanted to stay with him, even if for a little while. She wanted to feel calm again.

"Then you'll stay here with me. It is your choice." He smiled a tiny smile that made his eyes crinkle and his nose seem wider. It made Jasmin happy.

In the evenings, in their little tent, if she stayed quiet long enough, he would tell a story or two. His stories were always about a woman whom he said she reminded him of. This woman was brave, he said; she was brilliant, and she was a hero. Jasmin lived for these evening stories with the general, the soft dusk light falling on his face, the calmness of his voice.

"What did she look like?" Jasmin asked the first evening.

"She looked like you," Fujiwara said. Jasmin's ears perked with excitement. A hero who looked like her? "She was special. A lot like you, in fact. Very funny, full of love to give."

Jasmin felt her body swell with pride. Special, like you. She liked being special, liked knowing that he had picked her out; she who was not smart like her sister or handsome like her brother; she who always felt like an afterthought in her family, always having to earn her keep by keeping everyone happy.

"Was she pretty?" Jasmin asked. Sometimes in the books that Jujube used to read to her, there were pictures of shapely women with shining golden hair. Jasmin wondered if the general's brave woman too had golden hair.

"I think she thought she was ugly. But that is because the white people have made us think of beauty as only one thing. But she shone. And she always had so much hope."

Of the many things Jasmin liked about him, the best was that he talked to her like she was a grown-up. She didn't always understand what he meant; some of it confused her. But during these evenings, Jasmin could forget how her family had betrayed her, ignore the gnawing in her stomach when she thought about Jujube unscrewing the one lightbulb in the basement, leaving her encased in darkness.

"But how did you know her?"

"She . . . worked with me." His eyes were half closed as he leaned back in the chair with his drink. "You are a curious thing, aren't you?"

"Was she . . . . sec-katary?" Jasmin asked. That was what their neighbor Uncle Andrew Carvalho's wife had been before she went away. The family had whispered uncomfortably when Jasmin had asked about the aunty next door, her father settling on "Aunty Tina has passed away." Jasmin knew that meant she was not coming back. The only other kind of job she knew about outside the home was what her sister did at the teahouse, but that didn't sound very brave or exciting.

The general paused, then took a breath so deep Jasmin thought he had fallen asleep. "No, she was a patriot."

Jasmin had heard this word before. Her father sometimes used it to describe the Chinese men who lived on the edges of the jungle. She had heard her family whispering about how these Chinese men killed Japanese soldiers. They gave her nightmares, these men. She dreamed of them sneaking up behind her and wrapping dirty fingernails around her neck. Jasmin was confused because the brave, smart woman the general was talking about didn't sound anything like the angry men she imagined, but she kept this to herself, sensing that the general would not want to hear about Chinese men killing Japanese men.

"What did she do?" Jasmin asked.

"I'll tell you about the brave things she did soon," the general said, standing up. "But now it's time for you to go to bed."

While Jasmin looked forward to evenings with the general, the days were getting boring. She didn't have to spend all day in the basement, like she did at home, but the general confined her to the house, where her only company was the houseboy, who was nice but spoke mostly Japanese and generally ignored her. For the first few days, Jasmin had skipped around the house, exploring it from top to bottom, every corner, even the dusty ones that made the bottom of her feet black. She chased a cockroach around, enjoying the feeling of her feet skipping through the house that always seemed cool even when it was hot outside. Her peals of laughter alarmed the houseboy, who came running and shouted something in Japanese when he saw what she was doing. Then he smacked the cockroach to a pulp with his bare hand. Jasmin had turned away, stricken. At home, Jujube always had Jasmin catch bugs, even cockroaches, in little jars and let them out outside on the grass or in the drain.

But once the house had been explored, there wasn't much else to do. So, after lunch she decided to explore beyond the house, slipping out the back door when the houseboy was rinsing vegetables. He didn't even see her. At first she didn't know where she would go. Similar to when she was at home with her family, the general had her wearing boyish clothes, cotton pants and shirts, but he'd found clothes that fit her better, so the legs of the pants didn't drag on the floor and pick up dirt, and the shirt didn't fall off her shoulders. Also, the white shirt from the general had a little label on it. It was in Japanese, but he had told her it said, "Belonging to Fujiwara." He had told her to show the label to any soldier who stopped her, and she would be safe. Jasmin liked the idea that she carried a piece of the general with her everywhere she went; it made her feel important and protected. As she scampered down the winding driveway and onto the road, she giggled at the thought of the houseboy finding out she had run away. She felt a smidge of guilt that the houseboy might be scolded if the general found out she had left, but then she pushed the thought away. She would be back in the evening. It was not a big deal. She wouldn't even be missed.

The end of the driveway joined the main road. The ground felt hot under her slippers. Jasmin turned left and took a few steps, then felt her heart beating faster. Now that she was out in the open, she was scared. Jujube's words rang in her head: "They'll hurt you . . . there." Jujube. Thinking of her sister made her face hurt, and she was overwhelmed once more by the terror and anger at being locked in that basement with no light. She pulled back her shoulders and continued walking. She could be brave like that woman the general had told her about. The patriot.

The sun was beginning to grow into its afternoon strength, and she was tired after a few minutes of walking. The backs of her knees itched with the heat rash that she got when she became too sweaty. At home, Jujube had a tube of ointment that she would rub on Jasmin's neck and knees when the rash showed up. Jasmin hated the smell, but it always worked; it stopped the itching, and the mean-looking red welts would go away. She was about to give up, turn around, end her exploring, and go back to the general's house when she saw something familiar up ahead—the dented red sign—WELCOME. She had walked to Yuki's house! Jasmin sped up her steps in excitement. It had been days, and Jasmin missed her friend terribly.

Yuki's home was quiet when she arrived, different from the other night, when she had seen many girls and a few men milling around. Today it seemed as though everything sagged in the heat, and when Jasmin peeked into the doors of the open shacks, she saw girls splayed on the ground on their back or stomach with only underwear on, keeping cool and chitchatting with one another. Same as the other night, Jasmin swept by quietly, unnoticed.

She realized she didn't know where or how to find Yuki. But as she crept along the walls, she remembered. She saw a head moving under a faded bedsheet and a hint of blue near a rubber wheel. Of course, their wheelbarrow.

Yuki's face popped out, alert, eyes widening. "Mini! Where have you been? I went to look for you at your house, but I couldn't find you!"

Yuki pulled her into the wheelbarrow. They settled in, cross-legged, facing each other.

"Why weren't you at your house?" Yuki repeated. The eye on the unscarred side of her face was narrowed and angry.

Jasmin felt her chest open, like everything she had been holding inside was rushing out of her. She leaned forward, pulled her arms tight around Yuki. Yuki smelled pungent and a little vinegary, but Jasmin didn't care. She had her friend back.

—

Two days later, Jasmin returned to the wheelbarrow.

"Secret word!" Yuki whispered.

"Lala chaka chaka wooka!" Jasmin whispered back, stifling a giggle. The code was so funny to her. Yuki had come up with it, and they'd had to practice saying it over and over so Jasmin could remember it. Jasmin still had trouble remembering if it was "wooka" or "weeka."

"You can come in!" Yuki lifted the sheet and pulled Jasmin into the wheelbarrow. Jasmin hadn't brought Yuki to the general's house because she wasn't sure how he would receive her, and she definitely didn't want to meet Yuki outside her own house because she didn't want Jujube or her mother to catch them.

Jasmin was still confused by the sad-looking girls she encountered where Yuki lived but learned to avert her eyes when she saw girls and men walking by. Mostly she swept along soundlessly, sticking close to the walls, holding her breath until she got to the wheelbarrow.

Yuki and she played in the wheelbarrow, pretending they were English ladies at tea, or each wheeling the other around like a dead body, trying not to burst out laughing. Once when Yuki was wheeling Jasmin, she hit a small stone and the wheelbarrow tipped over. For a minute, Jasmin felt the wind knocked from her.

"Jasmin, Jasmin, please wake up!" Yuki cried.

Jasmin had held her eyes closed a bit longer, just for the fun of it, and when she finally opened them, giggling at her trick, she was shocked to see Yuki crying, tears catching in the scars on her face.

"Yuki," Jasmin said. "I'm sorry."

Yuki had looked away. "Leave me alone. I'm not crying over you."

Mostly, though, Yuki loved listening to Jasmin tell stories about her new home with the general. She asked about him constantly. "Tell me about his hair smell again. And about his house," she would say, face rapt. And Jasmin would tell her about his minty hair cream and his big, airy white house.

Jasmin was delighted to find that the houseboy didn't seem to notice when she disappeared after lunch, as long as she was back and cleaned herself before the general came home for dinner. Although she and the general continued their nightly chats, she had noticed that he was looking more and more tired. When she was trying to fall asleep at night, she heard him pacing. Often he turned on the radio after dinner, and although it was mostly in Japanese, she heard a few words she recognized. "Surrender." "Bomb." "End."

The night after she arrived, he'd asked her what she wanted to be when she grew up. The question had confused Jasmin, because for the longest time, she'd known her answer—that she wanted to grow up and become Jujube. Jujube was smart, and caring, and always knew the right thing to do. But now Jasmin didn't know anymore.

Noticing her silence, he'd asked, "Have you been to school?"

Jasmin shook her head. "I can read, though," she said.

"Do you like to read?"

Jasmin shook her head again. She preferred being read to, even if it had become harder to convince her mother or sister to sit down and read to her.

"You are different than your mother and me in that way," the general had said.

Jasmin had detected the smallest note of disappointment in his voice. It worried her. "But I can learn?" she said.

The general smiled wanly. "I'll make sure you do. No matter what happens to me, I'll make sure you are taken care of."

He reached out and Jasmin had thought he was going to hold her, but then he dropped his hands. "Good night, Jasmin."

CHAPTER FOURTEEN
—

JUJUBE

Bintang, Kuala Lumpur
August 24, 1945
Japanese-occupied Malaya

It had been seven days, five hours, and twenty-three minutes since Jasmin had disappeared. Jujube felt like she had searched every part of the town for her sister. The first few days she had started by going to visit neighbors and friends of the family. The Carvalhos said they hadn't seen or heard anything. The Tans speculated wildly, as they usually did, that perhaps Jasmin had joined a circus, perhaps she had been bitten by a dog and fallen by the roadside, perhaps she had stolen a rambutan from the magical rambutan tree in Uncle Robbie's backyard and been spirited away by tree ghosts. Old Aunty Swee Lan, who, rumor had it, was blessed with the gift of foresight, shook her head gravely when she heard, but Jujube couldn't get anything else out of the old woman. Each day a sicker, heavier feeling filled Jujube's stomach, bitter and sour, the bloat of dread.

In a fit of desperation, Jujube began looking in drains and big trash piles, unsure what she was hoping to find—a scrap of dress, a slipper, a finger, a girl. At night, on the little mattress she and her sister used to share, Jujube had nightmares about Jasmin calling out for her, but when she got close, Jasmin's face turned pale gray, dead. But it wasn't just death that haunted Jujube's waking hours. She worried about whether someone had gotten to Jasmin, whether someone had used her sister's body and left her to bleed out by the road, whether someone had found ways to break her sister without killing her.

When she got home that afternoon after searching for Jasmin, Jujube smelled bad, as rotten on the outside as she was on the inside, covered in specks of trash juice, simmering in the eleven o'clock sun. Before stepping into the house, she grabbed the slim bar of soap that their mother kept on the windowsill and scrubbed her hands and feet. The water was a relief, warm first from being sunbaked inside the hose, then cooling down once it started to gush out. Jujube stared at the stream of water sluicing its way on the ground along the grass before splashing into the narrow drain outside their house. When they were kids, everyone but Jujube had hated that drain. Abel often lost things in it. She remembered him searching for that tiger-striped marble in there, spending days sticking his hand in the drain trying to find the smooth glass ball. Jasmin was terrified of the drain, which roared when the monsoon storms broke the skies, with more power than one would expect of such a narrow channel. But Jujube loved the drain. She loved the ridged sides that were just the width of her legs outstretched. When she was younger, those early days before Jasmin was born, before the Japanese had come and broken everything, she would walk with her legs along each side, pretending the base of the drain was lava. On days when the drain was dry and the sun was hot, and she was tired of the noise everyone was making, she would sit in the drain, its curved ends shielding her from the world. In the drain, out of sight, she would read, escaping into stories of Enid Blyton, where trees could transport its climbers to different lands, or stories of plucky Dickensian orphans who would find their place in the world against all odds. In the drain, she would hear things too. Because it was just behind the kitchen, her ears would pick up her mother's voice—sometimes little songs she used to hum, sometimes giggling laughter, though Jujube never could see whom her mother was talking to. And when Jujube was called in for dinner, her mother would say, "Where did you go? I didn't see you for a few minutes," and Jujube would smile sweetly and say, "Nowhere, Ma, I was playing."

These days every sinew in Jujube's body seemed taut, vibrating, and on the verge of snapping. She was exhausted. Following the stream of water as if hypnotized, Jujube walked, squelching wet soil underfoot, to the drain. She swung her feet in, then her whole self. The dripping hose water had awakened the drain, the trickle wetting its base, unsticking leaves and bits of trash, smearing the dried bird shit on the side. It was getting disgusting, the smell beginning to rise in the heat. Still, she settled her body in the drain, the enclosed space a comfort. Just for a minute, she told herself, trying to catch her breath; she would sit there just long enough to figure out what to do, which problem to solve first, fix her head, slow her heart, be still. She closed her eyes, the sun beating against her eyelids like little angry hands on a door. "Wake up," the sun screamed, "you must find your sister."

"Jujube!" A familiar voice echoed along the sides of the drain from above, the sound of something heavy thudding to the ground and a *dringggg* sound, a bicycle and a bike bell. "Jujube, where are you?"

What in the world was he doing here? Jujube sighed, biting the bottom of her lip. Part of her just wanted to hide in the drain, hoping Mr. Takahashi would not find her, willing him to give up and cycle away. But the part of her that knew he was good, and that he was worried, pulled her to her feet. She leaned on the side of the drain, turning her face up.

"Oh, what are you doing in the longkang?" Beads of sweat dotted the top of his nose, and he was panting from the cycling. It was endearing that he knew the Malay word for "drain." She almost smiled.

"Come here, my goodness." He lifted her out of the drain, struggling to balance on the edge. He was not strong. Jujube had heaved herself out of the drain many times nimbly, without any help, but today she let herself fall limp in his arms. Once out, she found she didn't have the energy to stand, and flopped on the ground, the grass damp and hot beneath her face.

"What are you doing here?" she mumbled.

If he heard her, he didn't pay attention. "Oh, goodness, did someone push you in? Where is your mother? Ai, you are very wet!" Mr. Takahashi pulled Jujube to her feet, staggering as he did so, and slung her arm over his shoulder. "Come here, girl, let's get you in the house."

"The house is dirty," Jujube said, but she let him bring her inside.

The house was indeed a disaster. Initially, after the excitement about the Nagasaki bomb, Jujube's father had seemed almost like his old self, telling stories about how he imagined the overthrow of Japan would go, wondering aloud if he would get his old position at the public works department back. But Jasmin's disappearance seemed to have sapped any hope he'd summoned up. He walked around like a deflated ball, coughing up his own spit, and picking painful scabs off his hands, the result of cuts from the sheet metal he had to handle at the factory. After work he retreated to a corner of his room like a wounded animal, lying curled up in an unmoving ball at night, breathing in uneven intervals.

Her mother was doing worse. For a few days after Jasmin disappeared, her mother had taken to muttering under her breath about going to see a mysterious "him" to ask for help, but no matter how hard Jujube probed, she was unable to get more. Now her mother mostly confined herself to her room during the day. Jujube could hear her pacing, muttering incomprehensibly, coming out at intervals, all mad hair and wild eyes. Once Jujube had tried to drag her mother to the bathroom. She'd picked up the water dipper and tried to throw some water on her mother to quell the stench, but her mother had pushed Jujube away with surprising strength and then crouched in the corner of the bathroom, eyes wet and staring, until Jujube walked her back to the bedroom. Jujube tried to keep the house in order, but she had barely enough time to cook what meager rations they received, let alone the time to clean.

Mr. Takahashi did not comment on the rancid smell wafting out of the kitchen, though he did yelp at the thick black line of ants on the floor. Since her mother had spilled the oil and Horlicks on the floor, Jujube had been unable to rid the kitchen of the infestation. Depositing Jujube on a rattan chair in the small living room, he picked his way through the ants and the mess and set a kettle of water on the stove.

"Today I will make you tea!" he said. "I will help you, little Jujube. You sit. I been worried about you because you are not been at the teahouse for a few days, and I ask your manager about how are you . . ." Mr. Takahashi prattled on, mixing up his tenses, opening cupboards, finding cups and tea leaves.

Over the next half hour, Jujube watched as he planted a cup of tea in her hand, then fiddled around in the kitchen till he found a broom, a mop, and a rag, and tried to clean the floors and tables in their kitchen. He did not do a good job, Jujube noticed, leaving a layer of grease and oil floating on every surface, but she didn't care.

After he had finished his attempt at cleaning, Mr. Takahashi sat down opposite Jujube, cross-legged on the floor.

"No, sir, you can sit on the chair." Jujube rose.

"No, you are tired, girl. You sit." Mr. Takahashi handed her a fresh cup of tea; she had not noticed him refilling her cup. The tea was poorly made, weak and not steeped long enough, but the steam was calming. He stared up at her from the ground, eyes wide like a lost dog's. "Is no news of your sister?" he asked.

Jujube shook her head; there was nothing to say. Perhaps to fill the silence, to stanch his discomfort, she surprised herself by saying, "And what of your daughter?"

Mr. Takahashi's eyes lit up at the question, then clouded over. From her perch over him, she felt like she could see the machinations happening inside his head—the joy of his daughter being found, the guilt for her sister.

Jujube wondered about the ways in which girls and women performed for men by always knowing what it was men wanted and how it was they wished to be comforted, always engaged in the ongoing calculus of figuring out what sides of themselves they should show to a man and which parts of their grief were too unbearable for him. She noticed her mother used to do it with her father when he was excited by things at work, subsuming her own distractions or sadness to ask him about his day, then nodding and smiling at his enthusiastic chatting about soil and tides, performing the dutiful, happy wife.

"It's all right, sir, you can tell me," Jujube said. After all, Mr. Takahashi had been nice to her.

He needed no more encouragement. He pulled what looked like a crumpled photo and a telegram out of his pocket. "Here is Ichika!"

She wondered if he carried the photo with him all the time, or if he had been carrying it in hopes that she would ask about it. So Ichika was the girl's name, then, thought Jujube. His girl. She swallowed the familiar coil of anger in her throat and bent down, lowering her head so she could peer at the photo of a girl who looked a little older than she was, twenty-one perhaps, hair tucked behind her ears, wearing, to Jujube's surprise, a pair of pants.

"My daughter is a very modern girl. She goes to a university. She learns art. And also nursing," Mr. Takahashi said. Jujube noticed he pulled his shoulders back when he talked about Ichika, as though his pride and affection for the pants-wearing girl could not be contained by his chest.

How dare he, she thought. But to Mr. Takahashi, she performed the rites of the grateful girl, the girl who would listen to a man's relief and joy, subsuming her own breaking despair.

CHAPTER FIFTEEN

CECILY

Bintang, Kuala Lumpur
1937
Eight years earlier, British-occupied Malaya

To no one's surprise, Bingley and Lina Chan reintegrated into society with ease. With what Cecily assumed was the former Mrs. Yap's money, they attended social events at The Club and the resident's house, and hosted their own parties, entertaining senior British officials at their large and rather modern-looking house. It was startling to Cecily how short the collective memory of the British was.

"A year ago, no one would talk to her!" Cecily complained to Gordon. But Gordon loved them, Fujiwara-as-Bingley especially, greeting the couple like old missed friends. Cecily flinched at every party when Gordon bounded up and bellowed at Fujiwara; she watched how Fujiwara smiled thinly without his eyes, tolerating Gordon's worship. If Gordon only knew, she thought, her body taking her back to the day Fujiwara had slammed her against the wall. She thumbed a fading bruise on her wrist that he had inflicted and felt a prick of pleasure.

The Brits seemed to love Fujiwara too. As Bingley Chan, Fujiwara was all easy smiles and none of the awkward moroseness for which she knew him. Instead, he performed a self-deprecating humor that made her cringe.

"Mr. Chan, have you seen my wife anywhere?" she heard a British administrator say at a crowded event one day.

"Well, no, my good sir, these eyes are too small to see anything clearly!" And together they laughed uproariously.

He gave them permission to use him as the butt of their jokes, and that made them respect him. Here is a man, they seemed to think, who looks like one of *them* but thinks like one of *us*. Here is a man who allows us to give voice to the things we know we should be ashamed of but don't want to be ashamed of. Cecily wondered at the damage that would do to one's soul, to allow others to chip away at you, past the layers of defense, to gain acceptance. Even now, as the respected wife of a senior administrative official, she saw groups of white wives stop talking when she approached. Sometimes they would make snide comments about child-rearing.

"Did you know," Mrs. Landley, wife of Alistair Landley, a mid-level manager, said breathlessly, "that they let the girls bleed their monthlies all over the house?"

"Did you know that they let their children run around naked till they're teenagers?"

"Did you know?"

For Fujiwara to make himself the object of ridicule to gain admittance into what Cecily thought was a poor excuse for a society made her heart splinter for him—how much of himself he had to give in pursuit of his ideology, and how much of himself did he even have left to give? She did not want to feel pity, but she did.

Lina seemed completely at ease in her new role as a society doyenne. Cecily watched her wearing dresses that were as pale as her skin. She looked like a beautiful ghost floating through the throngs of people who delighted in greeting her. British officers, the same ones who had arrested her first husband and had, most likely, strung him up and beat him to death, met her with respect, then, when she turned away, stared at her body in open admiration. Cecily was outraged at the blatant hypocrisy and furious that Lina seemed willing to accept this shame as part of the equation of her existence.

For weeks Cecily avoided the couple. She watched them at the parties, arm in arm, wafting through crowds like movie stars. But where Gordon would rush toward them as though claiming an audience from royalty, Cecily would slink to the back of the room, trying her hardest not to be noticed. She observed them from her distant perch, hoping to read their body language. She tried to imagine the pressure of Fujiwara's arm as it grasped Lina's forearm. Could Lina feel his heart beating through his side? Did her body radiate warmth or coolness against his? Cecily willed Fujiwara to turn toward her. See me, she screamed. They had not communicated since the day in room 7A, but he mutated, virus-like, in her mind. She saw flashes of him everywhere, a corner of a linen pants leg disappearing behind an alley, the heady smell of mint hair cream lingering outside a shop, a hovering face in a crowded town center that disappeared as her eyes tried to distinguish him from the throng. She fantasized stupidly about him bursting into her house, scanning the corridors, sweeping her into his arms, taking her away. They made her cringe, these childish fantasies, though not as much as recollecting her brazenness that day in 7A. She still did not know what had come over her, and now she felt only the creep of shame.

Lina tried to break the ice a few times. She sidled up to Cecily at parties and even once when they passed each other on the street. "Where are you off to?" Lina said, pressing a cool hand on Cecily's arm.

"Just. Nowhere," muttered Cecily, flustered, rushing off in the other direction.

There was an unintentional encounter only once, when Cecily, Gordon, and the two children were walking to the playing field. Cecily spotted the Chans approaching, but with her hands occupied by Abel kicking the ground mournfully and by Jujube, who was so focused on her book that she required her mother's hand to lead the way, Cecily could not turn her family around quickly enough.

The men greeted each other with their usual boisterousness.

"Your baby is so cute," Lina said, squatting down to meet Abel. "What's your name, little one?"

Abel fluttered his eyelashes, already so long that when they detached, they fell into his eyes and irritated them. "Abel," he said shyly. "I'm"—he held up six fingers—"years old."

"No, dum-dum, you're almost seven," said Jujube, not even looking up from her book.

Cecily glared helplessly at her family: Jujube, who was right but needed reprimanding for her impertinence; Abel, whose face was scrunched up with distress at his sister's meanness; and Gordon, blustering and smacking Fujiwara on the back so loudly that everyone passing by turned to stare.

Lina clapped her hands and chuckled. "These children are so

funny, lah, Cecily!" Then, as though catching Cecily's distress, she tugged at her husband's arm. "Come now, Bingley. Let's not hold them up anymore. It's too hot, and the children will sweat in their nice clothes!"

"Not very friendly, is she?" Gordon grumbled into the Chans' retreating backs. Cecily said nothing, grabbed the children by the elbows, and walked forward.

"I know why you avoid her," said Gordon, wiping his sweaty forehead with a handkerchief. "She's not really our kind, even if she pretends with all those new clothes, you know? Low class," he said, pressing his hand to his hair. Cecily noticed for the first time that he'd started wearing it slicked back, like Fujiwara.

But in early February, Cecily decided she'd had enough.

She'd thought she'd washed both the ideology and the man from her system. Distance was a deceiver in that way, lulling her into a sense of stability and security, making her think she had adjusted fully to her new life as an upper-middle-class colonial subject. But Fujiwara and Lina's return had shaken things up again, and now, in between her bouts of shame and lust, she craved news about the Japanese progress, wondered how long they would take to arrive at Malaya's shores. She remembered how good it felt to have a purpose, to have a secret that was not shameful, to want something bigger than herself. She missed the part of her that Fujiwara had nurtured, and the sense that amid everyone around her, she alone was enlightened. It was a superiority that had comforted her every time she felt snubbed, by another wife, by her own husband. She missed being a woman who cared about something, missed being a woman who was more than just an extension of her house and family.

Cecily decided to handle her predicament. The idea arrived early in the morning and seemed so logical that she started baking what her mother called "European pie" as soon as she jumped out of bed, before she could find a reason not to. She sliced the luncheon meat, potatoes, button mushrooms, and quail eggs into the thickened chicken stock, then dropped a dash of the secret ingredient, Worcestershire sauce, the thing that made it "European," she supposed.

"What are you doing, my darling?" Gordon asked, stealing a slice of luncheon meat. She waved him away to work.

She tipped the whole soupy mess into an enamel baking dish, and into the crust pastry atop the pie, she etched "L&F" for "Lina and Fujiwara," before realizing her error and covering the F to make a messy "B" for "Bingley." She stood back to admire her handiwork. Even her mother, who had rarely been impressed by anything she did, would be proud of her, she thought.

Midafternoon, she folded the reports she'd found in the work folder Gordon had left carelessly on the kitchen table into an envelope and wrote "Chan, Bingley" on the front. Gordon was always misplacing his papers; he would just think he'd left them in the office or ask one of his many secretaries to procure another copy. Then she covered the European pie and started walking down the street. "Don't rain, don't rain, don't rain," she whispered.

When she reached the Chans' house, a pile of women's shoes was lined up against the front door. Good, Lina has guests, she thought.

She could drop off the pie, tell Lina that Gordon had a document for Bingley, and leave. No fanfare, easy.

Lina answered the door in a gold dress that was much too fancy for an afternoon tea.

"Oh, wah, look who it is!" Lina exclaimed.

Too exuberantly, Cecily thought. "Good afternoon, Lina, I just wanted to drop off some pie I made—"

Women's voices echoed through the house. "There are other ladies here. Why don't you come in and say hello?"

Cecily paused. She had not wanted to stay and make awkward conversation with women she didn't know well. From the quality of the shoes outside, shiny leather pumps with clean lines, she'd gathered it was a group of British wives. She was not properly dressed and not properly prepared for their condescension.

"I shouldn't. You have company—"

"No, lah, Cecily, come on in. Who is watching your children?"

"The servant," Cecily admitted reluctantly.

"Well, then, what are you waiting for? No need to talk out here in the hot sun!" Lina brandished her hands, ushering Cecily in. There didn't seem to be a way to get out of this. Cecily slipped off her brown shoes and, ashamed, pressed them underneath the pile of the other women's shoes.

The house was impressively sparse. Her own house, even though it was bigger after the renovation, was still a constant mess. But Cecily liked to think the mess was a comfortable one, chairs and cushions haphazardly arranged, lots of places to sit, mats on the floor for the children to play on, photographs of family on every available surface. The Chan house was pristine, the walls a creamy white, not unlike the dresses that Lina now favored. The front hallway opened into another room, and the floor was bare, the white tile shimmering and cool against Cecily's bare feet. Lina led her into what looked like a parlor, which seemed to have only one piece of decor, a large abstract blue-and-white watercolor that dominated the wall and the room. It seemed designed to draw the eye but refused to give the viewer anything else; it was even impossible to determine the center point of the painting. Three white women in floral dresses sat primly in straight-backed chairs, pinkies raised over tiny teacups. They looked like such a caricature that Cecily had to bite her lip to stop a giggle—she wasn't sure if from nervousness or the humor of the situation.

"Lady Worthing, Mrs. Chandler, Lady Lewisham. This is Cecily Alcantara, whom you probably know already!" Lina said. "She brought us a pie!"

Lady Lewisham was the resident's wife, the one who'd been so disapproving when Cecily pretended to faint last year during that mission with Fujiwara. Thinking of Fujiwara made her stomach ache. Cecily noticed that next to the tea saucers stood sweating glasses of clear liquid. From the juniper smell rising from the glasses, Cecily knew they contained very strong gin and tonics. The women were drinking.

The blondest one, Lady Worthing, sniffed at Cecily's covered dish and said, "No, thank you. I've already eaten." The other two nodded in greeting, then gave her a once-over. Cecily flushed, knowing they were judging her clothes and the pie she'd been so proud of just a few hours ago.

Lina steered her toward the kitchen, where Cecily set the pie on the table and the envelope of stolen documents next to it. "I have something for your husband from Gordon—" she began.

"Oh, this is so nice!" Lina exclaimed. She had removed the cover from the pie dish and was tracing with her finger the top of the crust—the "L" and the messy, corrected "B." Then, without wiping her finger, she clasped Cecily's hands in her own.

"Bingley told me your husband can be . . ." Lina paused as if looking for a delicate way to say something. "He said that Gordon can find it hard to overlook my past . . . transgressions."

Cecily was taken aback, not least by the fact that Lina knew and pronounced correctly the word "transgressions." And it seemed that Fujiwara had found a way to explain Cecily's reticence. She felt a twinge in her side.

"But I like you very much, and I'd like us to be friends. It was my ex-husband—not me—who did the bad things. I hope you can see that."

Cecily felt the beginnings of a clammy sweat on Lina's palms, a fissure in the other woman's perfectly coiffed image. It surprised her. After all, Lina did not need her; she'd re-ascended to the top of the social ladder on her own, with her easy charm. Cecily had meant her pie to be a way for her to reach out to Fujiwara, let him know she wanted back in. She had intended nothing more, certainly not this twitch of vulnerability on Lina's face, the naked hopefulness. Lina, with all her polish and her prowess, was looking to Cecily for something akin to approval. It was awkward yet somehow endearing.

"Come now, Lina," Cecily said. "We can't leave those three alone with the teacups. Who knows what mayhem they'll cause?"

Lina sighed happily and swung her arm into Cecily's, and they walked back out to the front room, where the three white women were tittering, teacups abandoned and faces pressed close together.

"What are we gossiping about?" Lina trilled, flopping down in the armchair. Cecily shifted from foot to foot, wondering where to sit, before Lina gestured at a rattan chair next to her. She sat down gratefully.

"Nothing at all," said Lady Lewisham, but from the way the corner of her mouth twitched, Cecily knew she desperately wanted to be asked again.

"Now, ladies, come out with it," Cecily said.

"Well," said the sniffy blonde, Lady Worthing. "We were discussing which of the men we would have our fun with if we weren't with our husbands."

"The local men, of course," said Mrs. Chandler, the prettiest and most soft-spoken of the group. She raised the glass of gin to her lips. The three of them burst into a peal of giggles.

"Oh, how . . . fun," Cecily said dryly. She felt her back straighten to its full rigidity, as though her body were involuntarily building a defense.

The three women began their judgments.

"Mr. Lingam? Much too short. And too dark," said Lady Worthing with a curled lip.

"Mr. Chong?" Mrs. Chandler asked.

"The shop owner? Absolutely not, you can smell the shop on him! Do you want musty anchovies on your bedsheets?" scoffed Lady Lewisham.

"Mr. Rahman, the assistant headmaster? Oh, yes," said Mrs. Chandler, closing her eyes.

"The perfect tan on his skin," said Lady Lewisham.

"I don't see what you see," said Lady Worthing, pursing her lips. "He's almost . . . too educated, too Westernized, you know? It's like having a darker version of one of our own."

Cecily choked. This was not the afternoon she'd had in mind. She had heard about British men who lusted over the local girls, called them exotic natives, brown-skinned tarts. British literature was certainly full of the rabid sexualization of nonwhite races. But in her mind, British women were filled with only two expressions—disgust and paranoia—and while these bothered her, she had adjusted to the disapproving curl in their lips and their arched, raised eyebrows when they were forced into any kind of encounter with someone darker than themselves. She had not been prepared for—whatever this was.

The women continued without pause. "Gordon Alcantara. Too—" Lady Lewisham turned to Cecily as though suddenly remembering her presence. "Mrs. Alcantara, I hope you won't mind us," she said. Cecily shook her head mutely. There was nothing good she could say.

"He's just too, too shouty and small, can you see?"

Cecily stared at a particularly shimmery corner of the tiled floor. They were crude, but they were not wrong.

"Now, your Mr. Chan!" Lady Lewisham gasped into her gin and tonic with the fullness of happy intoxication.

Cecily raised her eyes from the floor and watched Lina carefully. On the surface, Lina seemed fine, nodded and smiled keenly, as though the women were discussing something banal, like flower arrangements or the price of produce. But on her lap, Lina's fingers were twisted together, her knuckles white.

"Let's not be rude to our hostess, now, shall we?" Cecily said.

"Don't be a spoilsport, Mrs. Alcantara!" Lady Lewisham chortled, the smell of gin in the air around her breath. "Lina is used to us blathering!"

"That Bingley Chan. He's a short one, isn't he? Such a little man," said Lady Worthing, leaning back in her chair, settling in as though for a long discussion.

"But that voice, oh, la la! Sounds like they spat him out from boarding school. If you didn't look at him, you'd think it was a Harrow boy speaking." Lady Lewisham sighed. "Such a pity about everything else when he could be one of us. But I suppose you can't have everything."

"Now, Mrs. Chan, you must let me make amends in advance. But I absolutely would have him. He's an animal, isn't he, Mrs. Chan? Honestly, sometimes I wonder that he didn't end up with a white missus." Mrs. Chandler fussed with an imaginary out-of-place curl, then looked over at Lina.

"A scandalous creature you are, my dear!" Lady Lewisham's cheeks were flushed with the excitement of it all. Cecily wanted to slap her, rearrange her conceited, pinched cheeks.

Lina bent to pour herself a cup of tea, her smile even, her face the picture of composure. "More tea?" She gestured at the air.

The ladies ignored her, continued their chattering. Only Cecily saw the way the stream of tea shook against the teacup as Lina tilted the kettle. Only Cecily observed the little puddle of brown spillage on the saucer, saw the way Lina did not pick up the teacup because her hands were shaking so much.

"Ladies, I think I'm not feeling overly well. I might consider taking my leave. Mrs. Chan, will you walk with me part of the way?" Cecily said.

"My, my, you do fall ill a lot, don't you?" Lady Lewisham said. "I'd best be on my way as well. Lord Lewisham has invited guests over, and the local servants just don't run things the way they would in England—"

"Are you quite all right?" Mrs. Chandler said to Cecily.

"Yes, yes, I'll be all right. Just a little light-headed."

The British women gathered their things and made their way to the door. "What a wonderful afternoon, Mrs. Chan. You must have us visit again," Lady Worthing said, extending a limp hand for a shake.

"Indeed, indeed, yes," Lina said. But Cecily noticed she did not grasp Lady Worthing's outstretched hand, which retreated quickly.

"Goodbye now," Lady Lewisham proclaimed. And they were gone.

As soon as the gate slammed, Cecily turned to Lina, unable to hide her indignation. "How dare they—? How could you tolerate—? What insolent—"

"Now, Cecily," said Lina tiredly, sinking into the rattan chair that Cecily had occupied.

Standing over Lina, Cecily cast a shadow on Lina's curled-up figure; she realized how small Lina was.

"He— He says I must make good with them. They accept me now, you know?" Lina said. "It *is* tiring sometimes." She sighed a big, breathing sigh. "But thank you. For—making them go."

Lina's eyes closed. Cecily watched Lina. It occurred to her that this was the part of Mrs. Yap that she had carried through her transformation: performing strength in the face of a husband who expected her to fulfill a role, neither of them knowing the way it chipped away at her, the greater good of social capital superseding everything.

"These men, they don't deserve us, you know?" Cecily said. "We do so many things for them that they can't see."

"I get worried I might slip and embarrass myself," Lina said, eyes still closed, fluttering with tiredness. Did Fujiwara even realize, Cecily wondered, the consequences of the masks he forced them both to wear? And did he even care?

"I'll start washing up," said Cecily, collecting the empty gin glasses and half-full teacups from the table.

"No, no," Lina said, opening her eyes and jumping to her feet. "My mother would be ashamed of me. She's dead, but I swear she would rise from the grave and demand to know why I let a guest wash dishes."

"Mothers can be tough," Cecily said, picking up a stack of cups and walking it to the kitchen. "Mine always wished I was prettier."

"Mine wished I had a little dingaling!" Lina's laugh was loud, boisterous, a little bit more of the old Mrs. Yap breaking through the veneer. "She couldn't believe it when I came out and I was flat down there. She kept asking the midwife, 'Where's the kuku? Where's the kuku?' Turns out the fortune teller my parents had gone to told them their first child was going to be a boy. Must have been the worst fortune teller in all of Ipoh!"

Lina howled with laughter, and Cecily couldn't help herself; the images of an older version of Lina screaming about a boy's kuku sent her into a fit of giggles so persistent she had to choke down some of the cold tea to stop herself.

Behind them, the gate jangled and the smell of mint hair cream spread through the room. Lina's smile widened. "You're home, my darling! Thank god." She gestured at Cecily. "Look who's visiting!"

"Mrs. Alcantara," Fujiwara said without a moment's hesitation, without surprise, without expression.

Cecily wanted to shake him. "I'm here!" she wanted to scream.

"Do you not care?" But the mint scent was making her dizzy. "I brought docu—" she started.

"Lina, I heard you laughing from all the way up the road. What's so funny—?" Fujiwara said at the same time. He stopped. Cecily saw him breathe deeply, his throat vibrating, his eyes focused unblinkingly on his wife. He wouldn't look at Cecily.

"Gordon had some documents for you, darling. They're in the kitchen." Then Lina launched herself at Fujiwara's chest, enclosing herself in a hug so intimate that Cecily felt awkward and looked away.

"Is that so?" Fujiwara looked over Lina's silky head and for the first time at Cecily, dark eyes ablaze in inquiry and surprise.

Cecily supposed this was its own triumph. She was now the one acting unpredictably. She met his gaze and held it.

"Tell your . . . husband I'm glad he sent these by. It's been too long since we've had a chance to . . . catch up," Fujiwara said.

Cecily released the breath she didn't realize she had been holding and narrowed her eyes, not breaking eye contact with Fujiwara.

"Thank you for tea, Lina. I'm glad I stopped by."

CHAPTER SIXTEEN

ABEL

Kanchanaburi Labor Camp on the Burma/Thailand border
August 24, 1945
Japanese-occupied Malaya

"I have something to show you." Freddie's voice echoed against Abel's head like a drum. "Come on, come on, come on."

Freddie kicked Abel's side, wedging his toes in the softest part of Abel's stomach, trying to jolt him upright. Abel groaned. His mind was as muddy as the ground, and the suddenness of movement sent a wave of vomit through his system.

He looked up at Freddie, gagging. "See what you're going to make me do."

Freddie rolled his eyes. "Don't you dare, Abel. Not in here. The others will kill you."

"I don't care about them, they're not the boss of m . . ." Feeling the rise of his retch, Abel hurtled out of the living quarters into the banana plant and vomited, his bile yellower and riper than the bananas.

It had been about six days since he had killed Brother Luke. Abel found that if he ate little and drank a lot, he was able to keep the nightmares at bay, halt the creeping of his out-of-order memories—the splitting crack of the rebar, the spurt of blood on his bare feet, the angry clucking of the chickens, the roar of the boys, and then the resounding silence as everyone waited for Brother Luke to rise, the jeers when he did not. His torturer, Master Akiro, was barely around anymore—where previously he would seek out Abel just to smack him around, throw him in the coop, and come for him at sunset, now Master Akiro seemed to walk around in a haze, the skin on his face stretched with worry. He had come for Abel only once, when Abel was relieving himself, but the toddy took care of that too—Abel had felt hardly a thing. After the act was done, Abel had wandered out of the outhouse smelling like piss, wrists bruised from being pushed against the wall, and had fallen into a drunken nap under a tree.

Freddie had found him then, of course, had made him sit up so he didn't choke on his vomit, had dragged him back to their sleeping quarters and forced him to drink water so he didn't dehydrate. Their relationship had changed, and in the few moments of clarity that he had these days, this bothered Abel. There was an indignity to what was once a partnership between them—they no longer sat up together, painting and remembering. Instead, he knew that sometimes Freddie washed him, tried to make him decent when he fell over awkwardly in ways that exposed him. The other boys pointed, Abel knew that too, but it was Freddie who stepped forward, Freddie who dispersed the gawkers, Freddie who helped him feel human again on the worst days. The two of them had drifted, perhaps because the power between them had become so imbalanced in Freddie's favor, and no friendship could fully withstand such a sudden contraction. No friendship was founded on this much pity. In his own way, Freddie seemed to have grown. He was still quiet, never seeking the spotlight, but now he was also popular with the others. Even in Abel's drunken hazes, he would hear Freddie singing with the other boys, even laughing at times, a hiccuping laugh that made Abel smile.

The days were easier now that they didn't have to put in much work. Some of the harder-working boys would attempt to lay down tracks for a few hours each day, but there was barely any supervision. Most of the time, the boys simply scrounged for food, sat around dozing, or continued work on the new "theater," a structure of bamboo and palm fronds that Rama had them building for their nightly performances. Abel hadn't seen it himself, since most of his days had begun to blend together; he couldn't remember how to separate them anymore. But he heard that the nightly shows had become very involved, sometimes even competitive: talentimes, sketches, singing competitions, full concerts, tournaments like arm wrestling and long jumps. Freddie had told him that Azlan did a particularly hilarious drag performance of a British lady he called Mrs. Mills, who had, in Azlan's interpretation, large uneven knockers that the boys made out of cloth scraps stuffed with leaves.

Abel supposed that things were much better now. Perhaps the boys should rise up, take over the camp, Abel would think, but then he would see Master Akiro and a group of soldiers cleaning their large rifles, and the thought would shrink away. Still, he wondered if it was worth the effort to try to escape, to make the long, dangerous journey home to his family. He traced the toilet-paper sketch that Freddie had done of Jasmin, but the toddy made it hard to conjure her face in his mind. It scared him to think what might have happened to her—he'd heard about the horrible brothels where the Japanese threw young girls and forced them to—to— He pressed his eyes shut; he couldn't think about it. He'd even mustered up the courage once a few days before, gotten himself all the way to the edge of the camp, heart pounding, feet flying as though winged. He could do this. He *would* do this. He would leave. But as he stared out at the hot brown ground, flat as far as the eye could see, the toddy began to wear off and he was once again assailed by the curse of his memories: the rebar, the blood, the pain, the animal expression in Brother Luke's eyes. Toddy was easier. It helped him reach inside himself for the simplicity of inaction; it curbed the urge inside of him that always wanted to strive for better. Because the only thing to reach for in the miserable life he'd been given was survival. So he stumbled back to the nearest tree he could find and poured the bottle down his throat. Toddy helped him survive.

"Come on, let's go." Freddie pulled Abel to his feet and scrunched up his nose at what Abel assumed was the combined staleness of vomit, alcohol, and being unbathed. Abel resented being up this early—the sun was still at an angle, and it wasn't hot enough to be noon. He wanted to catch a few more hours of drunken sleep before the heat of midday made it impossible. He reached for a warm bottle on the floor.

"You don't need that," said Freddie, but Abel glared at him. Freddie should know better. Abel took a swig from the bottle, letting the warm liquid coat his esophagus, lighting a pathway through his body, bringing him back to life.

"Whatdoyouwant," Abel muttered, finally able to speak.

Freddie shook his head, sucked his cheeks, in frustration, in irritation, Abel wasn't sure. Swaying a little, Abel felt Freddie's arm under his shoulder, propping him up, the steadying touch familiar, because it was what Freddie did every time he found Abel passed out somewhere, in the chicken coop, under trees, after eating, after taking a shit. Their movements were practiced now, Abel taller, stumbling as his eyes struggled to focus, Freddie, shorter, knees locked, arms outstretched, steering Abel.

They walked down the path, the grass still wet from dew that the sun hadn't yet had the chance to dry. Looking down at his feet, Abel realized he was wearing slippers, but he didn't remember putting them on. Freddie must have put them on his feet. They stumbled past the mess hall, empty except for the one or two early risers who were preparing breakfast. Abel spotted Siu Seng, one of the boys who had commandeered the kitchen since the Japanese had stopped caring about feeding them. Now their breakfasts smelled better, steaming broths that Siu Seng was able to create out of very few ingredients and whatever herbs he'd managed to plant and harvest around the camp. They walked farther along and past the chicken coop, and Abel shuddered. All the chickens were dead now, even the stubborn brown hen. Siu Seng had found her clucking on her side one day, eyes glassy. He had carved her up, and every boy at camp was the recipient of a tiny sliver of chicken that night. Then Siu Seng had used her bones to make a broth that everyone except Abel had raved about.

Abel stopped. Even though he knew through Freddie that he came here every night, the proximity to the coop made his skin burn. Again the haunted sound of rebar on bone, passing between his ears.

"I have to go back," he said, struggling against Freddie's arms.

"We're not going in the coop, Abe, I promise. Just come with me."

Abel pulled a little, tried half-heartedly to extricate himself from Freddie.

"Come on."

Abel allowed himself to follow. Lately when Freddie spoke, it felt to Abel as though Freddie's voice swept through him, unclenching all the knots that lived in his chest. If he felt like he was spinning out of control, all he had to do was concentrate on Freddie's tenor, quiet, even, low.

As they stumbled away from the chicken coop, Abel began to feel stronger, standing straighter. "Where are you taking me, kiddo?" He punched Freddie in the shoulder, noting ruefully that he was so weak, it barely registered to Freddie. Before, his punch would've caused Freddie to double over.

"For a drunk, you talk too much." Freddie cracked a smile, and Abel felt the weight loosen from his stomach.

A few minutes later, they reached a tall structure, like a shed, palm fronds on the roof, held up by long poles of wood. The sides were open-air, but the ground was covered with more palm fronds, some lashed together like mats and others loose. At one end was an elevated "stage" made of crates, and behind it, brown-stained pieces of cloth, perhaps old shirts, that had been pulled over string to form a makeshift backstage curtain.

"Wow, they finished the theater!" Abel looked around in surprise.

"We just used some of the railway supplies. No one cares anymore. Come here, I have something to show you."

"This isn't what you're showing me?" Abel raised an eyebrow, but Freddie was already running to the other end of the shed.

Abel walked as quickly as he could to catch up with Freddie, but the effort winded him. He realized he hadn't eaten anything since yesterday. As he neared the curtain, a sound caught his ear, groaning, soft.

"Freddie, stop, there's someone behind the curtain."

"I know," said Freddie, clambering onto the stage. "Ready?"

Freddie drew back the curtain, and curled up on the floor, cuts on his face and arms, leaves stuffed in his mouth, wrists tied to ankles like a hog, lay a groaning Master Akiro, naked but for an undershirt.

"Freddie, what the—?"

"Abe. You can make him pay now. Get it all out."

"What do you even expect me to do?" Abel pulled himself onto the stage and squatted there, the loose palm fronds swishing beneath his slippers. He held his head in his hands.

"You can show this fool who's boss," Freddie said.

Abel stood up and backed away from Freddie, but he realized that the shed had become more crowded, the boys had gathered around like bees to honey, the prospect of a violent show bringing out the same carnal impulses that he had seen with Brother Luke in the chicken coop. Their eyes were trained on him, feet beginning their thundering.

"Are you a coward, Abel?" Freddie's voice was hard, higher than Abel remembered, not the low, calm tones that had always brought him back.

"You can't expect me to." Abel felt like falling and gripped one of the shaky poles holding up the tent for support. This was his fault. He'd become so pathetic that he'd made Freddie think this was the only way.

"He deserves it. Like Brother Luke did," said Freddie.

"I didn't— Brother Luke— That was for you!" Abel screamed.

Freddie's eyes clouded over, the blue darkening like a stormy sky. "You can't sleep. You can't go on like this. I didn't think—didn't know it would be this bad for you."

Abel wondered if that was why Freddie had stuck with him so religiously, dragged him from the depths of his despair. Maybe it was the guilt gnawing away at Freddie.

"Are you mad?" Abel yelled, surprised at the volume of his voice. "There are still Japanese here! Freddie, the Japanese will come for us."

"See, I told you he couldn't!" Rama yelled from the crowd.

"Look," said Freddie. "We'll do it together. All of us, you, me, the others. There's more of us than them now. It can be for all of us."

Master Akiro moaned from the floor, his eyes, those narrow close-set eyes that used to terrify Abel, filled with their own terror. Abel had to admit, there was something thrilling about seeing the pain in Master Akiro's face, the knowledge that something bad was coming, the same look Abel was sure Master Akiro had seen in Abel's own face many times.

Freddie lowered his voice, barely above a whisper. "I know what he did to you in the coop. He made you a dog. Forced you. You have to make him pay, Abe; you can't let him get away with something like that."

Abel felt the bottom leave his stomach, humiliation rushing through his body. So Freddie did know.

"I didn't tell anyone, Abe. But you need to show them—show me—you're . . . strong. I need you to get better." Freddie's eyes shone with the intensity of his plea.

He picked up a large stick off a pile in the corner, Master Akiro's uniform, and handed it to Abel. Because Abel was so weak, he needed to grasp the stick with both hands.

"A-BEL! A-BEL! A-BEL!" the boys began chanting, their pitch feverish, the shed hot with sweat, their shouts reverberating through his head.

Arms shaking from the effort, Abel lifted the stick over his head and Master Akiro screamed, choking through his mouthful of dried leaves, the muffled yell sounding almost childlike. Again Abel saw the blood pool at his feet, heard the crack of the rebar as it hit Brother Luke's face, all of it coming back to him in the right order, one after the other. Abel dropped the stick and pushed blindly past the boys, running as the retch of bile coursed through him. No one stopped him. As he vomited into the grass outside, he heard the thumps of kicking feet and the snapping of broken bones coming from the theater.

Master Akiro was dead anyway.

CHAPTER SEVENTEEN
—

CECILY

Bintang, Kuala Lumpur
1937
Eight years earlier, British-occupied Malaya

Cecily wondered if the only reason to endure frustrating men was to become friends with their better wives. Lina Chan was her opposite in all the ways that showed. Where Cecily felt unseen in crowds, Lina couldn't help but be noticed; where Cecily never said much and, when she did, never said what she meant, Lina couldn't help but blurt out every artless thought that popped into her head, tact be damned; where Cecily found it difficult to socialize with the others, blaming her isolation on their snobbery, Lina wafted her way through every room, leaving a cloud of entranced and charmed people in her wake. Still, as the August heat seeped into pores and sweated through clothes, Cecily found that with each other, she and Lina were their own opposites. It was as though Lina's exuberance and Cecily's reticence were disguises they could shed only when they were together.

They spent many afternoons in each other's houses, chattering so fast and so loud that sometimes they talked over each other.

They gossiped shamelessly about other women. They talked about the shared loneliness of being a daughter who could not turn to her mother when life betrayed her. And they confided in each other. Lina talked about a new aching pain she felt in her chest when she saw children running around, when she was handed newborn babies of friends to hold and coo over, and how sudden this feeling was, how new and perplexing the ache was for someone who had never enjoyed the presence and pastimes of children. Cecily found herself asking Lina how it was possible to love and hate the domesticity of one's life at the same time, and how guilty it all made her feel. They consoled each other, held warm bodies together in long, strong hugs. They whiled away these warm afternoons, sometimes forgetting to sip their sweet tea until the mugs were cold, the sugar and milk separated, chalky and sinking to the bottom, until the orange glow of dusky sunsets crept into the room. When it was time for them to separate, leave for their individual homes and the dinners they had to make for their families, Cecily always felt heavy and filled with a sort of dread, as though a spell had been broken and real life was an unwelcome intrusion. Perhaps this is what love is, she thought—a relationship that didn't require constant vigilance. With Fujiwara, she had to agonize over what he was thinking, but with Lina, she always knew. Without the burden of inscrutability, the women's friendship bloomed, easy and bright.

"You know, even though all these bad things happened, I wouldn't change anything," Lina said as she flounced through the door on one of these many afternoons, all perfume and breath.

"Well, hello to you," Cecily said. "Jujube, please watch your brother! Aunty Lina is here!"

"Hello, Aunty Lina," Jujube intoned from the kitchen, barely looking up from her book. Abel scampered through the door to say hello, then pulled himself away, shy at the last minute, peeping and waving from the doorway before running back to his sister.

Lina laughed at Abel before resuming. "I'm serious. I was thinking about it today. I think"—she paused to take a bite of the kuih that Cecily offered her—"that everything was preordained. Happened for a reason. One thing led to another . . ."

"You have no regrets? And you're not angry about what happened to you when they came for Kapitan Yap?" Cecily's body clenched. It had been a long time since she'd thought about Kapitan Yap, the price he'd paid for what she had done.

"I think . . . I think I had to go through all of that so I could meet Bingley. And then I got to know you! And it was worth it." Lina arranged herself on her favorite chair in Cecily's house, tucked her feet under her like a child. She sipped a mouth of tea. "Ouch, hot!" she squeaked, then laughed at herself.

What a strange and wonderful way to live, Cecily thought, to find the sun in all things. In Cecily, discontent was a constant state of being. She lived with a persistent gurgle of want, of longing for more of everything she could see but did not yet have. To be just content, Cecily thought. How simple it must be.

"Here." Lina put her cup of tea on the table and blew on her fingertips. "Give me your hand. My ah mah used to say that you can tell a person's whole life by the lines on their palm."

Cecily laughed and opened her palm. She didn't believe in things like this, but it was hard to say no when Lina was in one of these joyous moods. Her brightness was contagious. Lina ran a thin index finger over the longest line on Cecily's hand, the calluses on her fingertip leaving a pleasurable tickle.

"See here. Your lifeline is deep and long. My ah mah would say you'll live a very long time."

"Are you sure it isn't deep because I don't use enough hand cream? Maybe it's just dry," Cecily said.

"No joking!" Lina said. "This is serious. See here. Look how your lifeline separates into two."

"And what does that mean?"

"It means you have two sides, become two different people. And see here. That's the love line"—she pointed at the line closest to Cecily's fingers—"and that's the child line, and of course that's the lifeline we talked about. And wah, see here, that big line? It crosses all three lines at an angle."

"And what does that mean?"

"A big disturbance." Lina pursed her mouth so her bottom lip puckered.

"Sounds ominous," Cecily said.

"It means a big betrayal. Or a disruption. A lack of peace. So you better watch out!" She opened her mouth wide in mock fear. Then all the seriousness faded from Lina's demeanor. She started laughing hard, short, happy breaths pushing from her lungs. Cecily wished Lina knew, wished that maybe this whole time she'd been only playacting the silly ingenue whom no one took seriously. It would be so wonderful to bring Lina on, have Lina's wonder and excitement infused into Fujiwara's and her plan—the world would be so much brighter with her in it.

"Don't be scared, Cecily. Palm reading is a lie. See mine?" Lina flourished her hand at Cecily, tilted the palm under Cecily's nose. It smelled faintly like jasmine. "My lifeline is so short, see, it means I'm basically already dead." She flapped her hands in front of her face in a terrible approximation of a ghost. "Maybe I'm haunting you now, Cecily, woo!"

Cecily caught Lina's palms in her own. Lina was right. You couldn't read a person's future from her hand. Still, she enjoyed sitting here, pretending to be girls, laughing about the disruptions their palms were intuiting for their lives.

Around this time, Cecily and Fujiwara resumed their meetings at Oriental Horizons. Their first meeting was a stilted, nearly soundless pantomime. Cecily walked into room 7A with a sheaf of reports she'd taken from Gordon's desk, and Fujiwara thumbed through them before leaving in a cloud of sweat and mint without once making eye contact. The second time it was she who left first, refusing the role of the anguished, helpless woman gazing at the back of a retreating man. As she turned to go, she caught Fujiwara's face—eyes narrowed, cheeks pinched. He was biting the inside of his mouth; the gesture made her ache with want.

Their third meeting was the first time they slept together. It was bound to happen, she supposed, all that tension and anger with no place to go, though perhaps Lina was right—some women just weren't made for a peaceful life; she was someone who needed the simmering possibility of chaos. This time when Cecily arrived in 7A, she let him meet her eye, watched the cloud of desire break in his face. "It's happening," her body said to her as she felt her pelvis clench, then open, ready to receive.

Fujiwara was a considerate lover. For Cecily, unfortunately, this made the sex wan and mediocre. He was gentle when he laid on her on the musty bed, the sheets pilled and scratchy. He was slow when he extricated her from her undergarments, watching her intently, for what, she didn't know. She nodded encouragingly as he pushed into her, so tenderly and with so much care that she had to stop herself from rolling her eyes.

"Are you all right," he whispered, soft fingertips brushing her cheek. "I can stop if you want."

"Don't stop," she breathed. She closed her eyes and recalled the rage of the man who had thrown her against the grimy wall and wound his fingers around her throat, willing her desire back into her body, allowing it to push her beyond her cliff. She gasped as her body tried to reach for its climax, almost—almost. She opened her eyes just in time to watch the ripples of his orgasm crest through his body as he bucked against her, powerless, depleted.

Still, she told herself, the sex was not bad, and there were times, if she positioned herself at a certain angle, that it even felt like something. And there was a comfort in mediocrity, the balloon was punctured, the tension released. Sex became a part of their routine. Cecily would hand over whatever report she was able to snag from Gordon's files or repeat any useful information she had overheard from Gordon or his superiors. Then she and Fujiwara would undress quickly, without fanfare, and fall into bed. After he was done, shuddering quietly above her, they would, spent and sweaty, air out their bodies and discuss news from Japan. She learned about the ongoing stalemate the Imperial Army was facing in China, about the shakiness of the alliance with Germany, about alterations the Japanese had made to the military uniforms to enable quicker and quieter movements through jungle terrain. These were Cecily's favorite moments of their encounters, her cheek on Fujiwara's chest, the mingling of sweat and mint wafting off his body, listening to him breathe, his words whispered above her head, the quiet intimacy of it all. The sense that perhaps, finally, they were equal.

"How did you meet Lina?" Cecily asked one evening as it drizzled in confused spurts outside the hotel room. The sky had darkened, and the gray light made the dingy hotel room look strangely regal.

"You know how. At the resident's party from our mission that one time. When she was Mrs. Yap." Fujiwara sat up in bed and straightened his back against the wall. His face was shadowed, and his hair was sticking up, the strange gray light making it look like a misshapen coronet.

Cecily pressed: "Right. But after her husband was arrested. When you got to know her. Was it by chance? Or was she a mark?"

He pulled himself out of bed, stepped into a patch of light seeping in from the window. He poured himself water from the jug at the foot of the bed. "Want some?" He nodded at Cecily.

Cecily shook her head. "I mean. Did you plan the whole thing?"

Fujiwara turned and watched the large raindrops splashing against the window. Framed between the large windows, he looked surprisingly diminutive. Cecily remembered when he used to seem so much larger, straighter.

"Why do you care? I'm here with you."

"No, that's not— That isn't—" she stumbled.

He thought her questions were the jealous ones of a mistress, not the curious ones of a female friend. A bubble of embarrassment rose in her chest. The drizzle was turning into a tropical storm, and the wind shook the hotel's wooden beams. Cecily hoped it would pass soon; she wasn't sure the hotel was structurally sound enough to endure a lengthy monsoon rain.

"Here." He poured her some water and sat back down on the bed, avoiding a spot of dampness that they had created. "Look." He ran his hand along the inside of her thigh, tickling the tiny hairs on her body. "Lina doesn't know about us—about any of this. I needed her connections. She needed a husband to help her come back into society. It was just . . . easy."

"Do you feel guilty?" Cecily asked.

Sometimes she asked herself the same when Lina's wide, open face brightened with a joke or her eyes welled up. Lina cried easily, at sad stories, funny stories, happy stories. Cecily cared for Lina, guarded their happy afternoons fiercely, replayed their conversations when they were apart, chuckling to herself. That Lina loved Fujiwara—Bingley—was without question. Lina always said he was her savior, her second chance.

"Well, do *you*? Feel guilty?" Fujiwara said, his soft voice nearly drowned out by a bolt of lightning that cracked through the sky. He was once again at the window, watching the rain beat down. Cecily held her breath the way she always did during storms, waiting for the loud crunch of thunder that typically followed the lightning.

"Remember once a long time ago that I told you the German leader was a good man and a bad man. Remember what you said to me?" he said into the rising storm.

Isn't everyone both good and bad? she'd asked. She remembered how painfully bright the sun had been that day, how she had shivered from sheer proximity to Fujiwara, how different she, like the weather, had been.

Instead of thunder, another bolt of lightning parted the clouds. Cecily rose from the bed and joined him at the window. They stood together silently, without touching, watching the storm wreak its chaos.

In April, Cecily and Lina became pregnant together, and this was the first joy that they did not share. Lina was overjoyed in the frightened way that women become when they learn they're carrying their first child. She ingested herbs, stroked her stomach relentlessly, made offerings at both the Buddhist altar and the Catholic chapel, bowing and genuflecting for a little boy to carry on the family name. Women cooed and surrounded Lina in tight clusters, peppering her with unsolicited advice.

"If you eat a lot of fish, the child will come out a good swimmer!" Mrs. Low proclaimed. No one said anything because one of Mrs. Low's boys had drowned years ago in a mining pool.

"If you sleep facing the eastern window, the child will get more morning sun and have a sunny personality!" Mrs. Chin dictated. Everyone assumed that this must've been a mistake that Mrs. Chin had made herself, having mothered five sour, bad-tempered sons whom everyone avoided.

Cecily, on the other hand, didn't even notice she had skipped her period until nearly a whole second cycle had passed. When she realized, she counted backward frantically, but it was impossible to fully determine who the father was—she had consistently been with both Gordon and Fujiwara, the routine encounters overlapping in her mind, neither standing out.

When Gordon heard the news, he was thrilled. He had loved Jujube and Abel as babies, wondered at their tiny fingers and cooed at their curious, unblinking eyes, so the chance to do it again excited him so much he immediately began outfitting the extra room in their house for the new baby. Cecily spent evenings watching him flap his arms as he rearranged the old storeroom, muttering room configurations to himself, with Jujube and Abel running around asking him a million questions. Cecily knew the scene should have warmed her heart, that this level of domestic joy was enviable. Instead, she felt scorn. Gordon's clumsy thrill felt like weakness; his desire for the simple felt unambitious, dull. It was off-putting.

"I'm pregnant," she told Fujiwara during their next meeting at the hotel, on a sunny evening so morbidly cheerful that even the birdsong seemed louder than usual.

She studied the softness of his cheeks and the hardness of his jaw for micro-expressions, the way he'd taught her to read in others, to learn when they were lying. His chin remained still, but his lower lip curved down. Was it displeasure? Or shame? Or indifference? She had never been very good at this.

"I thought you always took care of things," he said, loosening his tie and draping it over the ugly green chair in the room. "After. You always washed yourself out?"

The audacity of this man, she thought, to find a way to both blame her *and* take ownership of a baby that may not even be his.

"Well, I didn't ask for this, if that's what you're saying," Cecily said. "And it could be yours. Or it could be Gordon's."

She knew she did not imagine the shiver that passed over Fujiwara's jawline, the micro-expression for hurt, or rage, or both. His knuckles unbuttoning his shirt whitened, but then, as quickly as it came, the expression was gone, his face slack once more.

"Well, then, that's settled. Another addition to your family. Give Gordon my congratulations," he said as he unbuttoned his shirt cuffs.

Her stomach sank, then twisted, the cold archness of his voice swallowing her. But even as she struggled to resist, she felt it—the widening space below her pelvis; his disinterest in distractions, his ability to scratch out the bother and look only forward, the ease with which he ignored the severity of emotion—it was delicious, unexpected, unsolvable. Perhaps this was what was wrong with her, to desire only men who held power over her, who simmered with anger and refused to partake in the care of others. She was wet and wanting. She pushed him on the bed and straddled him, her heat encouraging them both. That day with Fujiwara, her body undulated and writhed and gushed in a way that she had been able to achieve only by herself before.

—

Despite the congruency of their pregnancies, Cecily's and Lina's physical changes varied widely. Cecily's appetites increased in all ways, and Gordon joked that he didn't know if she would eat him out of house and home first, or if she would kill him from sexual exhaustion. Where before, her meetings with Fujiwara had been a routine of procedural discussions prior to sex, now she found she could barely wait. As their bodies slammed into each other, she would remember important intel and gasp it out as groaning desire roiled through them both.

Lina's body betrayed her in direct and indirect ways. She ballooned quickly and her curveless elegance disappeared, replaced with a chunkiness that enveloped her arms, thighs, stomach. She threw up so much that the blood vessels in her face ruptured, leaving it puffy and red. Her breath was laced with the sourness of bile; even a sip of water would trigger her heaving insides, send her rushing for the toilet, choking as the frothing yellow made its way up her body. She stopped hosting the parties she had become known for, and her appearances at balls became rarer. Some days, Lina said, the only person she saw was Cecily, not even her husband, because she was asleep from exhaustion by the time he got home.

Cecily felt sorry for her friend. It was often the case that Lina would vomit multiple times during Cecily's two-hour visit, emerging from the toilet red-faced and shaking before rushing back to vomit again. The first couple of times Cecily followed her friend into the toilet, held back her hair, and held her hand as the shudders broke through Lina's body. But as it wore on, Cecily found herself staying in the living room, flinching as Lina's gagging echoed through the house. In between gasps of nausea, Lina wept weakly. She was worried that she would lose her husband, that she could no longer be what he needed, that she could no longer charm in society, that all the goodwill she had built up, all the reinvention she had done, would be for naught.

"Does your husband take care of you when you're sick?" Cecily asked.

Lina smiled wanly. "He says that our child and I are the most important things in the world to him. He's sweet, he doesn't complain when I don't have dinner ready or when I'm just sick in bed. But—"

"But?" Cecily said.

"He's stopped looking at me when he says goodbye in the mornings."

—

In the last two months of 1937, the monsoons arrived as usual. They started out the same: fat, oily drizzles splattering against the roof of the house as the sky grayed and the clouds clustered in the darkening sky. Then, within minutes, a thunderous sheet of rain would vibrate through the walls, the drumming puncturing any hope Cecily had of calm. She'd read about peaceful rains that happened in English novels, light drizzles in the countryside of Jane Austen, damp, misty air from the ocean breeze in Enid Blyton's Cornish boarding school landscapes. But in Malaya, the rains shouted as though releasing rage, and it was a terrible inconvenience. Cecily was sick of it. The afternoon and evening rains, petulant and unpredictable, made it hard for her to schedule evening meetings with Fujiwara, made walking anywhere slow and treacherous.

On Tuesdays, Jujube and Abel stayed later after school; both had taken up sports—Abel unsurprisingly joining the long jump and running teams, and Jujube a surprisingly decent netball player. This meant that Cecily had a precise amount of time, two and a half hours exactly, to sneak away to the Oriental Horizons Hotel to see Fujiwara. It had worked well before the incessant rain arrived. She always returned home exactly on time to let the children in, start dinner, wash Fujiwara out of her clothes and hair, and greet Gordon when he returned from work.

But the monsoon season delayed everything. It flipped her umbrella, drenched her shoes, and soaked the folders of documents she carried when she walked to the hotel. It made Fujiwara late too, and they were always wet and sweaty, the humidity from their bodies filling the stuffy room air, the smell of damp feet sucking away their desire. He would watch Cecily wring the rain out of her hair as they talked, and often it felt like too much effort to heave their warm, wet bodies together when the rain reverberated through the beams, loud, intrusive, and determined to interrupt. Cecily's body was also becoming increasingly unwieldy, and although she had been pregnant twice before, it still exhausted her. Instead, they peeled off their soggy clothes, twisted out the water, and spread them out on chairs in front of the whirring fan. Then they would towel each other dry in a fond, almost spousal way, Fujiwara rubbing a gentle hand over all of her. He would stop sometimes and press his palm on her rounded stomach, eyes crinkling if he felt the baby kick. Cecily wondered if he mirrored the same actions with Lina, if he paused over her stomach as well, straining for signs of life. But she did not ask.

Still, it startled her sometimes how far she'd come with Fujiwara, what a stupid quivering girl she had been just a few years ago. The mystery of men and the causticity of their charisma really did lose its sheen once you could see the nakedness of their desire and the vulnerability of their physical need that seemed so easy to fulfill. She realized that she had simply wanted to solve Fujiwara, and now that she felt she had, her desire for him was no longer the same. It had morphed into something more. She respected and acknowledged his magnetism. Her body still rose to attention when he entered the room, she still admired the way he drew people to him, but his desire for her had become its own power. She may not have had his way of winning people, but she had him, and in solving the puzzle that was him, she had equalized the planes on which they stood.

Her mother had taught her that when you give yourself to a man, he ceased to respect you, that your virtue was all you had to bargain with as a woman, and once that was gone, a man had no more reason to stick around. But her mother had been wrong. Her treating sex like a man had made Fujiwara treat her like a man, even if he did not realize it. During those loud, rainy afternoons in the hot, dingy hotel room, they discussed futures and military strategies she knew she had no right to know. Here, instead of being the closed, morose, silent man she used to know, he was expansive, as though he held inside his body all the things he couldn't say to anyone all week, then blurted them out to her as a kind of release.

One of these afternoons, Fujiwara arrived at their rendezvous with an armful of maps. "I need to talk through this strategy with you, Cecily." He unfurled a long roll of paper on the floor, motioned for her to sit beside him on the carpet, then, remembering she was pregnant, pulled a chair out for her.

"What's this?"

"With the success in China, the emperor has put me in charge of the invasion strategy for Malaya. This is a big moment for me."

Cecily stilled her lips to hide her excitement. She had heard of this from the wireless—an extensive battle in Shanghai, months of a stalemate, but finally, finally, Japan had taken China. Still, when they discussed strategy, it was usually in more indirect, theoretical terms. But this was tangible. Fujiwara was speaking to her as though she were a commander in the army. This, she thought, was what she was fighting for: to stand side by side with a man, to have her ideas mean something, to effect change. She imagined standing next to Fujiwara as he introduced her to the emperor as the key to Japan's successful overthrow of the British, as the woman, the *woman*, who enabled Malaya to join its self-determining Asian sister countries. An image of Gordon, portly, sweaty, pleading for mercy, pressed against the back of her mind, but she dismissed it. Gordon would lose his job, but Fujiwara would save him, she would have Fujiwara find him another. Gordon would be all right as long as he had a superior to serve. Gordon was not like her. He would find a way to fit into his circumstances.

"Have you met the emperor?" Cecily asked. She'd seen a photo of Emperor Hirohito, a young-looking, handsome man with very stylish hair. The local papers described him as a monster, a killer of Chinese, and the Malayan Chinese population feared him.

"Only once," Fujiwara said. "I was invited along with my superior officer to the palace. But only he went inside. I stood outside. But now the emperor is asking me. That's why this is so important."

The unrolled sheet on the floor curled at the edges, and on it was a large map of the Malayan peninsula, dotted with red, to denote, Cecily supposed, military strongholds. On the outer corners of the map were Fujiwara's scribbles. They reminded Cecily of the terse, instructional missives he used to leave for her behind the sanitary napkins at the sundry store, before they were bold enough to meet, before they became entangled in each other in ways she could barely quantify. Crouched on the floor in an uneven squat, he looked up at her. At that angle he looked like a child, reminded her of Abel when her son was telling her one of his many illogical but funny stories.

"So you see, Cecily"—he gestured wildly at the map at her feet—"we need to disable the cannons on the southern border, or ships will be toast."

Cecily laughed at this Britishism, the bit of Bingley coming through. As he chattered on, crawling on the floor pointing at dots and pins, waving animatedly with his hands, Cecily crossed her ankles and allowed herself to wonder at a future with him, as a father, as a husband, as a man of the house. It had taken a looming war, a career as a spy, and devastating emotional turmoil to find someone who did not bore her. She studied the map at her feet, the green peninsula tip pointing at Fujiwara's big toe, faded blue ocean on three sides, attached at the top to the kingdom of Siam by a thin strip of land.

Many years ago, when she was in primary school, Cecily had asked the white nun who taught geography what the strip of land was called. The nun had not known and had been furious at Cecily for what she perceived as impertinence—being called out for her limited knowledge of the hot, horrible Southeast Asian region where she had been forced to live. Cecily had been whipped that day, the stinging lashes on her buttocks rushing up her spine, pushing tears out of her eyes. But mostly she remembered her anger at the indignity of bending in two, pulling her skirt up in front of the classroom, facing the very map she'd had the audacity to question.

"What about the north?" she asked Fujiwara, uncrossing her ankles, using her right heel to tap the sliver of land that had gotten her in trouble all those years ago.

"The north?"

"This strip—it's called the Isthmus of Kra."

"Don't be silly, Cecily."

She inhaled sharply to stop the frustration building at the back of her throat. Calm down, she told herself. She knew how to manage this—this tendency with men, whose first instinct was to dismiss, to put a woman down when presented with something unfamiliar instead of engaging in more inquiry. There was no need to lose her temper.

"You told me the soldiers are being trained to run through jungle terrain and handle heat. Perhaps they can run in from the north? If all the British weapons are in the south, pointing the wrong way . . ." She trailed off. A crease pressed itself between his eyebrows. Cecily fiddled with her thumbnail. Perhaps she had gone too far, acted outside of her designated role. She retreated: "But I don't know anything about the military, of course. Just a suggestion . . ." She curved her shoulders small against the back of the chair, shrugged a tiny shrug, shrinking herself, wishing she weren't so far above him.

Around them, the sky had begun its daily darkening. Fujiwara's crouched figure blocked the graying light from the window and cast a shadow over the map of Malaya. Her mother would have considered that an omen, Cecily thought, but from her position above him, she was able to admire the curve of his temple, which was beginning to gray. A fleck of dry skin stuck to his slicked-back hair. A wave of tenderness broke through her—she wondered if it was the pregnancy, turning her into a sentimental mess. Before she could stop herself, she reached over to flick it away. He turned when her fingers grazed the top of his ear, reached up to circle his arms around her waist, and lowered her to the floor with him. As he laid her gently on the map, Cecily watched their shadows dance across her country, then felt the map crease and crinkle beneath her as her back arched. He brushed his fingers across her cheek.

"You are a wonder, you know?" he said as his body pressed against, then into, her. As the storm reached its usual crescendo, she felt the map tear under her.

"Don't worry about it," he said from above her, urgency and desire pulling his face taut. "I need you more."

When they were done, the rain was torrential, the overwhelmed monsoon drains spilled into the streets, and Cecily was late. From their hotel window, she watched the water rush along the roads of their neighborhood, bits of garbage floating on top like tiny boats. The wind whipped violently and without direction. No one was on the streets. Everyone except her had the presence of mind to stay home and wait for the storm to pass.

Behind her, Fujiwara chuckled.

"What?" she said.

"Come here. You have map on your buttocks."

Cecily wriggled as he scraped bits of green topography and blue ocean off her skin while she hurriedly dressed. "I must go," she said.

"So fast? Come on, help me clean this up," he said, gesturing at the torn map and overturned trash can in the room.

Cecily shook her head.

"But," he said, looking worried, "the rain is heavy. You should wait it out."

"I can't. The children . . ." She trailed off.

He nodded. He never argued when she invoked her kids; it was a separate part of her life, one he did not encroach on and never tried to be a part of. Sometimes she wanted him to ask, wanted him to worry about her loyalty, to have even the slightest suspicion that she may be duplicitous. But she supposed she had given him no reason to doubt; when he called, she came. Besides, there was no time to worry about all that now. The children needed to be fed. Gordon would not want to arrive to a home without her in it. She pushed her umbrella open, and stepped into the flooding street.

The umbrella was useless. She had brought along one of those larger ones that promised not to flip, but the heavy winds meant the rain pelted her from all directions. The air was colder than usual, the wind had taken care of that, and she shivered in her already drenched clothes. As she angled her body against the gusts, she realized she had not put on her bra properly, and the front twisted painfully against her chest. She turned her face back to the hotel to see if she could catch a glimpse of Fujiwara—was he watching her from the window? But the swirling rain made it impossible to see anything. Besides, he couldn't help her anyway. They could not be seen leaving a grimy hotel together.

She focused on walking, one foot in front of the other, the wind pressing against her chest, then her side, making her sway. It was a ten-minute walk to her house normally, flat and easy through town, one she often did in slippers. She'd had the foresight to wear covered shoes that day, which thankfully gripped the ground better, but they were no match for the rivers of brown water on the street that had broken the banks of the overwhelmed drains. Big puddles washed over her feet, leaving her shoes heavy and soaking. Cecily grimaced from what she knew would be the stench later. She steadfastly held her umbrella above her head, out of stubbornness or a desire not to be recognized, she did not know, and pushed through the wind.

After an exhausting twenty minutes of being nearly blown off course twice, Cecily arrived at the gate of her house, soaked. Her hair stuck, heavy and lank, against her face. Every part of her felt weighed down, even more than usual. She was so tired. She pressed a hand on her stomach, but the baby was quiet, probably exhausted too, she thought. The rain pelted against her painfully as she fumbled with the gate, fat, wet drops sliding down her body, between her thighs, down her back. Her umbrella folded into itself, defying its own promise not to flip. The shallow drain in front of the house, the one that Jujube loved to sit in, was a rushing tide, spilling everywhere. Cecily glanced at her wristwatch to see just how late she was, but it had stopped, the second hand fluttering helplessly. She hoped the children had been able to get home from school before the rain started, but they also knew that when it stormed, they were to remain in the safety of the school until either the rain was over and they could walk home or Cecily could go retrieve them.

The latch of the gate clattered annoyingly as the rain dripped into her eyes. "Come on," she muttered. As the latch finally gave way, another gust of wind ripped through the air, pushing the flimsy gate hard against her.

"Ooof," Cecily yelled. Clutching her stomach, she stumbled backward, her foot twisting awkwardly in her soaked shoe, which she felt, too late, catch on the corner of the drain. Her ankle gave way. Before she hit the ground, she heard the children yelling, "Mama! Mama!" and a familiar, throaty scream, "Cecily *ah*!"

Then everything went dark.

―

When she came to, she was too hot. It felt like she was suffocating. She looked around in a panic, her eye passing over the familiar ceiling of her bedroom. She thrashed around, then realized she was wrapped in so many blankets that she was weighed down, almost pinned to the bed.

Jujube, Abel, she thought groggily. Where were they?

She struggled to pull herself out from under the heat of the blankets. When she managed to sit up, she realized she was in dry clothes, but around her, the damp, moldy smell of dirty rain persisted.

"Shhh. Rest." A velvet throb of a voice.

Startled, Cecily saw Lina sitting on the corner of the bed, a long white arm outstretched, handing her a cup of something warm. Lina's eyes, big and dark, were round with concern, and Cecily had to admit that even with the new pregnancy-induced puffiness to her face, Lina was still a remarkably good-looking woman. Cecily reached for the cup and was surprised to find that, despite the rest of her body sweating, her fingertips were cold. She wrapped her hands around the cup, which smelled like English tea, strong and bitter.

"You can relax, Cecily. Everything is taken care of," Lina said. Her voice lowered to a crack. "You really gave us all a scare."

As Cecily sipped, Lina rattled off the sequence of events. She, Lina, had swung by to say hello; it was the first time she had felt like herself in days. Perhaps it was a turning point for her body, what did Cecily think? Anyway. She had wanted to surprise Cecily, but then the rain had started, and she didn't want to walk home in the rain. And luckily Cecily's kids made it home just as the rain was beginning to splatter more dangerously, and they'd been squealing excitedly as if they'd been racing the dark clouds. So Lina had let them in, made them each a hot Horlicks, and told them stories about her days running her father's shop, which sold all kinds of live animals. Lina chuckled. "Yes, Cecily, don't be surprised, I know lots of things about all kinds of animals, and I even wanted to become an animal doctor, but, well, girls don't do that, do we? There were fish and chickens and cats and dogs, but the children were most interested in the different kinds of lizards that my father sold, one of them was even blue in the neck! But I'm losing my train of thought. Oh yes, Abel began to get sleepy, so I sent both kids to bed for a nap. Jujube grumbled that she was old enough to stay up later, so I allowed her to read in bed until she also fell asleep. By the time the children were safely in bed, the storm was in full force, and I was worried about you, Cecily, so I stayed. And then not even a few minutes after I had settled down in the chair, I heard the gate, but before I could come let you in, you hit your head on the corner of that *treacherous* drain."

"The baby . . . ," Cecily whimpered.

"It's all right. I called Dr. Buchanan immediately, and he checked on you while you slept. All is well, just a scare lah." Lina pressed a hand on Cecily's stomach the way Fujiwara had done many times before. "I even felt a little kick earlier. This is one tough one," she said, eyes softening, face relaxing. "Nah drink," she said, gesturing to the cup, and Cecily took a small, warm sip. Then Lina took the cup of tea out of Cecily's hands and put it on the table.

Unused to this much care, Cecily felt her eyes well up. She wriggled against the expanse of blankets.

"Oh, and your husband was falling apart. I sent him to the bar once the doctor said you were all right. Men, they can't take stress, you know?" Lina chuckled to herself. "And I made the children some noodles for dinner. You arrange your pots differently than me! I had trouble finding the biggest one!"

I have been wrong, Cecily realized. She had mistaken Lina's emotional duress and physical discomfort for weakness. But here Lina was, managing a whole panicked household with calm efficiency, with so much empathy. Cecily was awash with emotions—gratitude, amazement, but most of all, guilt. Cecily could still feel Lina's hand on her belly, feel the coolness of it transmitting care she did not deserve.

Cecily struggled to raise herself to a sitting position. "Thank you, Lina. I think I'm all right now. You can go back home. Your Bingley—he will be worried."

"Nonsense! I'm going to stay with you. I sent the doctor over to my house with a message. Told him I'll be with you tonight."

Cecily's throat caught in a panic. Seeing her distress, Lina said, "Oh, no, I didn't tell him you got hurt, of course. Men don't like those kinds of details!" She smirked, then closed her eyes, cheeks crumpling. It was a stark contrast, an expression of private turmoil so visceral that Cecily lowered her eyes. "These days he barely notices me anyway," Lina whispered.

Cecily patted the bed beside her. Lina moved herself from the bottom of the bed to the top and Cecily, finally freeing herself from the blankets, shifted over to the left, giving Lina space. Both panted from the exertion.

"Look at us, pregnant lumps," Lina said, and in spite of herself, Cecily laughed. Both women lay on their back, eyes raised to the ceiling.

The rain had finally stopped, and out of the window, the moon revealed its half fullness, pressing out from behind the clouds. Lina laid her head on Cecily's shoulder and breathed into Cecily's neck, trusting, tickling, not unpleasant.

"I'm sorry," Cecily began. She blinked back a tear that she hoped Lina didn't see. "I'm sorry he hasn't been there for you." Fujiwara, the shadow between them, a threat to this friendship she had been so surprised and grateful to build. "Why do you let him act this way?" As soon as the words slipped from her tired mouth, Cecily regretted them. It was not Lina's responsibility to police his actions; he was not someone who could be controlled, and she of all people knew it.

Lina pulled her head off Cecily's shoulder and turned on her side, faced away from Cecily so only her cheek was visible, skin nearly blue where the moonlight hit her face.

"That's love, isn't it?" she said. "To know badness lives in someone but to love anyway. It was the same with my first husband."

"You don't need him," Cecily said, pulling herself into a half-sit over Lina's side, feeling an ache in her chest so painful she had to grip her hands into fists under the blanket.

"Maybe I love him more for his badness. My mother used to say maybe love is just ignoring the bad things," she said. She looked up at Cecily, face shiny with tears and the moon. "Is something wrong with me?"

"No." Cecily was stricken. "You are the one thing that is not wrong."

Then, as quickly as her face had crumpled, Lina was smiling again. "Let's not talk about bad things. Lie down," she said.

Like a child commanded, Cecily lowered herself back onto the bed and curled her knees into her stomach, facing Lina. Lina flipped onto her other side and faced Cecily, body curved the same way, a mirror image. She pressed her hands against Cecily's hands, their bellies touching. They fell asleep, two shrimps, curled toward each other.

CHAPTER EIGHTEEN
—

JUJUBE

Bintang, Kuala Lumpur
August 25, 1945
Japanese-occupied Malaya

It felt familiar—in the days after Jasmin ran away, neighbors and friends had gathered around, performing the same vigil at the Alcantara house that they had done when Abel disappeared. All the neighborhood aunties, Mrs. Carvalho, Mrs. Chua, Mrs. Lingam, Aunty Mui, even the rich Aunty Faridah whom her mother couldn't stand, cooked pots of food and made sympathetic clucking noises, *she will be found soon,* they said, *she's a brave little girl and she will come home,* they exhorted. The neighborhood uncles organized searches, cursed the Japanese, swore to find Jasmin. But this buzz of activity lasted only a few days. After that, people just went about their lives as if nothing of significance had happened. Adults stood in line for food rations, swapped recipes—incorporating boiled tapioca, sweet potato, even paper into their rice rations—to make food last longer. Children played games, avoided the angry stares of the Kenpeitai soldiers. Neighbors leaned over the fence and reverted to simple gossip—that the Sequiera boy and Tan girl had been making eyes at each other, that no one could tell if the Menon woman was pregnant again or just hadn't lost the weight from the previous birth, that the soldiers seemed fewer in number these days, perhaps the Americans really had won.

When Abel had been taken, their fear and pity had lasted longer. Perhaps it was earlier in the Occupation and people had not yet been cauterized to accept pain as part of existence. Or perhaps, Jujube thought, there was recognition that the first time something like this happened would be the hardest, but subsequent tragedies were supposed to get easier—like a scabbed-over wound that split open—you were already supposed to know how to feel; you did not need the salve of extended sympathy.

In fact, some of the neighbors became crueler in their whispering. Jujube overheard Mrs. Chua whisper spitefully, "Something had to be wrong in the Alcantara home if the littlest girl had to run away!" The other aunties shushed her when Jujube walked by, but she could feel their stares eating into her back. Maybe they were right, Jujube thought, chest swollen with guilt. After all, it was she who had driven her sister away.

At home, the walls seemed to seep pain and tension. And it was unbearably quiet. Their household cacophony used to have its own melody: her father, loud but with words jumbling together always too fast to be understood on the first try; her mother, voice surprisingly melodic but dangerously low when she was about to lose it; Abel, uneven because it was sometimes low and sometimes high, cracking with puberty; Jasmin, reedy and nasally, as though she were pushing her entire voice out through her left nostril.

In the before times, Jujube had a school friend, Florence, whose house was always eerily quiet. After Florence's mother had died, her own mother had urged Jujube to visit and keep her company. But Jujube hated those visits because, during the day, Florence's house was completely silent except for the sudden bumps that occurred when Florence's father stumbled after drinking too much, his foot or arm clattering against a wall or a table. Jujube often wondered why they didn't play music or fill the silence with some sort of sound, but she had been too afraid to ask. Now her own house was silent in this way; the only sound puncturing the stillness was the shuffling of feet as someone walked on the creaky wooden floors. She understood Florence and Florence's father now. Grief sucked everything with it, left holes in the body that nothing, not even music, could fill.

It was even worse at the teahouse. After a week, she went back to work, just in time—her manager, Doraisamy, had already posted TEA GIRL WANTED signs on the door. She snatched one of the handwritten flyers, marched in, and handed the paper to Doraisamy, who shrugged without shame. He gestured helplessly at the kitchen, stacks of unwashed teacups and teapots balancing precariously on every available bit of space, the insides of the cups and pots swirling with stagnant brown water and clumps of tea leaves. Jujube shuddered to think about the hygiene of the teapots and cups he had been serving customers in her absence. She picked up a cloth rag and ran it under the water before she started scrubbing the cups. And just like that, Jujube resumed the mundanity of her life, even as the Jasmin-sized pit in her chest threatened to choke her alive.

―

The teahouse felt different. Rumors continued to fly: Emperor Hirohito was close to signing a surrender; the Japanese had run out of munitions and were ready to give up. Jujube began hearing more rumors about Chinese freedom fighters living on the edge of the forests conducting guerrilla strikes, attacking squads of Japanese soldiers under the cover of night, then disappearing back to the dark, damp forests in the daytime. Or at least she called them freedom fighters. Her father called them heroes and patriots. The British wireless dispatches called them Communists. Mr. Takahashi called them rebels, which was one of several things she had begun to hold against him. Still, Jujube couldn't trust herself to believe any of it was true. It was too much to hope for anything these days, and besides, things would never be the same. Even if the Japanese left, half her family was gone. What would a postwar life be without Jasmin and Abel? Would their family continue to exist in the horrific silence of their present, creaking around like tired apparitions in their own home, weighed down by the footfalls of their sadness? There was no more normal for Jujube. She did not know how to go home.

The soldiers had started coming to the teahouse alone, not in groups. They stared into space. Some buried their face in their hands. Their muddy green-brown uniforms hung off bonier shoulders and pronounced clavicles. Only their faces seemed to bloat, their breath smelling alcohol-bitter, the air stale with the rot of halitosis. In several of the soldiers, this moroseness manifested as quietness, which Jujube was grateful for. They would sit in the corner, sneak drops from a flask into their teacup, and sip with their faces bunched together. But in others, morose meant mean. Where before the occasional rowdy soldier would pull her in by the waist and breathe heavily down her neck, they mostly ignored her. But these days they watched her with greedy eyes, and when they pulled at her to ask for refills, they dug their fingers into her back, sometimes rolling those fingers up and down, pressing into the side of her breast and the indent in her waist, as though reminding her of all the things they could do if only they felt like unleashing themselves. And what is to hold us back now, they seemed to say; we do not have anything left to lose. When the first of these gropes had happened, she had looked for Doraisamy, eyes wide, silently begging for help. But he had looked away. She was on her own.

Before, she would have had Mr. Takahashi as a shield. But his presence at the shop had become inconsistent. He came at all hours of the day, sometimes multiple times a day, sometimes not at all for many days. The food coupons he used to bring for her became scarcer. He told her that his school had been shut down, that he no longer had a recess routine. When she asked him what he would do now that his people seemed to be in retreat, he would not meet her eyes, avoided the question. This irritated her. Did he presume to think she would care if he left and went back to Japan? That she would mourn him like a silly child? She was not a child; she did not need his bumbling attempts to take care of her. After all, he was one of them, cruel men who delighted in the suffering of her family. Sometimes the force of her bitterness shocked her.

And when he was around, he spoke incessantly of Ichika. Jujube regretted giving him permission to speak about his daughter, because now he would not shut up about her. The words fell from his mouth like sawdust from a hole at the bottom of a gunnysack, rushed, urgent, as though he had been waiting a long time to tell her.

The worst day was the day when he received a letter from Ichika.

"Finally," he said, pressing the envelope to his chest, his joy stinging Jujube like rays of sun that were too glaring for her eyes.

She knew he deserved this happiness—it had been months since he'd heard from Ichika, aside from the telegram informing him that she was alive. Ichika's letter was postmarked before the bomb, but it had taken over six weeks to arrive. Mr. Takahashi insisted on reading it aloud to Jujube, translating the Japanese in his halting English. She wished she had the courage to hit him across the mouth, smash his face into the table, silence him. Instead, she creased her face into a thin smile and motioned for him to proceed.

"She tells me that even though she has not yet received her nurse credential, she is volunteering at the hospital! There are many casualties, and she is helping!" His face was slick with sweaty joy, his eyes shining at the prospect of Ichika's future. Jujube had never seen such pride on her own parents' faces. Was it because they as children had not done anything worthy of such pride? Those opportunities had been snatched from them. Or did some parents love more than others? She did not know, but the shimmer in his voice made her insides clench. Ichika had sent a photo of herself standing in what Jujube assumed was a hospital ward—beds, people, doctors, and nurses in conical hats milling around her. Ichika wore her own clothes: those pants again, baggy but cinched at the waist, and a loose shirt with buttons, a man's shirt.

To slow the furious clenching in her stomach, Jujube tried to find fault with Ichika. Ichika definitely looked older in this photo than in the one that Mr. Takahashi had shown her before, Jujube thought smugly. Tireder. Perhaps she was fleshy in the wrong places, and that's why she wore the loose clothes, to hide herself. But even as Jujube tried to invent as many flaws as she could, she saw the brightness in Ichika's face, the crinkle in the corners of Ichika's eyes—this woman looked smart, lively, happy. Perfect Ichika, with her giving nature, her useful skills, her comfortable clothes, her ambition. Jujube wanted to strangle her.

After he had finished dissecting Ichika's letter and photo, Jujube waited for Mr. Takahashi to ask her how she was. She did not know how she would answer—there were not enough words to describe the depths of her pain, the gnawing she felt constantly in her chest, as though a rat were chewing away at her insides, reminding her that she, like her family, was not whole anymore.

She decided she would be aloof, answer with quiet confidence, "I am always fine." She looked forward to the crease of concern on his forehead, the one that appeared when he knew she wasn't telling him everything there was to tell. Then maybe she would offer a tidbit or two about what was going on at home, the mania of her mother, the illness of her father, the deep sadness that pressed on everything around her—just enough for sympathy but not so much as to invoke his pity. She would not have Mr. Takahashi pity her.

She waited as he folded Ichika's letter. Then he carefully slipped the letter and photo back into the envelope, smoothing it down against the table, his fingers as lined as his face. He ran the same hand through his hair, nervousness, she assumed, gearing himself up for the difficult conversation he was about to have with her. Anytime now she would be able to deliver her line.

Then Mr. Takahashi picked up his cup, finished his tea, nodded at her, smiled briskly, and without a word, left the teahouse.

CHAPTER NINETEEN

CECILY

Bintang, Kuala Lumpur
1938
Seven years earlier, British-occupied Malaya

Across the world, the German and Japanese advances had become significant. Through the wireless, the residents of Bintang heard tales of the quick sacking of cities, the Japanese breaking through careful Western defenses with ease, of some British commanders surrendering without a fight. Fujiwara told Cecily, eyes shimmering, about the military wins the Japanese accrued, one after the other, their strategies always several steps ahead of their opponents'. Advances that typically took weeks and months now took days.

In the city of Kuala Lumpur, in the town that was Bintang, the English were divided in their opinions. Half were steadfast in their faith in the empire, determined not to let what they perceived as a hoard of slant-eyed savages impact their lives. If anything, the parties and balls became more extravagant; plus, there was the expansive construction of "hill stations"—luxurious getaways in the hills of Malaya where temperatures were cooler due to the higher elevation.

British families would rush for these "out-station" getaways every weekend. But the other half were terrified, whispering that this was the end. They packed up trunks and bags and boarded ships that left Port Lewisham weekly, returning to the damp, cold climates of their youth.

As the year turned over into 1938, the monsoon breathed the last of its storms, then quietened. In its place a leaden humidity arrived. Cecily supposed a new year was to bring new optimism, but she was mostly just tired. Her thighs pasted themselves together uncomfortably as she walked down the Oriental Horizons' corridor.

She had barely pushed through the door when Fujiwara announced, "I'm leaving. They're sending me to China."

Cecily pushed the door closed with her elbow and immediately regretted it; the room felt like an airless void.

"Are you all right?" he asked as she flinched at the pain that coursed up her spine.

She placed a hand on her lower back and dropped herself into a chair with a heavy thud, her loose maternity dress puffing around her. He had arrived before her and was sitting on the floor, his back straight against a wall, the knife creases on his pants flattened against his legs, stretched out in front of him. She had never seen him do this; he was not a casual man, not a man who sat with his feet out on the floors of dingy hotel rooms.

Something had shifted between them again. He had never acknowledged the stormy night when she'd set out in the rain, the same night his wife had not come home and a doctor had appeared at his house with nervous reassurances. He did not ask what she and Lina talked about, did not acknowledge that she and Lina spent nearly every waking hour together when Cecily was not with him.

Their lives, the ones that they had tried so hard to keep separate, had begun overlapping, but it was as though he hoped that by ignoring the realities of their entanglements, by not acknowledging Lina and the babies who were to come, he could pretend nothing had changed.

"What will they have you do in China?" she asked, ignoring his question about her well-being.

"Probably train me, then have me train others so we can be prepared. The stalemate in China is finally moving in our direction. It's so close. I can feel it. Here"—he gestured widely at the air around them—"here, Malaya is next."

She could feel it too. She had always found her body mirroring his excitement, and this time her chest thrummed, overheating her in the already stuffy room. The warmth radiated across her fingertips, tickled through her body pressed uncomfortably into the chair.

But to him she said, "You know your leaving will break her."

Pools of sweat collected behind her knees. She felt two stray drops fall down her left calf, stopping at the ankle. She watched him shift his position on the floor, moving his weight from buttock to buttock as if preparing to stand up. Perhaps she had upset him; she wondered if he was going to get up and leave.

"I can't think about that right now," he said. He flicked his eyes to the carpet and then back at Cecily. She wondered if she imagined the shine of remorse that filtered through. He leaned back heavily against the wall. "It's the next step, Cecily. We have to take it. There's no other choice."

We. Even now, all these years later, it still gave her a jolt of pleasure when he referred to them as a single unit.

"I know."

This time she was not shocked. He had left before, and she had known the likelihood that he would have to leave again was high. But instead of simply vanishing, as he had done before, he had told her this time—it meant they had grown and evolved, co-conspirators, even partners, now. Still, perhaps it had been naive of her to assume that this moment would be simpler, that their lives would stay the same, unencumbered by the new layers connecting them: a woman they shared, children they could share. He had been unattached when they met. She cringed, remembering how she had been back then: the rawness of her desire, how she had wanted him, how girlish and simple her lust had been. She opened her mouth, almost formed, "What will happen to the baby?" But then she swallowed the words, pressed them down like an uncomfortable cough. It was not the time.

Instead, she asked, "What do you think the new world will look like?"

She watched him closely. He inhaled, pressed down the creases on his pants. "I imagine our world so self-contained that we do not rely on the West. Japan will lead Asia into a new era of modernization. Things will be faster. People will be more productive. There will be economic growth, more prosperity for everyone. We will eliminate exploitation, no more dangerous mines for children to drown in, no more laborers breaking their back in the estates. Eventually Malaya could even function as an autonomous country, coexist peacefully with Japan. Can you imagine it? Your country led by someone born within the borders of Malaya? As long as you have been alive, you have been ruled. Japan offers a new future for your country, one you cannot even imagine!" He stopped as though surprised by the ferocity of his own words. Then he looked at the wall, seemingly embarrassed.

Your country. Cecily knew she should not be surprised that he did not refer to Malaya as his country; he served the emperor and had always been proud of his Japanese heritage. But still, it stung. Did this mean that Fujiwara planned to leave Malaya as soon as the Japanese arrived? And would she go with him? Fujiwara's vision was political, economic, ideological. When Cecily couldn't sleep at night, her back aching from the baby, Gordon snoring softly next to her, she too imagined the future. But she was ashamed to describe her fantasies to him; they were far more commonplace, domestic, even. She dreamed of presiding over parties at Fujiwara's side, his eyes crinkling as he watched the children laugh. She dreamed of sitting next to him as they discussed strategies and legislation. She dreamed of opportunities for her children, for Jujube, already so brilliant, to go to university and become a doctor, a scientist, a woman with a vision not limited by her sex. Cecily shook her head. She should dream bigger, as he did. Here she was, thinking about Jujube's education, when she could be thinking of the education and prosperity of an entire nation.

She swallowed, reminded herself to focus. "How long will you be in China?"

"I don't know." He was back to his terse self. He sighed as though his outburst had exhausted him.

"Will you tell her?"

He closed his eyes for a beat too long, his lids twitching, a microexpression she had never encountered but understood. Determination. He was moving forward, shedding distractions, remembering what mattered, reminding her. "Cecily, this is everything we ever hoped for."

Maybe she wasn't that simple girl who talked and schemed and dreamed, the earnest woman who once watched a man lit by the moon tell her about a future that had seemed unimaginable. And yet it was impossible not to feel the vibrations of his excitement, the swell of the moment coursing toward them both, an idea so close to becoming solid, true. And as on that night, for a moment, it was just the two of them, unencumbered by the commitments of family, of futures, of Lina.

"Everything we hoped for," she repeated to Fujiwara. The air in the room thickened, and a sheen of sweat shone on her upper lip. The pinched muscle in her back twitched.

—

Fujiwara disappeared on one of those cloudy days that Malayan people liked—when it didn't rain but the temperature was cool enough that one could loiter in the street. A tiny breeze cooled the tops of arms, swished through errant hair. Children played; people conversed. And that night, as the sun set and the mosquitoes began their buzzing chorus, Lina burst into Cecily and Gordon's house, hair askew, feet falling out of gray slippers that were too small for her.

"Cecily!" Lina screamed. "Bingley didn't come home. He has never not come home before!"

Gordon shot up so quickly that he bumped his knees under the dining table. "Stop screaming," he hissed at Lina. "You're being hysterical."

Fujiwara had not told Cecily the exact day he planned to leave. "Better if I just go quietly," he'd said, and Cecily had wanted to ask, better for whom? But she had not pressed him. She knew he was right, it was too risky, and there was nothing she could've done to prevent the frantic terror she now saw roiling through Lina's face. She took a deep breath and pulled Lina to her chest.

Gordon said, "He's a busy man, Lina. Maybe he got stuck doing . . . What is it he does again for work? Selling things?" But above Lina's head that bobbed as quiet sobs pushed into Cecily's chest, Gordon wriggled his eyebrows. "Another woman?" he mouthed.

Cecily gritted her teeth and pressed soothing hands into Lina's shoulders.

Perhaps the real victim in all this was Gordon, ignorant of every pulsing tension around him, unaware just how quickly the world he idolized was going to change, how the child she carried might not even be his child. She should pity him; he deserved her compassion. But all she wanted to do in that moment was slam her knuckles into his face.

Just you wait, she thought. Her body, having steeled itself for days, felt prepared for battle, sharp and vicious, ready to pounce on whatever came next.

When word got out—and it got out quickly, because Gordon wouldn't stop talking about it—that Bingley Chan had disappeared seemingly overnight, no one seemed to question his motives or his safety. To them, it was all Lina's fault. She drove him away, she must've done something, she wasn't enough. After all, to lose a husband once might be bad luck. But to lose two? That was damning carelessness bordering on suspicious.

"She was never good enough for him," Lady Worthing said.

"Haiya, she didn't take care of herself during pregnancy, can you blame him?" Mrs. Low said.

Cecily was angered by the virulent gossip that surrounded her friend. The neighbors, British and local alike, lingered around the Chan house, trying to catch a glimpse of the distraught Lina. They whispered across fences and cornered Cecily at the store with prying questions. They tried to "drop by" with soups and flowers and interloping eyes and feigned offense when no one answered the door. Cecily found it all disgusting. Their tacit acceptance of Lina, with all her parties and prettiness, had been a masquerade for their envy. Now they felt far too comfortable letting their true feelings show.

First Lina worried that something had happened to Bingley, the same way it had to Kapitan Yap. But a second devastation was in store for her when she realized he had packed up most of his essential belongings, leaving dusty gaps on shelves where his things had been. Once she accepted that he had left of his own volition, she seesawed between despair and attempts at logic.

Cecily existed in a strange in-between space. It was surprisingly easy for her to be two people, to not just compartmentalize but truly feel the feelings she needed, to exist as the woman between Lina and Fujiwara. By day she stayed steadfast by Lina's side, listening as Lina recounted her conversations with Bingley again and again, trying to find clues. Lina talked in circles, repeating the same futilities over and over—he would never leave without saying anything, he must have business in Europe, he would be back for the baby. With Lina, Cecily relived and analyzed every gruff statement, every turned face, every unmet gaze, every eye-roll, every lip curl of displeasure.

By night, however, there was a second Cecily, the woman who was filled with adrenaline at the thought that *this was it,* the future that she and Fujiwara had dared to dream about, that it was all coming to pass. This Cecily spent hours tuning her wireless radio to the right frequency and standing in the kitchen with it pressed to her ear as loud and excitable newsmen expressed bewilderment at the pockets of rebellion and rise of anti-colonial sentiment percolating throughout the empire. This Cecily lay in bed at night wondering where Fujiwara could be—lying at the stern of a ship, gazing at the moon, the way she was? Or crouched in a muddy trench somewhere, directing an army? Sometimes the anticipation was so great she felt her skin itch. Her dreams became deliciously violent and vivid— she dreamed of smug white women being dragged out of Bintang by their parasols, of the resident, Frank Lewisham, being stripped out of his stuffy white suit as he trembled, quivering in his formless underwear, of the cavalry of uniformed men she imagined Fujiwara leading. She conjured scenarios in which she and Fujiwara laughed together as they surveyed the remnants of The Club, demolished to the studs, the beacon of British manhood stripped bare. These imagined victories would wake her up slick with sweat and want, fingers reaching around her stomach, taut between her legs.

Sometimes she even tried looking beyond these vindications, wondered what her life would be once this was all done, but those visions were fuzzier. She realized Fujiwara had only ever spoken to her of ideas; she wished she'd had the presence of mind to ask him more. Perhaps he would announce to his superiors that it was she who had made it all happen—hail her as his partner and inspiration. Perhaps he would burst into her house like a conquering hero, press her against a wall, his desire worn openly, while Gordon watched, pathetic and betrayed. But these scenarios all seemed unrealistic, ridiculous, even. At times little jolts of fear would skitter through her—she worried that when the Japanese were in place, life would become ordinary again, filled with the small fanfares of family:

children to be tamed, a husband to be tended to, the tragedies of dull domesticity rearing their ugliness once more. On these doubt-filled days, she wished she could suspend time, live forever in the bright moments of her and Fujiwara's imminent triumph, adrenaline coursing through her.

Then, as quickly as it started, the neighbors' interest in Lina died off. As their curiosity waned, Lina was simply cast out from social circles. Gordon urged Cecily to back away as well, worried that Lina's second social failure would rub off on them like a rash.

But Cecily ignored him. Every day she continued to trek over to Lina's house with food. Every day she listened to Lina's circular conversations. Every day she consoled, comforted, and hugged. And every day she wondered how much longer she had to wait before Fujiwara brought a whole new world to her.

CHAPTER TWENTY

—

ABEL

Kanchanaburi Labor Camp on the Burma/Thailand border
August 29, 1945
Japanese-occupied Malaya

When Abel was young, his mother had taught him that in history, leaders emerged in vacuums and chaos. She said it was because at the end of the day, men just wanted someone to tell them what to do. Abel had always disagreed with this premise—he hated it when someone told him what to do, and sometimes, even when he agreed with the instruction, he felt compelled to defy its instructor. When he told her this, she had laughed and said, "That just means you're going to be the leader."

It was a powerful thing, to understand the strength and bearing of one's charisma before one was old enough to put a name to the feeling. Abel learned that he had power, that something about him imprinted on people when he entered rooms, that they would talk about him long after he departed, that he was always someone people remembered. He was never old enough to understand the reason—after all, he was not the most athletic, or the funniest, or the smartest (though, depending on whom you asked, they might say he was the handsomest, but this was not a fact universally agreed upon)—however, at school he was the pack leader: the one whom people shifted over to accommodate, the one whom all the boys wished they were, the one who got away with mischief. One of his teachers who had let him off after a particularly egregious prank called him a charming rascal. He had asked his mother what that meant.

His mother had turned to him, smiling that indulgent smile she reserved only for him. "Your teacher is mistaking charisma for charm," she had said.

"Ka-rish-ma?" Abel rolled the word around his tongue, feeling its unfamiliar arc trapping saliva.

"Close enough." She chuckled, tugging his ear. And then, thinking he was out of earshot, "I knew someone like that once."

"Who, Ma?" he'd asked.

She flushed, the tip of her ears pinker than he'd ever seen. "Nothing. No one. Just a man I used to know."

Of course, it was this very need to defy and lead that had gotten him in trouble at camp in the first place. It was difficult for him to comply in the way that others did, to lay tracks, to carry heavy loads at an even pace, to be quiet and stay out of sight. It astounded him that the others just accepted the simple hierarchy of the camp: that the Japanese were enslavers and the boys enslaved. But, where at school his charisma was celebrated and other boys followed his lead, at camp it meant the boys were terrified of him. "You're going to get us all killed," Rama said to him early on. But charisma and defiance, like everything else, can be beaten out of someone. Every animal, no matter how fierce, how feral, can become a cowering shadow of itself if stoned sufficiently. Every animal can be silenced—in Abel's case, with the bitter sweetness of toddy.

"You used to be different," said Freddie the day after the incident with Akiro in the theater shed. Abel could smell the stench of shit around him, realizing too late that it was his own. The last thing he remembered was the sound of cheering, of kicking, of bones breaking, then the sweet darkness overpowering him.

"How could you think I could do that," Abel said to Freddie, but the words wouldn't form in his mouth. "Leave me alone!" he tried again, but Freddie just shook his head and nodded at someone in the distance. One of the boys came running. Abel felt the cold sharpness of water drenching him, then bucket after bucket continuing to stream down his body as the other boys, at Freddie's instruction, washed away the shit, his shit, and any last shred of dignity he had.

—

At first Abel had assumed that he would be treated as a pariah at camp after refusing to kill Master Akiro, that the boys would come and kick and punch him the same way they had Master Akiro, until he too begged for mercy. But the reality was, in many ways, worse. They began to treat him as some sort of fallen soldier, something weak, to be guarded, to be shut away, to be treated with gentleness. Every day he found food by his head when he woke up. Every time he got up to empty his bladder, several heads would whip around to make sure he didn't fall, and when he did stumble, which was often, someone was always there to offer an arm, lift him off his ass, pull him to his feet. Before, when this role had been held by Freddie, Abel had been able to endure the constancy of his friend's assistance. It had been calming, even, to have Freddie there when he woke from one of his drunken torpors, the soothing tone of Freddie's voice, a reminder that he, Abel, was still all right. But now, like a commander surrounded by lieutenants, Freddie seemed to have delegated that duty to every boy at camp. The other boys stared at Abel with pity, hushed their voice when he walked by, patted his back like he was an injured animal. The humiliation was devastating, to have his weaknesses laid bare and acknowledged in this way. It made Abel want to sink into himself and hide but also to break every consoling hand that patted him.

Through the whispers, Abel learned that after the deed was done, Freddie had instructed the boys to bury Akiro's body near the banana tree. The location was not random. Many of the boys believed in the folklore that banana trees were haunted by the spirit of a vengeful woman. This meant the boys generally stayed away from the banana tree at the camp, convinced that the spirit of an angry, dead ghost lady would jump out and cut off their genitals. Freddie, Abel supposed, had thought it a suitable punishment for Akiro to be haunted in the afterlife by a ghost intent on mutilation. Abel didn't have the same fear. His mother had raised him on a diet of history and science, so folk stories of ghost women did not frighten him. That banana tree had been his respite from everyone when he needed shade, solitude, silence, a place to drink without hateful stares. But now even the tree had abandoned him. The thought of resting near a decomposing Akiro in his shallow grave was horrifying.

The Japanese officers assigned to the camp gave the boys a wide berth. Abel didn't know if they assumed that Akiro had just deserted, like many others before him, or if they suspected or even knew what had happened to him. But whatever that truth, the officers stayed away, cloistered in their quarters, one or two emerging at night with stuffed packs, sneaking away, hoping for a better future on the road.

As the Japanese soldiers continued their desertion, supplies at camp—food and otherwise—were being depleted and not replenished. Before, trucks would arrive every few weeks with sacks of rice that the boys would have to balance on their backs and haul into the grounds without spilling a single grain or risk a beating. But these days, nothing came. At first the boys raided some of the deserted soldiers' quarters and were delighted to find unusual Japanese snacks and delicacies that they had never seen. They would sit in circles after their talent shows, each nibbling a bite of a crunchy alien snack, some nodding in delight, others screwing their faces in disgust at the unfamiliar tastes. But then those snacks ran out too. Some of the kitchen boys were enterprising, able to scavenge for herbs and plant matter from the roots and trees at the camp, but mostly they were hungry, and without the strictly enforced rationing by the Japanese, the boys reached for seconds and thirds, and soon food supplies began to run dangerously low. All of this Abel knew from whispering that he didn't partake in. He ate once a day now, because the less he ate, the quicker he was able to get drunk. Drink was the one thing that seemed not to go dry—crates and crates of toddy were discovered in the Japanese quarters, a fact for which Abel was grateful.

It was in this barren state of leadership that Freddie emerged, skinny, soft-spoken Freddie, who was, before, every Japanese soldier's target for a beating. Somehow this same Freddie became the leader of the lost boys of the Kanchanaburi camp. Even through Abel's haze, it was amazing to witness: Freddie set a schedule so there would always be three boys as sentries to see if someone other than one of their own was approaching. Before the last of the Japanese had left, Freddie had instructed one of the boys to steal a transistor radio that crackled with staticky Japanese words every few hours. Most of the boys did not speak Japanese, but the ones who did translated as best they could, extracting words from the static: "Bomb." "Surrender." "America."

The reaction at the camp was mixed.

"We're going to be saved!" some of them said.

"We're going to starve," said others.

"We're forgotten," said Freddie. "Which means we need to take care of ourselves."

They debated, voices drowning one another out, flies and heat buzzing, the air feral.

"Our food's running out," said Rama, patting his stomach ruefully. "I don't know how we get some more."

"The mudslides are getting worse," said someone else. "It's like we're being washed away."

Without work to do, without tracks to lay, the days at the camp grew longer and lazier. A restless energy bounced off the walls—the boys, used to terror and the exertion of finding ways to survive, now seemed purposeless. This excess nervous energy turned the boys into fighters. Every day, it seemed, someone was beating someone up for the slightest of offenses, the stupidest of reasons—you stole my food, you looked at me wrong, you cheated at a game. The scuffles ranged in severity. Though most of them were simple fights that left no one worse off than a couple bruises, occasionally someone would be lying on the ground bleeding, wounded, gasping for air. It was ironic, Abel thought, that all the torture, all the pain they had feared and dreamed about rebelling against, had turned the boys into the very thing the Japanese had wanted: men kicked into submission.

But he didn't need to worry about himself. To escape the pitying stares, Abel drank, and the other boys left him alone. Abel supposed he should be grateful; he was not in any condition to fight anyone. But once in a while, he wished someone would push him around. To avoid him was to assume he would lose, to assume he was so broken that he wasn't even worth considering as an opponent.

"I need you," said Freddie softly to him one morning. It was early, and somewhere a rooster crowed. The sky was still dark, the crest of orange far in the distance, the sun, like Abel, unable to lift itself. Abel was sitting outside the boys' quarters, his back held up only by the pile of wood behind him. He was like a hunted animal now, hiding inside, under, and around structures, hoping not to be found. But of course, Freddie had found him.

"Go away," Abel said. He didn't want or need a lecture. He couldn't look at Freddie without feeling the cringe of shame rushing through his body; it made him sick.

"I need to talk to someone. I don't know what to do. We need a plan. I think we're in trouble."

Freddie sounded calm, but his eyes, the familiar blue that once comforted Abel, betrayed the still overtones of his voice. They darted around in an unfamiliar way, holding, behind his irises, the anxious responsibility of nearly a hundred boys at camp.

"You don't have to take care of them," said Abel crossly. "Who died and made you Jesus of this camp?"

Freddie winced as if struck. "What happened to you? Why have you become like . . . this?"

Abel wanted to ask, "Like what?" but then he decided he didn't care what Freddie thought anymore. He took a sip from his bottle instead, felt the toddy slide through his empty stomach, leaving a slick burn. Abel imagined a shiny golden pathway glowing through his body.

But Freddie didn't say anything else, which infuriated Abel. He was sick of everyone protecting him, and the thought that Freddie was protecting not just his body but his feelings was too much to endure. He didn't need protecting, much less from skinny Freddie.

"LIKE WHAT?" Abel asked, surprised at the volume and clarity of his own voice. Let Freddie insult him. He'd show Freddie what was coming.

"We need to leave," said Freddie, voice barely a sigh. "Before it's too late."

For what? Abel thought. For whom? But by the time he'd collected his thoughts, Freddie had walked away.

—

The next couple of days were a hive of activity, and Freddie, of course, was at the center of it all. Abel watched incredulously as the same boys who were beating each other up just a few days ago became organized, forming assembly lines that created packs of supplies tossed in piles. Each pack contained food, water, rags that Abel assumed were for bandaging wounds, and other items he couldn't quite see. Freddie marched around as though he owned the place, supervising—more in this pack, work quicker, only essentials, *we need to move it,* and so on.

"What's happening?" Abel asked Vellu, who was trying to shove what looked like an accordion into his pack.

"We're gonna get out of here. Freddie says we have to go soon, get on the road."

The road, Abel thought resentfully. He'd thought of it first. A week ago, he'd wondered to himself if the boys should revolt against the Japanese and leave, make their way home. But drunken ruminations didn't count for anything. Abel supposed he should help—he agreed in principle that they needed to go, that any time now, some Japanese tanker was going to bust through the fences and shoot them all; they were not needed anymore. But these days even the basic act of standing made him dizzy. Sometimes, if he chose a bad spot to settle for the day, he found himself in the middle of the activities. The boys walked around him, carrying supplies, chatting loudly, and the buzzing stung his brain, made his head hurt, frustrated him. Occasionally someone would mutter, "Come on," and pull him by the armpit to a spot out of the thoroughfare. But mostly they ignored him; his drunken moaning rendering him useless to the process and therefore invisible.

Two days into their frenzied packing, Rama burst from the outhouse, his pants askew, clutching the transistor radio he had been listening to.

"Emperor Hirohito is going to surrender Malaya!" he shouted, his voice ringing through the camp.

Voices began shouting in earnest. "What do we do, where do we go, will they rescue us, who will rescue us?"

A breathlessness filled the camp. And as usual, through the rising tide of panic, the voice of reason.

"We'll leave tomorrow. We have enough packs." Freddie, his voice so quiet and calm that the boys were mollified. Only Abel detected a quiver at the end.

CHAPTER TWENTY-ONE

—

JASMIN

Bintang, Kuala Lumpur
August 29, 1945
Japanese-occupied Malaya

On the thirteenth day of Jasmin's stay with General Fujiwara, Yuki did not turn up at their wheelbarrow meeting spot. Earlier that afternoon, Jasmin had crept out of the general's house unseen, skipped her way along the road until she reached the WELCOME sign. The station had seemed a little busier than usual, feverish, and more soldiers were clomping around in their loud boots, but Jasmin paid them no heed. People did not notice her, and if they did, they did not care. She immediately noticed that the sheet was not thrown over the wheelbarrow per usual. Instead, it hung askew on the side, exposing half the brilliant blue of the cart. At first she'd thought that Yuki was playing a prank and pounced into the sheet laughing, assuming that Yuki was hiding underneath it, waiting to jump out on her. But the sheet had fluttered in its emptiness and fallen to the ground. Jasmin climbed into the wheelbarrow and waited. Yuki was just late, she reasoned, and would come by very soon. She pulled the sheet over the wheelbarrow, as Yuki usually did, and, as the moist, warm air unfurled around her, curled up and fell asleep. Nothing to worry about. Yuki would be back.

"Mini. Mini."

Jasmin's eyes flew open. She stretched her jaw to yawn and realized she was hot and thirsty, her tongue stuck to the roof of her mouth. "Yuki?"

Yuki was crouched in front of her in the wheelbarrow, spine curved into itself. There were large raised welts across Yuki's arms.

"Painful," Yuki said, just the one word. Tears leaked out of her eyes. Her nightgown rose with movement, and Jasmin saw a long jagged cut bisecting Yuki's left thigh.

Jasmin looked away from her friend. She couldn't bear it. "What happened, Yuki?"

"An uncle beat me today."

Yuki fell against Jasmin, who put her arms around her friend.

"Can we go away?" Yuki sobbed into Jasmin's arm. "I'm so scared."

They clung to each other, Jasmin's heart as broken as Yuki's body.

When the two girls got to the general's house that afternoon, they were able to slip in quietly, unnoticed. Jasmin could hear the houseboy pounding something with a mortar and pestle in the back, perhaps ginger or cili padi or another ingredient for dinner. The rhythmic sound as the round bottom of the pestle drummed against the mortar felt like a reassuring heartbeat to Jasmin. She was terrified, bringing Yuki into the general's house this way; she knew that the general wouldn't like it and that he wouldn't like Yuki. But she didn't know what else to do. She couldn't bear Yuki's sobs, and she knew that no number of silly faces, no jokes, no amount of giggling would make it better. She just needed to get Yuki away from the bad place with the dead-eyed girls and half-dressed soldiers, and she didn't know where else to go. Yuki had been silent walking over, leaning on Jasmin, breathing hard, as though it took all her energy to make the little steps. It was a far cry from the first time they had run side by side, when it had been Jasmin who'd struggled to keep up. Yuki's swollen eye had stopped bleeding, but a blue bruise had begun to bloom. It made Jasmin flinch every time she looked at her.

Now that they were at the general's house, Yuki stared around in shock. "This house is so big!" she whispered. "You get to live here?"

"Shhhh," Jasmin whispered, terrified that the houseboy would hear them.

They crept, hand in hand, to Jasmin's room. At the room door, Yuki stared, eyes raised, and Jasmin recognized the same awe on Yuki's face that she'd felt when the general had first led her into this room. Used to only the thin mattress that she had shared with her sister, Jasmin had been amazed by the presence of the bed, a thick mattress laid atop a sturdy four-poster structure. She had never seen anything so grand. She remembered sinking into the sheets and wondering if this was what fairies felt like in the clouds. And then she had slept so soundly that when she woke up the next morning, her face had felt creased.

The girls clambered onto the bed and Yuki lay down, spreading her arms like a winged bird. Jasmin noted that Yuki's grubby neck and wrists, and the blood from the cuts on her face, left small brown marks on the sheets, little stains spreading like germs. She frowned but didn't say anything, just lay down next to Yuki.

"I want to stay with you forever," Yuki mumbled into Jasmin's hair.

Jasmin bit her lip. This was what she had worried would happen, that Yuki would see how wonderful the general's house was and ask to stay.

"I don't know, Yuki," she stammered.

"You can just ask the general! There are so many rooms and places in this house!" Yuki exclaimed, as though it were the best idea in the world. "Then we can play every day!"

The conversation made Jasmin's stomach knot up. She loved Yuki, she really did. Yuki felt like half of her; when they were together, Jasmin felt complete, and when they were apart, she felt like she was less, pages flying loose and unbound in the wind. And she knew that something bad was happening where Yuki lived, and she wanted to help; she had to save Yuki, this half of her heart. But she also knew that the general would not appreciate scarred-face Yuki, that he would not want people in his space, and that only she, Jasmin, was special. She knew he hated dirt, hated disorder. She'd seen him berate the houseboy when he'd found a stain on his uniform. That night she heard the houseboy scrubbing the uniform for hours, the sound of swishing water lulling her to sleep.

Jasmin worried that bringing Yuki to the general, with her smells, and her dirt, and her loud voice, would turn him against her, and that if the general no longer favored her, he would stop telling her the stories, that this big comfortable bed would no longer be hers. And then what would she do? Where would she go? She would need time to explain things to him. She knew that Yuki couldn't stay, that she would have to get Yuki to leave the bed and the house and go back to the scary place. But she would take care of that later. For the moment, she reached for Yuki's hand and pointed at the tent of mosquito net, neatly piled above their head by the houseboy, the netting making an erratic pattern. "Yuki, what do you think that looks like? I think it's like an elephant's backside!"

Yuki exploded into cackling laughter and closed her eyes. Within minutes, she was asleep, and soon Jasmin felt herself drifting off as well, the musky smell of Yuki's greasy hair a shield around them.

CHAPTER TWENTY-TWO

CECILY

Bintang, Kuala Lumpur
1938
Seven years earlier, British-occupied Malaya

Cecily's baby arrived first, brown and bald, on a hot, clear January afternoon. When the midwife handed the baby to her, Cecily gazed at the little girl's red face and tried to discern her lineage, turned the swaddled child this way and that, looking for an indication that there was any bit of Fujiwara in her. She couldn't tell; how could you tell? she wondered. Much to Gordon's irritation, Lina burst into the house, pushing past the midwife, surprisingly light-footed despite the advancement of her own pregnancy.

"What are you doing here?" Gordon asked, mortified. He was still concerned that the brush that had tarred Lina socially would come for them too.

"Cecily! Oh, this beautiful little girl, look at her face," Lina cooed. It made Cecily smile; this was the first time she had seen any of the old joy in Lina since Fujiwara had left. "What will you call her?" Lina asked, pressing a soft finger against the baby's fat arm.

"We're thinking about naming her after my mother," Gordon said, pushing past Lina to reach for the baby. "Agatha. We can call her Aggie for short."

"No, no, no," Lina mouthed to Cecily behind Gordon's back. Even through her fatigue, Cecily chuckled; she hated the name too. The brown baby wriggled in the swaddle, which made Lina giggle. "See, she doesn't like it either," Lina whispered to Cecily when Gordon turned away.

Displeased with all the noise, Gordon left the room. Lina hauled herself onto Cecily's bed and lay down.

"What about yours?" Cecily asked.

"Well, if he is a boy, Bingley wants to call him Aston." Wants, Cecily noted. Lina had used the present tense. As though Fujiwara were still around.

"Aston? Like the English car?"

Lina's chin trembled. "Lately," she whispered, "I've been hoping it's a girl. I don't know if I can—if I know how to raise a boy . . . on my own."

Cecily reached under the thin blanket, slipped her palm over Lina's hand, and held it.

"I'm sorry . . ." Lina gripped her hand tightly. "It's your day. I won't bring my nonsense in here."

A pause filled the air. Cecily's baby coughed the tiniest of coughs, and Lina's face relaxed, eyes softening as she watched the baby move.

"What about flowers?" Lina said. "Rose?"

Cecily pushed the name around in her head. "Too overpowering."

"Lily?"

"There was a stuck-up girl at school named Lily. I hated her."

Lina chuckled. "I'm sure she deserved it."

"How about Jacaranda?" Cecily said.

"Absolutely not," Lina said. "You are not good at this at all! You're lucky you have me here."

And in the distance, the sun began its quiet dip, and still they lay there whispering to each other and to the baby. It felt just for the moment like everything was as it used to be, that maybe, just maybe, things would be all right.

Lina's baby arrived five days later, in the middle of the night, at the beginning of a lunar cycle when no moon was visible in the sky.

When Cecily received the midwife's terse, alarming message, Gordon had protested loudly and angrily. "It's so late at night. People will talk. Please, wait till morning."

But Cecily ignored him. Something about the message, scratched in uneven writing on a torn scrap of paper, unnerved her.

she's asking for you.

When Cecily arrived, the Chan house was eerily quiet, the unforgiving white from the overhead lighting reflecting off the hair follicles on her arm.

"Are you family?" A midwife emerged from the bedroom, a small woman who looked dry everywhere except on her cheeks, where the light reflected cruelly off oily pimples. "Are you family?" she repeated sternly. "I wanted to send for family." Cecily shook her head. "Will there be family?" she asked again.

Cecily looked away, unwilling to dignify the woman's probing with a direct answer. "I'm a friend. The closest she has. What's going on? Why did you send for me?"

The oily midwife spun on her heel without a word, and Cecily took this as an indication to follow.

Lina's bedroom smelled of blood, sweat, and exhaustion, not unlike how her own had just a few days ago. Still, Cecily recoiled as the strength of the smell hit her. It seemed to have absorbed into everything, made her feel nauseated and claustrophobic.

Lina's head was visible above a sea of blankets, hair sticking to her face, which was shining with sweat, eyes closed. When Cecily got closer, she noticed the unhappy paleness of Lina's face, the bluish hue of her chapped lips.

"Is it over? Where is the baby?" Cecily said.

Something in the pungent room creaked, and Cecily looked around in alarm. Everything was too still. When her child had been born, the house had been alive with activity, a frenetic energy swerving through the air, the children and other family members begging for updates in between her cries and contractions. But here in Lina's shimmering white house, a soundless heat obscured everything.

"Is something wrong?" she repeated.

The midwife gestured to a younger woman, who handed a swaddled bundle to Cecily. As she reached for the baby, her fingers brushed the woman's, which were cold and clammy; she did not meet Cecily's gaze.

The baby girl's face looked crushed, as though only one side of her face had remembered to inflate. The other side was dented in, ridged and mottled. She shifted in her swaddle, closed eyes fluttering. The eye on the scarred side of her face bulged.

Cecily sat down in a chair, not trusting her legs. "What did you do?" she hissed at the midwife. "Did you do this to the child?"

"The child was suffocating," the midwife said, voice low and shaky. She pointed at Lina. "She kept saying she needed to wait for her husband. She insisted. She kept holding the child in."

"Are you blaming her?" Cecily felt her eyes flash. It took all her self-control not to raise her voice in the rust-smelling room. Behind her, Lina stirred.

"I had to use forceps to pull the baby out," the midwife said.

"Is this the reason for the face? Or was she already like this?" Cecily demanded. It horrified her, the thought that the girl was already rotten inside, charred by the sadness of the life she hadn't even begun to live.

The oily midwife ignored Cecily's question. "I did everything I could. There was too much bleeding."

"Wait, do you mean—?" Cecily sat on the edge of the bed. She brushed her fingers over Lina's tired face, felt alarmed at how hot her cheeks were. She realized then why she had been summoned: not for the disfigured child but for Lina.

"How long does she have?" Cecily steeled her voice to prevent a telltale quiver.

The midwife looked away; her shoulders raised unevenly as though she were ready to defend herself. "It's not long now."

"He didn't come, Cecily," Lina murmured from the bed. "I wanted him to. I prayed for him to. I knew he wouldn't, but it's not—it's not bad to hope, is it? I tried to hope. For her."

"Shhh," Cecily said. As she handed the swaddled bundle to Lina, she could feel her heart splintering at the wretchedness of it all: Lina and this broken baby girl, the worst kind of collateral damage.

Lina stroked the side of the girl's face that was a smooth, unmarked, glossy cream.

Cecily made for the door. "You stay, Lina. I'm going to get a real doctor. They can't just leave you like this."

"No," Lina whispered. Her eyes opened. "Come here. Please."

Cecily returned to the bed, held her hand to Lina's cheek, the contrast between the milky white cheek and her brown-hued hand reminding her of the time long ago when Lina had pulled Cecily's hand into her own, then pulled Cecily through the party. Cecily recalled the wonder she had for this woman who seemingly felt no shame, who lit up every room.

"Don't go. The girls can be sisters. Come, we can think up names," Lina said weakly, patting a clean space on the bed. Seeing her friend hesitate, she said, "Cecily, how can you still be calling your daughter 'baby'? It's been five days." Lina chuckled, then closed her eyes from the exertion. "Please sit with me."

Cecily blinked through the tears she hadn't realized were slipping down her face. "Daisy?" she whispered.

"Too British." Lina's hand, which had been stroking her baby, sank heavily onto the blanket as though the effort had become too much.

"Hyacinth?" said Cecily.

"Do you—?" Lina's breath was slow and labored. "Do you want the girl to grow up to become a romance novelist?" Still, she smiled a small smile, a sliver of sunlight in the oppressive room.

Cecily blinked furiously; the tears were obscuring everything now. Her heart cleaved from a pain so great it made her shake. "Jasmine?"

"Jasmine." Lina rolled the name around her tongue. "I love

it. It's a quiet flower that smells like sunshine. You should . . . You should take it." Then she reached for Cecily's hand, held it in a grip so tight it hurt her fingers. "I'm so tired, Cecily. Please, you'll watch my girl until he comes back, won't you?"

―

Death took much longer than Cecily expected. For the next few hours, they held vigil, she, the midwife, and the midwife's frightened assistant. Lina's breaths slowed into unconsciousness. She lay there, a pale shell, unmoving for hours except for the thin hiss of breath becoming fainter and fainter, until the midwife, holding Lina's limp wrist in her hand, took the pulse and finally declared her gone. There was something indecent about the prolonged nature of it all—it felt as though they watched Lina's soul strip itself until there was nothing left but the most naked of humiliations.

"If you're not family . . . ," the midwife said, gentler now that they had been forced to spend the intimacy of dying together. "What should I do with the child?"

There was no more need for subterfuge, no more need to exist in the watery place of half-truths between Lina and Fujiwara, no more need to split herself in two anymore. It was time to make a choice. The room sweated, but Cecily knew; she had known the moment she'd walked into this room that reeked of brokenness, she had known the very moment all those years ago, under the white moon, when Fujiwara had told her about the new, brighter world he wanted to build.

"So?" the midwife said, picking up the swaddled bundle from the bed.

Cecily turned to face the wall, picked at the chipped off-white paint, the same color as the broken-faced girl. Then she nodded at the midwife. "I'm not family. I have three of my own. Make the arrangements. Other arrangements."

There had never been any other way, Cecily thought. Behind her, the scar-faced baby cooed.

CHAPTER TWENTY-THREE

CECILY

Bintang, Kuala Lumpur
August 29, 1945
Japanese-occupied Malaya

When the Japanese first arrived in December 1941, Gordon had been defiant, still reeling from the revelation that the charming merchant they'd known as Bingley Chan had turned out to be a conquering Japanese general. When the military convoy drove through town, Gordon refused to come out at first, squashing himself determinedly into a round rattan chair. "No," he said. "I will not bow to that two-faced crook."

It was only when Cecily explained, first patiently, then angrily, that it was necessary to show allegiance to the ruler of the moment, that Gordon did not have to jump for joy but did need to think about his future and that of their family, that he joined her on their doorstep, eyes trained to the ground, refusing to watch the approaching parade.

After that, for weeks, Gordon would gather with old colleagues at one another's houses, sipping what was left of their whiskey stores and making up strategies for how the British would retake Malaya from the Japanese.

"The Japanese have no ships, so it should be a marine approach," proclaimed Andrew Carvalho from next door.

"We are too important to the Crown for them to leave us to a bunch of barbarians!" Mr. Lingam said.

"In fact, I have it on good authority that MI6 has dispatched spies who will defeat the Japanese from within!" announced Mr. Tan, his voice loud and full of conviction.

What did he know about spies? thought Cecily spitefully.

But as the whiskey supplies dwindled, food became scarcer, and more of their British counterparts were captured and sent to Changi Prison, the men began to fear that they would be next. Stories of inhumane torture used against suspected traitors began to reach them. For Gordon, the last straw was when the Japanese soldiers came for the resident, Lewisham, and dragged the man away, arms tied behind him like a hog. Cecily watched Gordon's lips twist in agony, watching the white man he admired so much be reduced to begging for his life in his underclothes. In the days that followed, Gordon, whom she could not ever get to shut up, barely finished a sentence.

In fact, as the years passed, both she and Gordon changed. In Cecily, the change manifested as erratic conduct. She chattered incessantly or blasted around the house in fits of productivity—cooking and cleaning and mending—then abandoned her tasks when she felt the unbearable darkness taking over, leaving behind the detritus of home life: bits of meat lying half cooked in oil, clothes half washed in the bucket, jars of pickled vegetables open and covered with ants.

The worst of it was the rage. Cecily could feel it bubbling up inside her, coils of anger that bloomed outward from her chest, so strong she could feel the heat in her toes and in her ears, and even when she tried to control it and press it down, it would rush through her screaming for release. And release she did. Sometimes she wouldn't even remember what terrible things she had said, just the swollen feeling of gratification that followed when the hurt registered on Gordon's or the kids' faces. It was their desolation that stayed with her, so much that she took to her room for days afterward. Like when Gordon had gone to get rations and been able to bring home only a bull's testicles, resulting in the scream of Abel's boyish laughter. She had shouted so loudly her head rang with the echo, watched her son's face color with pain and shock. Later that night she woke up and walked over to her sleeping son to brush his wiry curls off his fair, open face, and had cried for all the pain she could not hold in. She didn't know how to tell them that her anger was not at the things they did but at what she herself had done to make everything the way it was.

While she expanded with rage, Gordon shrank, bags of sagging skin hanging off places that used to be filled out, under his chin, his arms, his eyes. But even more than that, his personhood shrank. Gordon had been a man obsessed with climbing the British institutional and social ladders that had governed their lives. Without those institutions, he was unmoored. Still, unlike Cecily, he did his duty. Every morning he would faithfully make his way to the sheet-metal workshop to which he had been conscripted and return in the evenings with torn-up hands and a bag full of meat rations. But it was as if a switch had been turned off in him. He retreated out of their bed, curled himself on a mat at the far end of their room. Nothing seemed to get through to him; his eyes were shadowed. The only thing that even momentarily tethered Gordon to the world was

Jasmin, who always knew how to crawl into her father's lap and hum an off-key song, which would bring a tiny smile to his drawn, empty face. So when Jasmin ran away, Gordon ceased to exist, his light extinguished completely.

The doctor was shaking his head. "Perhaps," he said, addressing Jujube so he could avoid looking at Cecily, all wild-haired and without undergarments, "it is for the best. More peaceful for him this way."

When the coughing first started, Gordon was worried, would study his just-coughed-on palm or handkerchief for blood, wondering if he had consumption. But when it became habitual, he stopped covering his mouth, just let the coughing fit reach its wheezing, panting conclusion. After a while, the echo of Gordon's cough became as much a sound of their home life as any of the children's voices.

When Jasmin had been gone ten days, Gordon's wheezing had become so bad that his lips took on a purplish tinge. Her husband was an academic man meant for clerical work and numbers; he was not suited to the forced labor; his work at the sheet-metal workshop had taken its toll—gone was the man who used to irritate Cecily with his plumpness and pomp, and in his place, a tired, coughing ghost. And then Gordon slipped into a coma. It was so uneventful, so without fanfare, that Cecily knew he could not have planned it.

"What do you mean?" Jujube demanded, always exact, needing the precision of the doctor's words.

Cecily watched her eldest daughter rub her hand harshly over her eyes, not allowing herself even one tear. Unlike her parents, Jujube had not cracked and was the only thing holding their home together. It was she who found ways to keep food on the table, it was she who had called the doctor when she wasn't able to rouse her father, it was she who still, Cecily knew, searched every day for Jasmin. Cecily wanted to reach out and hold her eldest, remind Jujube that she was still a child, that she was allowed to crack, to feel. But Cecily held her arms by her side. Jujube's sorrow, like everything else, was Cecily's fault, and no amount of consolation was going to help.

"His lungs are not working well. It will be less painful this way, and he can be in his own home, resting," the doctor said to Jujube, running two fingers through his hair, refusing to state the obvious. It dawned on Cecily that once again, as she had seven years ago with Lina, she would wait for an innocent to unknowingly cede his life to a cause that she saw now held no more meaning.

"Will my father . . . die?" Jujube asked, blinking rapidly.

"Yes," said Cecily as the doctor said, "Just— just keep him comfortable."

Then the doctor left their stinking, cramped house in a hurry, eyes trained anywhere but at the two women.

In the coma, his sallow face cradled by pillows, his breaths uneven and whistling through parted lips, Gordon looked almost at peace. And maybe he was, Cecily thought. She wished she could switch places with him, wished she could extinguish the horrific realization that her family, once five, was now just Jujube and her.

"Why is this happening?" Jujube whispered. This time she did not rub her eyes quickly enough, and tears escaped them.

Cecily felt the admission on the tip of her tongue, the whole long, tedious story of her betrayal pushing its way through her, her daughter's sorrow compelling her into honesty. Grasping the tip of her tongue between her teeth, she bit down, tasted blood. No, she told herself. In three years, their family had lost three people, the cost of the lie of a new Asia. Jujube would not, would never, understand.

Then Gordon coughed, a loud, phlegmy hack that echoed through the room. Jujube whirled around. "Pa," she said, her eyes hopeful, willing her father awake.

But Gordon's eyes remained closed and stayed closed. They did not know it yet, but a week later, he would stop coughing and breathing entirely.

CHAPTER TWENTY-FOUR

August 30, 1945
Two weeks before the Japanese surrender in Malaya

ABEL

On the rare mornings he was able to wake up early, Abel liked watching the sunrise. It was the one time the camp was quiet, and the one time he didn't feel like an overwhelming disappointment to himself and to others. He would sip from a bottle of toddy, imagining it was the bitter black coffee his mother used to make in the morning at breakfast, the coffee that he would drink too hot because he could never wait, the torture of the burn down his throat almost pleasure. Some mornings at the camp, Abel felt a shiver of wind creeping through the distance, its swish nearly but not fully drowned out by the chirping of the crickets. But this particular morning, it was drizzling, slim drops of rain that pinched his neck and back. All of it reminded him that, at the very least, he was alive.

Because the truth was, even if he drank to forget all his pain, the unwelcome memories requiring more and more toddy to push them back, he did not want to die. He often moaned that he wished the others would leave him to kill himself, an exhortation that made Freddie look away sadly. But it was always a lie.

The camp had made Abel confront his mortality every single day. Some days, when Akiro had beaten him harder than usual, he'd wished he were one of those people who wanted to die. It wouldn't have taken much, with his body so weak and riddled with injury. It would've been as simple as climbing up and throwing himself off a tree or slashing his wrists with one of the many sharp implements that littered the camp. Yet the uncertainty of death scared him. He wondered about the people he would have to leave behind. His family loved him; his mother loved him especially. The idea that his death could intentionally hurt her made him seize up inside; he could not bear the thought of her sorrow.

So this fear of dying needled him into basic survival. This meant remembering to eat occasionally and finding safe spots for shelter, away from the dangers of landslides or falling pieces of wood. It meant that this fateful morning, as the drizzle fogged up the gray sky and made the air humid, it was Abel who was the first to spot the planes, their wings swooping through the air in formation, like a gale of white birds against the creeping ball of orange sun struggling to rise. The toddy swirled in his stomach, the familiar sourness creating a knot of gas and the buzz beginning its resonant whir through his head. But even in his haze, he knew. He *knew*. His body untangled itself, intent on surviving, his knees cricking painfully as he rose to his feet, moved one foot in front of the other.

Run, his body screamed. *Run*.

JUJUBE

It was not an exaggeration to say that everything in Jujube's life was fissured with despair. Jasmin had been gone for nearly two whole weeks, and some days Jujube felt so overwhelmed by terror over what could've happened to her sister that she couldn't breathe. Her father's illness had become so acute that he lay motionless in his bed at home, eyes shut, comatose. He had a few days, the doctor had said the day before, and after the doctor left, Jujube had held vigil by her father's bed, willing herself to talk to him, to remind him of her voice, to beg him to come back. But she hadn't known what to say, how to express the burning fury that choked her every day as she wondered what they'd done to deserve everything their family had to live through. Instead she had sat silently, watching the dark shadows on the wall, her father's labored breathing the only echo in the room.

Her mother would be completely silent for days on end, barely eating, barely moving from her stool by the window in her bedroom. Then suddenly she would begin talking, an incessant stream of confusing, jumbled information. She muttered in a manic way about "going to see him" and "this is what he does to women." At first Jujube had thought Cecily was referring to Gordon and tried to reason with her mother. "Pa is sick and needs to rest." But her mother would wave her away impatiently, unseeingly. "He owes me," she would mumble. And Jujube would walk away and close her mother's door quietly, resignedly, behind her.

Jujube had hoped that, as in the past, her mother would come around. But this time, things seemed to be escalating. Her mother had grown gaunt from eating infrequently but also puffy from her inconsistent sleep schedule. At night Jujube would hear her pacing up and down, the wooden floorboards creaking like there were rats in the walls. And then by dawn, exhausted, she would fall asleep for an hour or two before restarting her vigil by the window.

At the teahouse, Doraisamy came out of the kitchen and snapped his fingers obnoxiously in front of her nose. "Hello, hello, are you here, Jujube? Are you going to do your work? You know I can get a thousand girls to replace you?"

It took all her willpower not to bite Doraisamy's curling fingers. Instead, she pulled the tea towel and her apron off and dropped them in his hands. "Sorry, sir, I have to go back to my house for lunch. I'll come back quickly, sir."

"I swear I will sack you," Doraisamy shouted at her retreating back. Then, as though rethinking his options in real time, he yelled, "You better come back within an hour!"

When Jujube reached the house, the sun hung hot in the late-morning sky. Her shirt pressed against her back, and she knew that unsightly sweat stains pockmarked the cotton, rendering the already thin material see-through.

"Ma?" she called out. She did this out of habit. Her mother, cloistered up in her room, almost never responded these days. "Ma, I came home early. I can make some lunch!"

A clattering. Jujube froze. Her mother emerged from her bedroom in a brown dress with a faint yellow stain on the front; Jujube didn't want to know what it was. Her mother smelled like rotting fish, and her hair was lank with grease and tangled into knots.

"Ma," Jujube said, heart pounding. "You came out of the room today. How are you feeling?"

"I'm so sorry, my girl. I have to tell someone."

"Tell someone what? Ma, please."

Jujube pulled her mother into the bathroom, tried to scoop some water from the tank with the red dipper to throw it over her mother's stinking hair. But her mother struggled free, wriggling past Jujube with surprising strength.

"I know someone who can find your sister. It's all my fault. But he can help us. He will," her mother burbled incoherently.

"Ma, you're making no sense. You know Jasmin ran away. And it's my fault, not yours." That was the first time Jujube had admitted that out loud. She swallowed the guilt wedged in her throat, blinked away the image of Jasmin's tearful, pleading face as she was being shoved into the basement.

"Years ago I helped a man, and he was a bad man, Jujube. I have to make things right," Jujube's mother continued without appearing to hear her.

Jujube's exhaustion rolled through her. She couldn't argue with her mother like this anymore. "Please. I'm just going to get you into bed, Ma, and I'll make us some food. Stop it." She pressed an arm into her mother's back, perhaps a little more roughly than she had intended. She was just so, so tired.

Without warning, Jujube's mother shoved her hard, across the wet bathroom floor. It was bright behind Jujube's eyes when she heard the crack ring through her, but before she could fully register the sound of her own head hitting the cement floor, the world faded out.

CECILY

The familiar smell of grass and jasmine assailed Cecily's nostrils as she approached the large white house. Cecily still thought of it as the old resident's house, where she first met Fujiwara as Bingley Chan. The house didn't look as different as its current circumstances would imply; it still loomed above everything at the edge of town, its driveway long and steep, its lawn well maintained. The clean white exterior was a little worn by the years, but generally its majesty had not diminished. To think she had once come to this house as a guest of the British resident, dressed in beautiful clothes, important enough to be feted, to stand on its porch and inhale the fresh scent of rain as music rang through its halls. Cecily looked down at herself. Her toes were dry and exposed in her worn slippers, and the nail of the first toe on her right foot was ridged and green-gray with a fungal infection. She was wearing a brown housedress—one she had been wearing for days as she'd lain unbathed, rocking back and forth in her room. The smell of herself wafted to her nose. She was sour, bitter, rotting, a shadow of the woman Fujiwara once knew, hysterical where before she was quiet, broken where before there was strength.

As if pitying her, the late-morning sun dipped behind the clouds. Cecily took big steps and pulled her legs up the steep driveway meant for automobiles, not the shaking legs of a breaking woman. Even without the sun, the air was hot, and her housedress clung to her body in patches of sweat, under her arms, behind her knees, between her breasts. She tasted a drop of sweat rolling down her upper lip into her panting mouth.

She knew she should have come to Fujiwara sooner. But when her brain was muddled the way it was, time passed strangely, as though everything were misted with dreams. Jasmin would walk into the house so soon, so very soon, she thought every day, and sometimes she managed to trick herself into believing she could hear her daughter's chirping laugh echoing through the house. But then she'd wake up, and despair would root her in place, and she would be reminded over and over what had happened. And how she had set it all in motion.

At the top of the driveway, she stepped onto the familiar porch, the same porch she'd stood on, listening to the incandescent strains of Billie Holiday, all those years ago.

"Ma'am?" A houseboy dressed in gray stepped onto the porch and looked Cecily up and down.

"I need to see your Sir," she said, stepping toward the boy, who raised his hands as if to protect himself, from her, from her smell, she didn't know.

"Stay," said the houseboy to Cecily, as though she were a dog. He stepped backward into the house.

But Cecily did not have much to lose anymore. Ignoring him, she marched toward the boy and crossed the threshold into the house even has he pleaded, "No, no. Stay." She stood in the entryway.

The house looked different when it was not draped and decorated for a party. The ceiling was high and arched, and an inviting breeze seemed to whisper along the walls, keeping the place cooler inside than it was outside. It was both a relief and a disgusting reminder of her body's grease as her scent surrounded her. Cecily muttered to herself, practicing her lines: "She could be your daughter, your blood. Please help me find her."

JASMIN

In the four-poster bed in General Fujiwara's house, the stomachs of Jasmin and Yuki growled hungrily in unison. They'd slept for so long that it was already deep into the next day. Jasmin felt the squeeze of the acid pinch at her insides. Yuki giggled, but Jasmin shushed her, worried that someone would hear. The room was thick with humidity, and Yuki had become even more pungent in the stagnant air. Jasmin, addled with the drowsiness of sleep, still hadn't figured out what to do about Yuki.

"I'm hungry," Yuki said.

The long cut on Yuki's leg had stopped bleeding, a scab beginning to form. Jasmin looked away from her friend. She felt for Yuki, but she was also frustrated. She was taking such a risk to bring Yuki to the general's house. And Yuki had never once said thank you.

"Please, quiet," said Jasmin.

"But I'm so hungry I could eat your arm!" Yuki replied and, to illustrate her point, lunged for the fleshiest part of Jasmin's right arm, pretending to bite into it. "Nyam nyam!"

"Stop it!" screamed Jasmin. She was not in the mood for Yuki's silly games. There was too much at stake, so many thoughts swirling around in her mind that she felt she couldn't control them. She was scared because she knew the general would come, and a mounting terror was threatening to suffocate her—she worried she would lose them both, Yuki and the general, once the time came.

"Why are you being so horrible!" Yuki screamed back. The red welts on her arms stared accusingly at Jasmin.

CECILY

The piercing yells of girls punctured the air. Cecily rose from the rattan chair, almost tripping in her slippers. It was unmistakable. She could not make out the words, but the girls were young, a pitch that belonged to the reedy, gurgling voices of children.

The houseboy had also heard; he came running toward Cecily, confusion ridged across his youthful face.

"Who is that?" Cecily asked loudly, slowly. "Are there girls here?" She had never thought that Fujiwara was one of *those* men, like the horrible men who had come to the house looking for *guniang*, the kind who would imprison little girls in his house. The houseboy began walking briskly down the corridor, and Cecily rushed after him.

"No!" he said to her, waving helplessly, his English not sufficient to give strength to his admonishment. Cecily ran to the end of the corridor, to the room where the sound of girlish yelling was becoming clearer and clearer. As she drew closer to the door, her rage became absolute—she could kill Fujiwara, she thought. He who always left a trail of death in his wake. And to take innocence in this way. She balled her fists.

"No!" the houseboy yelled again, rushing to catch up with her, pulling at her housedress.

Cecily turned to shove the boy's hand away; her purpose was singular now, she had to get to the girls. The door to the room creaked open, eyes emerged in the white light of morning, the swish of a nightgown.

"Mama?"

JUJUBE

Jujube didn't know how long she was out, but when she came to, her mother was gone, the front of Jujube's body was drenched, and the red water dipper lay on her chest like a bleeding crater. Ears ringing, she pulled herself off the slick ground and somehow stumbled out of the house to the sundry shop, where Aunty Mui was stacking jars and Uncle Chong was repainting the sign.

"What happened, girl, what happened?" Aunty Mui yelled, rushing out from behind the shelves with surprising agility for an old woman. Jujube, overcome by dizziness, pain, and exhaustion, simply sat on the shop floor, noting with some satisfaction that a few drops of blood fell on the ground in perfect circles. Aunty Mui dispatched Uncle Chong to the chemist, and he returned with a paper bag full of ointments, creams, and gauze. Between the two old people, they deposited Jujube on a stool, rubbed a smelly cream onto her head wound, and wrapped it up with gauze. Aunty Mui clucked the whole time, "We need to take you to the doctor," and "Where is your mother," and "Did you eat today," but Jujube simply sat silent, "face like a mask," Aunty Mui would later tell anyone who came into the shop.

An hour later, back at the teahouse, Jujube pressed her fingers into the gauzy dressing that Aunty Mui had taped on the side of her head, feeling it absorb the stickiness of her wound mixed with the ointment Aunty Mui had applied and noting the disgust on Doraisamy's face.

"What happened to you? You can't go out on the floor like this," he said.

It seemed ironic to Jujube that she couldn't go out on the floor bleeding a little when these days the men came into the teahouse in various stages of injury: some wounds self-inflicted by drunken stumbling, some wounds the result of fighting guerrillas at the jungle edges, some bruises on their faces from punching each other. The desire to bruise, Jujube supposed, was born out of the desire to control an outcome, to see the certainty of the blue bruise spreading across a swelling cheek. Because these days, no one had control over anything—radios scratched with updates about surrenders, about gigantic losses suffered in Nazi-occupied areas, about local uprisings in Japanese territories. These thimbles of news were supposed to give her hope, but the idea of being free of the Japanese had become a concept so alien to her that she could no longer imagine it.

She trudged through each day, alive to be sure, limbs and body intact, but it was becoming harder to hold on to her thoughts. At night, during sleep, they rushed around her head like termites in a wall, never still. Sometimes they were so obvious as to be laughable, images of broken bodies she recognized as her siblings' but without faces; sometimes more insidious, staticky words mumbled through the radio or pages of books where she could not see or hear the words; sometimes glimpses of herself staring back at her, the reflection as disappointed in her as she was in herself. But one thing the dreams were not, was hopeful. They never knitted together a future in which her family was whole again.

CECILY

Cecily's first thought was: This is too easy. A clean, happy version of her daughter Jasmin stood before her, face upturned and arranged in childish incredulity. She didn't realize until that moment how much she had missed the innocence of Jasmin's voice, its nasal tenor, as though she had one nostril pressed down at all times. The world seemed to tilt as Cecily's body suddenly acknowledged all the pain and neglect it had been through, her stomach empty and her mind fuzzy with the onslaught of relief and terror. Operating only on instinct, Cecily crouched down and pulled Jasmin into her arms. She was breathing angry gasps, which, once they escaped her, she realized were actually sobs, into Jasmin's narrow shoulders. She tugged at her daughter's hair, which had grown in a little bit since the last time she'd hacked it off with scissors, inhaled the milky scent of Jasmin's skin, the scent she never seemed to lose even after she left babyhood.

"Come," she said into her daughter's hair. "We must leave this place now."

Cecily had many questions. Had Fujiwara been keeping Jasmin here? Had Jasmin stumbled in here? Had he done something to her? She could kill him, Cecily thought. And she would. But first she had to get Jasmin out. And away.

The walls had grown shadows that indicated an afternoon storm was brewing. The air hung heavy and still as it waited, and a break of lightning lit up the darkened corridor. Cecily saw Jasmin flinch, but she didn't cower the way she used to every time she saw lightning. Her little girl had grown brave.

Cecily hadn't made a plan beyond this point. She'd thought she would have to beg and plead with Fujiwara to help her find Jasmin. She hadn't expected that Jasmin would simply be here for the taking. They could walk right out of this cursed white house. Cecily didn't know how they'd escape detection or how she could stop Fujiwara from coming after them. But it didn't matter; there was only her family, and she had to bring them back together. Jujube would be so happy to see her sister, she thought. Her heart sank when she remembered her last confrontation with her eldest. She knew she shouldn't have hit Jujube, but she had just been so angry, so animal, she had felt like someone else entirely, unable to stop herself. But it would be all right. She would make it right when she brought Jasmin home. All would be forgiven.

"Come," she said again, pressing hard fingers into Jasmin's thin wrist. "Mama is going to make it better."

―

JASMIN

Jasmin had seen her mother in various stages of a breakdown before. When Abel hadn't come home, Jasmin had watched as her mother crouched by the window each day like an animal waiting for its owner to return. She would jump at every noise, ask everyone who walked by if they had seen or heard about the boys disappearing from town. And when she got the tiniest bit of information—for instance, that someone had seen a truck full of boys driving out of the neighborhood, or that one of the teachers at Abel's old school might have been tricking the boys into leaving with the Japanese—her mother would rush out, gesturing feverishly as she interrogated all these tenuous sources of information about Abel. But the days went by and neither Abel nor news about Abel showed up. Jasmin would hear her mother crying out in her sleep, the volume of the sobs ranging from quiet sniffles to loud screams that her father would try his best to shush.

But a departure from cleanliness had never been a symptom of her mother's anguish. For as long as Jasmin had known her mother, all her nearly eight years, her mother had always risen early in the morning, gotten dressed, and maintained a very orderly household and self. As the Japanese occupation wore on, some of the other neighborhood mothers had a tendency to look harried, but her mother was always simple, clean, ironed. Today, however, she stood before Jasmin in a housedress that Jasmin had never seen look this dirty, and she smelled like the fish that sometimes died in their dry drain after a storm.

"Who's that?" Yuki mumbled behind her. Jasmin pushed Yuki farther out of sight, back into the darkness of the bedroom.

The houseboy made a guttural sound, which Jasmin knew was his equivalent for "Who's in there with you?" He gestured with both hands in agitation at the multiple unwanted guests, and everyone knew he was worried what the general would say if he crossed the doorway. In the distance, the sun had ducked away as the sky readied itself for rain.

"I was looking everywhere for you!" Jasmin's mother said, her voice pitchy and cracking. She did not appear to have noticed Yuki. Then, to Jasmin's confusion, her mother started crying, whooping, loud sobs that echoed through the house. She reached for Jasmin, tried to fold Jasmin into her arms, but Jasmin shrank away. The smell was too bad. How could this be her mother?

Everyone heard it as it happened: the sound of a door opening and closing, the tread of footsteps coming down the hallway. The houseboy started choking, rushing down the hallway to his approaching master and blurting out a string of Japanese words that Jasmin did not understand. Behind her, Yuki stiffened.

"He's saying there's a madwoman in the house," Yuki whispered to Jasmin.

Jasmin said, "She's not a madwoman. She's my mother."

The general took two large strides and crossed the corridor, forcefully moving the houseboy out of his way with his hands. He stopped and took in the scene in front of him. Behind Jasmin, Yuki stepped farther into the shadows.

"So. Everyone is here, then," the general said, his face still, his voice so even it made a nervous urine stream press against Jasmin's bladder. From the shadows of the room, Yuki gripped her wrist tightly.

CECILY

It was his posture that Cecily noticed first. Although not tall, Fujiwara had always stood straight and stiff, a man without the flexibility to lean languidly. It was the ramrod posture of a man in control, a man who compartmentalized and enjoyed order, a man with unwavering commitment to whatever it was that gripped him—idealism, or loathing, or faith. But the man who stood before her in the house was a curved man, as though someone had taken a screwdriver to the base of his spine and unwound the taut string holding him together, causing his shoulders to slouch forward. To anyone else, he looked like a man with a bit of a hunch, but the hunch astonished Cecily. The slouch gave his gait a lumber that she was unaccustomed to, a clumsiness that surprised her with its fragility.

The second thing she noticed was the absence of scent. The minty hair-cream smell that had always followed him and his shiny, coiffed hair had been a signature, a way for her body to respond, an enslavement in itself. But the only scent that surrounded them was hers, sour and oily and unbathed. General Fujiwara's hair lay flat and unstyled against his forehead, the fringe making him look like a boy trapped in the body of an old, old man. He glared at her with steel in his eyes. No matter how he had evolved, this was still a man who liked to do things on his terms, and she had intruded, broken into his home, brought her madness, her stains, her smell, to his turf.

"Cecily—"

But Cecily would not let him have the privilege of the first word. "What," she hissed, "are you doing with my girl?" She reached for her daughter and pulled Jasmin roughly to her.

"No, Mama, I don't want to," Jasmin squeaked. Cecily was surprised at the strength of Jasmin's resistance, the force with which her youngest twisted away. This, the same child who had spent her whole life living to please everyone around her.

"You see, it's not I who have been keeping her here. She's always been free to go," Fujiwara said.

Cecily felt something unspool inside her, as though the tiny threads that cinched her sanity together were coming apart; Fujiwara had made her this woman, this wretch who had nothing left in her but screams. The final thread snapped and she lunged at Fujiwara, hands outstretched, all limbs and wild hair.

"Mama, no! No!" Jasmin shouted. "He didn't do anything to me!"

Fujiwara pawed at Cecily, swatting her arms away, his face unmasked in its disgust—at her stench, at her abhorrent display of emotion. The houseboy shrank into the darkness of the corridor wall, yelping, the chaos overwhelming him. And Cecily thought she heard the distinctly childish voices of two girls screaming.

"Stop it, stop it," a girl's voice yelled, and when Cecily looked down at the creature clinging to her leg, trying to pry her away from Fujiwara, it was not Jasmin. Instead, her eyes landed on the top of a small head with a receded hairline. When the child turned her face up to look at Cecily, she saw a stretched eye and a pale cheek marked with angry divots and mottled scars. She met the face of a secret she had considered long dead.

JUJUBE

At the teahouse, Jujube unwrapped her dressing gingerly. Although the cut had dried, it throbbed, insistent. Jujube pulled her wavy hair out of the pins that usually restrained it, letting it fall over her face. Her hair was a mess, but it would do to cover up the wound. Exhausted from the effort, she sat in the teahouse kitchen, contemplating the raw tapioca root that poked its head out of the bag on the counter, its sinewy brown skin a shade not unlike her own.

Her mind—which had, since Jasmin disappeared, become a well of constant agitation—felt different, calmer. It was as though the smacking of her head on the cement bathroom floor had knocked back the singular focus and immense rationality for which she had always been known. It felt like she could see clearly again, that she knew the way to wrest control, to create her own concrete bruise on someone, to compose a pain she could press, feel, observe, and hold in cupped fingers.

Jujube had thought the inclination to murder was gradual, a creeping mist that built in one's mind until the fog was so thick it had to be let out. But for Jujube, now, the impulse was sudden. It struck with no warning and imprinted itself so indelibly that it was all she could think about. She knew, of course, that murder was a sin, and to contemplate it, also a sin. But this mental clarity excited her. For so long she had felt rudderless, consumed by the breadth of her emotions and unable to see past them, but now everything seemed simple. Besides, it seemed fair. There was no god who would let them live like this, focused each day only on trying not to die, while their oppressors were allowed the dignity of hope. She thought bitterly of Mr. Takahashi's beloved Ichika, with her ambition, her carefree clothing, her desire to help people so evident because she was fortunate enough to have space in her heart for empathy.

At the teahouse weeks earlier, Mr. Takahashi had pronounced himself a pacifist. "I don't believe in their methods. There are better ways."

"But their methods tell us they don't think we deserve to live," Jujube had said.

Mr. Takahashi either didn't hear her or chose not to. He blew on the top of his tea. "It should not be the way of the world that the white men win everything."

But what made people like Jujube and her family prizes to be won, cattle to be slaughtered, daughters to be raped, animals to be starved? Enslavement did not just mean different-colored people buying and selling each other. Your enemy looking like you—recognizing yourself in your enemy—made it so much worse because it mirrored back to you all the darkness you held. Every day there were people carved up like steak on the street, killing fields filled with buried bodies, some still alive when they went in the hole on top of one another. She had nightmares of her brother and sister clawing through a narrow hole of bodies futilely, gasping for air. The hole in her heart threatened to engulf her if she didn't do something, anything, to feel a little power, to remind herself that she still had something the Japanese could not take away.

Had Mr. Takahashi changed? Or was it she who had been altered by everything she had lost? Or was the cleave in their fortunes—that his daughter got to live while she had yet another person taken from her—the wedge that would live between their friendship forever? Mr. Takahashi may have been a good man, but a good man who believed in a bad thing was a bad man, and she did not know how she could ever forgive him, or them.

CECILY

The girl with the mottled face hung back, one eyebrow squinched to the center of her face, the other, on the broken side of her face, unmoving. Cecily noticed that her arms were covered with the remnants of a beating, welts, bruises, and restraint marks crisscrossing the pale skin.

"What? Who is this?" Fujiwara asked.

The houseboy looked alarmed and frightened, worried probably about allowing not one but two feral strangers into the general's orderly house. Outside, a soft drizzle had begun to fall.

Cecily knew that in her place, most people would have thought frequently about the child she had left behind, the deathbed promise to Lina that she had explicitly broken. But while the guilt had been profound in the beginning, it had diminished over the years to little twinges she had been able to push back.

"You've taken so much from us. You have to let us go," Cecily said.

"Taken?" Fujiwara's voiced dipped dangerously low. "All I've ever done was try to make the world better. Once upon a time, you understood that." His lip curled in distaste.

Her daughter, her tiny, thin daughter, stood framed in the bedroom doorway and stared at the two adults with confused, wet eyes. Cecily's heart was pounding. She didn't know what game Fujiwara was playing at here, but she did know that she had to get her girl away from him, or Jasmin would be sucked into the toxic vortex that she now understood Fujiwara to be, a man who splintered women who loved him so they became warped versions of themselves that they could no longer recognize. She had thought him transformative, a man who had given her ideals, a purpose, made her bigger, but she saw that the problem was he thought so too: believed he had made her, and Lina, and the world around them, better. His delusion—that he was a good man, an idealistic man who simply did what was right—was what had broken them all. She had to protect Jasmin from that—Jasmin, as innocent and as accepting of love as the woman who had named her all those years ago.

Jasmin's lower lip started quivering, and instinctively Cecily reached for her. But Fujiwara was faster, enfolding Jasmin against him, her nose pressing against a button on his uniform.

Fujiwara addressed Jasmin with a tenderness that surprised Cecily. "So, Jasmin, who is your friend over here, and why is she in the house?"

Jasmin pulled herself off Fujiwara and stood as straight as her small form could muster. "Mister General," she started.

In spite of everything, Jasmin's serious desire to meet the moment tugged at Cecily, inviting a smile. Then she saw that Fujiwara was gazing at Jasmin with a soft indulgence that she'd never seen. Cecily steeled her lips straight, the smile gone. This was not the time.

"Yes, Jasmin, what can we do for you?" Fujiwara folded himself to a kneeling position to meet Jasmin. He angled two fingers under her chin. Cecily could feel those fingers, knew how the calluses on the tips contrasted with the smoothness of the joint.

"This is my friend Yuki," Jasmin said, pointing at the other girl. "Something bad is happening to her and I want to help her."

Yuki. Cecily turned the name over in her mind, pulled her knee into her chest, and realized that she too had sat down on the floor. The other girl remained standing, arms crossed on her chest. Fujiwara frowned, shifting his gaze to Yuki and taking in her tattered dress and scarred face.

Jasmin barreled along quickly. "She lives at the place over there, behind the welcome sign, and there are girls everywhere and they look sad and there are men and they look angry, and sometimes Yuki gets hurt and it makes me so sad and she's my best friend and canshecomestaywithusplease?"

The words tumbled out of Jasmin along with the beginning of childish tears. She reached for Yuki and they both perched in front of Fujiwara, cross-legged, fingers intertwined, sitting straight up like two determined toadstools.

There were other ways that this should have happened—that she would bump into the girl on the street, lock eyes with a familiar face, hurry away, and live with that guilt forever. Or that one day a policeman would come to her door with a death certificate, press her hands behind her, and arrest her. That the girl herself would come to the door and demand to know why she had been abandoned. But that it should all come together in such a tidy, poetic way—at the airy white house where she had first met Fujiwara, the two girls swinging arms and proclaiming themselves best friends—seemed cruel in its triteness, the circularity of narrative so perfect as to be absurd. Yet perhaps the only inevitable truth was that all lies eventually rise up to meet their makers. A broken child stood before them, and she and Fujiwara had made it so.

"Do you see Lina in her?"

Cecily was surprised at the ice in her voice, the steadiness with which she delivered what she knew would change everything, break the seal of the secret that she had kept hidden for so long.

"Are you happy to finally meet your daughter?"

ABEL

Sunlight broke through thick clouds. Abel's eyes adjusted as he ran, looking frantically for Freddie. The rumbling from the planes had gotten louder as they swooped lower, vibrations echoing through the camp. Other boys started emerging from their quarters, rubbing their eyes sleepily, staring in confusion at the sky. The planes had arranged themselves into formation, a neat V; one of them stopped directly in front of the sun, a mechanical eclipse.

"Freddie!" Abel called, his voice hoarse and creaky, unused to being used. "FREDDIE!" He passed by the pile of packs and supplies that Freddie had the boys gather at the center of the camp, in preparation for their journey today.

"Down, get down!" someone screamed. Abel pulled his body to the ground, and around him, boys ran out of the shacks and flattened themselves beside him. White circular balls that looked like eggs began dropping from the planes in diagonal lines, aimed, Abel realized, at any structure visible from the sky. First to go was their makeshift atap theater, then one of the outhouses.

"Liberation planes!" someone screamed. "The British are here to free us!"

"Then why are they shooting us?"

"Aren't they here to let us go?"

Rama came running out of the sleeping quarters, tripping over a bedsheet on which he had scrawled in mud: "POW!"—prisoners of war—"Stop Bombs! We r on your side!"

The boys pulled the four corners of the sheet taut, aiming the words at the sky, begging for the pilots to see. Around Abel, the air began to fill with smoke as the falling white eggs turned into orange balls, scorching everything they touched. One of the kitchen boys, a kid named Davidson, stood up and waved. "We support you, we sup—!" he yelled before his voice was cut short by a piece of flying debris that tore through his arm. Soon all the yelling, first joyous, then confused, turned into screams, high-pitched and bracing to the ear. The ground thudded with running feet and falling boys.

In all the chaos, Abel still couldn't find Freddie. Normally Freddie was everywhere, giving instructions, quietly leading. Abel began imagining the worst. His feet screamed in pain. It felt like he had been running around for hours, even though he knew it could not have been more than a few minutes. The ground seemed to weep with something corrosive that burned; whatever it was shredded the bottom of his slippers, nipped through the skin of his feet.

Still, he ran, croaking, "Freddie, where are you?" The landscape of the camp was changing before his eyes. An orange light suffused everything, almost an exact replica of sunset, except for the burning smell that accompanied the light, and the flecks of ash that coated the air and the inside of his nose. His eyes stung too from smoke, and the world looked filtered and dusted with a dusky romance, except that was the burning of bodies, of buildings, of the melted metal from the train tracks the boys had laid. There was an undulating roar; even through the ringing in his ears, he recognized the cacophony of groans and screams. Boys were doubled over, boys were lying on the ground with unseeing eyes, boys were armless and limping through the smoke, boys were dragging their bleeding bodies across the ground, boys were crying for mothers, and fathers, and sisters, and each other, arms, legs, torsos smeared with clumps of clotting blood, like jam baked too long. As Abel panted from the exertion, he was assailed by a new smell, sour, rusty, a hint of citrus. It came at him from all sides, so overwhelming that he felt that familiar roil in his stomach—nausea—but this time, for once, not the result of his drinking.

Freddie had been right, as usual. The British had come for the camp and bombed it to hell, to wipe out any way for the Japanese to transport supplies. And yet the only men who lay on the ground in piles of ash and limbs were conscripted boys who had, against the odds, survived the Japanese torture only to die at the hands of their supposed saviors. The familiar looked unfamiliar. Abel passed the dining hall, which had become—from a place of beatings to a place of laughter to what it was now, a pile of sticks and smoke. He passed by the collapsed structure of the theater where Freddie had offered him Akiro. And then, outside the chicken coop, he saw a familiar blue-eyed boy, crouched over and digging in the ground.

"Freddie!" Abel yelled, trying to get his voice to reach through the chaos around them. As he got closer, he saw that the ground was littered with scraps of yellow-brown paper, and on them, the familiar faces of his family and of the boys at camp: all the toilet-paper paintings that he and Freddie had done late at night by the light of the moon, Abel describing the people he loved and Freddie bringing them to life.

"What are you doing here, Freddie, we have to go!"

"I had to get the drawings, Abe, I had to, you know I had to. To remember, like I said . . ." His voice, usually soft, trailed off into a whisper, and his squat collapsed, knees hitting the ground, damp from the morning dew. In a single bound, Abel reached Freddie and caught him before he fell over.

Freddie was hurt, Abel saw now. There were gashes on his wrists that had bled and stained his palms a fading brown. But most concerning was the large circular wet patch on his right leg that looked fresh. The circle was surprisingly symmetrical, its edges unnervingly smooth.

"Freddie, you're bleeding."

"It's one of those that won't stop, Abe."

At the camp, none of the boys were doctors, but they had all, through force of necessity, become reasonably well versed with the severity of injuries and wounds. They knew the superficial cuts from the deep wounds, they knew how to tell bruise patterns apart, they had learned to spot the beginnings of sepsis. And they knew when a hit or cut had broken through a crucial artery, when the blood didn't stop and there was nothing they could do. This was one of those. Freddie's injury was deep, and the blood made steady, languid inroads down his leg, showing no signs of clotting.

"Does it hurt, Freddie?"

Freddie shook his head. "Take these," he said to Abel, handing him the scraps of toilet-paper drawings, some torn at the ends. His voice was resolute.

Abel held the paper drawings awkwardly in his hand for a second before pressing them into the waistband of his pants. "Freddie, I'm gonna get you out. You need to do this. You dragged me everywhere in this shithole, and now I'm gonna drag you."

Freddie chuckled at Abel's attempt at the weak joke, but his breath came out like a hiss, a kettle that had been boiling for so long there was no more water for steam.

CECILY

Darkness fell, and the houseboy, at Fujiwara's instruction, turned on a series of haphazard lamps, which created long silhouettes of their bodies, their shadows gesturing angrily against the walls. Crickets began chirping and a chorus of mosquitoes buzzed. One flew against Fujiwara's eyebrow. He smacked it absently, leaving a smear of carcass and blood on his forehead. Cecily pressed her hands against her sides to stop herself from reaching over to wipe his face. Even now, even in her all-consuming rage, her body willed itself to touch him. Behind Fujiwara, the girls clustered together, Jasmin's arms around Yuki. They were a single amorphous unit.

"Aunty Woon always told me my father was a big-deal man!" Yuki screeched, her first words in a while. Then she turned to Jasmin, good eye blazing with joy. "Now I can live here with you! Foreverandever!"

Outside, as though exhaling a long-held breath, the storm began in earnest, no thunder, no lightning, just ceaseless loud, large droplets of rain.

"I don't understand. Jasmin says this girl"—Fujiwara gestured at Yuki—"has been living at the comfort station."

Cecily squinted into the darkening corridor and studied Fujiwara's face as he tried to make sense of the information coming at him.

"You let my daughter rot in a brothel?" His voice rose to a volume that for most people was normal but Cecily knew from experience was dangerous. "You just left her there?"

"*You* left her," Cecily said, leaning heavily against the wall and hearing the broken sob escape her throat. "You left them both. All of us."

"It's okay, Mama, don't cry, I'll take care of you," Jasmin cried, leaping up and burying herself in Cecily's stomach, hugging her in such a familiar way that it sent hopeless shivers up her spine. Jasmin, always wanting to make everything better, even the things she could not understand.

"She wants to live with me, Cecily. I can give Jasmin a better life." Fujiwara's voice switched back to its usual volume, barely above a whisper, so everyone, even the houseboy, craned forward involuntarily. Even now, Cecily realized, he was a whirlpool of his own wants, taking only what he desired—Jasmin—and ignoring Yuki, the daughter before him.

"You can't just take Jasmin. That's not how being a father works."

"I've done everything the right way this whole time, and I've got nothing to show for it . . ." His voice trailed off and he pressed his hand against his forehead, smearing the mosquito even more. "Things have changed." He gestured around. "It's all coming to an end, you know this, with the Americans . . . A man starts to think about his legacy."

Jasmin's head whipped back and forth between the adults, her face absorbed in concentration, trying to read the unsaid. "Will I get to choose?" she asked. "Will Yuki get to choose?"

Even with the evening shadows glancing over his face, Cecily could see how his eyes sank with sadness. The curtain rose briefly, and under it she saw his desperation. For a minute, Cecily wavered. She reached out to rub the mosquito blood smear off Fujiwara's forehead, but then she dropped her hand back to her side. There was no redemption arc for her and Fujiwara. The war had made them, and the collateral damage they had inflicted was personified in the small human who stood before them.

"No," Cecily said, pulling herself to her feet, shouting above the cracking thunder that had belatedly joined the storm. "This is not a matter of choosing. I'm your mother."

"Well, who's going to let me bring Yuki?" Jasmin pushed her hair off her face impatiently, and a cowlick stood straight up. Cecily itched to press it against Jasmin's head, but before she could, Yuki launched herself at the general, burying her face in the exact spot in his chest that Jasmin had just a few minutes earlier when he had pulled her into a hug.

"Mister General, I wanna choose you," Yuki breathed.

JASMIN

Jasmin knew Yuki was copying her—she'd seen the general pull Jasmin into a hug, and she was miming the action, hoping the same thing would happen to her. But Yuki had gotten it wrong. Jasmin knew that the general was not like other grown-ups.

"No, Yuki, no!" she yelled, trying to pull Yuki off the general.

Jasmin watched as he glared at Yuki clinging to him. With Jasmin, he had wrapped his arms around her body, and it had been uncomfortable at first because his uniform was hot and a bit scratchy, but then, as she'd melted into it, she'd felt lighter, and all her fears about what he would say about Yuki had melted away. But now, of course, Yuki was going to ruin everything.

"Let me go! Why do you get everything!" Yuki screamed at Jasmin, her voice muffled by the general's uniform.

Most of the time Jasmin felt that Yuki knew so much more than she did, but not in this moment. Her heart sped up; she panicked and doubled over.

She heard her mother say, "No," and then, "Jasmin, are you all right?" and before she could reply, she heard a ringing sound echo across the room. When she looked up, she saw Yuki stumbling back, holding the marked side of her cheek, and Fujiwara massaging his hand. Yuki fell backward, then on her side. Jasmin heard the screams coming out of her own throat, felt them vibrate through her body.

What scared Jasmin most was that Yuki did not scream, did not say a word, simply lay on her side as if she were dead, clutching her cheek as a red print bloomed across the scars.

Jasmin rushed over and squatted above Yuki.

"You hit that little girl!" screamed her mother, stepping toward Fujiwara.

"At least I didn't leave her to die like a stray," he said.

It was all too much; Jasmin didn't understand any of it anymore, and at her feet, Yuki let out a small piteous yelp.

The houseboy rushed over with a cloth and some warm water. He looked to the general for permission and, seeing the barely perceptible nod, pulled Yuki into a sitting position and began to pat her cheek with the warm cloth.

Behind Jasmin, her mother and the general were arguing. Jasmin only caught snippets, her mother saying, "I had no choice," and "You didn't want her," and the general saying, "She's ruined anyway."

Jasmin didn't want to know what was going on anymore. She looked at Yuki cradling her cheek, which had begun turning blue. The houseboy gestured for the girls to wait as he stood up carefully with the water bowl, pressing his palms against the sides to prevent the water from spilling over the edge. He turned to go back to the kitchen.

As soon as his back was to them, Jasmin pressed her hand into Yuki's. Her mother and the general were engrossed in each other. She watched them turn away, their whispers sharp, as they walked toward the porch. Jasmin knew what to do. It was time. She linked her arm into Yuki's. They rose as one unit, gathered their dresses under their armpits, clammy hands leaking into each other's, and ran for the back door.

ABEL

Abel tried everything. He tried to lift Freddie but wasn't strong enough, and the movement made Freddie's bleeding thigh gush more. He tried to drag Freddie by the arms, but his friend screamed as his injured leg scraped the ground. He attempted to pull Freddie to his feet and help him walk, but Freddie collapsed on him.

"You have to move, Freddie!" he cried, feeling the shame of frustrated tears pressing against the back of his eyes. "Why are you being so stubborn?"

Freddie, he noticed, tried to glare at him, but even that seemed to take too much effort. His friend said nothing, just slid himself jerkily against the outside wall of the chicken coop, leaving smears of red against the brown sandy ground. Abel looked around for someone else, another boy, anyone to help him lift Freddie. The planes seemed to loom lower, but the air was clearing. Maybe he could run out and find someone. He didn't like the idea of leaving Freddie at the coop alone, but he had no choice.

"I'll be right back, Freddie. Don't worry."

Heat pummeled Abel's body. Panic surrounded them, shouting and yelling filled the air along with, unexpectedly, the tang of ginger and herbs from the garden that Rama maintained behind the chicken coop.

"Stop," Freddie said in a voice so commanding in its calmness that Abel turned around. "Please. I don't want to be alone."

So they sat together, thin backs wedged against the outside walls of the coop—the coop that had once broken Abel down into little pieces, now the only thing holding Freddie up. Around them, planes rumbled and sour death filled the air, but in their cocoon, it felt oddly placid. Maybe it would be all right to die here, Abel thought. Bits of ash tickled at his nose and throat, and he looked to see if they were irritating Freddie too. Freddie, who had his eyes closed as though in peaceful sleep, opened one eye and whispered, "I know I'm handsomer than you, there's no need to be jealous."

In spite of himself, in spite of the severity of the moment, the corners of Abel's lips curved upward, and his stomach contracted into a laugh, the first he'd had in months. Then Freddie leaned his head against Abel's shoulder. "My neck hurts," he said.

Abel leaned away to give Freddie more room on his shoulder. His back itched against the back of the coop, but he held himself still.

"I'm sorry." Freddie coughed.

Abel felt the spray of saliva against his neck. It smelled sour and bitter, but still Abel did not flinch.

"I'm sorry about Akiro. I just . . . I just wanted you to feel better."

"Quiet, Freddie, you need to stop talking so much." Abel pressed his fingers softly into Freddie's cheek, feeling the clog of dust and sweat under his fingertips.

"I hope my mother will be there . . . wherever I'm going after this," Freddie said hoarsely. "I'm afraid."

"Stop saying stupid stuff, Freddie. You're not going anywhere." Abel felt the thin body on his shoulder shake, felt a deep intake of breath.

"Maybe I won't get to see her because of what I did to you."

The dark circle around Freddie's leg had grown bigger, its earlier symmetry destroyed. There was no fighting it, Abel knew. This was all the time they had.

"'When you wish upon a star,'" Abel sang, Freddie's favorite song. He chewed the inside of his cheek to stop a telltale quiver from entering his voice. Absolution came in different forms. It was his turn to give it.

"'Makes no difference who you are,'" Freddie whispered in response, his sour breath blowing against Abel's cheek.

Freddie went silent before Abel finished the song, his breathing short and raspy. But Abel continued singing, one song after another, the songs they loved, a kind of hymn. Then Freddie's breathing evened into soundlessness, the sour breath no longer tickling Abel's neck, and he knew, he knew, he knew.

JUJUBE

"Jujube," Mr. Takahashi called from the front of the teahouse. His voice carried through the kitchen.

Doraisamy turned to glare at her. "Jujube, are you watching the customers?"

"Yes," she said. Her head pounded.

"Please put your things in your own space. I don't want any contamination," he said.

Jujube reached for the tapioca root that lay exposed on the countertop and nodded, a mask of meek acquiescence. Maybe she should get Doraisamy as well, she thought, but no, that would be mad, and she was not mad, she was simply vengeful. There was a difference. She watched Doraisamy's retreating back, sweat snaking a line down his white shirt.

Then she walked out to the teahouse floor, the fingernails of one hand carving crescent moons into her palm. "Would you like some more tea, sir? I can boil more water."

"Thank you, yes." Mr. Takahashi's voice, cheery. He did not notice the sticky wound on her head, inexpertly covered with her hair. He was distracted, had strolled in that evening with a sheaf of papers under his arm, late-arriving correspondence from Ichika that had been held up, arriving all at one go. He planned, he told Jujube, to arrange the letters in order and read them one by one so it would seem like Ichika was telling him a story, the order of the narrative round and complete.

Back in the kitchen, Jujube poured more water into the ornate blue kettle and put it on the stove. She opened the lid and watched as the bubbles began first at the sides of the kettle, then made their way to the middle until they were larger, popping, boiling. Then she tossed in the tea leaves and watched the water turn a muddy brown.

She turned her attention to the tapioca root. She thought about how her mother used to boil the root to remove the cyanide that existed in its raw form. Then she would mix it into their rice, and they all—when they were still a family of five—ate the gluey mixture they could barely swallow, lying to each other and saying they were full, then listening anxiously to the wireless for news. It had already felt barren and hopeless back then. Little did we know how much worse it would get, Jujube thought.

Jujube had not yet decided if she would stand over his body, owning the murder, or if she should run away before the cyanide took effect. She supposed they would eventually find her, and it would be obvious it was she who had poisoned him. Easiest perhaps to just own the action, watch him convulse, watch him bleed out of his nose and mouth as his stomach burned itself, watch him watch her and know it was she who had done the deed, watch the hope extinguish from his eyes as he died, knowing that Ichika would never see him again.

Jujube grabbed a knife from the drawer and admired its serrated edge. Like most things, it looked a lot more harmful than it was; the serrated edge was actually dull and in need of sharpening. As a tool of defense, it would be useless, but for her purposes, it would do fine. She scraped a powdery sliver of raw tapioca into Mr. Takahashi's favorite green teacup, careful not to spill any on the saucer. Then she poured the tea into the cup, over the sliver of tapioca, which floated like a tiny, unmoored boat among the stray tea leaves that had escaped the kettle's spout, before sinking. She scooped it out with a spoon, stirring any residual powder on the bottom.

Then she strode out of the teahouse kitchen and onto the floor, green cup in hand. The fans whirred, the afternoon humidity stuck to her back, an old man tapped his foot against the leg of a table with some impatience.

Her mind felt clear.

CECILY

There were rattan chairs on the porch, cushions fluffed and ready for someone to sit on, but Fujiwara removed his heavy military boots, lined them up behind a pillar, and lowered himself slowly and stiffly onto the wooden floor, crossing his legs under him. Cecily was surprised; she'd expected their screaming confrontation to continue. The storm too had passed, and the moonlight, bright and white, shimmered against his bare feet, fair, delicate but for a blister on the heel, probably from his hard boots.

He gestured at the space across from him. "Look. We need to handle this. They don't need to see us fight." His face was shrouded in shadow, cheeks sunken. Cecily mirrored him, crossing her legs under her body.

Cecily had never been a big believer in ghosts. It was true that sometimes nighttime noises, alien creaks, and the sounds that came with the expansion and contraction of old wooden houses scared her, but she wasn't one of those people who worried themselves about the dead watching. Still, some nights when things felt particularly bleak, she wondered if Lina hovered around the edges of the shadows, if Lina cursed her to the life she had, to the fates she'd brought upon the ones she loved.

"So why do you want a family now?" Cecily asked, twisting her fingers together. "Not before?"

"I think maybe this is the end," Fujiwara said. The moon lit one side of his face and darkened the other, his nose rising like a shadowed mountain. "The end of all we've worked for." He leaned back against one of the porch pillars and sighed quietly, his breath pressing into the still night air. "It's important for a man to leave a mark on the world."

"This is not what you said it would be like." Cecily was so angry she couldn't find the words. How did one articulate the years of broken promises and broken lives, that nothing had added up to the equation they had intended?

"I just wanted to see what it would be like for me, us, to have a family. I thought just for a few days, I could show her more." He paused for so long Cecily wondered if he had fallen asleep. Then he whispered, "She doesn't deserve a world like this." Before Cecily could reply, he said, "I didn't know about the other girl. You have to believe me."

Cecily pulled her knees to her chest, her housedress pressing into her legs. Perhaps this was as close as she would get to an apology, to regret. She didn't know if it was enough, but she could feel the bitterness of his guilt, almost taste their combined sorrow.

"She's a good girl, isn't she, little Jasmin?" he said. "But the other one . . ."

She searched his face, but it was his body that told her more. Most of the moon had ducked behind a cloud, so all she could see was the unevenness of his shoulders, the weight he carried. Perhaps for the first time, Cecily understood him, a man who had taken everything but had nothing left.

"Maybe we deserve this," Cecily said, gesturing at herself, all dirt and wildness, and him, all pain and stoop. She looked directly at the moon, which was so bright it hurt, not unlike looking directly at the sun.

He was silent but for a small whistling breath.

"I have to take them back," Cecily said, facing Fujiwara. "They need a home."

He nodded. "The English will come for me soon." His voice was calm, soft. For a brief moment, it felt like the old days, just the two of them, whispering about a future they had thought would come to pass. Cecily pulled herself clumsily to her feet, shaking out the foot that had fallen asleep. Fujiwara lay back on the porch, spread his arms out, tilted his chin at the sky.

Behind her in the house, a shout from the houseboy, shrill and panicked, pierced the night air.

JUJUBE

Ichika's letters floated like jellyfish on the ocean-green surface of the teahouse's table. Jujube watched as Mr. Takahashi carefully extracted each letter. He smoothed them out, then laid each neatly atop its corresponding envelope. Having been folded for so long, the letters stood half-pleated on the table like little accordions. The sheets were of varying quality. Some were stained, some of the ink smudged, but Ichika's looping penmanship, large and sure of itself, was unmistakable.

"Whoa, whoa, be careful," Mr. Takahashi exclaimed as Jujube prepared to place the teacup on the table. An urge to tip the hot water onto Mr. Takahashi or onto the letters swelled through her, but she breathed it back. It was not the time or the plan.

"I'm sorry," Mr. Takahashi said, patting her arm. "I do not mean to shout at you. Just so excited." The faint creases at the corner of his eyes deepened as he smiled. She placed the refilled teacup down in an empty space away from the letters, stepped back, and nodded, acknowledging his apology.

"Please," he said, "sit with me." He gestured at an empty stool next to him.

Jujube hesitated. This was not supposed to happen; she had not anticipated his affection. She gestured helplessly at the teacup. "Your tea, sir."

"If the manager comes out to scold, I tell him I am ask for you," he said. "Please, sit down. I want to . . ." He paused, searching for the word. "I want to *share* with you. A joyful moment."

There was nothing else she could do. She sat down next to him, curled her toes under the stool, pressed them against her shoes nervously. Steam from the teacup rose quickly; it would get cold soon, but Mr. Takahashi was distracted.

"Where shall we start?" he asked gleefully. "Why, at the beginning, of course." Chuckling at his own joke, he reached for the letter perched at the top-left corner of his arrangement. He cleared his throat and started reading aloud.

Ichika's letters were mundane, filled with day-to-day details.

Today I went to the hospital and the patients were nice to me. A doctor was impatient, but of course, he has a lot on his mind. When I went to the market, I was excited to be able to buy our favorite root vegetable, with which I will use to make broth. It was chilly today as the weather is changing. I drew the sky today. I wished to paint but we do not have supplies so I am content to draw without color for now.

Ichika wrote very generally; she was not, Jujube noted with smugness, a good writer, able to evoke feeling and presence on the page. Her letters were stilted, like a child's, prosaic statements of fact, no judgments, no poetics, no dramatics, descriptions of things, not feelings. Yet Jujube couldn't help but be enraptured, listening to Mr. Takahashi's halting translations. He would silently read a line or two, his eyes blinking quickly across the page, then slowly translate each sentence to English, stumbling over tenses, contractions, and pronouns.

From the letters Jujube learned that Ichika had moved away from Nagasaki to a smaller town, where she led a quiet life, despite the war. Still, her life, simple as it was, seemed to provide satisfaction and clarity and, the most alien of all, happiness. Jujube filled in the blanks in Ichika's letters—in her mind, every day Ichika rose around the same time, as the yellow sun pressed its rays determinedly through the clouds. She lived with an elderly aunt with whom she would consume breakfast, a mug of tea and pickled vegetables on rice, the steamy tea cutting into the sourness of the pickles, somehow making them both sweeter and more tart. Then Ichika would change into her loose, stylish man-pants and leave for the hospital, where she ran around for hours doing all manner of things, from tending the wounds of soldiers, to reading books to the injured, to ferrying papers across the hospital, to and from doctors and nurses. She would be tired, the arches of her feet aching as she curled her toes under, trying to loosen the tight muscle at the foot's base. After work, she would have dinner with her aunt, read her books, draw her pictures, then write these letters to her father filled with calm prose and girlish hopes that he would return.

Jujube also wondered about all the things that Ichika did not tell her father. Girlfriends whom she might hold hands with, browse new dress designs with, giggle with at cafés when handsome, lanky, studious men walked by. Or, for that matter, the men who might stop her on the street to compliment her long dark hair, or gaze at the pinch in her nose that made her look as though her face were always just a second away from a laugh. She might even feel the punch of desire blooming below her stomach that confused her when the narrow-eyed nurse at the hospital pressed her fingertips into Ichika's wrist and held them there a second longer than she needed to, eyes trained determinedly on Ichika, though Ichika couldn't or wouldn't look up. The ache in Jujube's head faded, replaced with a deep want. There was poetry to Ichika's inner life, filled with love and desire and happiness and wonder, and Jujube longed for more of it, for all of it.

JASMIN

Jasmin could hear Yuki breathing next to her in the dark wheelbarrow as they lay side by side, arms parallel with their bodies, hands fisted in tight balls. Jasmin was sure that the gears in Yuki's brain were working as quickly as her own, puzzling through all the grown-up shouting, all the back-and-forth, all the confounding emotions of the last few hours.

It was strange that they were not touching now, not clasping hands the way they had the entire time they ran from the house to here. Even when the mosquitoes, which came out as the sun set, began buzzing and nipping at her arms, Jasmin had not let go of Yuki. She had swatted the mosquitoes away with one arm and shaken her head vigorously, to the point of dizziness, to stop them from buzzing in her face. But now Yuki just lay next to her in the wheelbarrow, not saying anything.

"Yuki, are you hungry? I'm soooo hungry!" They had eaten the fishy snacks that the houseboy had given them, but those were airy and unfilling; she longed for the heaviness of rice, something to press against her belly and make her doze with happy fullness.

Jasmin clutched her stomach with both hands to emphasize her point, then realized that Yuki couldn't see her. She let her hands drop back to her sides, brushing against Yuki's arm. But at her touch, Yuki shrank away, turned on her side in the wheelbarrow, and curled into a crooked C. Jasmin could feel the spiral of Yuki's spine against her elbow. "Yuki?"

Yuki stayed silent but breathed louder, as though exhaling from both her nose and mouth at the same time. It sounded like a cross between a grunt and a sneeze, something that would normally make Jasmin giggle, but that she decided might not go over well. When Yuki spoke, her voice was scratchy, like Jasmin's was in the morning when she was thirsty or hadn't said anything in a long time.

"It's not fair! How come you get to have two pas and a mama. And I get, I get . . ." She didn't finish her sentence. Instead, she said, "If I were you, I wouldn't have run away."

Jasmin felt the tips of her ears turn red, fury rushing to her face. Yuki didn't understand what it was like being locked away in the basement; she didn't understand how everyone had changed since the Japanese arrived, and her whole family had turned into balls of sadness, and how it felt to look into her mother's empty eyes, and even now how hard it was to see her mother as the wild thing she had become. Yuki didn't know how it was to have to find ways to be constantly entertaining, responsible for keeping everyone in her family happy. She didn't know what it was like to watch people change before her, becoming broken pieces of themselves, and not be able to do anything about it. It was too difficult to explain, too wild and too big and too painful. Jasmin lay back down in the wheelbarrow and turned away from Yuki. Her stomach gnawed. Behind her, Yuki exhaled angrily.

JUJUBE

Jujube had been sitting with Mr. Takahashi for nearly forty-five minutes. The sun had completed its descent, and the teahouse was artificially lit with the stark ugliness of fluorescent lights. When Jujube looked up at the dusty light tubes attached to the ceiling, she could see little black shadows against the white phosphor coating, carcasses of the dead insects that had the misfortune to fly into the light and get trapped. Doraisamy had been shooting her dirty looks every time he came out onto the teahouse floor, because she was not serving other customers. But because she was with Mr. Takahashi, the most regular of regulars, he left Jujube alone.

Mr. Takahashi had finished reading four of Ichika's letters, each several pages, without stopping once for a sip of tea. Mr. Takahashi's reading was nothing like her mother's effortless weaving of nightly tales; it was halting and stilted, full of pauses, as he translated from Japanese to English for Jujube. His voice wavered over words he found tough. "My daughter, she says there is a little boy who lives near her, a neighbor child, who is . . . more than naughty. What is the word? Extreme mischief, she says. She thinks he cannot be reformed."

"Incorrigible," said Jujube.

"Incor—" Mr. Takahashi tried, then gave up. "Very naughty," he said, chuckling. "You understand."

Jujube wondered if she would dream about Ichika that night, get to relive Ichika's purposeful and honest letters, get to playact a life with actual possibility.

Mr. Takahashi cleared his throat volubly. "My voice is tired." He gestured at his throat. "But I am glad to read the letters to you. They bring us a little escape, yes?" He smiled a quivering smile, indulgent, trusting. "Well, what do you think, Jujube?" he asked.

"Of your daughter's letters?"

"Of my daughter."

Jujube wondered what Mr. Takahashi wanted her to say or, more precisely, what he wanted to hear. Perhaps he wanted a simple validation that his daughter was well bred, that she was as good a person as he thought she was, that he had done the right things to see she was raised to become a woman who was a credit to him. Perhaps he wanted reassurance that Ichika would be all right, that he would get to see her again, that their life as a family was not irreparably broken by this war, that one way or another they could be whole again.

"Your daughter is a good person," said Jujube. "You are very lucky."

Mr. Takahashi looked away, his face sinking, tired. "This war," he started. "This war."

The hole in Jujube's chest, the one that had opened the day Jasmin disappeared, pinched inward, painfully.

Mr. Takahashi cleared his throat unevenly. "There is no fairness. I don't know what will happen with this war," he said, pressing his lined hand onto hers.

"What will you do if you see her again?" Jujube asked Mr. Takahashi, withdrawing her hand. She imagined them together, him and Ichika reunited, telling stories to each other, and Jujube a distant, nearly forgotten memory.

"I hope—" he started. He picked up one of the envelopes and smiled at Ichika's handwriting, wistful. "I hope we will—start a small printing business. Not books, that is too difficult. Maybe notebooks, or calendars, and we will print Ichika's art and photographs inside."

"A quiet life," Jujube said.

"A quiet life," he repeated back to her. "No more hospitals, no more dead."

Doraisamy had begun clattering loudly in the kitchen, banging the dishes, knocking the mop handle repeatedly against the wall. He wanted to close up the teahouse.

Mr. Takahashi coughed a little, finally reaching for the teacup. Jujube imagined the cyanide tentacling its way through the tea, purifying with poison.

"I'll finish this tea and leave. I think your manager is telling me to go." He smiled weakly. "I am sorry for my . . . outbursting," he said. Looking at her directly.

"Outburst," said Jujube involuntarily.

"What will I do without you?" Mr. Takahashi said, bringing the teacup to his lips. He blinked a little, as though expecting a burst of steam, then, realizing the tea was now cold, smiled to himself and tipped the cup toward his mouth.

Without thinking, Jujube shot her arm out, her fingers crossing the sea of letters. She swept her hand against the teacup, which wobbled against his fingers.

"Jujube, what . . . ?" He looked at her, alarmed.

"No," she said, and hit the cup again, this time tipping it over. Murky brown water spilled over his fingers in waves, sweeping across one of Ichika's letters. Ink washed across paper, and the accordion folds of the letter flattened as it lay dead, smudged and unreadable.

Mr. Takahashi jumped up and backward to avoid the wave of spilled tea dripping its way to the edge of the table.

"What did you do?" he said, voice shaking, cheeks reddening, the closest to anger that she had ever seen from him. His eyes widened so much that his hairline looked stretched against the side of his head. He reached for the wet letter, fingers arched to peel it off the table.

Jujube wedged her body between him and the table, the tea dripping quietly off the edge onto her skirt. She raised her hands so he couldn't get past her, couldn't touch the wet surface.

"I'm sorry," she said. Then, not knowing what else to say, "It's better this way."

When his cloudy brown eyes met hers, she didn't know if he knew what she had nearly done to him. She wondered if she should crow, make him feel the fear she had intended for him, make him feel the pain she wrestled with every day. Instead, she murmured "I'm sorry" over and over as he silently gathered up Ichika's undamaged letters and tucked them under his arm. When he was done, he looked at her, then at the ruined letter in the puddle of tea and ink. She opened her mouth to say something, but there were no words. She felt her breath whistle through her nose.

He walked slowly out of the teahouse.

In the kitchen, Doraisamy knocked the mop into the wall again. Jujube grabbed a rag, peeled the ruined page off the table, and mopped up the mess. When she finally left the teahouse that night, the moon hung low and full in the sky, a perfect fattened orb, bathing her in its cool light. Anyone else would have taken it as a sign of hope, or absolution, or something good to come. Anyone else would have swung her face up to gaze at the wonder of the moon's unthwarted splendor. But Jujube simply wondered what other horror the silvery moon would illuminate that night, and every night to come.

ABEL

A new kind of confusion had descended upon the camp. The planes had stopped their bombing and lowered themselves to the ground, and once they landed, out of them spilled white men in military uniforms, cheering, arms raised in the swell of victory. The British had arrived, Abel thought. Japan had indeed lost the war. Flashes of light burst through the ashy air; the pilots were taking victory photographs. Abel watched them put their arms around each other and pose, a wall of RAF uniforms, with his dead friends as the backdrop. Did they assume everyone they had killed was Japanese? Did they not care, the carnage simply collateral damage? Cameras clicked over piles of limbs. They were singing as they stepped over the bodies and debris, one song Abel recognized, the anthem "God Save the King," something he'd been forced by Brother Luke and others to sing at school.

Soon the British soldiers were rounding up the boys who were alive. The boys' eyes watered with smoke and panic, their clothes were torn, they were skinny and bleeding. Abel saw Azlan stumbling, eyes glazed. He saw Rama being led by two others, limping, each with a forearm under Rama's armpits, to hold up his heft. The soldiers lined the boys up together, rubbed a rag over some of their faces.

"Now come on and smile!" they shouted. "We've liberated you! God save the king! Don't you heathens know freedom when you see it?"

The cameras clicked and clicked.

The British hadn't seen him yet, crouched inside the coop. When

Freddie died, Abel had sat nearly catatonic, unable to move himself, determined to hold his friend up, unwilling to let his shoulder collapse. But eventually his body had twitched, his shoulder no longer able to withstand the deadweight of Freddie; he'd caught Freddie's head as it slipped off his shoulder, laid his friend's head carefully on the ground, the angle odd, twisted. The toilet-paper drawings crinkled unpleasantly at Abel's waist as he crawled on all fours into the coop to calm himself.

As he squinted through the coop's wire fencing at the scene unfolding before him, he knew there was only one thing he could do, one thing Freddie would've done. Tightening the drawstring of his pants so the drawings hugged against his body, he pulled himself to his feet and ran, as fast and as quietly as he could. He ran away from his friends lined up like dolls, away from the clicking camera lenses, away from the English soldiers jubilant in their victory, away from Freddie twisted on the ground like string. His body screamed from the exhaustion, from the many hours he had not eaten or had a sip of toddy. Survival was unlikely, that he would be able to even get past the soldiers and to the gate was unlikely, that he would find a way to walk across Thailand seemingly impossible. But still, there was nothing else to do. It was time to go.

―

JASMIN

When Jasmin woke up, it was still night, but Yuki was gone. The bedsheet was thrown back and her face was damp with dew, arms covered in mosquito bites. Her stomach was painfully empty. She didn't know if she'd expected Yuki to be there or not;

she'd fallen asleep to the sound of Yuki's breathing silence, a big hole of unsaid between them. But now she was scared. The last time she had woken up alone in this wheelbarrow, Yuki had come back hurt, and she'd had to take Yuki to the general's house. Now she wasn't sure even she could go to the general's house. She wasn't sure she had any house or anyone she could trust. Her throat screamed for water. She needed to get up and make a plan. She pulled herself unsteadily to her knees and pushed the rest of the sheet away. Humid night coolness pressed into her face; it was quiet, and there was no one around.

She tried to collect her thoughts, which were all rushing through her head and making her feel sick. So many people needed her attention—she had to find Yuki, she had to figure out what was wrong with her mother—but most of all, she was so hungry she felt like she couldn't stand without falling over. She clambered out of the wheelbarrow and looked at her feet, but it was too dark to see anything. Her shoes felt so tight against her toes that she took them off and left them inside the wheelbarrow. Her feet pressing against the still-cool ground, Jasmin stumbled slowly toward one of the shacks. Perhaps there would be some food, something to drink, perhaps one of the girls would help her. Then afterward she would find Yuki.

She knocked gingerly on the door of the first shack. "Hello?" she said softly, terrified.

She heard a rustling inside, then a light turned on and the door swung open. A man stood at the door. He was a little taller than the general, wore the same uniform top, though his was far dirtier and had fewer stripes on the shoulders than the general's. Jasmin noticed that his legs were bare; faint black hairs dotted his pink upper thighs. He said something to Jasmin sleepily, but she didn't understand because it was in Japanese, then he raised his voice and turned his head toward the shack, called for someone. Jasmin knew to run. Her whole body hurt and her uncovered feet pressed into the ground. The softest spots on her arches stung as bits of garbage, twig, and dried mud dug into them. Dots appeared in front of her eyes, little black spots on white, then little white spots on black, dancing. She stopped, heaving big painful breaths, air whizzing through her body.

She leaned against the side of another shack, making sure to stay out of sight of the front door. She felt like all her senses were firing, but so much so it rendered her helpless. This whole place made her feel unsafe in a way that nowhere else did. Deep inside, she knew if she didn't keep running, didn't stay out of sight, she would end up a dead-eyed girl, like all the others she saw around her. She felt so hopeless and alone, and so hungry. Even Yuki had left her, Yuki whose stubby fingers she could still feel in her hand when they ran together as one. Yuki was taller, but her fingers were shorter, her hands smaller, so Jasmin was always able to wrap her hand fully around Yuki's, something that made her feel like she could take care of Yuki.

As the spots in front of her eyes became bigger, she smelled the familiar oily smell of Yuki's hair and heard her friend's shrill whisper: "Where did you go? I thought I lost you!"

"I was looking for you," Jasmin murmured, weak, burying her head in her hands and then into her knees as she squatted on the ground.

"I went to Aunty Woon's private room and got this." Yuki waved what looked like a bun underneath Jasmin's nose. When she bit into it, Jasmin nearly cried—the bun was warm, soft.

She looked around and saw that Yuki was squatting in front of her with her own bun. A man's moan from the shack behind them punctured the rhythm of their quiet chewing. Jasmin jumped, and Yuki made a disgusted face.

"You're my sister, you know, no matter what." Yuki stared at Jasmin before throwing her arms over Jasmin's shoulders. Jasmin felt every bit of her body grow, but most of all her heart, which was so filled with happiness that she thought it would burst out of her chest. She'd always known it, and now it was confirmed. She didn't care what the grown-ups fought about. Grown-ups were always muddled and unhappy, it seemed they had so many things to think about that they often forgot the most important thing. And the most important thing to Jasmin was the simple thing—that she and Yuki would always be together, and nothing, no one, would ever separate them again.

After they finished their buns, Yuki helped pull her to her feet, which, while a little wobbly and sore, were a lot stronger after eating. They flitted back to the wheelbarrow, pulling the sheet over them, arms and legs intertwined like a single entity.

"It's hot in here," Yuki said, extricating one arm to fan herself.

Through the thin pilled sheet, Jasmin thought she saw a spark, a bright orange wisp, and then she too felt hot. Around them a noise began to build, the sounds of footsteps running, people yelling. Yuki looked confused, tried to pop her head out from under the bedsheet to figure out what was going on.

"Everyone's running, Mini," Yuki said. Vibrations rolled through the wheelbarrow, the heavy sound of many feet around them. "It's scary."

"I don't care," Jasmin said to Yuki, to everyone. It was getting hotter, stuffy, the roaring was getting louder, but she was tired of running, tired of counting on grown-ups to make it right; they never did. She pulled Yuki down onto the wheelbarrow floor with her—they were the only ones who mattered. Arm to arm, shoulder to shoulder, face-to-face, the girls allowed the rising, pulsing heat to lull them into a deep sleep. Outside, the flames snaked across the ground as the comfort station burned like a fever.

CECILY

Of course the girls had run away, Cecily thought. How many times had adults disappointed them, left them to fester in their own confusion, while selfishly chasing their grown-up highs—rage and lust and everything else that poorly masked the deep sadness of their lives? When the houseboy came running to tell them the girls were gone, she saw, for the first time, panic and fear crossing Fujiwara's face. He knew that the world he had created was no match for two girls who looked only for love and happiness. They would go the wrong way, make the wrong choices, trust the wrong people. He berated the poor forlorn houseboy—which direction did they run, how could you not have heard anything, how could you have let them go—questions the two of them should have been asking each other.

"Where?" Cecily screamed. "Where did they go?"

The houseboy pointed lamely into the distance. But Fujiwara seemed to understand. "The comfort station," he said, his eyes blazing. "Let's go."

Then the acrid burning started to float through the air around them, and Cecily was struck by how familiar it smelled, like Port Lewisham all those years ago. Behind the smoke, little reaching hands of orange flame lapped through the darkness—a fire, like the one that the Japanese had set all those years ago to the RAF planes at the port, a fire, growing bigger, brighter, hotter, nearer.

She looked at Fujiwara in alarm. "Where is that coming from? Where?"

"Oh no," Fujiwara said. "No, no, no, no, no."

Toward the fire they both went, coughing as the smoke thickened in their lungs. Cecily ran around haphazardly, throat in her stomach, pushing her voice through: "Jasmin! Yuki!" Fujiwara had somehow commandeered a group of young Japanese officers who systematically walked through the streets. Together, the two of them pushed toward the heat, and against the throng of Cecily's sweating neighbors fleeing in the opposite direction toward fresh air.

JUJUBE

At the entrance to the comfort station, Jujube saw her mother and the man. Purely on instinct, she'd run toward the fire—unsure if it was curiosity, a desire to help, or something else entirely. But now, as her mother approached, the cut on her head where she'd hit the floor of the bathroom started pulsing again, angrily.

"Jujube, oh my god." Her mother stared at her sorrowfully, and Jujube wondered if she remembered what she had done, if it hurt her mother as much as it hurt her. But her mother blinked, and the moment passed. "Quick, Jujube! We have to find your sister. The general says she could be in here."

Beside her mother stood a weary version of the Tiger of Malaya who'd sliced through the street, straight-backed, in the welcome parade for the Japanese three years before. It didn't make sense. What was her mother doing with the general?

"We have to go; we have to go!" her mother screamed.

The smell of burning and charred flesh salted Jujube's nose. The air was murky with floating bits that got stuck in her eyes. She ran alongside her mother, their slippers squelching in the mud. She ran past a clot of pubic hair covering a pelvis lying next to the lopsided entry sign that used to stand in front of the comfort station, half the letters burned off, no longer WELCOME, just OME.

They were screaming their voices hoarse, "Jasmin! Jasmin!"

Jujube and her mother became separated from the general, who, last she saw, was running around barking instructions to people. He kept saying he did not know how the fire was authorized, that he had not given the go-ahead, and the refrain made Jujube want to push him into the fire. The excuses, the remorse, it was too little too late, his people did this, a last erasing violence before they were forced to leave, as though it would cover up everything they had done.

Jujube wanted to stop to catch her breath; her side felt like its organs were about to disengage from her body. But she did not allow herself to stop—Jasmin could be anywhere. She and her mother ran and ran, past shacks filled with khaki pants hanging on the doors, past bloodied girls, past burned girls. They scanned each live face for the sugar-shiny eyes of Jasmin, for the smile that could light up a million planets. Together, they shouted and shouted and shouted.

"Jasmin! Jasmin! Jasmin!"

CHAPTER TWENTY-FIVE

December 1945

There is a knock at the front gate, *tock tock tock,* so faint at first that Jujube thinks she is imagining it. It is dusk but it's hard to tell inside the enclosed house, windows and doors shut no matter what time of day or how hard the heat raps against its brown walls.

Tock tock tock, the gate goes, insistent, louder this time. And then a voice: "Ma! Ma!" A pause. "Jasmin!"

Raspy, cracking, yet unmistakable. Jujube throws the window open to look, but before she can say anything, her mother, who for the last three months has not stirred from her bedroom, rushes out, unlatches the gate, and catches her son before he falls to the ground.

Abel is too thin. His gray eyes and light hair seem dead and brittle, the bottoms of his sandals have worn off, and there are scabs all over his arms. Still, he is not the worst one who has walked through Bintang in recent days. All sorts have come stumbling into town since the war ended three months earlier, every person broken and gasping, tired and bleeding. Jujube runs outside to help her mother, and together they scoop Abel up, the bones in his back and shoulders curving erratically, sticking out through his skin at such odd angles, Jujube thinks it is a wonder he has managed to hold himself up.

Jujube and her mother clean Abel silently. Jujube is stricken by the number of weeping cuts and sores all over his body, how it looks like a hundred mosquitoes have bitten him. He is somehow taller than he was eight months ago; she can't tell if it is because he has become so thin or because somehow, despite everything, he has managed to grow. When Jujube and her mother are done, Jujube tries to ask Abel what happened to him.

"Where have you been?" she pleads. "How did you get home?"

But her mother puts a hand over Jujube's mouth. This makes Jujube shrink back. The memory of her mother's touch is always tainted by the day her mother pushed her in the bathroom and split her head open.

Abel sleeps and sleeps. He wakes up to eat a little but doesn't speak, just sleeps, for a week.

―

Abel's dreams are peppered with Freddie. Sometimes the dreams are so real that he wakes up startled, sure that Freddie is right there beside him, humming. But then he sees instead the bare room, the worried eyes of his mother and sister bearing down on him. Finally he asks the question he already knows the answer to.

"Where is Jasmin?"

Jujube bites her lip so hard he sees a cut begin to form. "What matters is we have you back," Jujube says. "Jasmin and Pa would be happy."

Who, Abel wonders, gave anyone the right to make these kinds of decisions, to devise this soul-for-a-soul arithmetic in which he, a worthless drunk, a killer of men, a coward, was allowed to survive? That this is worth the life of a sister and a father. There had been many opportunities for his own death when he'd trekked for weeks across the horrible terrain until his slippers tore through, crawled across the Thai border into Malaya. Around him, stragglers fell, the wounded starved, the starving died, an army of the broken. Still, somehow, he'd been the one to make it.

He feels cold, even though the afternoon is searingly hot. He looks around in a panic. "The drawings," he cries. "Where are they?"

Jujube again. "I'm sorry, Abe. Here they are."

She had gathered them into a tidy pile at the foot of his bed. She hands them over to him, the scraps of toilet paper, the crude sketches now dried brown and smudged, musty-smelling.

He shows Jujube a sketch, the one that Freddie drew from Abel's memories so long ago. "Does it look like Jasmin?" he asks.

The edges of his baby sister's face have become so distant; it frightens him, being unable to hold on to her memory. Jujube nods, and for a moment he is filled with hope. He wants to remember; he wants her to remember for him. But before he can say anything more, Jujube collapses in a heap on the floor, lower lip trembling. His mother stumbles out of the room. He has noticed how they both carry anguish in their body. It crushes his mother so she no longer stands straight, her shoulders sloped as though the slightest weight would knock her over. It presses into Jujube's face so her eyes are puffy and half closed with sadness.

It is then that Abel knows Jujube is lying, that he is simply being indulged, that the sketch does not look like Jasmin, that he cannot remember what Jasmin looks like anymore.

Over the next few weeks, Abel's wounds heal, but the haunted look in his eyes does not. When he is able to walk, he holds on to Jujube's arm and limps through town. He stumbles often and clenches his fingers into her. They leave marks, little indented bruises, on her arm, but she does not mind. They are marks of the living, proof that he is there. Sometimes she catches herself staring at him. When she blinks, she is terrified that when she opens her eyes, he will be gone.

"Stop staring at me," he mutters.

As they walk around Bintang, Jujube points out old landmarks to her brother. "See here, that's where the sundry shop used to be. The Chongs' boy volunteered to fight the Japanese, and no one thought he would make it, but he did, though he's lost both thumbs.

"See here, that's the school, and it's open again. You should go back; they will take you."

He pays no attention. Instead, he asks everyone he meets if they know about a boy called Freddie from another Eurasian family. When asked to describe Freddie, Abel clenches on to Jujube's arm and recalls bright blue eyes, a serious disposition, a favorite song about wishing on a star. When word gets around, all sorts of people begin coming to the Alcantara house. They claim to be Freddie's mother, father, cousins, distant relatives. Abel's face fills with hope—he must, he needs to, find this boy's family, he says. The strangers push through the gate, crouch at the entryway, claim to know a blue-eyed boy. They gaze at Abel hopefully, thinking he has money or some other kind of reward to give them. But when Abel hands them the grubby, smeared toilet-paper sketches, they slink away, disgusted.

And then a new year, 1946, dawns. The monsoon rains come every single day of January, as though trying to wash away the shards of history. In the days leading up to what would have been Jasmin and Yuki's eighth birthday, Cecily dreams of them, two ghost girls. She dreams of flames licking at the corners of elbows, of white nightgowns catching fire. Sometimes she dreams of the girls singing silly songs together, but that is quickly replaced by flashes of running through the comfort station, screaming their names even as the stench of hopelessness surrounds her. She relives the crack of pain that incapacitated her when she realized the price of this war was innocence, and the girls had paid, without knowing why.

Alongside Jujube and Abel, she buries bits of bone and ash that they find in the rubble of the comfort station, not sure if the bones and ash are Jasmin or Yuki or neither. In the end, the two little girls are indistinguishable, sisters separated in life but together in death. Among the ethnic Chinese neighbors, there is a tradition where, after the bodies of the dead are cremated, the living use chopsticks to gently extract the tiniest bone fragments, put them in an urn, and bury them with other members of the family, so that they may all be together in the afterlife. Cecily and her family are not Chinese, but they do the same. They pour some of the bone fragments they hope are the girls' into the divots of Jasmin's favorite congkak board and bury it under the bougainvillea bush. And, although it seems morbid, Cecily cannot help herself—she keeps a fragment of bone in a small Horlicks tin that she places on a windowsill, where it glows in a patch of silver light when there is a full moon. She likes to imagine Jasmin and Yuki staring up at the night sky, little faces lit with moonbeams, arms intertwined, white nightgowns tangled, as they giggle together at everything and nothing. In a way, this too is a constant reminder of the absolution their family will never get.

There is a ceremony, of course. The Japanese flag is lowered, and the Union Jack is raised once again. That day, the air is still and pregnant with humidity, making the blue, white, and red flag hang limp against the pole. Cecily and her neighbors stand in an open field without shade. The sun beats down on their necks as they wait, facing a crude wooden platform.

Finally it begins. Cecily does not recognize the first two Japanese officers who are led toward the Union Jack. They are instructed to hand over their rifles to the British officers as a symbol of surrender, and they do so with appropriate contrition, eyes lowered to the ground. Around her, people clap; the residents of Bintang are supposed to feel relief that their benevolent colonizer has returned.

"Ma," she hears Jujube hiss. Her daughter is frantically nodding at her hands.

Cecily grits her teeth, feels the anger ache in her jaw, but she does what she is supposed to, brushes her palms together, mimes grateful applause.

When Fujiwara appears on the elevated platform, Cecily doesn't even recognize him at first because his nose, high and aristocratic, is broken. It makes his face seem uncentered. She has not seen him since that terrible night at the comfort station. She has disjointed memories of him shouting, "Who authorized this raid?" and "Find the girl," but they were quickly separated.

She looks around to find Jujube watching her. Jujube has never asked her a single question about why she and Fujiwara were together that night, but today her daughter's eyes seem to bore into her, and for the first time since that awful night, Cecily feels something other than despair. Fear. Her daughter must never find out. So Cecily keeps her eyes down, doesn't look up at the platform, will not let her face betray her. She hears the clatter of a rifle handed over, hears feet pound on the rickety platform, and watches Fujiwara's ankles as he is led away. She learns later that, in the following months, he will be tried and then hanged for war crimes in the Philippines, but that day, for the first time ever, she does not meet his gaze.

When she finally looks up, Jujube is no longer staring at her. Instead, her daughter's eyes are trained elsewhere. Cecily sees her daughter watching her son—Abel is holding the Horlicks tin close to his face and whispering to it.

"They're arresting the bad men, sis. I wish you were here."

The bones of two girls listen.

When they return to the house, a drizzle is quickly turning into a storm. They see that the postmaster has been by. A tattered parcel tied in string sits, sodden with rain, at the gate. Abel raises his eyebrows because the return address and stamps are Japanese, and the package was mailed more than three months prior, close to when the Japanese surrendered. Jujube and her mother look quizzically at each other and shrug; they have no idea what it could be or who sent it.

Once they have brought the wet parcel into the house, they all just look at it seeping onto the table. Abel is the first to crack. He puts down the Horlicks tin and reaches to tear the parcel's damp brown paper strip by strip, as though peeling fruit. He pulls out something that looks like a bound book, and opening the cover, they see it is a calendar. Each month is illustrated with a different photograph of a different flower—sunflowers, morning glory, lotus flowers, lavender, chrysanthemum, camellia, cherry blossoms, tulips, and others they cannot identify. Each day has a number and, next to it, the kanji equivalent. The paper is thick, high-quality, the images are sharp, the petals so bright they invite you to bring your eye close to the page to study each flower.

"What is this?" Jujube's mother asks.

Jujube ignores her mother, hands shaking so much she can barely grip the calendar. There is a storm of recognition in her chest, but she has to be sure. She roots around for a letter, a note, something to explain the flower calendar, and then she sees it—shaky handwriting on the inside cover.

Takahashi & Daughter Printing

Outside, the rain begins to subside, and from behind the clouds, the creeping sliver of a crescent moon emerges. Another day has come and gone. Jujube hangs the calendar by the window, and next to it, Abel places Jasmin and Yuki's Horlicks tin. Her mother turns both items toward the moonlight.

ACKNOWLEDGMENTS

To my family, without whom I am nothing. My late mother, Diane, who squinted to read early passages of this novel I would furtively post on Instagram and shamefully delete an hour later, and who showed me that life is only worth living if lived meaningfully. My father, Lawrence, who taught me to read and love books and who was instrumental in fact-checking this novel. My aunty Bernie, who taught me how to be funny and who has been proud of me even before I could walk on my own. My uncle Henry, who mailed me the book of early Malaysian photographs when he heard I was writing a historical novel. My grandpa, who drove me to and from English literature classes and who always believed. My grandma, who told the stories, and wrote the stories that inspired this novel.

To my agents, Stephanie Delman and Michelle Brower, whose shining eyes when talking about this book will always inspire me and who are the most formidable advocates. To the whole Trellis team, including Allison Malecha, who sold this book around the world. To Nat Edwards and Khalid McCalla.

To my editor, Marysue Rucci, for loving the imperfections of both my characters and my book, and for making both infinitely better and also, quite frankly, for changing my life by choosing my book. To Andy Tang, for your help with this book but also for your friendship, texts, and laughter. I am lucky to have met you.

To the teams at Marysue Rucci Books, Scribner, Simon Element, and Simon & Schuster, including Clare Maurer, Jessica Preeg, Elizabeth Breeden, Ingrid Carabulea, and Jason Chappell. To the audio team. To Michael Taeckens. To the many others who make a book a reality.

To the current and former teams at Hodder & Stoughton in the UK, including Phoebe Morgan, Lily Cooper, Maria Garbutt-Lucero, Alana Gaglio, Alice Morley, Charlea Charlton, and countless others.

To Samantha Tan, who has brought the audio version of this book to life, keeping all the Malaysian nuances intact.

To Fadilah Karim, Vi-An Nguyen, and TAKSU Gallery for the remarkable cover art. To Jon Gray for the stunning UK cover.

To the international teams across the world and the translators who are bringing this book to life in so many languages—I am always indebted to you.

To Gina Chung, who is always ready to scream, who woke me up in the middle of the night because she could not wait till morning to tell me how much she loved this book. To Katie Devine, for countless pep talks, vent sessions, for reading early and often, for understanding how to write about and through grief. To Jemimah Wei and Grace Liew, my SEA soul sisters, who remind me to write about our home with pride.

To the New School, where I met some of my earliest writing friends—Kate Tooley, Lauren Browne, Vic Dillman, John Kazanjian, who wrote and created with me during the strangest and bleakest of times.

ACKNOWLEDGMENTS

To Mira Jacob, who taught me how to write, but also how to become a writer and how to live in this world with words, thank you for your mentorship and friendship. To Marie-Helene Bertino, who helped me start this book, then urged me to always protect it. To Alexandra Kleeman, who read the earliest, roughest of chapters and still found lovely things to say.

To the Sewanee Writers Workshop and the wonderful friends I met—Marcela Fuentes, Jamila Minnicks, Kirstin Chen, Jon Hickey, Angeline Stevens, Mary South, Nancy Nguyen, David Villaverde, Alysia Sawchin, and so many others. To the Tin House Summer Workshop, especially the Nicole Dennis-Benn workshop, whose participants read the first chapter of this novel. To Alexander Chee, who was the tough voice I needed to let go of my novel.

To Seyron Foo, Vaughn Villaverde, Charmaine Wong, Kena Peay, Stephen Downey, Rosalyn Lau, Sonny Nguyen, Jerome Sicat, Diana Halog, Carlo Delacruz, Chris Juan, Jamil Walker, Elisabeth Diana, Alan Williams—thank you for being friends with me in California as I figured out who I was supposed to be. To Yves Gleichman, for deciding all those years ago, even before I knew, that I would be a writer and for your friendship and encouragement as I learned to be one. To Aram Mrjoian, for the puns and for our time at *TriQuarterly*. To Alan Karras, Kevin Kwan, K-Ming Chang, Jenny Tinghui Zhang, Jami Nakamura Lin, Jessamine Chan, Dawnie Walton, Jessica George, Rowan Hisayo-Buchanan, Tracy Chevalier, Nguyễn Phan Quế Mai, Daphne Palasi Andreades, Qian Julie Wang, Michelle Young—thank you for the various ways you have contributed to the creation of this book.

To Malaysia—for being the idiosyncratic place of my birth, for always being a literary inspiration.